OVER THE MISTY MOUNTAINS

★ ★ ★

OVER THE MISTY MOUNTAINS

★ ★ ★

GILBERT MORRIS & AARON MCCARVER

BETHANY HOUSE PUBLISHERS
MINNEAPOLIS, MINNESOTA 55438

Published by Bethany House Publishers
A Ministry of Bethany Fellowship International
11300 Hampshire Avenue South
Minneapolis, Minnesota 55438

Printed in the United States of America by
Bethany Press International, Minneapolis, Minnesota 55438

Library of Congress Cataloging-in-Publication Data

Morris, Gilbert.
    Over the misty mountains / Gilbert Morris and Aaron McCarver.
    p.   cm. — (The spirit of Appalachia ; #1)
    ISBN 1–55661–885–9
    I. McCarver, Aaron. II. Title.
III. Series: Morris, Gilbert. Spirit of Appalachia ; #1.
PS3563.O8742O94   1997
813'.54—dc21   96–45907
                                                                  CIP

Dedication

This book is lovingly dedicated to my parents, Jessie Lee and Jean McCarver.

To my dad for all the things you did to ensure that my sisters and I would have a life just a little bit better than you did, for all the extra hours and the many Saturdays spent working. They were noticed and greatly appreciated. Thanks also for pushing us to get all the education we could and for supporting me in a decision that looked questionable at the time because of what it would cost, but look where it led! I especially thank you for making sure that we all attended church "every time the doors were open."

To my mom for always being there for a son that she understands better than anyone. I appreciate what you quietly took from others when you decided from the beginning that my sisters and I were more important than the things that money can buy. (I still would rather have you at home with me, waiting at the door with a kiss when I got home from school—as you still do!) But I especially remember you reading the Bible to us and praying with us each night. It was your love and strength that made our house a home.

Thank you, Mama and Daddy, for giving me a Christian home and for teaching me that the only thing in this life that really matters is having a relationship with our heavenly Father. To Him be all the glory, honor, and praise! This book and any blessings it may give belong to the One who made it all possible!

GILBERT MORRIS spent ten years as a pastor before becoming Professor of English at Ouachita Baptist University in Arkansas and earning a Ph.D. at the Univeristy of Arkansas. During the summers of 1984 and 1985 he did postgraduate work at the University of London. A prolific writer, he has had over 25 scholarly articles and 200 poems published in various periodicals, and over the past years has had more than 70 novels published. His family includes three grown children, and he and his wife live in the Rocky Mountains of Colorado.

AARON McCARVER is the Dean of Students at Wesley College in Florence, Mississippi, where he also teaches drama and Christian literature. His deep interest in Christian fiction and broad knowledge of the CBA market have given him the background for editorial consultation with all the "writing Morrises" as well as other novelists. It was through his editorial relationship with Gilbert that this book series came to life.

Contents

PART I: HAWK

1. A Loss of Faith   13
2. Incident at *The Brown Stag*   27
3. Unto the Hills   43
4. Cry of a Hawk   57
5. Sequatchie   67
6. Trouble at Fort Loudoun   79
7. Encounter at a Stream   89
8. The Cherokee War   97

PART II: ELIZABETH

9. The Martins of Beacon Street   111
10. Patrick MacNeal   121
11. Charlotte Van Dorn   131
12. Dreams of a New Life   139
13. Discovery in the Library   147
14. Conspiracy Unveiled   155
15. A Mended Heart   169
16. Appalachian Destiny   175

PART III: WESTWARD JOURNEY

17. Watauga   181
18. Hawk's Son   191
19. The Journey Begins   199
20. Sabotage!   211

21. Amanda   223
22. Through Storm and Flood   235
23. Living Water   247
24. Another Loss   257

PART IV: AS THE DEER

25. New Homes, New Lives   265
26. The Settlers of Appalachia   281
27. A Frontier Christmas   287
28. Spring Returns   293
29. The Regulators   301
30. Hawk and Elizabeth   307
31. Rhoda and the Preacher   315
32. Mercy and Grace   321
33. Jacques Cartier   325
34. Never Thirst Again   335

Notes to Our Readers   345

Character List

In the eighteenth century, America's first pioneers left their homes and families and ventured beyond the seaboard colonies. With nothing but their faith and their dreams to sustain them, they struggled to carve out new lives on the rugged frontier . . . *Over the Misty Mountains*.

Jehoshaphat "Hawk" Spencer—Devastated by tragedy, he leaves his home in Williamsburg and travels over the Appalachian Mountains to lose himself in the wilderness.

Elizabeth Martin MacNeal—Daughter of the Martins, a prominent family in Boston, Elizabeth gives up a life of wealth to follow her husband's dream.

Patrick MacNeal—A Scottish immigrant, he came to the American Colonies with a dream of one day owning his own land.

Sequatchie—A Cherokee Indian chief who knows the true Way. He has prayed many years for someone to come to his people to read the Word.

Paul Anderson—A lifelong friend of Jehoshaphat Spencer, he is led to carry God's message of salvation over the mountains to the Cherokees.

Rhoda Harper—A beautiful woman caught up in a horrible life working in a tavern, she looks for a way of escape.

Jacques Cartier—Driven by his hatred for Hawk Spencer, the Frenchman follows a path of destruction that could engulf them all.

PART I

Hawk

November 1755 – October 1761

Lo, then would I wander far off,
and remain in the wilderness.

Psalm 55:7

A Loss of Faith

One

A rough, tearing wind ripped through Williamsburg during the night. Powerful gusts tore down shutters and rattled the windowpanes so hard that the inhabitants feared the glass would shatter into a thousand shards. Overhead, huge ominous-looking clouds descended upon the small city like a mantle of doom. Even as the gusty torrents of cold rain pelted slantwise into the buildings and across the terrain, sharp forked whips of lightning reached down from the ebony heavens and scratched across the roofs of the drenched houses. Loose bricks from chimneys were dislodged, shakes and shingles were ignited by touches of lightning, and then went out with a hissing as the driving rain poured down from heaven like a second deluge.

The Spencer house stood up boldly to the artillery of thunder and the crackling of silvery lightning, for it was a well-built house, designed specifically to withstand harsh weather. An oversized structure, it had a steeply pitched roof with five gables that shed the rain that ran down in torrents. Tall, narrow windows painted pale yellow stood out like jaundiced apparitions in the darkness of the night, and the extremely high, ornamented chimney looked like a soldier rigidly holding himself at attention. It was a red two-story house in the Federal style with windows evenly spaced, and in the front a double-paneled door stood firmly shut and bolted against the rampages of the weather. It might have been a country house, except it was built in the center of Williamsburg, which somehow gave the impression of its being slightly out of place.

Although the hour was long past midnight on November twenty-fifth, flickering yellow reflections from whale oil lamps illuminated the windows on the first floor. To the right of the entrance itself was the largest of the rooms, a rather ornate study, most unusual for the year 1755. The walls were lined with walnut bookcases, their rich grain catching the gleam of bayberry candles that guttered in sconces along their lengths. A cherrywood desk dominated the room, the top littered with books, maps, papers of various kinds, giving the appearance of a busy office rather than a private study. The fireplace crackled with the cheerful sound of poplar logs as they sizzled.

Two men sat opposite each other, one at the desk, his fingers drumming on the polished surface; the other sat rigidly upright, staring blankly at the rows of leather-bound books that lined the walls. The man behind the large desk was James Spencer. At the age of forty-five, he possessed the same general looks of the young man sitting across from him. Though streaks of gray lined his hair, he scorned the wigs so treasured by many of his countrymen and fellow citizens. He was heavy in the middle, and an air of authority and aggressiveness lined his stern face and showed in the firm actions of his body whenever he moved.

James Spencer leaned back now in his chair, his attention momentarily diverted by a blinding flash of lightning that illuminated the garden trees more brilliantly than any sun-filled day. He waited for the crash of thunder, and when it came, his eyes closed slightly and he shook his head. "We haven't had a storm like this all year," he murmured. When he received no answer, he leaned forward, picked up a quill, and stroked it with his left forefinger. "It hasn't been a bad year for storms," he remarked, not expecting any answer. He studied the face of his son, then said abruptly, "Don't worry, Josh, she'll be all right."

A strange, harsh expression flickered across the face of the young man who sat in the stiff Windsor chair. He sat with his feet planted flatly on the floor, his hands clasping his thighs almost as if he were prepared to leap to his feet and jump into action. Jehoshaphat Spencer was twenty years old, an even six feet, and a clean one hundred and eighty pounds of lean strong muscle. Thick jet black hair covered his head almost like a cap, with a slight wave that allowed a lock to fall around his broad forehead. He lifted his dark blue eyes to his father, and there was a blackness in them, almost as brooding as the night outside. His eyes were shaded by long thick lashes, and there was a firmness and a compactness in the man that spoke of years of hard labor. He had a dark-complected square face, a strong chin with a cleft, and a straight English nose. He was a handsome man, though not apparently aware of it.

"It's taking too long," he said tersely.

Quickly James Spencer looked over the desk and sensed what lay beneath the iron control of his son's face. Josh's nerves were as tight as a violin string and ready to snap. "It was the same when you were born," he murmured. Hoping to be encouraging, he tossed the plume down, adding, "It will be all right." They were useless, meaningless words, for when a child was born in the Colonies in 1755, there were no guarantees. Childbirth was a hard, difficult, dangerous thing, and many homes were filled with children who had never known their mother, having lost her in childbirth.

"It's taking too long!" Josh grated. "She should've had the baby by now!"

Spencer, knowing this was nothing but the exact truth, still tried to reassure Josh. He knew that both Faith, his daughter-in-law, and Josh had never been able to bury their fear about this child, as Faith had miscarried two times before. A grimness came to James Spencer's mouth, and desperately he searched his mind, trying to think of some way to comfort his son. James and his wife, Esther, had talked this over many times. Esther had said only the night before, "Josh's faith isn't very strong, James. If anything happened to this child, I'm afraid it would go ill with him. He might lose all of his faith in God."

"Nothing's going to happen," James had assured her. However, he had disguised his own fears, and now looking at his son, James sought desperately for some way to put a better face on the matter.

Without any idea as to what to say, he suddenly reached over and picked up a thick Bible that lay close at hand. He opened it and began to read from the book of Psalms. It had always been his favorite book, and whenever he found trouble overwhelming him, he would open it to this section. Now the timeless words of comfort began to roll off his lips, and he lost himself in their meaning.

Josh listened for a moment, then got up and walked over to the window. The drone of his father's voice went on and on, and soon the very meaning of the words themselves became blurred. He had heard the Bible all of his life—from the pulpit, from his father, from his mother. He had even read it himself, but now the fear of the loss of another child that he longed for so desperately loomed up inside him like a dark specter. It sickened him, almost nauseated him, and yet he knew that he could not show his father the struggle raging within him.

Outside, the rain fell in long, slanting silver lines, illuminated by brief lightning flashes. The raindrops made a monotonous drone as they hit the shingle roof, then fell off to the puddles below. There was a soporific effect about it that would have made him drowsy if the fear had not driven him to distraction. The lightning crashed again, blinding him momentarily. He shut his eyes, and as he did so, his mind went back to the first time he had met Faith Hancock. . . .

The girl standing in the school yard was small and overly shy. Josh, who was not very good at guessing ages, asked, "How old are you? Ten, I'll be bound."

"I'm twelve."

The girl's face was pretty, but her clothes and hair were plain looking. From the first day she had come to school in Williamsburg, Josh had watched her carefully. He was bothered by how the other students made fun of the way she dressed. She was wearing a shapeless linsey-woolsey dress of gray that had no trace of beauty. Her hair was drawn back tightly, and she wore an equally shapeless white cap on her head. She had dark brown hair and brown eyes, and there was a frailty and vulnerability about her that attracted Josh Spencer.

Even as he stood talking to her, Malon Jones came up and said, "Got yourself a lady friend, Spence?"

"We're doing all right without you, Malon," Josh said sharply. He did not like the heavyset, bug-eyed boy. He had had trouble with the bully on several occasions.

Malon reached over and grabbed the material of the girl's dress. "What's this made out of, a cotton sack? Well, I wouldn't even use it for that."

"Take your hands off of her, Malon!" Jehoshaphat said sharply. The other boy was two years older, stocky, and had administered two severe beatings to Josh already.

Now Malon grinned roughly, a cruel light glinting in his muddy brown eyes. "You ready for another thrashing?"

"You can try it if you want to!"

"Come on then! Outside!"

The two went outside and soon were rolling in the dust, gasping and throwing blows at each other. Only when they had battered each other into insensibility did the schoolmaster come out. He grasped them each by the collar, yanked them up, and said, "Fighting again? Maybe a caning will make a difference to you!"

Josh did not wince even once under the strict punishment administered by Mr. Highliger. Malon squealed loudly as the cane repeatedly struck, but Josh uttered not a word.

Afterward he sat down, his back burning from the strokes of the hickory cane. His lower lip was bleeding where he had bitten it during the thrashing, but he said nothing. After the school day was over, he slowly got to his feet and walked out of the room, moving carefully.

"I'm . . . I'm sorry you had to take a whipping."

Josh turned around and saw that the girl had followed him. Her name, he knew, was Faith Hancock, and he shrugged, saying, "It wasn't so bad."

"I bet it was. I bet it hurt like anything."

The two turned and walked down the dusty street. The August heat was dying down now, and as they walked along Josh began to grow curious about the young girl. "Who are your people?" he asked. Williamsburg was a small place, and he knew almost everyone who lived there.

"I . . . I don't have any people. I'm an orphan," she said, looking down.

Josh had known a few orphans before, but somehow the sadness in the girl's voice struck him. "Sorry," he mumbled.

"What about your people?"

"I'm a Spencer. My father's name is James, and my mother's name is Esther."

"Do you have any brothers or sisters?"

"No. Just me."

The two walked on, and finally she stopped in front of a cobbler's establishment. "I'm staying here with the Mayhans. I'm going to be bound to them for six years, until I'm eighteen."

"Maybe we'll see each other again. I don't mean at school." Josh suddenly felt shy and awkward. He was not good at making conver-

sation with girls. Most of the time he felt clumsy and uncertain around them, but when the young girl lifted her eyes and smiled, a shock went through him. There was a gentleness and a sweetness in her face that he had not seen before.

"Well," he said, "I'll see you tomorrow."

Faith hesitated and then suddenly reached out and, with a rather daring motion, took Josh's hand. When she leaned forward her voice was almost inaudible. "Thank you for looking out for me."

The touch of her hand was gentle and soft and gave Jehoshaphat Spencer a feeling of pride and power. Clearing his throat, he said huskily, "Oh, that's okay! I'll see you tomorrow, Faith."

"Tomorrow, Josh . . ."

"Esther—!"

Josh's reminiscences were broken off abruptly when he heard his father call his mother's name. Instantly, he sprang out of his chair and turned to face the woman who had come into the room. "How is she, Mother?" he demanded.

Esther Spencer was only two years younger than her husband. She was a small woman with brown hair and clear brown eyes. She was pretty rather than beautiful, but now there was an air of trouble in her usually placid expression. Something in her eyes, in the set of her lips, or perhaps in the way she held her hands together tightly, brought a surge of fear into Josh's heart. "Is it bad?" he demanded, rising and grabbing her arm quickly. He was a strong young man, not knowing his own strength, and he saw pain flicker in his mother's eyes. "Sorry," he whispered, then stood there waiting for her report.

"Dr. Twilliger isn't as happy with her progress as he would like," she said evenly.

"I wish Dr. Hammond were here," James Spencer said. He rose and moved jerkily across the room. There was no smoothness about his movements. All were quick and rather awkward. He slapped one fist into a palm and shook his head, almost viciously. "Why did Hammond have to choose *this* time to go to Richmond for that meeting?"

Ignoring his father's outburst, Josh stood staring down at his mother's face. He noticed the taut lines on each side of her mouth that only appeared when she was troubled. "What does Twilliger say?"

"There's . . . there's something wrong with the way the baby is placed."

"Can he do anything?"

"He's trying, dear!" Esther Spencer reached up and pushed the errant lock of hair from her son's furrowed brow. She knew well the tumult that was tearing this tall son of hers apart, and she yearned to do something about it. Quick flashes of memory of how the other two pregnancies had ended in miscarriages rose in her mind, but she did not want to create any more fear in Josh. "You two sit down. I'll go make some tea and perhaps something to eat."

"I don't want anything!"

James Spencer gave his wife a quick look. They had lived together long enough so that each understood the other's unspoken words by a mere gaze. In those few seconds, it was as if he said, *He's going to pieces, Esther.*

Looking at her troubled son, then back at her husband, Esther gave him a look that said, *We'll have to be strong for him. He is not as strong in the Lord, so it will be up to me and you, James.*

Esther forced Josh to sit down and said, "There's nothing to be gained by fretting yourself. Now, I'll fix some tea, and then later Dr. Twilliger will come down, and I'm sure he'll have good news."

Two parallel lines appeared between Josh Spencer's eyebrows—signs of anger or disturbance, or both. His parents recognized it instantly. Beneath their son's rather casual good humor lurked a stratum of temper that neither of them quite understood. Both of them were placid, easygoing people, as were most of their family. From time to time during Josh's young life, a temper and an intolerance had flashed out, almost from nowhere, that they both feared. As Esther left the room, James sat down with a cautious look at his son and shook his head. "It'll be all right," he said. "It's natural that men would be worried about their wives at a time like this."

Lifting his steady gaze that was troubled and flecked with an inexpressible emotion, Josh Spencer regarded his father. *You don't know anything about this, Father! You've never lost two children. You've had an easy life. You just don't understand!* He sat back, however, and his father began reading from the Psalms again. As the words flowed across to him, filling the room with the sounds and cadences of Old Testament verses, Josh leaned his head back, closed his eyes, and involuntarily, almost, began to think of how he had married the woman who was now suffering such terrible pangs upstairs in this house. . . .

———————

The dance was the biggest in the county, and it was being held in the home of a former governor. Josh Spencer was not a young man who often attended parties. He had spent far more time in the woods surrounding Williamsburg hunting the elusive deer, the coon, and the possum than he had on polished dance floors. Still, his mother had insisted, saying, "It's your duty to go, Josh. There won't be enough young men there, and the young ladies will be wanting for partners."

Josh had laughed at her, but then had obeyed by going to the best tailor in the city and being fitted with a fine suit. Now, an hour before the dance, he was standing before the full-sized mirror, admiring himself and feeling rather like a fool. "I never did care much for fancy clothes," he murmured as he studied his reflection in the mirror.

The suit coat was made of faille—a light, soft, ribbed fabric woven in silk—with light and dark green stripes, and was worn open. Under the coat he wore a white silk shirt with ruffles at the chest and at the wrists. The waistcoat was short, single-breasted, tan in color with a trim of dark green, and had silver buttons down the front. He had on white satin breeches that fastened just below the knee, white-and-green-striped stockings, and low-heeled black shoes with silver buckles. He was carrying a pair of white gloves in his hand.

Finally shrugging, he said with a half grin that turned one corner of his lip upward in a peculiar manner, "At least I won't be sniffing snuff out of a silver box. I draw the line at that!"

Wheeling swiftly, he left the room, his stride smooth and even. He moved more easily than most men, the result of long walks in the forest. Going down the stairs, he met his mother and laughed when her eyes widened. "Well, what do you think, Mother?"

"You look beautiful!"

"Women are supposed to look beautiful! I'm supposed to look handsome!"

James Spencer emerged from the study and made his way down the hall. "Well, that suit cost enough. You should look both beautiful and handsome. Come along. Let's go. You better let me drive. I wouldn't want you to spoil those white gloves with anything as crude as the lines of a buggy."

They arrived at the governor's house, which was illuminated with what seemed to be hundreds of lanterns, and Josh said, "Some house the governor's got here! It looks like a Greek temple." He studied the portico of Doric columns that outlined the huge building on three sides, noted the balustrade on top, and shook his head. "His father would've been happy in a log cabin."

"Times are changing." James Spencer grinned. "But I agree with you. I find it a bit ostentatious myself."

Stepping inside, they heard the sounds of violins, dulcimers, and a clavichord filling the house with music.

The foyer was a large, well-lit room with a domed ceiling and a large chandelier of cut glass. On each side of the front door was a floor-length window covered with white silk damask, faintly caressing the highly polished white marble. A sky of light blue, with fluffy white clouds floated overhead, and the illusion carried on down the walls with trees and the landscape of an old English garden.

At the far end of the foyer, a pair of great oak doors opened onto a large ballroom. The ballroom had a very ornate domed ceiling made of gilded tinplates depicting scenes of angels and other flying cherubs. The walls were white, broken up by floor-length windows alternating with long gilded mirrors that reflected the candlelight of silver wall sconces next to each one. Queen Anne walnut chairs with crimson silk damask lined the walls of the room. Doors to the right of the ballroom led to a formal dining room, where many tables were laden with refreshments. At the back of the ballroom French doors led to a garden filled with fountains, statues, and many beautiful rose bushes.

The ballroom was an array of swirling colors—reds, yellows, greens, blues—as the ladies' evening gowns swished by in step to the soft music. Their jewelry glittered, catching the reflection of the chandeliers overhead. Jehoshaphat enjoyed the dances he had with several of the local girls. Finally he saw a young woman over to his right with her back to him. He admired the way the rich chestnut hair was done in a French style that he knew was called a chignon. She was very attractive, and a sense of adventure and daring suddenly took Jehoshaphat. He moved over toward her and said, "Miss, may I have the next dance?"

The young woman turned, and a pair of bright brown eyes suddenly laughed up at him. "I thought you'd never ask, Jehoshaphat!"

"*Faith!*" *Josh had not seen Faith for six months. She had been to Boston, and now looking at her in a lovely dress, it seemed that he had never seen her before. "Why, you look like a grown woman!"*

"*And what did I look like when I left, an old mule?*"

Josh knew that she was teasing him, something she often did. They had become close friends over the past few years, but they had spent more time studying books in dusty schoolrooms or going for walks in the woods than attending parties.

"*I've never seen you in a party dress,*" *he said.*

"*Do you like it? I made it myself,*" *Faith said, twirling around.*

The dress was a simple gown but exquisite, made of a pale pink silk in the Watteau style. It had a low-cut neckline with a dainty white lace frill around it. The bodice fit tightly in front, and in the back the material hung loosely from the neckline, falling into folds all the way to the hem. The elbow-length sleeves were finished with a wide ruffle of lace at the end. The overskirt was of the same pale pink silk, which hung to the floor, trimmed also in exquisite white lace. A delicate pearl necklace, white gloves, and pink satin shoes added the finishing touches to the elegant ensemble.

"*You look absolutely beautiful!*"

"*Why, Josh, I believe you've been practicing up on young ladies. Have you gotten to be a gallant?*"

"*I don't believe I have.*"

"*Pardon me. I believe this is my dance, Miss Faith.*"

Josh turned with annoyance in his eyes. A tall young man was standing there, and before he could say a word, Faith was swept away.

She sure has changed, he thought to himself as he made his way to the refreshment table, where his mother was sipping from a crystal cup.

"*She's very pretty, isn't she?*"

"*Faith? Why, I didn't even recognize her!*" *Josh said, then glanced back toward the couple dancing in the middle of the ballroom.*

"*She's always been pretty, but you've never noticed.*"

"*Well, I noticed tonight.*"

"*Did you know she made her own dress? She's a very resourceful one. A steady young woman. A fine Christian, too.*"

Josh did not miss his mother's comment, but at this stage in his life, he was not particularly interested in Christian girls at all. He was, however, impressed by Faith, and as soon as the tall fellow relinquished her,

Josh swept her back out onto the dance floor. "Tell me what you've been doing," he said.

"No, you tell me what you've been doing. I've missed our walks together and our studies, too."

The dance went on for hours, and for Josh there was only one person there, Faith Hancock. He had difficulty when the tall young man kept insisting on claiming Faith for another dance.

"Who is he, anyway?"

"Why, he's the son of the governor of New Hampshire. He's down for a visit."

"A nutmeg Yankee? Don't have anything to do with him!"

"Why, Josh, don't be silly. He's actually very nice."

"He's not as nice as I am." Josh grinned. "I'll prove it to you."

Josh set out to prove that he was nicer than the son of the governor, and from that moment on, everything in Josh Spencer's life was geared toward courting Faith Hancock.

Perhaps that was the way of it with Jehoshaphat Spencer. He became a single-minded young man when he wanted something. When he set out to become a hunter, he practiced until he became the best hunter in the county. When he decided to be a rider, he had to ride the fastest horses and win the most races. And now he had settled his mind on Faith, and for the next two months he was practically ubiquitous where the young woman was concerned.

Faith was thrilled, although she never admitted it. For years she had been secretly in love with Jehoshaphat Spencer, whom she never called anything but Josh in her own mind, and now she recognized that he was falling in love with her.

The time came, then, a mere six months after the ball, in a gardenia-fragrant orchard when the two stood together. They had been silent for a long time, and finally Faith turned to him and said, "You're very quiet, Josh. Is something wrong?"

"Yes."

"Can you tell me about it?"

"I'm afraid I'm going to die."

Faith gasped and her eyes widened. Her first thought was that a terrible disease had been diagnosed. "Oh, Josh!" she cried and put her hand on his chest. "It's not smallpox, is it?"

"No, it's worse than smallpox." There was a mournful expression *in Josh's eyes, and he reached his hand out and said, "I'm afraid it's much worse."*

Fear came over Faith, and she said, "What is it, Josh?"

Reaching out, Josh pulled her up against him, holding her to his chest. "I'm in love with you, Faith, and I'm going to die if you don't marry me."

For a moment Faith could not think, and then she realized he was teasing her. She reached out and slapped his cheek sharply. "You are awful!" she cried, relieved and half angry.

"I'm serious, Faith. I love you with all my heart, and I want to marry you." He leaned down and kissed her. It was not their first kiss, but there was something about this one that was different. Faith realized it and came to him with a willingness and a yielding she had never shown before. Her arms went around his neck, and she pulled him closer, and for a time the two stood there in silence. Finally Faith drew back and said, "I love you, Josh. I always have—and I always will. . . ."

The shrill cry of a newborn child suddenly shook Josh to the core. It jolted him back out of that pleasant past when all had been good and sweet and easy, and now his eyes wildly met his father's. Both men jumped to their feet and ran out of the study. Scrambling upstairs, they stopped outside the door, which opened at once, and Esther Spencer stepped out. Her lips were tight, and there was a nervous blink in her eyes. "You have a fine son, Josh."

"A son!" Josh's eyes grew dim with tears. Everything was all right. He began to shake, and he held his hands together tightly, squeezing them to control the joy that ran through him.

He felt his father's hand on his shoulder, then heard his voice congratulating him. Then he shook himself and said, "Faith! I want to see her!"

"Son—"

Something in his mother's voice brought Josh up short. A sudden fear seized him, touching something in the inner part of his heart and running along his nerves. His mother was a steady woman, but this was fear that he saw in her eyes, not steadiness.

"What . . . what is it? What's wrong with Faith?"

"Josh, she's in a bad condition, I'm afraid."

Josh stood there frozen, as if the world had fallen around him. The joy over his new son left, and all he could think was, *Faith's dying.* He shoved inside the door, and the doctor, who was standing over the bed, turned to him.

"Mr. Spencer—"

Josh pushed him aside with one rough sweep of his arm and fell on his knees. One look at his wife's face and he knew the worst. Her eyes were sunk back in her head, her mouth drawn back from her teeth. *She looks dead already,* he thought. Grabbing her up in his arms, he held her and began to weep. "Faith—"

He felt her hands touching him feebly and heard her voice whispering, "Josh."

Holding her for a time, he laid her back down gently and said hopefully, "You'll . . . you'll be all right, Faith."

But Faith Spencer knew that her life was almost gone, and all that kept her alive now was determination to speak to her husband. "Let me hold the baby," she whispered.

The doctor moved quickly to the side of the bed and placed the small bundle in her arms. Pulling back the blanket, she looked at the tiny morsel of humanity.

"His name is Jacob," she managed to get out.

"Yes . . . yes," Josh said, his voice choking.

Faith Spencer reached up one thin arm, touched Josh's cheek, and her voice was so still that he had to lean forward to hear it. It came just as a wisp of breath. "You must . . . not blame God, Josh. He's taking me home, but . . . you must not blame Him. He's giving you . . . part of me to keep."

"No!" Josh said. "No, you can't leave me!"

She turned and tenderly kissed the red face of the child, who lay with his eyes tightly closed as if he, too, were leaving. The dying woman looked once at the baby, then her eyes reached up and touched her husband's for a lingering moment. "I must go with my Lord," she said, "but I leave . . . Jacob with you. Good-bye . . . my husband. You have been . . . always my . . . dearest one. . . !"

Those were Faith's last words. She lingered for a few more minutes, then the thin chest heaved once and was silent.

The doctor moved forward, picked up the infant, and whispered, "I'm afraid she's gone, Mr. Spencer."

"Keep your hands off me!" Josh overflowed with blind, unreasoning rage. It was the strain which lay deep in him that his parents had never understood. Now it arose like a black cloud. Ignoring the baby, he rose and walked stiff-legged to the door. His parents stood frozen, watching fearfully.

"The baby's all right, son," his mother said. Josh stared at her as if she had said something in a foreign language. Without a word, he pushed past her. His father reached out and grabbed his arm, but Josh shook him off and left the room. He walked down the stairs blindly, reached the front door, and without pausing for a coat, stepped outside. The wind blew fiercely in his face as the cold rain mixed with the tears of anger and tragic loss he refused to shed in front of others. A flash of lightning lit up the scene as he moved down the walk. He had no idea where he was going. All he knew was that he felt betrayed by a God he had tried to serve, and he went out into the night. Nothing in the blackness of that night was darker or more ominous than the bitterness and despair that filled Josh Spencer's heart.

Incident at *The Brown Stag*

Two

$\mathscr{S}$ ince a considerable percentage of people in the Colonies could not read, tavern owners soon learned to follow the English custom of identifying their establishments with a picture. The crudely drawn brown deer with a crown of awkward-looking antlers represented Dutch Hartog's tavern, *The Brown Stag*. The sign hung from a cast-iron shaft, and as the remnants of the stormy wind tossed the clouds about in the sky, the faded icon creaked as it swung on its hinges.

Inside the tavern, the proprietor stood behind the bar, polishing a glass listlessly. His smallish pale blue eyes were fixed on the customer who sat with his back braced against the wall staring blindly at the thick brown bottle on the table in front of him. Dutch Hartog was one of the roughs. Not over forty, his thick blond hair had receded halfway down his skull, and his mouth had the look of a catfish, twisted to one side, drawn up by a scar that traced its way down his left cheek. He had served in the British Royal Navy, leaving his right foot and lower leg at one of the furious battles fought by His Majesty's forces at sea. A stout peg furnished the deficiency, but the loss of his leg had made Hartog a gloomy man indeed. He had made his way to America using what money he had to buy *The Brown Stag* at Williamsburg. Now he leaned back and considered, with some dissatisfaction, his establishment.

The tavern was a dark, low-ceilinged place—low enough that a tall man could bash his head against one of the greasy timbers that supported the second story if he wasn't careful. Half a dozen rough-hewn pine tables and a motley assemblage of chairs and stools completed the furnishings of the room, all faintly illuminated by two small windows that allowed dim rays of light to filter in from the outer street. Four tin lanterns with intricate punched patterns suspended from pegs augmented this light with a pale yellowish gleam. The smell of cooked meat, grease, sweat, and alcohol formed a pungent aroma about the place. To the left was a door that led to the kitchen where Dutch's woman did what cooking was necessary.

A flight of stairs nailed to the side of the wall gave access to the upper part of the tavern, which consisted of four bedrooms. One was used by Dutch himself and whatever woman he kept at the moment. The other three were for rent—usually for short term.

"Dutch, you ought to make him go home."

Quickly Hartog turned to fix his pale blue eyes on a young woman who had entered the room from the kitchen. She was wearing a green tight-fitting cotton dress, cut low as befitted a tavern girl. She had dark brown hair and eyes, and just above her lip, on the right side of her cheek, was a beauty mark. Her complexion was covered with more makeup than most women wore.

"Ain't my job to run good customers off!" Dutch grunted. He shoved his weight against the bar and placed his meaty forearms down, staring at his powerful hands. "As long as he's got shillings, he can stay here and drink."

Rhoda Harper was not happy with his answer. She stood there hesitantly, the dim light of the lanterns highlighting her rather prominent cheekbones, and her lips twisted with dissatisfaction. "He's been drunk long enough, Dutch. Tell him to go home."

"You take him to raise?" Dutch jeered. "Why don't you take him upstairs. He's got money, it seems. That's what you're here for, girl."

A slight flush touched the young woman's cheeks. True enough, she was a tavern girl—the lowest level of life in Williamsburg, no more than a prostitute. Still, despite the hardness of her expression and the tenseness of the set of her shoulders, there was something about her that spoke of a past that was different. "He needs to go home," she said stubbornly.

Dutch Hartog was slightly puzzled. When Rhoda had first come to the tavern, he had considered her no different from any of the other doxies that came and went from time to time, driven like dead leaves by an aimless wind. They appeared, some sickened and died, and a few actually found men who cared little enough about their past to marry them—or at least to take them away under some understanding. Dutch had taken Rhoda for one of these and had been surprised by her behavior. At times she would drink heavily, falling into the usual alcoholic stupor that many of the tavern girls did. At other times, however, brief flashes of education and hints of culture that did not go with her profession would surface. Several times Dutch had questioned her about her background, but she had been sullenly reticent. Now he saw that her guard was down, and he nodded his big head toward the lone customer, asking, "You know 'im, Rhoda?"

A slight hesitation, and then Rhoda nodded shortly. "I . . . used to, but it was a long time ago. His name's Jehoshaphat Spencer."

"Who is he?"

Again the hesitation. "His people are respectable."

"How would you be knowin' respectable people?"

Rhoda tightened her lips and turned her head to glance at the slumping figure of Spencer as he drunkenly tried to pour from the brown bottle into the glass. "I knew him when I was a little girl."

"Here in Williamsburg?" Rhoda's eyes seemed to grow misty for a moment, a sign of weakness that Dutch had rarely seen. He studied her carefully and waited.

"That's right, Dutchie. We grew up together. Went to the same school."

"Oh, I figured you was educated more than most. What about him?"

But Rhoda had said more than she intended. Pain came to her eyes as she seemed to remember things from the past. Long ago she had given up all hope of a better life—still, from time to time, she thought wistfully of how things could have been different. She had hardened herself and given herself over to the life of a tavern wench with no hope beyond that. However, when Josh Spencer had come into the tavern out of the storm, she had been shocked at the clarity of the memories that had stirred her. Josh apparently hadn't recognized her; it was true that her appearance now was vastly different from the innocent young girl he had known long ago. He would have remembered a quiet young girl, sweet faced, the eldest of seven children. Perhaps he might have recalled helping her with her lessons more than once.

But all that was in the past, before her father had deserted the family, leaving a frail and sickly mother and a houseful of children to fend for themselves. Rhoda Harper had struggled vainly to keep the family together, but it had been a hopeless task. She had been honest at first and kept herself from the advances of men. The endless struggle finally wore her down, and then bitterness had come, along with a sense of futility. She had gone the way of so many young girls—which explained her position at *The Brown Stag*.

"I'm gonna take him home."

Dutch stared at the girl, mystified as he had sometimes been by what lay within her. He had led a hard life, and his opinion of women was not high. Nevertheless, he had formed a grudging respect for the girl. At one time he had considered taking her for his own woman, not as a wife, for he had two of those somewhere, perhaps dead, but he had been educated by them to the extent that he wanted no permanent attachments.

"A funny way for you," he commented only. Then he stood there and watched as Rhoda went over, pulled a brown, worn cloak from a nail, put it about her shoulders, and pulled the hood up over her head.

"Come along, Mr. Spencer. Time to go home."

Josh heard the voice, but it seemed to come from far away. He looked up blearily and tried to focus his eyes, but all he could see was a woman's face. Dimly he seemed to remember a tavern girl had been filling his glass and bringing him fresh liquor, but she meant nothing to him. All he could think of was: *My wife is dead. . . !*

"No, not . . . goin' home!"

"Come along."

Josh felt his arm pulled, and he angrily pushed away. "Get away! Leave me alone!"

Rhoda stood there, staring down at the man. Memories came back, trooping across her mind like faint specters—how in another life he had been kind to her. She had heard of his marriage, but she had never seen him since those early days. Now, she realized that whatever had brought him to this place, to drink himself into oblivion, was more than he could handle. Silently she watched him for a moment, then finally murmured, "All right," then turned and walked away.

Josh watched her go, blinking to clear his eyes. Something came to him, and then he felt shame. "Shouldn't have done that," he muttered. He half rose to go apologize, but the room seemed to swim. He tried to hold himself upright, but suddenly he became terribly sick. He lost his balance, grabbing wildly at the table and overturning it. The bottle crashed and broke, and he heard a male voice curse loudly. Strong hands reached under his arms, and he felt hands moving through his pockets.

"I'll take what you owe me, but I don't need you in the place anymore. You want a room, or you want me to help you out?"

Josh desperately tried to keep his churning stomach from rejecting the raw liquor that he had poured into it. Shaking his head, he blinked at the innkeeper, then grabbed his hat and pulled it over his head. Weaving as he moved, he headed for the door. As he stepped outside, he heard a woman's voice say, "Good-bye, Josh—" And then he was outside in the darkness. He turned blindly into the wind, hoping it would clear his head, but as he made his way along the streets of Williamsburg, he knew that he had lost that which could never be restored.

"Faith!" he moaned. "Why did you have to die?"

A bolt of lightning etched its way across the sky and lit up the tormented face of Josh Spencer as he reeled and staggered along the cobblestone streets.

———

Awkwardly Paul Anderson held the red-faced infant and smiled down into his face. Seeming to take this personally, the baby opened a wide mouth, exposing a fine set of gums, and rent the air with a loud scream.

Anderson blinked with shock. He was a young man of twenty, thin and wiry in build, and no more than five feet ten inches. Ordinarily there was a smile on his face, but the shrill screams of the child shattered his composure.

"What's wrong with him, Mrs. Spencer?"

Esther Spencer had been watching the young man after handing him the baby. "Why, nothing, Paul. He's just exercising his lungs."

Anderson gave her a look of surprise, then turned his light green eyes back on the infant. "He might make a shouting Methodist one day. He's got a good start on it."

"Let me have him, Paul." Esther reached over and took the baby, who stopped crying instantly. She cuddled him with a loving motion, traced the ruddy cheeks, then whispered, "He's a fine child. I never saw a healthier baby."

James Spencer had been standing to one side, staring out the window. He turned now and came over to stand beside the pair, looking down with them at the baby. "Jacob Spencer," he murmured. "My first grandson." There was pride in the older man's tone—still, his eyes were troubled, and when he reached out and touched the fine dark hair on the baby's head, he shook his head slightly. He started to speak, then pulled his lips tightly together.

Anderson had caught this motion, and his eyes went to Esther, who shook her head slightly as if to warn him not to speak. However, Paul Anderson was not a man to stay silent long. After a few moments of commenting on the baby, he asked, "Josh isn't here?"

"No." The monosyllable from James Spencer and the sharpness of the tone revealed the turmoil that was going on in the older man. "He hasn't been back since . . . since the funeral." Anger crossed his face, sweeping it momentarily, giving it a hard cast. "I'm surprised he even came for that!"

Esther reached over and put her hand on her husband's arm. "We must be patient, James."

"Patient? I think we've been patient long enough! It's been two weeks since Faith died! Where is he? Probably down at the tavern, drunk again!"

"That doesn't sound like Josh," Anderson said quickly.

"He's not the same man that you knew, Paul!" James said bitterly. "I never thought I'd be ashamed of my son, but he's not taking Faith's death right. He's got to learn to live with grief, as all of us do. I wish he would draw on the Lord for strength, but he seems to blame the One who could help him the most. Why, he acts as if he's the only man in the world who ever lost a wife! It's common enough, and he's got to learn to deal with it."

"Aye, it is common," Anderson said, "but Josh was so much in love with Faith. I guess it was harder for him than for most men."

"I can't see that!" James Spencer said stubbornly. "He's turning his back on God and everything he has believed in." He ran his hand through his hair and moved restlessly back to a window, staring outside. The bitter winter had struck in earnest now, and snow drifted down in flakes as big as shillings. Williamsburg was an attractive town, and the coating of snow gave it a pristine appearance, something of a fairyland look. The streets were glistening with a soft mantle of white, and many had put runners on their wagons and carriages, and bells on their horses so that there was almost a festive look to the city. None of this held any charm for James Spencer, however, as he stared, glowering out at the whiteness of the streets and the houses that were peaked with small castlelike pyramids on the chimneys. Smoke came out of most of them now, curling slightly upward, and the town seemed at rest.

Esther rocked the baby in her arms and began to feed him with a cloth which she dipped in rich goat's milk that she had obtained from one of the neighbors. The baby sucked it lustily with his tiny fists clenched together as Esther crooned to him for a while, saying those sweet nothings.

Paul leaned back in the Hepplewhite chair, balancing on the back legs, watching as Esther fed the child. His mind, however, was on Josh Spencer. The two of them had grown up together and had gotten into the usual troubles of young men. They had courted the young women of Williamsburg, attended church together, hunted together, and now that tragedy had struck his friend, Paul Anderson felt a sense of helplessness.

If I'm going to be a minister, he thought almost angrily, *I've got to learn how to handle crises better than this!* He thought of his father and his three brothers, all of them given over to running what was rapidly becoming the most successful business in Williamsburg. They had branched out from one store to three, and now they were talking of opening another in Savannah. Paul had learned early on that he had no aptitude, nor inclination, for business.

His parents had not been disappointed, however, by his decision. "It would be good to have a minister in the family," Paul's father had said fondly when his younger son had announced his call to the ministry. He had been less happy when Paul had spoken of his interest in someday going as a missionary to the Cherokee Indians.

The Cherokee Indians were not popular in the Colonies in the year 1755. The savage forays of the Indians against the settlers along the borders of the Colonies infuriated as well as terrified the colonists. Paul Anderson's announcement that someday he would be a missionary to preach the gospel to the Cherokee had not been popular with his family—nor with anyone else.

As if reading his mind, Esther Spencer said, "Are you still thinking of going to preach to the Indians?"

"Yes, I am, Mrs. Spencer. God's put it on my heart, although I don't know when He'll open the door for me to go."

"They have their own gods, don't they?" James Spencer said.

"They don't have the true God," Paul answered softly. "They need Jesus Christ as much as you or I."

"I suppose so!" James snapped. He ordinarily was a kind man, but his son's behavior of late had left him ill-tempered, and he could not see the future as being pleasant. He came over and stared down in the face of his grandson and said, "I don't know what's the matter with Josh." He shifted his glance to the young man sitting in front of him and said, "Will you try to talk to him, Paul? You two always got along well."

"Yes, of course I will. I thought I'd find him here."

"You'll probably find him down at *The Brown Stag.* He's carrying on there, I think, with some woman."

"You don't know that, James!"

"Why else would a man take a room at a tavern and stay away from his family and his newborn son?"

"I think he's lost, and he doesn't know what to do," Esther said.

"You always defend him! You always do!" However, Spencer's tone gentled, and he put his hand on his wife's shoulder. "And that's as it should be. I'm sorry, dear. I don't mean to be strict, but I'm worried about him."

Paul Anderson got to his feet and said at once, "I'll go find him, and I'll promise you this—I'll stay with him and try to keep him out of what trouble I can. He's a stubborn one, though." He frowned. "You know that better than I."

"Do the best you can, Paul. He's always thought a lot of you."

"Of course. You stay here and pray—and take care of this fine young fella—while I go see what I can do with his father. . . ."

Josh looked up at the man who had entered, and his eyes brightened at once. "Paul," he said, smiling. "Come and sit down. I want you to meet somebody."

Paul Anderson was relieved. He had expected Josh to be drunk and belligerent. Now, as he squinted his eyes and waited for them to adjust to the murky atmosphere of the tavern, he said quickly, "Hello, Josh, good to see you." He took the hand the other man extended, felt the strength of his grip, then took a seat at the table.

He's been drinking some, he thought, *but it's not as bad as I thought.*

"This is Daniel Boone, Paul. Boone, this is a good friend of mine, Paul Anderson."

Boone was not a large man, but there was something compelling about him. His face was clean cut, Paul saw, his eyes were bright, and his nose was slightly bent. He wore a hunting shirt of fringed deerskin, and there was an alertness about him that was lacking in most men.

"I'm glad to know you, Mr. Boone. Are you from these parts?"

"No, I'm from Carolina."

"He just got back from the frontier, Paul. He was involved with Braddock's campaign against the French at Fort Duquesne."

"On the Monongahela?" Paul asked quickly.

"Yes," Boone said. There was a glass in front of him, but the drink did not seem to contain alcohol. He lifted it and said, "This is good cider, Mr. Anderson. Better try some of it."

"Thanks, I will." Paul looked up and waved at the girl, who came over at once. She was an attractive woman, but with a hard look about her. She seemed remotely familiar to Paul, but when he couldn't place her face, he just shrugged and asked, "Could I have some of the cider that this gentleman has?" He waited until the girl brought him some, filled his glass, then he tasted it. "That's good." He leaned forward and said, "We've heard a lot about the battle, but I hear different stories."

Boone sipped the cider and shook his head. " 'Twas a mess," he said simply. "Braddock never should have gone there in the first place."

"I heard George Washington was in the battle. Is that right?"

"He was there, all right, but he'd been pretty sick. He got out of a wagon when the fightin' started," Boone said.

"I can't understand how British regulars could lose against savages. There weren't many French regulars there, were there?"

"No, but General Braddock, he didn't believe in listenin' to advice. Colonel Washington, he tried to tell him he couldn't march troops like they was on parade grounds," Boone said sadly, "but Braddock, he wouldn't listen to him."

"Tell me about it," Paul said. He wanted to hear about the battle, but he also wanted a chance to study Josh Spencer, so he listened as Boone described how Braddock had taken a large force through the heavy woods, having to chop a road to haul the guns and heavy wagons.

"They call it Braddock's Road now," Boone said. "When we got to the Monongahela, I thought it might be all right, but as soon as we crossed, they started shootin' from the cover of the trees. Braddock tried to get the men to line up like it was formation on a parade ground." Boone shook his head sadly, sipped at the cider, and said, "But it was no good. The general, he got shot almost at once. If it wasn't for Colonel Washington, I guess we'd all have lost our scalps there. He formed a retreat and got us out of there."

"What will happen now?" Paul asked.

"I reckon the Frenchies and the English will battle it out, and us Americans will be caught right in the middle."

Josh had listened to the story, which he had already heard, and said, "Tell Paul about the land on the other side of the mountains, Boone."

"Well, I reckon I could do that," Boone said. "I ain't what you call a settled man, Mr. Anderson. I don't like to be cooped up, so I've been wandering around over the mountains." His eyes grew dreamy, and he said, "You ain't never seen nothin' like it, sir! Not nothin'! Why, there's cane fields that go for miles. Game so thick that you just let your gun off and somethin' falls to the ground. The ground's so rich it almost drips with fat."

Paul listened as Boone spoke with glowing enthusiasm of the territory over the Appalachians. He knew his geography well enough to know that the English were spread out along a thin strip of the eastern seaboard from Georgia to New England. The mountains bounded them in there, and the country on the other side was claimed by the French. That was what the fighting between the English and the French was about—who would control that territory west of the Appalachian Mountains all the way to the Mississippi River.

"But you couldn't live there, could you?" Paul asked, leaning forward. "That's Indian land."

Boone gave the young man a smile. "Indians don't much believe in owning land. They just live on it."

"But it's really theirs, isn't it?" Paul insisted.

"Maybe," Boone said, "but there's white settlers now, spreading out all over that part of the world. Sooner or later there'll be trouble."

"Are you going there, Boone?"

Daniel Boone fingered the coonskin cap that lay on the table and did not answer for a minute. "I'm a wanderin' man," he said. "Can't stand to see the sight of cabin smoke close to me. There's millions of miles out there. I figure there's someplace for me and my family, and lots of others feel just like me. Over the misty mountains," he said.

"The misty mountains?" Paul asked quickly. "What's that?"

Boone seemed somewhat embarrassed. "That's what they are sometimes early in the morning when the sun comes up. They're just misty. They look almost like ghostly mountains." He laughed shortly and put his hat on his head, the coonskin tail dangling down his back. He drained the rest of his cider. "I reckon it's big enough even for me," he smiled. "Suits me, anyhow."

"That land, it can't belong to no white people!"

A harsh voice had broken the relative silence of the tavern, and all three men turned to look across the room to the man who had spoken. He was a big man, well over six feet, with curly red hair and a beard to match. He had strange blue-green eyes, and his dirty buckskins were very much like those Boone wore. He had been listening, apparently, to the conversation, and now lifted the bottle in front of him and drank from it, his throat convulsing as the raw spirits hit him. He slammed the bottle down and wiped his mouth with the back of his sleeve. Rhoda Harper had come to stand beside him to replace the bottle. The trapper, for such he appeared to be, looked up at her and said, "Ah, sweetie, bring Jack some more whiskey."

He waited until the girl turned and left to go to the bar, then he stood to his feet and moved over to where the three men were sitting. He stared at Boone and said, "I heard of you, Boone. The Cherokee, they don't like you much." Suddenly he struck his chest with a powerful fist. "I'm Jack Carter. The Cherokee, they like me very much. I treat them fair, not like you!"

Boone appeared unconcerned by the threatening appearance of the huge trapper. "I've always treated the Indians square," he said quietly.

"Square? No! You take their lands and give them cheap beads. You call that fair? You're a cheat!"

"Maybe you better go back to your table, Carter," Josh said. He did not like the intrusion of the trapper, nor what he implied. Coldly he said, "Nobody invited you over here!"

Carter stared at Josh Spencer and said, "You ever been across the mountains? No, I think not! All you do is drink whiskey. You wouldn't last two days among the Cherokee!"

Rhoda had brought the whiskey back, and Carter turned and grasped the bottle with his right hand. With his left, he pulled her close, and before she could protest, he planted a kiss noisily on her lips. "Now," he said, "you've got a real man!" He turned to look at the three Englishmen and sneered. "These are not men! These are women!"

Boone said softly, "I wouldn't be saying things like that, Carter, if I was you."

"Why? Who's gonna stop me?" Carter kissed the girl again. He hurt her, and she let out a small cry.

Josh moved to his feet at once. "Turn her loose, Carter," he warned.

Jack Carter laughed loudly. "Who's gonna make me? You?" Using the hand holding the whiskey bottle, he reached out and shoved Josh backward. Caught off balance, Josh became entangled with the chair and fell to the floor. He scrambled up quickly, and when he moved forward, Carter's eyes glinted wickedly. Looking at Rhoda, he said, "You wait over there. I have a score to settle with this fellow, then you and me, we'll go upstairs and—"

"Wait a minute," Paul said, "there's no point in starting trouble."

Without a moment's hesitation, Carter's left hand flashed out. It caught Paul across the mouth and drove him to the floor. Instantly Josh threw himself forward. The large trapper took the blow that hit him in the chest, but it did not seem to stir him. Moving quickly, especially for such a big man, Carter lifted the bottle and brought it down over Josh's head. The bottle did not break, but the force of it drove Josh to his knees. Carter drew his leg back to kick the helpless man, but at that instant a loud click echoed through the room. Jack Carter looked up to see that Boone had picked up his musket and had drawn the hammer back, and now the weapon was pointed directly at his stomach.

"Old Betsy here might make a pretty good hole in you, Carter," Boone said, almost pleasantly.

"You put that gun down, and we'll see who's the best man!" Carter growled. He dared not move, for the large bore of the musket stared at him menacingly. He knew what one of the large slugs could do to a man's insides.

"Suppose you just take your bottle and leave," Boone suggested. "Otherwise, I might have to waste powder and lead on you."

For one moment it appeared that Jack Carter would not listen, that he would throw himself forward, but something in the light blue eyes of the smaller man who faced him apparently changed his mind, for he moved back a step. He swallowed hard, then forced a laugh. "He is whipped already, and I will see you sometime, maybe out in the woods, Boone, when I have my gun."

"I'll look forward to it," Boone said.

"Come on." Carter grabbed Rhoda by the arm and dragged her across the room. She looked over her shoulder at Josh, who was struggling to get to his feet, but then she turned to watch where she walked as Carter dragged her up the stairs, where they disappeared at the top of the landing.

"Are you all right, Josh?" Paul asked as he helped Josh stand to his feet.

Josh reached up and felt the bump on his head. "I didn't make much of a fight of it, did I?" he mumbled. He knew that his reflexes were gone. The days of steady drinking had robbed him of that. He looked over at the two men, and shame filled his eyes. "Come down in the world, haven't I? Fightin' over a tavern wench." He touched the bump gingerly, then nodded. "Thanks, Daniel."

"Well, he wasn't much of a man, but I'd watch out for him," Boone said. "He's the kind that would shoot you in the back if he got a chance."

"Come on, Josh. You've got to go home. You've been neglecting your family far too long already." Paul's eyes searched Josh's earnestly.

Josh looked at Paul and after a moment's silence he said wearily, "I suppose you're right." He put his hand out, saying, "Thanks for your help, Daniel. And thanks for telling me about the other side of the mountains."

"Maybe you can do me a turn one day," Boone said. "See you

on the other side of the mountains, maybe."

The words seemed to catch at Josh Spencer. He stood absolutely still for a moment, as if a new thought had come to him, then he murmured, "Maybe so."

The three men left the tavern, and on the way back to the Spencer home, Josh said nothing until they neared the street where he lived. Then he stopped abruptly. "Paul, I want to tell you something."

Paul Anderson stopped. "What is it, Josh?"

"Were you listening to what Boone said about all that land on the other side of the mountains?"

"I guess everybody knows about that. I'm going there myself one day, to the Indians."

Josh Spencer stood silently for a moment, and then said, his teeth almost clenched, "I'm going there, too, Paul." He looked around the streets of Williamsburg and thought of Faith. He could not bear spending the rest of his life where everywhere he looked he would be reminded of the woman he had loved above all others. "I'm going there, too. I'm leaving Williamsburg, and I'm never coming back!"

Jack Carter, whose real name was Jacques Cartier, lay back on the bed and watched Rhoda dress. "I gave it to that fellow, didn't I? I should've hit him again! I'd have stomped him to bits if that fellow Boone hadn't put a musket on me!"

Rhoda finished buttoning up her dress. She was tired and angry, and ashamed, as always, when this sort of thing happened. Without a word, she started to leave, but Cartier came up off the bed. "Wait a minute," he said. "Don't leave until I tell you to. Sit down!"

Rhoda did not resist, for the giant's hand was like an iron clamp on her arm. She sat down and stared at him. His flushed face was filled with jaded lust, and she felt the nagging shame for allowing herself to slip into a life like this.

"You need a man like me, Rhoda."

"I don't need any man, except for his money!" she said bitterly.

"No, you need a good man like me. Now, you take that Spencer fellow. He's no good. He's weak, and so is the other one with him." An angry flush touched the broad cheekbones of the Frenchman and he said, "Boone, he won't live long, you bet! When he crosses the mountains, I'll see him, or I'll tell some of my Indian friends to take his scalp."

Rhoda sat there numbly, listening as the trapper rambled on. He drank from the bottle from time to time and spoke of things she did not understand. She had known him for some time, for Cartier had come to Williamsburg on some sort of business. Some suspected him of being a spy for the French, but nobody could prove anything. Finally, he drank himself into insensibility. The last thing she heard him say was, "That Josh Spencer, I am not finished with him, you bet! No, not yet!"

Rhoda saw that he was passing out. Quickly she arose and left the room. She was puzzled about Cartier's hatred of Spencer and wondered if, perhaps, she ought to get word to Josh.

She knew that he had never recognized her, and a bitter twist came to her lips. *Josh wouldn't want to hear from me, not a tavern wench!* The thought ran through her, leaving a pain, and she was shocked that after all she'd gone through, there was still a longing for purity that lay deeply buried in her spirit.

Unto the Hills

Three

A sullen sun had risen halfway up over the low-lying mountains as Josh Spencer took stock of his equipment. He was in the room that had become as familiar to him as his own hands, and as the feeble rays of light filtered through the cloudy panes of glass, he looked up from the musket he was holding and let his eyes run over the furniture, caught for a moment by fond memories that lay deeply embedded in his mind. The room itself had a slanting ceiling, and the floor was made of hard pine of varying widths, worn smooth by years of the passage of bare feet. Two handmade rugs, red and blue, made by his mother, were now worn, and he suddenly remembered how luxurious it had been when at eight years old he had for the first time gotten out of bed onto the warmth of the wool instead of the cold, bare floors.

There won't be any rugs where I'm going, he thought abruptly and lifted his eyes to the miniature portraits of his father and mother that stood out against the pale green print of the wallpaper. He studied their faces for a moment, and a frown formed two vertical creases between his eyebrows at the thought of the sharp differences he had had with them since the death of Faith and the birth of his son. Quickly he passed his hand across his face, closing his eyes as if to shut the memory out, but his love for his wife had been the most consuming passion in his life, and he could not shake the memories. Night after night he had lain in his featherbed tossing and turning, many times getting up and walking the floor, often leaving the house and going out in the bitter cold, trying to tire his body out so he could finally fall asleep. Even when sleep did overtake him, he dreamed of Faith, of their days together, brief as they had been, all etched on his memory forever. He heard a scratching at the door, and rising, he walked over, still holding the musket in his hand. When he opened it, a large shaggy dog with a massive head and curly red fur pushed his way through the crack, reared up on his hind legs, and tried to lick Josh's face.

"Get down, Charlie!" The words were rough, but Josh reached out and fluffed the floppy ears. He had found the dog in an alley and brought him home and fed him with warm milk soaked on a wet rag. The puppy had now grown to a monstrous size, and he had every bad habit a dog could possibly display, including tearing up furniture with his huge teeth and large claws. Seemingly, he was impervious to being housebroken, and he brought fleas from the outside as if it were his duty to infest the house.

Shoving the dog back down, he said, "You lie there and behave yourself!" Josh sat back down and began looking at the equipment he had piled up. The musket he held was a good one. It had been a present on his sixteenth birthday, made by Dave Devinny, one of the finest musket rifle makers in the state. He moved the hammer back on half cock and looked down at the frizzen, noting the smoothness of the action. Picking up a flint, he inserted it into the mechanism, pulled the hammer back to full cock, then pulled the trigger. The machinery clicked sharply, the flint struck the frizzen, and sparks flew. If there had been black powder inside, it would have exploded instantly, setting off the charge in the interior of the musket. It was a good piece, and he examined the flints, of which he had over a hundred. They wore out with use, and a piece shaped into a standardized form by a skilled flint worker was good, on the average, for some twenty or thirty shots, then was discarded.

Josh pulled the rifle up to his shoulder, closed his left eye, and sighted down the barrel. Under normal conditions a good musket would misfire once, perhaps, in twenty or more shots. Sometimes because of a poor, worn-out flint, often because in the rain it was practically useless. At other times the touchhole through the barrel became plugged with powder, fouling the priming flash, which in turn would fail to ignite the charge.

Placing the musket down carefully, he picked up the powder horn and the bullet pouch, weighing them carefully in his hand. He had spent the last two nights molding the bullets out in the work shed. First shaving the lead into an iron pot, he then set the pot in coals. When the lead had melted, he would ladle it out into the bullet molds, watching as the hot lead flowed in a slithering, shining stream into the molds. The liquid metal fascinated him. He had always felt a strong urge to touch it, for it didn't look hot at all—it looked silvery and cool. Once, he had tried it and, to his dismay, raised a blister the size of a shilling on his palm. When the bullets had finally cooled, he had taken them out and trimmed the roughness off with his knife. Now he removed the bullets one at a time from the pouch, rubbing them with an old piece of deerskin that was worn and slick. When he finished the last slug, he put it back in the deerskin bag and pulled the drawstring tight.

Standing up, he moved over to the nail driven in the side of the wall and lifted the deerskin jacket that he had bought from a trapper. It fit him loosely, and he held it for a moment, fingering the soft texture. It had an intricate design of porcupine quills and beads. As he stood there, his eyes went over to the suit that he had worn at the last ball he had attended. Somehow he knew that this change of clothes marked a change in his entire life.

"I've got to get away," he spoke aloud, almost frantically. "I just have to!"

Quickly he gathered up his supplies—including blankets, bullets, powder, underclothes, extra boots—and wrapped them into a blanket in a roll. Then with one final look around the room, he turned quickly and went out into the hall. He passed by the door to his parents' room and heard their muffled voices. The temptation was strong in Josh to leave without saying good-bye, for he knew there would be a scene, but he could not do that. Reaching out, he tapped on the door, and almost at once it opened, and his mother faced him. "It's time for me to go, Ma," he said.

"Come in."

"No, I don't want to."

His father was there almost instantly. "Your mother said come in, Josh!" James Spencer's voice was harsh, but there was pain in his eyes. "We've got to talk before you leave."

Josh hesitated, then put his bundle down out in the hall and stepped inside the bedroom.

James stood watching his son, and a sense of hopelessness swept through him. However, he felt he had to try. "Son, this is a foolish thing you're doing," he said.

"That may be, Pa. But I have to do it! I've got to get away!"

"Why do you have to go now?" Esther Spencer came to stand beside her tall son. She was not a tall woman, and she had to turn her head upward to look into his face. Her tone was pleading, and with something close to a mixture of pity and worry in her voice, she said, "You've got a family here, Josh. You've got a son to raise."

He could not meet his mother's eyes or his father's stern gaze. Quickly he glanced over at the cradle where the baby lay sleeping quietly. Suddenly he felt an impulse to go over, look down, and even pick the child up. He knew that was the right thing to do.

Josh was not a hardhearted young man. On the contrary, he was gentle and compassionate to those less fortunate than he. But the death of his wife had snuffed something out in him. It was as if a candle had been burning brightly, and then suddenly a snuffer had closed over it so that nothing was left but a smoldering, evil-smelling wick. He hated what he had become, but each time the dark cloud of despair and hopelessness settled on him, he had found it easier to run to the tavern and drink it all away than to face it.

Quickly he shook his head. "You'll be a better mother and father to him than I'd be. Right now I just can't think straight." He saw the hopelessness on his parents' faces and quickly added, "I'm just going out to see what the country looks like west of here. Maybe I'll do some trapping or just wander around for a spell." When he saw a lack of comprehension in their faces, he said, "I can't explain it, but I need some time alone."

"How long will you be gone?"

"I . . . can't say, Ma."

The three of them stood there, and a silence fell across the room. The feeble rays of the sun slanted downward on the patterned carpet beneath their feet, and millions of tiny dust motes danced in the bars of golden light. The slow, monotonous ticking of the Seth Thomas clock on the mantel was the only sound in the room for a time, and then suddenly the baby, as if startled by the silence, awoke and began to cry.

"Don't you even want to hold your son once, Josh?"

Josh glanced quickly at his mother. Again the impulse came to go over and hold the tiny bundle. He knew that, even as little as he had seen the child, he would remind him of Faith, and this, perhaps, was what stopped him. He could not bear the thought of another reminder of the great love that had been torn away from him. "No! It would just make going harder! Maybe when I work through this, and he's older, I'll be able to handle it."

"I think you're going against God's will," James said firmly.

A hardness came over his face, and he looked at his father and said, "Pa, don't try to talk to me about God. If God's so good, why did He take Faith away from me?"

"Wiser men than you or I have pondered such questions," James Spencer said. "We're living in an evil world, and I can't explain it. Job struggled with it. Why did evil things happen to him when he had done nothing wrong? The only answer is the verse that says, 'Shall not the judge of all the earth do right?' "

"Do right? You think it was right for Faith to die?" Josh snapped bitterly.

"I think this world is full of evil, son. But one day it will all be taken away."

"Well, I can't wait for that!" Josh said harshly, then immediately was sorry, for he saw his mother's face become contorted, and he knew she was fighting to keep the tears back. Awkwardly he reached out, put his arms around her, and held her close. He kissed her cheek, felt the wetness of the tears, and whispered, "I might be back, Ma, and maybe things will change." He released her quickly, put his hand out, and when his father took it, he squeezed it hard. Swallowing convulsively, he said to both of them, "Try not to think too hard of me." Then he turned and left the room as quickly as possible.

When the outer door slammed, Esther said, "He's gone, James."

James walked over to his wife and put his arms around her. "We'll have to trust God. We've tried our best to raise Josh, and you know the promise. You raise up a child in the way that is right, and when he is old he will not depart from it. We'll have to hang on to that."

"There's another one, too. I came across it just last night. Let me show it to you." Releasing herself from James' embrace, Esther walked over and picked up the Bible that lay on the rosewood table beside the bed. It was open, and she said, "Here. Read this one."

James Spencer took the Bible and read the lines that Esther had marked with a thin spidery line. Aloud he read, "All thy children shall be taught of the Lord." Tears came to his eyes, and he whispered, "It's hard to believe, but we'll have to trust God. His promises never fail, do they, sweetheart?"

"No, they never do." Esther turned, went to the cradle, and picked up the baby. She held him tightly, and he stopped crying at once. "Jacob," she whispered, "you're going to grow up to be a fine man. And someday your father will come back to teach you how."

The large dark eyes of the child studied her thoughtfully, then without preamble a gurgle came, and the infant seemed to smile.

"Look at him! He's laughing!"

James leaned forward, studied the baby's face, then reached out and traced the silky cheek. "By gum, I think he is! He looks like Josh, doesn't he?"

"Except the nose. He has his mother's nose."

"There's some of both of them," James nodded. "You know, as long as this baby's alive, there's something of Faith alive, too. That's the way it is with children. They're the heritage of the Lord."

The two stood there, looking down at their grandson. Their thoughts were with their son, who was running from his pain and his responsibility of being a father—and his Lord. Inside, both of them were praying the same silent prayer. *Lord, teach him—and then bring him back home again.*

Anderson's General Store stood out both by its size and ornate design from the other businesses on the main street of Williamsburg. Silas Anderson, Paul's father, was a man astute in catching the winds of business. Before designing his own, he had visited several large stores in Boston and New York. As Josh entered the establishment, his ears filled with the hum of many voices, for the inside of the store was almost cavernous. Merchandise of all kinds was stacked and neatly organized in sections, and everything from French lace curtains to plows and fancy harnesses were available.

At once Josh was greeted by Paul Anderson, who had seen him enter through the front door. Anderson was wearing a black wool frock coat with a pair of matching knee britches and white stockings. The brass buckles on his shoes glistened, and the cravat that rose high around his throat was of a pristine whiteness.

"Josh! It's good to see you!" he said. He stopped abruptly when he saw the coat Josh had on and asked, "Are you going hunting?"

"Let me talk to you privately, Paul."

"Why, of course. Come over here." Josh's friend led the way to a deserted section of the store that dealt primarily in blacksmithing supplies. "How's Jacob?"

A slight hesitation broke Josh's speech, which told Anderson a good deal. He had spoken with James and Esther Spencer often, and he was aware of Josh's reluctance to enter into his responsibilities as a father. Now he saw the rather adamant cast of Josh Spencer's tanned features and knew that nothing had changed.

"He's fine. A healthy child." The words were short and clipped, and at once Josh changed the subject, saying, "I'm leaving Williamsburg, Paul."

"Leaving? Going on a hunting trip?"

"Yes, a long one. Maybe all the way over the mountains."

Paul Anderson was speechless for a moment. He ran his hand through his sandy brown hair, which was clubbed in back, and a stubborn expression clouded his light green eyes. "It's a bad time for you to be leaving," he said simply. "I know you've had a hard time since losing Faith, but—"

"I didn't come here to discuss anything, Paul!"

The terseness of Josh's words stopped Anderson short. Paul was a rather stubborn young man himself, but he had good insight into people. He saw now that Josh was waiting for him to argue, and he knew that it would be useless. "Well," he said tentatively, rubbing his short nose with a forefinger, "maybe it'll be good for you to get away from things for a while."

"I want to pick up a few more things."

"Of course, Josh. What do you need?"

For the next thirty minutes, Josh carefully looked over the stock of items, picking things carefully, for he knew that he would have to carry all of the equipment he would need on his horse. Finally his eyes lit up, and he said, "I want one of those, Paul."

Anderson looked over quickly and smiled. "A coonskin cap! Tail and all!" Picking it up, he said, "See if it'll fit you. It's the only one we've got."

Josh took the cap, which was lined with heavy silk, and clapped it on his head. "Perfect fit," he said, grinning. He turned his head from one side to the other, feeling the tail brush across his shoulders. "Well, I look like a long hunter, even if I'm not one." *Long hunter* was the name being given to those men who left the East and plunged into the dark and unknown recesses of the western lands past the Appalachians. Men like Daniel Boone.

"Add it all up, Paul."

Paul shook his head. "Nope. It's a going-away present from me."

A moment's silence fell, and then Josh smiled. "Why . . . thanks, Paul." He hesitated, then added, "I know you think I'm crazy, or worse."

"No. Just a bit confused. We all get that way sometimes, and you've had about the roughest blow a man could get." Paul Anderson had a great affection for Josh Spencer. The two of them had spent most of their lives together, and though they were far different in temperament and inclinations, there was still a bond between them that was not easily broken. As he wrapped up the purchases Josh had selected, he said quietly, "You'll be back."

Josh took the package, then lifted his eyes to his friend. "I just don't know, Paul."

"You will be. Your parents are praying for you, and you can depend on my prayers, too."

Josh considered Paul's words for one moment, then he shook his head and appeared to put the whole thing out of his mind. He reached forward suddenly and grabbed the smaller man and gave him a hug. "I'll think about you when I'm out, hiding from the Indians and the bears." Then he turned quickly, as if he was afraid he would say too much, and left the store.

Standing still, Anderson watched him go, and a regretful look touched his countenance. Once again he rubbed the bridge of his short nose with his forefinger, and a long thought came to him about the ways of God and man. He was not a theologian, and yet suddenly he knew that the fate of Josh Spencer was somehow tied up with his own life. He thought of the baby—the innocent child, the victim of the tragedy—and said a quick prayer for him, then for the grandparents, and finally for Josh himself.

The bitter cold numbed Rhoda Harper's fingers. She stuck them into the muff that she carried to warm them. Her face felt stiff. She had walked aimlessly for over an hour down the main business street of Williamsburg, looking in the windows. Once she went into a dress shop and looked at the items of clothing. She had been well aware of the proprietor's disapproval. The owner was a tall lemon-faced woman with a pair of muddy brown eyes set too close together. Her words had been like bait in a trap when she had asked, "Yes? What is it?"

Rhoda, accustomed to such treatment from the respectable members of Williamsburg society, had grown stubborn. She had saved enough money for a new dress. She met the woman's stare and said coolly, "I would like to see the materials that you have."

"I don't think you could afford them."

Rhoda pulled out her purse and let the gold sovereigns clink in her hand. "I can afford it, but I doubt if you have anything good enough for me."

It had been a clash of wills that had somehow symbolized Rhoda's life. In the end, she had walked out of the shop angered by the woman's attitude and somewhat surprised at her own tenacity. *You'd think I'd be used to being treated like dirt*, she thought as she made her way through the snow that covered the sidewalks. Sleds passed on the main part of the wide streets, and there was a strange quietness as the snow muffled ordinary sounds.

Her head ached slightly, for she had drunk far too much the night before. Jacques Cartier had appeared after one of his long absences and had forced her to get drunk with him. As always, the remembrance of what had ensued shamed her, and she thought, not for the first time, of some way to flee from the life that she was leading. Her family came to mind now, scattered and making lives of their own. She knew they would be ashamed of her if they knew she had become a common doxie. As she moved along the street, she forced her mind to go blank.

One day is just like another, she thought, *and it'll never be any different.*

"Hello, Rhoda."

Looking quickly around, Rhoda saw Josh Spencer, and her eyes lit up. "Hello, Josh."

"Going shopping?"

"Just looking mostly." Rhoda studied his attire, taking in the coonskin cap, the long hunting coat that fell to his knees, and the heavy leggings and moccasins. "What are you all dressed up for? Going hunting again?"

"I'm leaving Williamsburg, Rhoda."

A sense of disappointment came over her. She had never referred to the past, for she was sure he did not remember her as a child. *All he knows*, she thought bitterly, *is that I'm a loose woman in a tavern.* However, he had always been kind to her, and perhaps because he had never bought her services, she had learned to admire him very much.

She looked up quickly, wondering if he still remembered the brawl he had had with Cartier, but she did not mention it. "Where are you going?"

With a wide gesture of his arm, Josh said, "Over there!"

She followed his gaze and said, "Over the mountains?"

"That's it. Going to see some new territory. Maybe I'll look up Daniel Boone. I'm tired of being cooped up in a town."

Without thinking, Rhoda said, "I wish I could go with you. I hate this town."

Josh looked at her suddenly. She was wearing a deep blue cloak and a hat that came down over her cheeks and ears. "You wouldn't like it out there, Rhoda." He reached out and grinned, touching her dark brown hair that had escaped from her bonnet. "It's dangerous trying to live on the frontier."

A shiver ran through Rhoda as she thought of the stories she had heard. "Aren't you afraid? Of the wild animals, I mean?"

"Well, I don't intend to get too friendly with 'em." The two walked along, and Josh was cheerful enough now that the die was cast and he was on his way. "I guess I won't be seeing you for a while."

"I'll miss you."

Something plaintive and sad in her voice caught at Josh. He stopped suddenly and turned around. When she looked up at him, he saw more than he had ever seen before. He had always thought of her as a pretty girl. She displayed very few indications of the effects of her rough profession, and although he did not know her age, he guessed she could not be over seventeen or eighteen. Her eyes were opened wide, and he noticed how doelike they were and the thickness of the lashes that shaded them. She had very smooth skin, now paled by the cold weather, but her lips were rich and red. A thought came to him, and he let it stay in his mind for a moment, thinking hard before he spoke it out. "Why don't you get away from here, Rhoda?"

"Get away?" His statement surprised her. "Where would I go?"

"Anywhere away from here. Do something else. You're too nice a girl to be living the kind of life you do."

"Are you going to preach at me like all the rest of the preachers in town? Your friend Paul Anderson came by and tried to talk to me the other day."

"I guess I'm no one to preach to anybody, Rhoda," Josh shrugged. "I believed for a time . . . but here lately, it's just . . . well, life's pretty short. It's a shame to waste it."

The same thought had occurred to Rhoda many times. She had a longing to do something different, but she had no idea what adventures the world even had to offer. She hadn't pursued an education other than being able to read or write. She was left to the confines of her own little world. And since her world was limited to that of the tavern, she heard very few fine sentiments. Now she looked up at Josh and said simply, "I don't know anything else to do."

Josh said, "Why, I'll help you. You could get a job somewhere else. Out of Williamsburg where they don't know you. Start all over again like I'm going to do."

"Would you take me with you to the frontier?"

Instantly Josh knew he had gone too far. "I couldn't do that, Rhoda. In the first place, I'm a greenhorn. I don't know what I'm doing. I've hunted a little bit around here, and I consider myself a pretty good shot, but the frontier is a harsh and unforgiving place. I've listened enough to those who have gone and returned to know how dangerous it is. A man has to be smarter, and quicker, and stronger than the wilderness to survive. I don't know if I will or not. I couldn't take a woman into a place like that."

Josh saw the glimmer of hope die in Rhoda's eyes. She turned again and started walking slowly away. Watching her go, he said, "I'll see you when I get back." But she did not turn. Somehow the incident troubled Josh Spencer. She was no more than a common prostitute. But there was a different quality in this one, and he hated to see her life come to ruin. There was something in the girl worth saving. Shrugging his shoulders with resignation, he headed toward the misty mountains.

"Where have you been?"

"Just out walking," Rhoda said. She had entered the tavern again and found Cartier sitting at his usual table with a bottle of whiskey before him. He looked rough and irritable.

"Fix me something to eat!"

"All right. What do you want—eggs and bacon?"

"Anything. My stomach feels like it's been cut open with a Chickasaw knife." He glared over at the proprietor and asked, "What's that rotgut you're sellin'?"

"If you don't like it, don't drink here!" Dutch Hartog turned to face Cartier. He was in a rough business, and tough characters came and went. He waited for Cartier to respond, his hand on the counter. All he had to do was drop his hand to come up with either a knife or a bung starter, both of which he had used often.

Cartier stared at the thick-bodied proprietor and decided it wasn't worth the trouble. He shook his head and went back to his drinking. When Rhoda finally brought his breakfast, he gulped it down wolfishly, making guttural sounds until it was all gone. Shoving the wooden chair back, he grabbed her and pulled her down onto his lap. He kissed her roughly, and she submitted without enthusiasm.

"Here," he said, reaching into his pocket and pulling out a gold coin. "Go buy yourself a new dress or something. A bonnet."

Rhoda took the coin and bit it. She had seen that his pocket was full. "Where'd you get all that money, Jack?"

"Never mind. There's plenty more where that came from."

"Do you ever go over the mountains?" she asked, suddenly thinking of Josh Spencer.

"Why are you askin'?"

"I just saw Josh Spencer. He's headin' over that way."

A crafty look crossed the face of the trapper. He said something in French under his breath, then asked in English, "When did you see him?"

"Just now. Before I came in here."

"Which way was he going?"

"He didn't say. Just over the mountains. He mentioned something about Daniel Boone."

The memory of the brawl came suddenly to Cartier, and his brutal face hardened. He was not a man to forgive easily, and filed away in his mind was the notion that someday he would get even with both Boone and Josh Spencer. "You been beddin' down with Spencer?"

"What business is it of yours?"

The massive hand of the trapper closed on Rhoda's back. He clenched the flesh together hard and she cried out, "Don't! You're hurting me!"

"I asked you a question!"

"What do you care? I don't belong to you!"

"You do when I pay for you! Now answer me!"

"No! Let me go!"

Jacques Cartier slowly released her. Rhoda got up and gave him a frightened look, then turned and left. Cartier began drinking more heavily. He was a shrewd, crafty man who saw men like Boone and Josh Spencer as a threat to his business, which he kept mostly to himself.

"I'll find him out there," he said. "Then we'll see!" he muttered. Shuddering as the raw whiskey hit his stomach, he continued to drink and began to make some kind of plans for revenge.

When Rhoda returned later in the day, she asked Dutch, "What happened to Jack Carter?"

"Don't know. He left right after you talked to him."

"Where was he going? Did he say?"

"He never says anything. I don't trust that fellow," Dutch said. "I could do without his business."

Rhoda stepped outside of *The Brown Stag* and looked up and down the street. It had begun to snow again, and she shivered. She thought of Josh, and for one moment her heart seemed to lose some of its hardness. "I wish I could've gone with him," she whispered— then she thought of what she was, and she shook her head, bitterness tingeing the sheen of her eyes and twisting her lips into a sarcastic line. "But he wouldn't want the likes of me."

Cry of a Hawk

Four

The face of Faith Spencer appeared as sharply and clearly in Jehoshaphat Spencer's dream as if it were a painting set before his eyes. Unlike most dreams, in which scenes and faces floated through his mind in a ghostly fashion, the features, so long beloved, were suddenly just *there*. In one of those inexplicable moments of the dream experience, Josh simultaneously knew he was dreaming, but the face that he saw was conjured up of memories drawn from the past and had the reality of a canvas painted by a master.

He lay quietly, aware of the bitter cold that encased his body, which was no less real than the warmth that came from the image of Faith. He studied the dark brown hair that fell to her waist and was conscious of the fine lace of the light pink party gown that he had seen her wear on several occasions. Her eyes, brown and warm, and flecked with tiny touches of gold, studied him provocatively, and the lips that he had kissed a thousand times softened with compassion and then opened to speak. He was conscious also of the frailty that had drawn him to her as a young woman—yet at the same time of the spiritual strength that had been an element of her makeup as much as the color of her eyes, or the straightness of her nose, or her delicate cheekbones.

From somewhere far away, he heard sounds, high and keening, and even as the sounds brushed against the levels of his consciousness, he tried to hang on to the sensation as though it were reality. She seemed to smile at him, and then her features began to fade, and a pale iridescence gathered around her in a halolike fashion. Then slowly, but with a tragic finality, the face began to break apart. It was like an image in water that had been suddenly stirred. As the sound became louder, and the face and the image of his wife withdrew and dissolved, Josh cried out, "Faith—!"

The sound of his own voice was hoarse and desperate. Vaguely hopeless, and coming out of sleep with a rush, he was suddenly frightened—for nothing was familiar. He had gone to sleep next to the fire that he had built under a towering hemlock tree beside a frozen stream. For a long time he had lain awake watching the stars as they did their great dance across the velvety blackness of the sky. He remembered seeing the snowflakes joining the stars, different only in that their movements were faster and more active than those distant orbs of frozen fire that dotted the heavens.

Now as he came out of sleep, bitterly disappointed by the loss of the vision of Faith's features, he was aware of a weight pressing down on him. He panicked as the thought brushed across the edge of his conscious mind, *I've been buried alive!* Frantically he lunged, and with a sob of relief, his arms broke through the blanket of snow that had fallen upon him. The snow was no more than six or seven inches deep, and was so light that he sat upright with a gasp and a shudder. As he brushed the snow away from his face with his forearm, he stared around in a confused fashion.

Everything was changed. It had been snowing, it seemed, all night, and now the hemlock tree overhead was laden with a shimmering mantle of white velvet. Throwing his blankets aside, he saw that at some point the branches overhead had dislodged a load of snow on the fire so that everywhere he looked a plush carpet of glistening snow met his eyes. He squinted against the brilliance of the scene and stood to his feet as the morning sun touched the tiny grains, reflecting them like jewels. He had slept in his clothes, as he had every night during his journey. Looking around he saw his horse stamping and pawing at the ground where he had tied him out with a long piece of rawhide the night before. Josh's blankets and saddle and few belongings made a lump on the smoothness of the ground, and at once he felt a wave of disgust mixed with humor begin to rise within him.

"If you can sleep through a snowstorm, there'd be nothing to stop an Indian from walking right up to your camp and slitting your throat!" he muttered to himself.

As he began to clear away a place to build a fire, he considered the journey that he had made from Williamsburg. It had been an exhilarating time for Josh, and the farther he got from civilization, the more aware he was of the outside world.

This new world consisted of trees that grew ever larger as he moved farther west. High overhead, he could hear birds calling out as squirrels scampered through the branches. A few times he caught sight of a shy Virginia deer, which he had stalked, once successfully, and feasted on the meat for several days. The absence of human voices was a pleasure to him, and for days he had not spoken with a single soul. Once he had seen a party of hunters and had turned his horse into a grove of magnificent first-growth firs simply to avoid their company. He had had enough of human relationships for a while, and despite the bitter coldness and hardships of the trail, he welcomed the challenge and the distraction the solitude brought him. The silence had sunk into his spirit like a soothing balm.

From the distance came the mournful cry of a timber wolf, and Josh held himself still, savoring the wildness of the sound. Somehow he felt a kinship to the big lobo, for he had come to love the wild and untamed forest that spread out like a large carpet over the land.

"I missed something," he murmured. "All those years I stayed in town, I was in a prison—and didn't have the sense to know it!"

The thought amused him, and he smiled stiffly, his lips numb from the breeze that bore tiny fragments of ice. Since moving from the world of men into the world of beasts, he had found himself more aware of the ironies of life. He'd always had a keen sense of humor, but it had not been kind—as humor often strikes at the weaknesses of others. But the months of solitude had caused him to look down deep into his own heart, and he had learned to smile at his own foibles as he did now.

Standing to his feet, he looked toward the creek. "Bit of fish might go down nice," he said, and the sound of his voice seemed loud in the silence of the glade. Moving his pack he pulled out a small leather pouch no more than three inches square. He opened it and removed his fishing tackle, which consisted of a hook and thin strong line. Removing his gloves, he blew on his fingers, then threaded the line through the eye of the hook. Pulling a small chunk of bacon from his food sack, he made his way to the creek.

The narrow stream was no more than six feet wide, shrunken to its wintery dimensions, though in spring when the ice melted it would be much larger. Taking his hatchet, Hawke hacked away at the ice until he'd roughed out a ragged splintery hole, then baited his hook and dropped it into the frigid waters. The ice was too thick and opaque to see through, but an instant tug on the line brought a yell from the solitary fisherman.

"Got you!"

Quickly he pulled on the line, and when he got the fish out of the water, he carefully grabbed it by the lower jaw and ignored the flopping of the bass. "Well, I guess you'll do just fine for breakfast!"

Making his way back to his campsite, he quickly cleaned the fish, throwing the head and entrails into the brush. His horse snorted and bucked, startled at the unexpected noise.

"Calm down, boy," Josh said. "You wouldn't begrudge a man a good breakfast, would you now?"

Raking back the snow, he cleared a small spot, then rose and moved into the brush. The weeds were dead and dry, rustling under his feet. He began to break off small stems, and when he had a double handful, he moved back and made a small pyramid of them. He made two more trips, each time bringing back larger twigs, until finally he had a pyramid nearly a foot in diameter. His hands were numb, and when he pulled out his powder horn, he could hardly feel the smoothness of the horn. Pouring a small amount of powder on the pile, he capped the powder horn carefully—very carefully. His life depended on his rifle, and if it had no powder, he was helpless.

His face was rapt and intent as he worked. When he pulled flint and steel from his possible bag and struck it, a spark fell on the powder, igniting it with a small puff of sound. "That's it," he muttered as he nursed the tiny blaze.

Carefully he fed small twigs onto the growing blaze, adding larger ones, then he sat back on his heels and stared at the orange and red tongues of fire with satisfaction. Holding his palms out, he felt the warmth slowly creep into his frozen hands, until finally he singed his left palm and jerked it back.

He impaled the fish on a sharp green stick that he had sharpened to a point, then held it over the fire. Soon the delicious smell of seared fish filled the air, and his stomach knotted. Pulling the fish back, he added a pinch of salt, then pulled off a piece of the flaky white flesh with his thumb and forefinger. He juggled it around until it cooled, then popped it into his mouth and savored the hot meal. He devoured all the fish, then said, "Should have caught another one—reckon I can cook me up another breakfast. Two breakfasts never hurt a man." He moved to the creek, drank thirstily, then filled the small sauce pan with creek water.

Walking back to the fire, he dug into the leather sack that held the rest of the ingredients for his meal. He kneaded the dough on a clean slab of bark, wetted it with the river water, added a pinch of salt, and then rapidly and skillfully molded it into cakes. After setting them on a flat stone and moving the stone into the heat of the fire, he took a handful of dried meat from another pouch. Taking a long piece of curled bark, he laid the meat on it and poured water over the strips to soften them. When he had laid out half a dozen strips, he stretched them across the prongs of a forked stick. Hunched by the fire, he held the stick of meat over the coals. When the meat sizzled out its fat and curled crisp and brown to the edges, he pulled it off the stick, onto another piece of bark, and then began taking up the cakes, shifting them rapidly so he would not burn his fingers. Finally he picked up the iron pot, moved over, and sat down.

Hungrily he devoured the food, and then for a while he sat there thinking of where he was. He had a mind that could hold a piece of country in it, almost as if it were on the pages of a book. He had gone over it carefully, retracing the steps and the route he had taken since leaving Williamsburg, and he knew that he was now close to Holston country near the Watauga River. Soon he would be reaching the area Daniel Boone had told him about. There had been something about the man that had drawn Josh, and now he thought of the lean face and the light blue eyes with something almost mystical in them. He smiled as he thought of the time he asked Boone, "Were you ever lost, Daniel?"

"Lost? Well, not so's you'd mention it. Of course"—the blue eyes had lit up with mild amusement—"I was a little bit *confused* once for about a week—but not so as you might say, lost."

"Must be nice to be like that," Josh said aloud. "Most of us stay lost all of our lives." His quick shift from the physical to the spiritual was a habit of his. The lostness of a man in a woods was a simple and uncomplicated affair—unlike the kind of lostness that had fallen upon him when Faith had passed out of his life. The thoughts disturbed him, and he quickly arose, made up his pack, and after feeding the horse a bagful of oats, he swung into the saddle and made his way along the creek. Josh's eyes moved from side to side, for he had already developed the habit of watching, as much as possible, for any movement that might signal danger.

He had a sudden memory of Saul Elliott, an old backwoodsman who had taught him, when he was just a boy, much of what he knew about his woodsmanship. "Don't ever fix your eyes on an object, Josh," Elliott had said. "Kind of shift 'em back and forth, from side to side, and as far ahead as possible. If you get to starin' at somethin', you can be trapped. Kind of freezes you, like."

Moving briskly through the deep woods, his mind studied the trees and their various uses. Some of the ash trees grew a hundred feet high, and he knew they would be good for paddles and for oars and for leaching lye. It made good wood for a puncheon floor because it whitened under use. Then there was hickory, the best of all woods for an ax or a hatchet handle. He saw the stands of oaks, and already his mind was thinking of the cabin he would build somewhere. Once he saw a young elm bordering on a hazelnut thicket, and he thought, *I remember Ma saying that makes a good poultice for cuts and bad wounds.*

All day long he moved forward steadily, not pushing his animal, but simply soaking in the silence of the dense woods about him. He saw a few animals, but no bear. *They'll be all holed up.* A humorous thought struck him. *I wish a man could do that. Just go hide out somewhere and sleep all winter long, and come out in the spring all fresh and ready for the world. Don't reckon I'd miss too much if I did that.*

Once Josh saw a flash, a movement by a frozen stream, but by the time he had unlimbered his musket, the small animal was gone. *Must have been a fisher or a mink or maybe a rabbit. . . .*

Worry suddenly crept like a worm into his thinking. Even in the peace that had enveloped him like a warm cape since leaving Williamsburg and putting his life behind him, somehow arose the thought, *What am I going to do with myself? I can't wander around the woods until I'm an old man.*

The thought nibbled at the edges of his consciousness, and he could not get rid of it. One part of him was imaginative, creative, but the other was analytical—his mother had once said to him with exasperation, "I do declare, Josh! You have to organize everything and put it into a compartment—like a woman storing her spices!"

Josh had never forgotten that statement, and now he tried desperately to throw off all thoughts of the future. Reaching down, he patted his horse on the shoulder, saying firmly, "I don't want to have any more worries than you do, Rusty. As long as you got something to eat, you're all right. I envy you that."

Still, the little voice that served as a spokesman for the analytical side of his spirit said, "But a man's not a horse. He can go back and relive the past. And even more, he can jump ahead in his mind and know that something lies out there ahead of him."

Turning aside from the disturbing thoughts that gnawed at him, Josh deliberately forced himself to think on his immediate needs. *Need something for the pot tonight,* he thought and checked the priming in his rifle. Tying the horse out, he fed him some of the oats, noting that one more feed was all the bag held. He moved on into the deep thickets. Finally he found a trail with some tracks and stopped with his back up against a huge beech tree. He held the rifle loosely but firmly in his hands. That was another secret Elliott had given him. "When you're huntin', boy, just become a tree yourself. Animals see movement quicker than they smell things. So if you can just be still long enough, something's gonna show its head."

For thirty minutes Josh remained absolutely still. An itch developed on his lip, but he would not even reach up with his lower teeth and bite it. It was a test, and he knew that the Indians had the ability to hold such a position for hours. His legs grew cramped, and once he almost cried out with the pain of a knotty swelling in his calf, but he gritted his teeth together and thought, *If an Indian can do it, I can do it!*

Finally he was rewarded for his patience. A tiny sound came, and he shifted his eyes slightly, catching a flash of movement. A buck stepped out of the thickness of the forest, his head held high, and his eyes looking constantly, searching the whiteness around him. Josh remained absolutely still. The rifle was cocked, and his finger was on the trigger. His left hand held the barrel, and though he had lost all feeling in that hand, he knew that he would have only one shot. He could not, for a moment, decide whether to slowly move the musket into position or to raise the rifle with one snap movement and get the shot off. He chose the latter, and even as the rifle rose he saw the buck whirl. Judging accurately the direction of the leap of the animal, he pulled the trigger. The shot knocked the deer down, but the animal jumped up at once and disappeared in the corridor of snow-covered trees.

Josh ran quickly and gave a sigh of relief when he saw the bright red trail of blood in the snow. "Hit hard," he murmured, feeling his blood pumping through his veins and his heart beating faster. Josh began to move through the snow at a steady pace, trotting, and after half a mile his breathing had hardly increased. *Getting tougher*, he thought. *My legs are gettin' stronger every day.*

He saw the body of the deer lying in a clump of cedars up ahead, and he smiled with satisfaction, advancing carefully. One of his friends had rushed in on a buck that had leaped to his feet in his dying throes and cut the man to pieces with his razor-sharp hooves and antlers. But this one was dead, so Josh quickly pulled out his skinning knife and began to butcher the animal. He was not as good at this part of hunting. Carefully he removed the skin, and then cut off a quarter. He kept the liver also, which was a favorite of his. He made his way back to where the horse was tied. "I'm gonna fix up a good supper, Rusty. You can't enjoy a good steak, but I'll feed you the rest of the oats."

It was a feast, for there was nothing Josh liked better than deer liver. He made a stew and also put a huge chunk of the fresh meat on a forked stick. The savory smell as it sizzled above the fire made his stomach growl. Finally when it was done, he gorged on the meal. He tore off chunks of the steak with his strong teeth, and when he could hold no more, he leaned back against a tree and said, "Now all I want to do is lie down and sleep."

The next morning he fried up another piece of the steak and moved ahead, glancing up at the sun. The sky overhead was blue, and there was no sign of snow. An hour later he sighted some small animals bouncing from tree to tree, and he thought, *Squirrels! I could do with a little squirrel stew.* He tied the horse, patted him on the rump, and said, "See if you can find some dried grass under that snow, Rusty." Leaving the animal tethered, he moved underneath a canopy of towering evergreens. Overhead, the thick branches kept the snow from falling to the earth so that only an inch or two crunched beneath his feet. It was still bitter cold, and as he moved forward a sudden thought came to him, one that he had had before. *There might be Indians in this part of the woods.*

He had not gone fifty feet before he stepped into a hole that was covered over with a layer of snow. He fell awkwardly, twisting to hold his musket clear. Even as he was falling he caught a glimpse of movement to the side. Fear ran through him, for whatever it was stood only a few feet away. He cried aloud and brought the musket to bear, but even as he did, he was struck in the face by a stream of the vilest-smelling liquid he had ever encountered.

Skunk!

Gagging and coughing and clawing at his eyes, Josh let his musket fall to the snow. He was blinded, for the stench of the skunk's spray had struck him full in the face and on the front of his jacket. Some of it had even gotten on his lips, and it burned like fire. Wallowing in the snow, he took handfuls of the powdery fluff and washed as well as he could.

Finally, he got his eyes clear, and peering through half-shut lids, he saw the skunk—white stripe down his back and his plumed tail raised high—regarding him with a pair of beady black orbs. Josh grabbed his musket, leveled it, and then could not see, for the burning scent clawed at the tender tissues almost like needles. "Go on!" he muttered, and gathering his musket, he half groped his way back through the woods toward his horse.

"Well, this is just great!" Josh said bitterly. "I'll probably smell like this for days!"

The rest of the day he stopped several times at streams and tried desperately to wash off some of the stench. He had brought a bar of lye soap, and he heated water and washed as well as he could, but he knew that the stench would not come out of his hunting shirt. It was ruined forever, so he tossed it aside. Josh knew he needed to find some place to shelter for the winter. Turning Rusty toward the mountains, he decided to head there to look for a cave.

Just as Josh kicked Rusty's flanks, a piercing crack shattered the eerie silence of the thick snow-covered forest. A searing pain ripped into his back, and he toppled off his horse. He vaguely remembered being astonished as he hit the ground. *Why . . . I've been shot. . . !*

The dark pit into which he plunged engulfed him without a trace of light. When he awoke hours later, it was snowing again, and he was burning up. He tried to sit up, and a streak of fiery pain shot through him. It was as if someone had driven a white-hot iron through his chest. He looked down and saw that his woolen shirt was soaked with dried blood, and the movement had started it bleeding again.

He struggled to a sitting position and tried to think, but the fever was already making him light-headed. He got up slowly and looked around. There was no sign of the horse.

"Got to find some shelter," he muttered. The afternoon sun cast long shadows across the ground as he stumbled along, falling more than once. A root caught his toe and he fell headlong. Josh was a strong man, and he was shocked to discover that he did not have the strength to stand up. He could not move. He lay there on his back, turning his head from side to side in his efforts to rise.

He began to lose consciousness, and he thought, *This is death.* Even as he slipped into the darkness, he thought of his parents— and then he thought of the son whom he had turned his back on. *God's striking me down. I've been so wrong!*

He had no time to think more, and just before the last bit of consciousness ebbed from him, he heard a strange noise keening high in the air. Glancing up, he saw a red-tailed hawk circling in a wide gyre. Even as the hawk screamed again, Josh slipped into an utter, complete, ebony blackness.

Sequatchie

Five

$\mathcal{S}$ometimes the darkness was unbounded—blacker than a hundred midnights down in the swamp! At other times it seemed that he was drifting through a heaven filled with light so intense he could not open his eyes. And just as varied as the darkness and the light were the sensations of heat and cold. His body would shake so viciously that his teeth chattered, and he thought he was buried under tons of snow. Then the biting cold would fade and something warm and soft would envelop him and a voice would speak. Often he would be drenched in sweat and would cry out, for his body burned as if it were in a furnace. At times like this he tried vainly to throw the soft warm covering from his heat-parched body.

Finally lucid moments began to come to him, and he opened his eyes to mere slits. Racked by fever, he could not distinguish between the wild dreams and what seemed to be harsh reality. He knew there were people near, for he had heard their muffled voices, and he could smell the odor of bodies—mixed with acrid smoke, old hides, and smells that were foreign to him.

"Ho! Sit up and drink!"

Josh was drawn roughly from a trancelike dream in which he had been pursued by a large animal that he could not identify. He opened his eyes and started violently, for there, not a foot away from his face, was the countenance of a man he had never seen before—which at first seemed to him part of his nightmare.

An Indian!

Instantly, wild stories flashed through his mind, stories of captives who had been burned at the stake and pulled apart, their flesh stripped from their bones while they yet lived. He opened his mouth to speak and put out his hand to defend himself, but then he saw a smile break across the dark face, and the obsidian eyes glinted with humor. "You decided to live awhile."

The voice spoke in a pleasant baritone, and there was nothing threatening in it. Josh reached up and threw his arm across his forehead, which was dripping with sweat, at the same time studying the dark features so close to his own. The face was bronze with a distinct copper tint, and the long beam of sunshine that came down through an open door to Josh's right revealed a long face with a broad forehead. The Indian had an aquiline nose, high, prominent cheekbones, and a square jaw. His head was totally bald except for a patch of hair ornamented with feathers and porcupine quills that disappeared behind the man's shoulders. The cheeks were smooth, and the man, who wore only a breechcloth, seemed to have no body hair.

"Where . . . where am I?"

"Don't talk. Drink this."

A cup made out of birch bark was thrust to Josh's lips. The odor of the liquid was pleasant and aromatic, and as he drank it thirstily, he found it had a taste somewhat like English tea. He drained it to the bottom, then held it out again, whispering, "More."

Again a humorous light touched the dark eyes of the Indian. He turned and handed the cup to an Indian woman who suddenly appeared out of the darkness at the side of the room and filled it without a word. She looked older than the man, in her late fifties, and was rather tall but more delicately built than most of the Indians Josh had seen. His mind was clearing quickly, and he took in the oval-shaped face and the jet black hair of the woman. She wore a short leather skirt, deerskin moccasins, and a blouse made out of some sort of lightweight material.

"I am Sequatchie," the man said and sat back on his heels, regarding Josh.

Josh drank the rest of the tea and nodded. "That's good," he whispered. He found that his voice was hoarse, as if he had not spoken for a long time. He cleared his throat and looked around the room, then back to the Indian. "My name is Jehoshaphat Spencer."

The Indian considered him and shook his head. "Too much name," he said, then turned to the squaw and said something in his native language. At once the squaw moved toward the fire that was sending up a thin spiral of smoke over to one side. She removed something and brought it back to Josh. He was surprised to observe that it was on a pewter plate. The Indian, seeing that Josh was looking at the plate, grinned suddenly. "I stole that from the British when I was a young man. No steal anymore, though."

"You speak English very well," Josh said. He reached for the knife that Sequatchie handed him, and pain suddenly ran through him, as if a sword had passed through his body. He grunted but gritted his teeth to keep from crying out. Looking down he saw that his bare chest was bound with cloth, and memory came flooding back to him. Holding the plate and the knife, he said, "I was shot."

"Yes, you almost died. Look." Sequatchie leaned forward, reaching over Josh and touching Josh's back. "You shot from back. Bullet go through, come out up high." He touched Josh's chest and shook his head. "It is a good thing you not taller. You would be dead by now, and in eternity."

Josh felt the Indian's hands, and a strange sensation went through him. He had never been this close to an Indian—certainly never touched by one—but there was something in the tall, lean figure, and especially in the rather stern countenance that somehow gave him confidence. "You found me?"

"Yes."

"How long have I been in this place?"

The Indian seemed to count mentally, then held up his hand. "Five suns," he said. "You believe God?"

The question shocked Josh, and he blinked with surprise. "Why . . . certainly I believe in God."

"You thank Him then. If it had not been for my mother, Awenasa, I think you would die." He turned to the Indian woman and smiled. "She knows how to make anyone well, even animals."

Josh turned to the woman whose face was impassive. She stood back in the shadows, saying nothing, and Josh hardly knew how to speak to her. "Thank you," he said. "I'm grateful."

Sequatchie translated his words, and when the Indian woman said something, he turned to face Josh. "She says you thank your god, not her."

Something about the situation disturbed Josh. When he had ridden out of Williamsburg, he had left behind his relationship with God. When Faith had died, he had walked away from all that. Now here in a rough cabin in the middle of the wilderness, he was suddenly confronted, in the stolid face of a Cherokee woman, with the concepts of God and living and dying.

"I do thank God," he said quickly. He struggled to throw off the blankets and said, "I'm too hot."

"Your fever was bad. We had to wash you down with cold spring-water to keep you from burning up," Sequatchie said. "You eat. You hungry now."

Josh tore at the meat with an almost animal-like viciousness, barely pausing to chew it. He was starved, and even as he ate, he could feel the strength seeping back into his body.

Carefully he said between bites, "Do you know who it was who shot me?"

"White man," Sequatchie said, staring at him calmly.

The brief words startled Josh, for somehow he had assumed that it had been an Indian. "Did you see him? What did he look like?"

"Big man. Heavier than you, and a man of the forest."

"But what did his face look like? What color were his eyes?"

Sequatchie shook his head. "I saw only his footprints in the snow. He wore white man's shoes. He waited for you and shot you from where he hid. He took your horse, too."

A pang went through Josh. "He took my Rusty?"

"Yes, if that is what you call your horse."

"I'll miss that horse," Josh said briefly. He handed the plate back and asked, "Could I have some more of that tea?"

Sequatchie turned and spoke to the old woman, who quickly came and filled Josh's cup.

He drank it and said, "What is it?"

"Chuckaberry, very good for you," the woman said.

Josh was surprised that she spoke English. "It was very good." He hesitated, then said, "I hate to be so much trouble."

Neither of the two who watched him responded. They stood there looking down on him, and finally Josh found that despite himself, he was drifting off into sleep. "Can't stay awake."

The last thing he heard was the woman saying, "Good. He live now."

"Yes, until he gets shot again."

Sequatchie's voice seemed to come from far away. Josh wanted to argue that, but sleep spread over him like a warm blanket and he drifted from the land of consciousness into that other place where the spirit seemed to be hidden in deep mist.

"Good. You strong man." Sequatchie had pulled the bandage off of Josh's chest and studied the raw, puckered scar.

Josh moved his shoulders carefully. There was still pain, and he knew he would have discomfort for some time. Yet for the past three days he had grown steadily stronger. He looked across at Sequatchie, who was sitting on a log outside the cabin. It was cold and snow covered the ground, but the Indian wore only a thin doeskin vest, a pair of leggings over his breechcloth, and a pair of calf-length moccasins. From inside the cabin, Josh heard small thumping sounds. He knew it was Awenasa pounding corn to make meal. "Maybe I could help with that," he said. "I would like to do something."

"Woman's work."

"I wish my mother had thought that way," Josh replied.

Sequatchie smiled briefly. There was a sense of humor in the man that had surprised Josh. He had thought of Indians as being stoic and devoid of humor. However, the few days he had spent with these two and others from the village who came to sit and watch him from time to time had convinced him otherwise. As he observed them, he discovered that their humor ran freely when strangers were not present. They had learned through sad encounters with the white man to keep themselves behind a stolid wall of seeming indifference.

Josh was sitting on another log that was chopped halfway through. He picked up the hatchet that had been used to do the job. It was a rather flimsy instrument made of inferior metal. He looked at it and at the log. "You need a good ax. You could cut through a log like this a lot quicker with one than with this hatchet."

Sequatchie shrugged. "That my father's tomahawk," he said, as if that settled all things.

Quickly Josh looked up, and a thought came to him. *These Indians. They don't like change. He'd rather chop through a tree with this tomahawk and take two days than have a new ax.* Josh was, however, aware that Sequatchie was interested in the white man's ways, for he asked many questions and seemed willing enough to answer Josh's inquiries. One of the first things Josh had asked was, "Did he take my gun—the man who shot me?"

"Yes, take everything you have. Except your clothes."

Sequatchie looked at Josh again, his face steady in the bright sunlight. There were children playing around the other cabins, their thin voices sometimes laughing, sometimes crying out in anger. The adults of the tribe, especially the women, were busy moving about their work. There were no men in sight, and Josh asked, "Where are the rest of the warriors?"

"Gone hunting. Bad winter. Not much to eat." Sequatchie puffed on the pipe and watched the blue smoke rise slowly. "Your name is Jehoshaphat." He pronounced it slowly, breaking it up into syllables. "What does it mean?"

Josh blinked with surprise. "I don't know that it means anything."

"White people not very smart about names."

"I guess not. What does your name mean?"

Sequatchie puffed contentedly on the pipe. "A man's name is power. He doesn't give it away to others easily because it would give that man power over him."

"Oh!"

Sequatchie, however, nodded and said, "It is only one of my names. It means Possum River."

Josh suddenly grinned. "That's a funny name."

"Among my people we have naming ceremonies. Every name someone gives has to be used. Someday I may tell you some of my other names."

Josh picked up a knife and began whittling on a stick. It was a poorly made knife, and he looked at it, saying, "This isn't much of a knife."

"No. Trader's goods. I give two beavers for that knife."

"Two beavers?" Josh stared at the thinness of the rusty blade and shook his head. "You were cheated, Sequatchie."

"Yes, Indians get cheated regularly by your people."

Sequatchie's words embarrassed Josh, and he dropped his eyes. He continued to whittle on the stick, and finally a thought occurred to him. "Did you see anything else when you found me? Anything that might help me find the man who shot me?"

"No. He rode a horse without shoes and led a pack animal." Sequatchie studied the young man and said, "The hawk showed me where you were."

Confusion swept across Josh's face. "An Indian named Hawk?"

"Hawk—" Sequatchie pointed up at the sky. "Bird with red shoulders and a red tail."

"Oh, that kind of hawk. What do you mean he showed you?"

Sequatchie considered the white man carefully. He had learned that white people made fun of Indian beliefs, and he himself made light of some of them. However, his heritage ran deep and he said, "I was out hunting, and I heard a hawk far off as the sun dipped low in the sky. When I climbed the hill, I saw a big red hawk. He kept circling and circling high overhead. I kept waiting for him to fall to make his kill, but he did not."

Josh sat waiting for the story to go on. He had learned that Indians did not like to be rushed, and so he was as patient as he could be.

Finally Sequatchie said, "I knew this was not just a hawk. So I went through the woods, closer to where he circled, and when I got under him I found you there." He waited for one moment and said, "That was when I gave you your Indian name."

"What's that?"

"Hawk. It is a good name. Better than Jehoshaphat—which means nothing."

Josh smiled. "You may be right about that. I never liked it much myself."

The two men sat there talking, and finally Sequatchie's mother called out, "Come and eat." They moved inside the cabin, which had very little light. The village had been a surprise to Josh. It was not large, having no more than twenty houses. He had learned that it was part of a network of Cherokee villages. The Cherokees all built one-story log cabins. The logs were stripped of the bark and notched at the ends, and grass mixed with smooth clay was plastered over the walls. They were roofed with bark and long broad shingles or sometimes thatched. Only a few had a window. Sequatchie's was partitioned to form two rooms, with animal skins covering the doorways from within and without. Just outside the dwelling was a smaller, partly buried winter house where the family slept during the coldest weather. Sequatchie had told him that these were called "hot houses" by the white traders because of their stifling heat and smokiness. The floor of the hot house was dug two or three feet below ground level and was twenty to thirty feet square. Large upright logs formed the framework, which was covered with clay plaster. Cane couches for sleeping were built along the walls. One wall had a small scooped-out fireplace, which often burned day and night. Josh learned also that the hot houses were used by medicine men to treat certain diseases.

Josh ate the stew hungrily and asked, "What is this, Awenasa? Possum?"

"Puppy."

Josh had a mouthful of the stew, and for one moment considered spitting it out, but the dark eyes of both of his hosts were watching him intently. He managed a smile and said, "It's very good."

"Puppy dog stew not bad," Sequatchie said. Again humor gleamed in his eyes. "Some white people don't eat dogs."

"I heard that some men from over the sea eat snails," Josh said. "The French people."

Disgust crossed the face of the Indian woman, and she said, "White people have no sense! Eating snails!"

From time to time, Josh sensed a difference in the spirit of the two who had taken him in. They did not speak of themselves a great deal, but one thing he discovered was that they were very religious. It was two weeks after he had awakened from his coma that he finally asked Sequatchie, "You talk a lot about God. How do you know about Him?"

Sequatchie was making a pair of snowshoes. He had stretched thin strips of wood around a frame and now was boring through one of them with a sharp awl made out of metal. He worked slowly, for time did not mean much to the Indians. If it took two weeks to make a pair of snowshoes, that mattered little. There was nothing else to do during the winter except hunt. The question that Josh had put forth hung in the air for some time, and he waited as usual.

Finally Sequatchie said, "Many moons ago, when I was a very young man, no more than a puppy in the tribe, a man came to trade with us. His name was Elmo McGuire. He was a small man, and he knew nothing about our ways." Carefully he finished making a hole through the thin piece of wood, then he blew the chips away and grunted with satisfaction. "We made fun of him at first. He could not shoot a bow. He could not even run as fast as some of the squaws. But one thing we saw—he never grew angry. Once we put a snake in his bed, not a bad one, just a green snake. He was terribly frightened of them, and I expected him to strike out. He was so frightened that he became ill, but he didn't say one word to us." He held the partly finished snowshoe up to the sky and peered at it critically. "There was something different about him. Any Indian I knew would have fought over the things we did to him—but he never did."

"Where did he come from?"

"From across the water. He spoke funny. Not like you speak. He said his words differently. He said he was Scottish. Do you know Scottish?"

"Yes, way across the big waters, Sequatchie. Very fine people. What was he doing living among the Cherokees?"

"He came to tell us about his God."

"A missionary!" Josh exclaimed.

"What is that?"

"One who goes to another land to tell people about his God."

Sequatchie continued working on the snowshoe. Far off a wolf howled, and Sequatchie's eyes swiftly turned in that direction. He had the habit that most Indians had of always being aware of his surroundings. The tall Indian said nothing, but the animal was on his mind, Josh knew. "Had you never heard of his God before?"

"No. He talked about Jesus all the time. Do you know Jesus?"

Josh hesitated, then said, "Yes, I know about Jesus."

"He is a good God, is He not? He died for all men, red and white."

"That's right," Josh muttered. "You got converted then?"

"What is converted?"

"You put away your old gods and followed the Jesus God."

"Yes." Sequatchie's face grew troubled for a moment, and his eyes narrowed. "It was not easy. My people like the old ways, most of them. But I listened to McGuire for many moons. He stayed three years. Not one single person would come to believe in his God, but he never gave up."

"He sounds like a strong man."

"No. He was very weak. Always sick, but he was a good man. He did what he could to help. He did not understand our ways, but he didn't make fun of them either as many white people do."

A long silence passed, and Josh saw that Sequatchie was thinking hard. Finally he said, "What happened to Elmo McGuire?"

"After a long time, some of us began to believe him. Every day he would come and read to us from a book. Then he got sick and died. Everyone was sad. I still have the book."

"Could I see it?"

Without a word, Sequatchie got up and entered the cabin. He came back, almost at once, carrying a small object wrapped in flexible doeskin, soft as velvet. With careful hands, he unwrapped it and handed over a dog-eared, worn book that had the words *Holy Bible* on the front. "This is the book of Jesus. I cannot read it." He handed it to Josh, who opened it and saw that the first page had an inscription in a coarse handwriting: "To my son, Elmo McGuire. May he serve God all the days of his life." It was signed, Amos McGuire. "From his father," Josh said. He thumbed through the Bible, noting that the pages were worn very thin. Then looking up, he saw Sequatchie's eyes fixed upon him.

"You can read in book?"

"Why, of course." Josh hesitated for a moment, then said, "Would you like for me to read some?"

"Wait! I get other Christians."

Sequatchie got up instantly and went quickly from cabin to cabin, and soon everyone in the village, mostly women and children, with only a few old men, had come together. Most of them did not speak English, but Sequatchie said, "You read book. I say in Cherokee."

Josh opened the Bible to the first page. "In the beginning," he read, "God created the heaven and the earth." He stopped then, and Sequatchie, in the strange, guttural language of the Cherokee, translated it carefully. He sounded as if his mouth were full of mush, but his eyes were alive as he looked quickly to Josh.

"What say now, Hawk?"

It was the first time his new name had been used, and from that moment on, Jehoshaphat Spencer was known among the Cherokees as simply Hawk. All around him, eager eyes watched, waiting for him to continue. Somehow he knew that this would be a new way of life for him. Looking down at the page, he read the second line from the Scriptures. "And the earth was without form and void; and darkness was upon the face of the deep. And the Spirit of God moved upon the face of the waters. . . ."

Josh read line after line, waiting each time for Sequatchie to translate. Each time he looked around at the dark faces and saw that they were turned to him expectantly, and a sudden thought occurred to him. *It must be awful not to be able to read. These people can read the face of nature. They know so much about the skies and the woods and the ways of the wild creatures, but they can't read the Word of God.* Something in the hunger of the people stirred him, and he thought with guilt, *I'm a hypocrite! I've given up on God and the Bible, and here I am reading it, just like a preacher!* But he could not stop now, for the hunger in the eyes of these simple people was evident on every face.

He read for over two hours, and finally when he closed the book, Sequatchie dismissed the people. After everyone had returned to their cabin, the tall Indian turned to Josh. "You want to be a long hunter?"

Josh nodded. He had shared this much of his dream with the Indian, and he waited now to hear Sequatchie's comment.

"You are not a very good hunter."

"No, I'm not. I was raised mostly in a big town—a big village."

Sequatchie sat thinking for a moment, then he turned and said, "Every promise the white man has ever made to the Cherokee they have broken. I have given up on making treaties."

"I can't say as I blame you, Sequatchie."

Sequatchie hesitated, then said, "I will make a treaty with you. It was what McGuire called a covenant, an agreement between two men."

"Yes. That's what a covenant is." He was puzzled and said, "What kind of covenant do you want to make with me?"

"You read the book of Jesus to me and teach my people, and I will teach you how to be the best hunter in the mountains."

Josh sensed the solemnness of the moment and hesitated. He knew he was getting a late start. Daniel Boone had learned how to hunt as a young boy, but Josh had missed out on most of that. Suddenly a burning desire touched him to become a great hunter like Boone—a man who could move through the woods as silently as an owl! Josh realized he was being offered a great gift. "You don't understand, Sequatchie. I . . . I can read the book, but I have turned away from the God that the book speaks of."

"I know that. It is not in your heart—this Jesus that died for all men. You have a bitterness in you. Something is eating away. You're like a tree with a bad disease on the inside. Outwardly you look strong, but inside something is bad."

Hawk could not answer for a moment, for Sequatchie's words had surprised him. This simple Indian had described the inner struggles of his life better than any white man could have done. Hawk dropped his head and stood there silently. Finally he lifted his eyes. "You're right, Sequatchie. So you would not want me to read the Bible."

"The book is true no matter who reads it," Sequatchie said. "Will you covenant with me? You will read and teach my people, and I will make you a hawk indeed. The hawk is the best of hunters, and you will become like him, like your name."

It was one of those moments when life seemed to hang in the balance—as when a man reaches a crossroads and must choose which path to follow. Jehoshaphat Spencer hesitated only for one moment, then he smiled. "My name is Hawk," he said. "I will read the book, and you will teach me how to be like you."

Trouble at Fort Loudoun

Six

*E*sther Spencer was well aware that the Scriptures strictly warned against pride. She would have been taken aback, however, if anyone had accused her of being guilty of this particular sin. Actually, this "evil" was centered almost altogether in one area—her kitchen and the meals that she prepared in it. All of her life she had been a cook, and although she read practically nothing in the form of books, journals, or periodicals, she had a large collection of recipes bound together under leather covers, all carefully arranged. Some of them went back to her ancestors in England, back to Devon. Nothing gave Esther Spencer more pleasure than reading the spiderlike scroll of brown ink that set forth the making of a mint pie or another delicacy of that age. It delighted her to be able to reproduce those dishes that her great-great-grandmother Ophelia had set on tables for her men back so long ago in another time and another place.

The October sun was waning as Esther moved about the kitchen unconsciously, taking in every item and every inch with a pair of sharp brown eyes. Her grandson, Jake, was napping, and Esther was enjoying the quiet moments to herself. "I declare," she said aloud. "I think I'll make a pudding."

Esther went into the storage closet and began pulling the items she needed off the shelves—a small bottle of rosewater, flour, a tin of sugar, and an assortment of spices as well as some cream, ten eggs, and a crock of butter from the springhouse. Returning to the kitchen, Esther looked around the large whitewashed room and decided to use one of the pine workstands placed between two windows that were curtained with a pale yellow muslin. She reached up to one of the many pine shelves lining the walls of the kitchen and pulled down a large copper kettle and two bowls. Carrying the kettle to where the water was stored, she filled it and hung it on the crane in the fireplace, which had a cheery fire burning since morning in order to prepare for the evening meal.

Turning around, Esther looked about the large room, smiling as she did so, then returned to the workstand to begin the preparations of the pudding. Picking up the cream, she measured out a pint and poured it into a bowl with the eggs she had already cracked over the edge of the bowl. The recipe called for three egg whites to be kept separate. So she took these and put them into the smaller bowl next to her. Reaching up, she plucked a wire whisk from the shelf and began to beat the egg whites until they looked foamy. She poured the contents of this bowl into the other bowl containing the cream and eggs, and to this she added three spoonfuls of fine flour. Once again she beat this mixture well so that there would be no lumps, and then added some cinnamon, nutmeg, and ginger for seasoning. Esther then took a cloth, buttered it, and spooned the thick mixture into the cloth. She tied the bundle and placed it into the kettle of boiling water. The mixture needed to boil for about a half an hour, so Esther took a few minutes to relax and wait.

Sitting down on the high-backed elm settee next to the brick fireplace, Esther took in her surroundings. She loved this bright, cheery room. Her eyes went to the last rays of pale yellow sunshine slanting in through the four small windows that lined the walls. The soft light made small circles on the yellow oilcloth that covered the wood floor of the kitchen. Her eyes drifted to the plain Dutch table made of rosewood, where she kept the English tea setting that her mother had given to her long ago, and then she gazed at the four Windsor chairs that were painted green and had cushions of yellow woolen moreen. Looking at these brought a smile to her face, for there were many fond memories of the times spent with her family in those chairs. Esther lifted her eyes to the ceiling where strips of apples, peppers, and squash were hanging and now filled the room with their fragrant aroma.

Realizing it was almost time for the pudding to come out, Esther moved back across the room to the workstand, took up a small bowl, and began mixing the sauce for the pudding. She cut off a small portion of the butter, put it in the bowl, poured a little rosewater and sugar in, then began to beat the mixture with the wire whisk.

As she was beating it, she glanced to the far end of the room where an oak dresser stood. Her eyes moved over the engraved pewter plates and cups and then to the top shelf. Esther stopped mixing for a moment. She seemed to relish the time as she looked at her most treasured dishes, a set of fine Chelsea plates, painted in soft shades in the center with a floral bouquet. Quickly she looked back down at the workstand and finished what she was doing. Then she walked over to the fireplace, removed the bundle from the boiling water, carried it over to the workstand, and opened it. Placing the hot pudding in a bowl, she poured the freshly made sauce over it and added a few blanched almonds.

Just as she put the finishing touches on top, the door opened. She looked up to see James enter with a newspaper in his hands.

"That smells good," he said with a pleased expression. "What is it?"

"What do you care? You eat whatever I put before you, and you never taste anything!"

James laughed and came over and put his arm around Esther's waist. "That's because your beauty takes my mind off of what I'm eating." He kissed her heartily, and she flushed.

"Will you get away and leave me alone, or I'll never get this meal ready!" However, as he grinned at her and left to take his seat at the Dutch table, she thought, *Not many women my age have a husband who's kept a little romance in his soul. I hope he never loses it.* Aloud she said, "Well, what does the paper say? Nothing good, I suppose."

James laid the broadsheet flat on the table, pulled a pair of silver-framed spectacles from his inner pocket, and placed them methodically on his nose. "I don't expect *good* news from a newspaper," he announced. "That's *not* news. Politics, floods, wars, murders—that's what folks want to hear about."

"Not me!" Esther said firmly. She put a kettle on the fire and pulled the English tea setting out and sat down while the water was boiling. "What's the bad news this time?"

"Well, let's see. Robert Clive has recaptured Calcutta. That pretty well gives England control of India. He's quite a fellow, that Clive!" He ran his eyes down the paper and said, "Says here Ben Franklin's gone to England. He'd like France better."

"Why do you say that, James?"

"Oh, Ben's quite a ladies' man. I'd think he'd find the French females more to his taste than those frozen English fillies."

"Not in my kitchen, if you please, Mr. Spencer!"

James laughed aloud and said, "Sorry!" and continued to read the paper. "I see the tide's beginning to turn against the French. The British have taken the Forts Duquesne, Frontenac, and Louisbourg."

"I never understand these things, James. What kind of a war is it, anyway? It has so many names." The teakettle began to whistle and Esther got up and poured two cups. Coming back to sit down she said, "Why can't they have just one name for it?"

James scratched his head thoughtfully. "It is complicated," he said. "Basically, France and England are fighting to see who will control this continent over here. All of the ruling monarchs have had little wars named after them—King George's War, Queen Anne's War, and some call it the French and Indian War. But basically it all boils down to this." He shook the newspaper out and a grim look clouded his face. "Before it's all over, everybody in this country will either be speaking French and kissing the pope's ring—or else we'll be speaking English and staying Methodists, Episcopalians, and Anglicans."

"Here, drink your tea before it gets cold."

As they sat there drinking their tea, James tried to explain to Esther what was happening in the war all along the frontier. She had little interest in political matters, and he had almost given up trying to explain the portion that the Indians played. However, he tried again. "There's an Indian called Attacullaculla," he said slowly. "He's nicknamed the Little Carpenter."

"Why do they call him that?"

"Why, because when he works out a treaty he can join the two parties together as easily as a carpenter joins woods."

"Is he friendly to the English or to the French?"

"To the English. He's about the best hope we've got. Look, let me show you something." He rose, went into his study, and came back with a large map, which he spread out on the plain wood table. "Look. You see right here? This is a new fort called Fort Loudoun. It's garrisoned by British troops, put there to protect the Cherokees—their women and children, and the old people. And it's important that we hold it. Look. Here's a map of it. . . ." He found another sheet of paper, and Esther leaned across the table to stare at the map of the fort. She listened as he explained how it was one of a chain of similar forts along the frontier to safeguard the settlers from attacks. Finally they finished their tea, and James said, "Fort Loudoun is important. If it falls, the Cherokees will lose all confidence in the English. Most of the other tribes hang with the French, anyway."

"Why do they do that?"

"Because the French want the Indians to keep their ways. That way they can keep buying their furs, which is all they want. Our people want to settle the land and make farms and towns. When that happens the Indian way of life will disappear."

"I'm surprised the Cherokees would be friendly to that idea."

"Well, frankly, so am I. If it wasn't for the Little Carpenter, I think they would have attacked our settlers on the frontier already."

"Well, that's it. Fort Loudoun." Hawk shifted the bale of furs on his back and turned to look at his companion.

Sequatchie was carrying a smaller bundle, and he was staring at the fort that seemed to rise up out of the ground. Then his eyes came back to Hawk, and Sequatchie thought, *Two winters ago he couldn't have carried that much weight, much less walked so softly for so far.* Sequatchie felt a fondness for the strong young man. The time that Hawk had spent in the village of the Cherokees had been good for both men. They had made many long journeys together deep into the forest, and Hawk had quickly grown in the knowledge and the ways of the Cherokees.

Hawk glanced over now and, as if reading his companion's thoughts, said, "It's a good thing you found me that day I was on the ground with a bullet hole through my back." He had not spoken of this all of these months, but now as they moved slowly toward the stockade, he said, "I know Indians don't like to be thanked very much, but my people like to say that. I owe you a lot, Sequatchie."

Sequatchie shook his head. "We are brothers. Someday you may save my life. Until then we will speak of it no more."

The two men entered the fort and stopped just inside the gate. It was the first time that either one of them had ever seen the inside of such a place. They stood looking at the perimeter, which was roughly star-shaped. The walls were formed of tall logs, six inches or more in diameter, with the tops sharpened to needlepoints to discourage enemies from climbing over. At various positions there were bastions with cannons pointed out. They stuck out from the walls so that they could sweep the walls themselves of enemies who attempted to scale them. Inside, along the walls, houses had been built—lean-tos, for the most part—which served as dwelling places for those inside the fort. Pigs and chickens roamed about, and in the middle of the structure was a large parade ground that was swept clean. Even now a group of red-coated soldiers was drilling under the direction of a harsh-voiced guard.

"That looks like the office over there," Hawk said. "Let's go see if we can peddle some of these furs we worked so hard for." Fort Loudoun had become the most convenient place for the Cherokees to come to do their trading. Their enemies, the Chickasaw and the Creek, dared not attack such a strong fort, and so an active trade went on within its walls.

As they drew near to the building that housed the traders' supplies and the bales of furs, Hawk suddenly drew up short.

"What is it, my brother?" Sequatchie asked. His dark eyes traveled in the direction in which his friend was staring. "Do you know that one?"

"Yes. His name's Jack Carter. Boone and I had trouble with him back in Williamsburg."

"I've heard of him. He is a bad one. He cheats the Indians. He sells firewater to them and gives them cheap beads for good furs."

"I doubt if he'll remember me," Hawk said. He was mistaken, however, for as soon as the two men stepped up, Jack Carter's eyes flew open wide. He seemed to gasp for breath, and Hawk could not understand why he was so shocked. He remembered well the fight that he had had with Carter at *The Brown Stag*, and his thoughts went at once to Rhoda Harper. He only said, "Hello, Carter. I didn't expect to see you here."

Carter seemed to get control of himself. He was wearing what appeared to be the same dirty hunting shirt, and his red and curly whiskers were longer than ever. "Hello, Spencer."

"You remember me? I suppose you remember Daniel Boone, too."

"I remember both of you. I'm not likely to forget."

Hawk studied the man's face and saw a crafty light had come into the trapper's eyes. He almost asked about Rhoda, but not wanting to stir up more trouble, he felt that might be unwise. "Come along, Sequatchie. Let's get rid of these furs."

"Wait a minute," Carter said. "Sell 'em to me. I'll give you a top price."

"Make your offer," Hawk said. The two men watched as Carter pulled out some cheap beads, poorly made tomahawks, and a pile of shoddy-looking blankets.

"Is that all you got to offer? I think we'll look a little further." Hawk nodded, ignoring the anger in Carter's face. They moved down the line toward another trader, a Scotsman with red hair and freckles. "You buying furs?"

"Yes, man, I am. Let me see what you have." The Scotch burr rang clear in the man's voice, and when he saw the furs that Sequatchie and Hawk had brought in, he exclaimed, "Why, these are prime! First-rate! Will you have goods or silver?"

"Silver," Sequatchie said at once.

The Scotsman, whose name was McDougal, nodded. "That's good sense. Might I know your names?"

"I'm Sequatchie. This is Hawk."

"Hawk, that's your Indian name?"

"Yes, my English name is Jehoshaphat Spencer."

McDougal nodded and offered his hand. "Glad to see you here. I hope we can do more business in the future."

Hawk and Sequatchie looked over the goods that were for sale and made some purchases. McDougal had sold them most of them, and Sequatchie whispered once, "This man, he talks like Elmo McGuire. His speech is the same."

Hawk nodded. "Both from Scotland," he said. He turned and asked, "Do you know a man named McGuire?"

McDougal turned quickly. "I know three McGuires. Which one do you speak of?"

"Elmo McGuire," Sequatchie said.

"Ah, yes. I know the man. He came from my part of the world back in the old country. He was a preacher there. Do ye know him?"

"He is gone to be with God," Sequatchie said.

Sorrow came into McDougal's eyes. "Too bad. He was a bonny preacher. How did he die?"

Sequatchie shook his head. "Of sickness," he said briefly. He hesitated, then said, "He was an honest white man."

McDougal smiled suddenly, rather ruefully, and nodded toward Hawk. "Our reputation's none too good with the Cherokees. I suppose we've earned most of it, though."

"Not you," Hawk said at once to McDougal. "You too are an honest man. Have you heard news of the war?"

"Ah, it's still the French talking the Indians into making raids along the frontier. Not ten miles from here two families were massacred and their homes burned just last week."

"It wasn't the Cherokee," Sequatchie said at once.

"No! They were Creek, I think. They're in thick with the French."

"They're wrong. The French will lead them astray," Hawk said.

The three men spoke for a while, and Hawk noticed that Jack Carter had been eyeing them steadily. "What about that fellow there, McDougal?"

"Ah, nobody knows about him, but he's not good for the Indians. Trades them cheap whiskey for good furs."

At McDougal's words, Carter's countenance turned cold and his eyes narrowed. He did not speak again that day to Hawk or Sequatchie.

Later that night Carter crept outside of the fort. He made his way silently through the forest. When he was far enough away from the fort, he stopped and made a cry that sounded almost exactly like a hunting owl. Far off in the distance the screech of another owl answered him. Soon he saw a shadowy movement and spoke out in Creek, "It is I, Jacques Cartier."

Figures stepped out from behind the trees. Three of them were Indians, and one was a white man. "What 'ave you found out, Cartier?" the man said with a heavy French accent.

"The fort can be taken. How many soldiers can you get to attack?"

The French lieutenant studied the face of Cartier and shook his head. "Right now, not enough. But our time, eet will come."

Cartier turned to the three Indians and said, "There are two men inside. They will leave the fort. Probably tomorrow. They will have much silver. I will send you word when they leave. Kill them and you can keep the silver they carry for yourselves."

"What do they look like?" asked one of the warriors.

"One is Cherokee. The other is a big white man with black hair, black eyes. Kill them! Plenty of silver to buy whiskey."

The Indians all nodded. Two of them were Chickasaws, the other a Creek, all sworn enemies to the Cherokees. "Come, Lieutenant," Jacques said. "I will show you the trail that leads to the fort. When you lead your forces here, I will come with them. I can get inside the fort anytime. They trust me there. When the attack starts, I will see to it that the gates are open."

The lieutenant nodded eagerly. "We must take this fort," he said. "That would put the Cherokees into our arms. They must believe that the English are powerless. The taking of Fort Loudoun will prove that!"

Early the next afternoon, Hawk and Sequatchie were saying their farewells to McDougal. The Scotsman said, "I wish ye wouldn't go now. There's been reports of Creeks and Chickasaws in the area, maybe French forces, too. We'll need every gun if we get attacked here."

Hawk looked at the small Scotsman. "I wouldn't mind staying. What about you, Sequatchie?"

"No, my people need these supplies. They are hungry after the long winter." He had bought a horse and loaded it down with sacks of grain and food supplies.

"I guess I'll go along with Sequatchie."

"Watch your scalp," McDougal said.

At that moment, Jacques Cartier stepped outside of the factor's office. He had been drinking heavily, and he had been thinking of Rhoda Harper. For the two years he had thought Spencer was dead, he had been at peace. Now his mind went back to the brawl they'd had. And now Spencer had snubbed him to buy goods from a filthy Scotsman. He felt the hatred burn within him. He could not handle liquor well, and now he staggered across the parade ground, murderous intent on his face. Hawk did not see him approach. When Cartier lunged forward, Sequatchie simply stepped up and, reversing his tomahawk, struck the trapper between the eyes with the blunt end. Cartier uttered a gasp, his eyes rolled upward, and he fell limply to the ground, the knife he had intended to use on Hawk falling beside him.

Hawk wheeled and saw what had happened. Reaching down, he picked up the knife and studied the face of the unconscious man, then looked up to Sequatchie. "Thanks," he said.

"Why does he hate you so much?" McDougal asked.

"I think he hates everybody." Hawk hesitated for a moment, then leaned forward with the knife.

"You're not going to—" McDougal gasped, for Hawk had removed the trapper's fur cap and had grasped his long, thick red hair. "You're not going to scalp him!"

"Not really," Hawk said, smiling grimly. He took the knife, held the thick hair up, and cut it off close to the scalp, without drawing blood. He stuck the red hair inside his belt and looked around at those who had come to watch the scene silently. "Tell this coward that Hawk has his scalp. Tell him I'll swap it to a squaw for a bowl of stew."

McDougal watched them as they left the fort, his eyes on the tall form of the man called Hawk. Then looking down at the unconscious form, he said, "He'll be like a mad animal when he wakes up. Hawk would have been better off if he'd put a knife in his throat. He'll have to do it someday, I fear."

Encounter at a Stream

Seven

$\mathcal{O}$ctober of 1757 brought a beautiful fall. As Hawk and Sequatchie made their way through the towering trees, Hawk remarked, "Somehow, I always liked autumn the best, even though there's always something of death in it." He looked up at the garish colors of the season—the reds, yellows, and oranges—colored the forest, and he became more philosophical than was his usual manner. "I guess there has to be death or there wouldn't be life," he murmured. "Every year autumn comes, and then winter, and everything seems to be all over. The ground's hard and frozen, and the trees look dead. Nothing but dead grass, but then spring comes, and new green shoots begin to break their way through the hard ground. The trees sprout their new growth, and the first thing you know the earth's all renewed again."

Sequatchie, who was plodding along beside Hawk leading one of the pack animals, nodded and said, "That's the way it's always been. Death and life. Does the Book say anything about that?"

Hawk was accustomed to the Indian asking him questions about the Bible. He had read the Bible through more than once during the two years he had been with the Cherokee, and now a verse came to him. "The Lord kills and the Lord makes alive. I guess this is His world," he remarked, looking at the white clouds scudding across the blue skies overhead.

Hawk was silent for a long time, and Sequatchie knew that his white friend was thinking of the things in the Book, as Sequatchie called it. He had an instinctive knowledge that Hawk was a man who was deeply unhappy and dissatisfied. Once he had said to his mother, Awenasa, "My brother Hawk is a man who wanders lost.

He has learned to find his way through the woods—but he has not found his way as a man."

Awenasa had agreed at once. "He needs a squaw and sons, and little ones about him. No man is complete without that." She had given Sequatchie a reproachful look, for it was a constant argument between the two about Sequatchie's own lack of a wife. He had been married once, but his wife had been killed in a raid by the Creeks, and he had never spoken of taking another wife. He had looked at his mother, knowing what was in her thoughts. Ignoring her hints about his own marital status, he said, "Hawk was married. He did have a squaw."

"He told you that?"

"Not in so many words, but I know it." There was a deep wisdom in the Cherokee, and he knew well how to read the hearts and minds of men, especially one such as Hawk, with whom he had been day and night for almost two years. "But it is not a squaw he needs— he needs the Jesus God of the Bible. He reads about Jesus, but he does not believe."

Now as the two rode on, Sequatchie thought of the conversation he had had with his mother. He said no more about it, but as they wound their way through the forest, he spoke of plans to come. "There will be food now," he said. "The buffalo will come again. We will have venison, wild turkey, and bear. The fish will be in the streams, and I will show you how to catch them with white oak fish traps."

They paused early in the afternoon, and Hawk used a Dutch oven that he had purchased from the Scottish trader, McDougal. He made plump loaves of bread from the flour and corn, and that night they drank coffee and ate fresh trout plucked out of a stream. They also enjoyed the pulpy meat of the persimmons that had fallen to the earth in abundance, for both men loved sweets. Sitting by the small fire, they talked late into the night, and just before turning in, Hawk said, "I will go in the morning and get a deer. There are tracks around the stream everywhere."

Sequatchie nodded, and the two men rolled in their warm blankets. Hawk went to sleep almost at once, which was unusual for him, and slept dreamlessly. When he awoke there was no yawning or stretching or coming awake slowly. One moment he was deeply asleep, then his eyes opened, and he was completely alert and aware of his surroundings.

Rising silently, he picked up his gun and left the camp, marveling at how he had learned to travel through the woods making no more sound than a cloud drifting overhead. It had been a hard lesson to learn, but Sequatchie had taught him well. He knew that it was a skill that might save his life one day, and as he moved through the forest, his eyes never stopped moving from side to side. He had also learned from the Cherokee that life in the forest often hung by a hair. The tribes that surrounded the Cherokees were cruel. Some of them were treacherous and could appear at any moment, rising like ghosts, killing, butchering, scalping, and then fading away back to their own territory.

By the time Hawk reached the creek, the sky in the east was tinged a faint milky gray. He took a stand beside a huge beech tree and checked the priming of his rifle. Holding his rifle loosely with both hands, one finger on the trigger, all he had to do was sweep it up, aim, and pull.

He was acutely aware of the sounds of the forest. He had never known how much he had missed until he had learned to still-hunt. After a time, he heard the tiny singing sound that he knew came from a mouse, called the "singing mouse" by the Cherokees. It had small white feet, and its song could only be heard if a man remained absolutely still. Overhead, an owl drifted by on his last cruise for food before daylight. His thick feathers deadened the sound of his flight, and yet the quick ears of the hunter heard it faintly. Hawk did not move, but turned his eyes upward without shifting his head and saw the great hunter glide across the sky. There was something ominous about the great bird that carried death in his mighty talons.

Time passed and only the tiny sounds, faint and mute, continued to catch his attention. Hawk's mind suddenly went back to Williamsburg and he had a clear vision of his son's face as he had seen it the day he left home. It came to him sharply now. He saw the round red face, the chubby fingers, and marveled at the perfection of the tiny fingernails. He remembered the dimples beside each knuckle of the red hands that were clenched tightly together. The hair was as black as his own, and he wondered if it had grown lighter. Sorrow came to him as he realized that this part of himself—this part of Faith, the fruit of their love—was alive and so far away. By this time the child would be walking and talking and becoming whatever was in him. *Would he be like Faith? Would he have a dimple such as she had in her right cheek? Would he have her sense of humor? Will he become tall like me or short like her?* The thoughts flashed through his mind, although he remained perfectly still. It was painful for him to think of his son, and more than once during his two years he had suffered agonies, knowing that he was wrong to leave the child alone. He thought of his own father, and his memory went far back as he recalled how he had depended on him and learned from him. He stirred faintly, shifting his weight from one foot to the other, driving the memories from his mind and concentrating on the scene before him.

Even as he did, a slight sound caught his attention. Without moving his head, Hawk swiveled his eyes, and at that moment a magnificent buck stepped out from behind some alders and lifted his head.

As always, since Hawk first saw a deer, his heart started to beat like a trip-hammer. There was something regal about a full-grown, powerful buck, and he remembered back when he had shot his first deer. His hands had trembled so that he could hardly pull the trigger. He was more experienced now, having killed many bucks, and his finger tightened on the trigger. He knew he had to move quickly to swing the rifle into position, for one move and the buck would be gone, springing away at a flying gait.

Careful now. You'll only get one shot, he warned himself. He took a deep breath, held it, then suddenly the deer lowered his head and began drinking. Hawk could've taken the shot then, for the deer's eyes were, of necessity, down close to the stream and he could not see his enemy. Yet there was something so peaceful and quiet and right about what he saw that Hawk could not move. He took in the strong shoulders, the heavy rack of antlers, and when the deer suddenly lifted his eyes, Hawk snapped the rifle into position. He expected the deer to leap away, but nothing happened!

Of all the times he had hunted, Hawk had never experienced anything like this before. The slightest move, and a deer ordinarily would explode with a blinding speed and bound away, but the liquid brown eyes regarded him calmly, and Hawks's finger on the trigger remained still. *Why, he seems not at all afraid of me. I've never seen such a thing. . . !*

As if to reinforce this, the deer suddenly lowered his head and drank again. Hawk could hear the sound of the deer lapping the water. Although the rifle was held in his hands with a rocklike steadiness, still, he did not pull the trigger. The deer seemed to be aware of him, yet showed no fear at all. Hawk noticed an oval ring of white fur on the deer's haunch.

Well, old man, he thought, *I've never seen one like you before. I guess I'll wait for the next one. It would be like killing a man, almost.* He suddenly dropped to one knee, expecting the deer to bolt, but the buck did not move. The silence of the moment was shattered by the sound of a musket exploding. In the next second, a branch over his head suddenly split with a crack and fell onto his right hand, which he held over the trigger of the musket.

Instantly, the deer exploded into action, but no faster than Hawk as he quickly threw himself to one side. He came to his feet with a lunge and hoped that his hidden enemy was alone. If so, he would not have time to reload. Hawk dashed through the forest, dodging the saplings and the larger trees, and at once caught a flash of a figure as it darted into a thicket. Running at full speed, he held his right hand over the mechanism of the musket so that the powder in the pan would not be blown away. His legs pounded, and he made no attempt to move silently now. Ahead he heard the crashing of a body as whoever fired the shot ran desperately.

Only one of them, Hawk thought with exultation. *Now let's see what kind of a runner he is!* He threw himself ahead, ignoring the branches that scratched his face, his moccasined feet striking the earth as he flew through the forest. Soon he saw his assailant. It was, as he suspected, an Indian, and he saw also that it was a Chickasaw. Hawk had learned enough from Sequatchie to identify the men of this tribe. As they came out into a clearing, he could have shot the man. Instead, he ran all the harder. The Chickasaw was a small, wiry warrior, and he turned now to look over his shoulder. Fear filled his eyes, for he knew that he was a dead man. Hawk was less than thirty feet away and could not miss. Hawk called out in the Cherokee language, "Stop or I'll kill you!"

The Chickasaw threw down his musket and ran harder. Hawk took a quick shot that veered left, then tossed his gun down to run more easily. It was a short race, for Hawk was a strong runner. He caught the Chickasaw, who tried to dodge, and wrestled him to the ground. The Chickasaw pulled a knife from his belt, but Hawk grabbed his wrist and twisted hard. The Indian cried out sharply as the bone snapped under the sudden strain. The knife dropped to the ground, and Hawk picked it up. Holding on to the injured wrist, he held the blade under the Indian's throat. "Don't move and you'll be all right," he said, speaking again in Cherokee.

The Chickasaw's eyes flew open wide, for he fully expected to be gutted, but Hawk said, "Come along. You're going with me. Who put you up to this?"

The Indian's face went blank, and though he obviously understood Cherokee, he did not say a word. Hawk cut several thongs from his hunting jacket and with them tied the man's hands behind his back. Then he led him back through the clearing, where he picked up both muskets. He shoved the Indian along, leading him back to the camp.

Sequatchie was alert and had his own musket ready, for he had heard gunshots and now the sounds of two men coming. He said nothing, but his eyes searched the Chickasaw carefully.

"He tried to put a bullet in me over by the creek."

Sequatchie said, "He's not part of a war party."

"No, he was all by himself." Hawk shrugged, and suddenly his eyes narrowed. He reached out and yanked a deerskin pouch hung by a thong from the Indian's neck. It jingled slightly, and he opened it up and saw what was inside. "These are French coins, Sequatchie," he said grimly. He looked at the Chickasaw and an idea came to him. "Did you get these for shooting me?" he demanded.

The Chickasaw put his lips together in a taut line and stared straight ahead. He expected to be tortured, for that is exactly what he would have done had he captured one of his enemies.

Sequatchie studied the thin face of the Chickasaw and said, "We'll take him back to Fort Loudoun."

"That's a good idea. I think the commanding officer there might like to know that the Chickasaws are carrying French money." He looked at the Indian and said, "I think they might shoot you for that."

Sequatchie said suddenly, "Why did you try to kill this man?" There was no answer, though, and Sequatchie shrugged. "We will take him back to the fort."

The English commander received the prisoner, and when he saw the coins that the Chickasaw had carried about his neck, he said, "I've been afraid of this. There's money being spread among the Indians by the French. All the more reason for you to stay, Hawk, you and your companion. We could use a few more good men around here."

"No, we must get home," Hawk said. "What about Carter?"

"He left shortly after you did." Lieutenant Matthew's eyes narrowed. "Do you suspect him?"

"I'd suspect him of anything," Hawk said. "If you see him around here again, I'd lock him up, if I were you."

"I may do that," the commander said.

After Hawk and Sequatchie rode away from Fort Loudoun, they passed the spot of the attack but said nothing about the Chickasaw. Hawk did say, however, "I forgot to tell you. A deer saved my life right there by that creek." He related the story of how the deer had watched him carefully and seemingly without fear.

"I never saw anything like it, Sequatchie. He looked at me like— well, almost like he was trying to tell me something."

Sequatchie suddenly said, "From the Book you read two nights ago about the deer. You remember?"

"Oh yes. It was from the forty-second psalm." Hawk nodded and quoted it, "As the hart panteth after the water brooks, so panteth my soul after thee, O God."

Sequatchie turned his dark eyes on his friend. "Do you remember the second thing?"

"No, I can't remember it off hand."

Sequatchie said, "The Book says, 'My soul thirsteth for God, for the living God: when shall I come and appear before God?' "

Hawk was amazed at how the Cherokee seemed to have a memory that clung to the words of Scripture. "You remember that?"

"As you read it, the Spirit of God said to me, 'This is for your friend.' " His voice grew gentle, but his eyes were intent as he said, "I think those words are for you. I think you thirst for God, although you won't admit it."

"They're just words, Sequatchie."

"No. The Book is different from other words. They are the words of God." He trudged on, his eyes searching the forest ahead, and finally he said, "God sent the deer to save your life, my brother."

"It was just an accident. A coincidence, we'd call it."

"I know not what that means, but I know the deer does not freeze when a hunter points a gun at him. He runs away at once. This one was sent from God to save your life."

Hawk stared in astonishment at Sequatchie. He had not thought of this, but now the whole scene flashed before his eyes. As they moved through the forest that day, and for the next several days on their way back to the Cherokee camp, Hawk thought of the eyes of the deer many times, and the words of Sequatchie came back to him, *God sent him to save your life.* On the last night before they reached the Cherokee village, he lay awake looking up at the stars, unable to sleep. All he could think about was the deer, and he remembered clearly the white fur on the deer's haunch, an oval ring. He had never seen that before. Finally he said to himself angrily, "I'm just getting superstitious! Indians always have these myths!"

Still he could not sleep, and the last thing he thought of before he finally did drop off was the intent, liquid eyes of the deer staring at him in a way that he knew he would never forget.

The Cherokee War

Eight

The struggle known as the French and Indian War continued without letup during the beginning of the 1760s. Little Carpenter, the skillful Cherokee chief, had won a victory of sorts by persuading Virginia and South Carolina to build forts for the protection of the helpless Cherokees. Fort Loudoun was the first European-type fort built in this part of the world. It was named after the Earl of Loudoun, the new commander of the British forces in America, and for some time it served as a protection for the Cherokees from their enemies.

The British attempts to gain Cherokee support failed, however, primarily due to British mistreatment of the Cherokees in a campaign against Fort Duquesne. The Cherokees, who had been practically the only Indians friendly to the English, turned against their former allies, and with French supplies and encouragement, they captured Fort Loudoun. One of the few survivors of the siege, and of the massacre that followed, was the British Captain John Stuart. Stuart was saved by the interception of Little Carpenter himself and was later named Indian Superintendent for the South.

The different nationalities that fought over the Ohio Valley and the vast continent that lay to the west in America did not agree on how to deal with the Cherokee Indians. The Spanish and the French viewed them as a curiosity who posed no serious threat. Most of the British and almost all the colonists saw them simply as ignorant savages to be wiped out as quickly as possible. The frontier settlers regarded the Indians as an uncivilized enemy. To the Europeans, land was a commodity to live from, an object of barter and trade. The vast wilderness of the Appalachian West offered rich farmland, plenty of trees for building cabins, and forests filled with wild game, offering food for the larder. To the early settlers it seemed to be free for the taking.

The Cherokees, who felt they were superior to all other peoples, looked upon the settlers as weaklings with an unhealthy color. They were cowards who screamed under torture, people who never kept their word, and fools who would sell their worst enemy a gun with which they themselves could be shot.

The Cherokees could not understand people whose ruling passion was to get money or own land. They believed that the land had been given to them by the Great Spirit, and therefore it was not to be sold or traded or even owned by an individual. They saw themselves as custodians sharing the land with all living creatures, a land held in trust for generations yet to come. At first the Cherokees were willing to share the use of the land with the newcomers. But as more and more settlers arrived, the natives were soon powerless to combat the legal methods employed by the land-greedy whites. They painfully discovered that no treaty the white man made with the Indians was ever final, or permanent, or kept honorably.

With all of these differences set in place, it was inevitable that a cultural clash would occur. And this clash, which developed into a bloody conflict, began with an attack on Fort Loudoun by the Cherokees. The victory of the Cherokees in taking Fort Loudoun was perceived as a disgrace by the English. An expedition was sent at once to recover the fort, but it failed miserably. A second plan was put into action, with the future of the frontier hanging in the balance. . . .

———————

The lieutenant who finally caught up with Hawk after a month's search among hundreds of square miles of hunting lands looked as though he had just stepped off the parade ground at St. James's Palace.

"I am Lieutenant Geoffrey Hurst, sir, and I can't tell you how happy I am to finally make your acquaintance."

Hawk had just come in from a long, tiresome journey all the way across the far mountain ranges. He had lost his razor along the way, and his dark beard now framed his face, giving him a rather fierce look. He had been surprised to find British soldiers so deep in Cherokee territory, and he wondered what could have brought them there.

"How do you do, Lieutenant?" he said amiably, nodding slightly. The coonskin tail brushed his back, and he thought as he looked down on the immaculate soldier, *He looks like a toy soldier. I hope he can fight better than he looks.* None of this showed in his face, however, and he waited to hear what Lieutenant Hurst had to say.

"I've been sent here with a force to recapture Fort Loudoun, Mr. Spencer." Hurst had a narrow face with a fine black line of mustache covering a rather small mouth, but there was determination in his gray eyes, indicating that despite his small size there might be something to him. "I suppose you're aware that our loss of the fort was frowned upon by the king."

"No, I didn't hear about that. His Majesty didn't care for it, I take it?"

"He did not, sir!" Hurst snapped. "Nor did I, nor did any of the officers in His Majesty's army. To be defeated by a bunch of savages is an unthinkable disgrace! I wish that I had been there."

Hawk thought back over the terrible siege and the bloody massacre that had followed the loss of Fort Loudoun and drawled, "I don't reckon you could've helped much. From what I hear, the defenders put up a good fight. They were just outnumbered, Lieutenant."

"Ten of His Majesty's soldiers can defeat a hundred of these cowardly savages!"

Being somewhat accustomed to the British attitude toward the Indians, Hawk said only, "Well, they might be savages, but if they're cowards, I don't guess anybody ever found out about it. All I've known have been brave men."

Surprise washed across the lieutenant's face. He was new to this country, having come directly from England with orders to capture Fort Loudoun without any delay, and he was determined to do it. "Well, we will not argue that, sir. In any case, I am commissioned to make you a handsome offer to join our forces. We need an experienced guide and someone who speaks the language of the Cherokee."

Hawk shook his head at once. "Sorry you've been to so much trouble, but you got the wrong man, Lieutenant."

"But you haven't even heard our offer."

"I don't need to hear it, Lieutenant Hurst. Maybe somehow you got the wrong word. Of all the men to help run the Cherokees down, I'm the last one you should ask. I'm a blood brother with Sequatchie, one of their chiefs, and a good friend of Little Carpenter."

"Oh! I heard something about that, but look here, Mr. Spencer. You wouldn't stand against your own people with these Indians, would you?"

"Yep! I would."

The brief answer seemed to shake the bottom out of Lieutenant Hurst. His pursed little mouth grew tight and he said, "Why . . . I'm disappointed to hear that. I'd hoped for better things from an Englishman."

For one moment, Hawk stood there considering what he'd heard and finally said, "I'm not sure I'm an Englishman, Lieutenant. I've never been to England in my life. Never saw the king. I guess you might say I'm more of an American than anything else."

"But the Colonies belong to His Majesty, and you're a subject just as I am."

"Somehow, when you cross over these mountains, the king of England seems mighty far away."

Hawk's answer infuriated the British soldier. "We fought for years to keep the French out of your country and paid a high price for it—and now all you can say is that you're not willing to help us keep the land clear for white settlers!"

"I don't want to be argumentative, Lieutenant, but I don't reckon King George and Queen Anne and the rest of the English monarchs over there did all this fighting out of the goodness of their hearts. The way I see it, and the way things seem to be shaping up back in Boston and in the rest of the Colonies, King George seems to be ready to bleed us dry with taxes."

"You're suggesting that you shouldn't pay taxes?"

"I'm not a politician. I'm just a long hunter," Hawk said wearily. "I'll never go back to Boston or New York or any of those places. I'm headed west, and the farther west I go, the farther I'll be from crowns and kings, and that'll suit me fine. Sorry, Lieutenant. You'll have to find yourself another man." Hawk turned and walked away rapidly, ignoring the sputtering and the arguments that flew from the officer's lips.

Later on, when Hawk found Sequatchie, he related the British officer's offer and laughed aloud. "Can you imagine those English trying to get me to go against my own people?"

Sequatchie's face underwent some sort of a change that Hawk could not interpret. "What's the matter?" he asked. "You don't think I did wrong, do you?"

Sequatchie squatted down suddenly and picked up a stick and began to draw designs in the dirt. Knowing that something was on his friend's mind, Hawk squatted beside him, then waited for some time. It was obvious to him that Sequatchie was troubled. The two of them had been together for years now and knew each other as well as two men could. Sequatchie, he knew, had been torn by his dislike of what the English way of life brought to his people, yet he disliked the French even more.

"The only hope for my people, especially those of us who are Christians, is to make close ties with the English."

Hawk stared at the coppery face, shock running through him. "I . . . I don't understand that. You know what the English do. They take your lands and push you farther out into the wilderness. Sooner or later there's an end to that. There's only so much wilderness out there."

"You speak truth, Hawk, but my spirit tells me that something is happening. My fathers lived and hunted on this land for many years. But now the white men come like the locust. More and more arrive every year. And you say there are many thousand more over the great water, more than I can count. They are coming, and nothing can stop them."

"That's not the way most Indians think. Dragging Canoe, Little Carpenter's relative, says he's stirring the tribes up to fight to the last man to keep the land only for the Indian."

"He is a fighting man, and all he knows is to kill. But when every Indian is killed, the English will still come. No," Sequatchie said calmly, "the only way for my people to survive is to change. Whether this can be, I do not know. It is a hard thing. The Good Book says that we are to submit to one another, and for an Indian to submit to those forcing him off the land is the same as death."

Hawk smiled briefly. "You're not very good at giving up. I've noticed that." He squatted in the dust, thinking hard, and said, "There's more to this than you're telling me."

Sequatchie looked up and nodded. "Somehow my brothers must

be won to the knowledge of the Jesus God. They cannot do that if they are involved in a war, killing others. Our way of life must go. I see it clearly. In the Scriptures Jesus said, 'Take my yoke upon you,' did He not?"

"That's what He said," Hawk admitted grudgingly. "I find that pretty hard to do."

"And He said, 'Turn the other cheek.' "

"He said that, too," Hawk admitted. He could not say more, for he knew himself too well. The fiery temper that lurked deep within his spirit was not suited to follow the teachings of Jesus on submission and turning the other cheek. Finally he said heavily, "I cannot agree with you. I think we should at least take your people and go as far west as we can."

"And what would we find there?"

"Eventually another big water."

"And when the white man catches us there, what will happen?"

Hawk could say no more. He had seen long ago that the Indian way of life was doomed, and now Sequatchie himself had agreed. Hawk did not agree with Sequatchie's ideas on surrender, but he listened quietly as Sequatchie spoke.

"If it takes submission to win eternity for my brothers, then it is worth the cost."

The two men talked for a long time, and finally Sequatchie said, "I ask you to help my people, Hawk. They are your people, too. We must teach them to work the land like the whites, to become what they are not by nature."

"You mean farmers? I don't think they could ever learn that."

"They can if we help them, but in the meanwhile we must prove to the English that we are worthy of trust."

Hawk thought of Lieutenant Hurst and gritted his teeth at the prospect of going back and humbling himself before the man. "The last thing I want to do is ask Lieutenant Hurst for his help."

Sequatchie smiled. "It'll be good for the pride that is in you. Come, I will go with you. We must help my people."

———————

Hurst, despite his small size, was an excellent soldier, and he knew men better than Hawk had guessed. The small force that he had brought with him was well disciplined and trained to obey at a moment's notice. They had brought two small cannons, and though they only threw two-pound balls, a steady barrage would eventually break down the walls of the fort.

"That's the way you destroy forts, Mr. Spencer," Lieutenant Hurst explained as they approached Fort Loudoun. "One cannon is all you need. The walls are what keep the invaders out. One cannon, no matter how small, if you have enough ammunition, can blow an entranceway. Once that's breached, the fort is doomed."

"I suppose that's so, Lieutenant," Hawk said as they rode side by side.

The defenders inside the fort had known, of course, that the enemy was coming. No small military force of soldiers could cross that territory with red coats flashing and cannons being dragged by heavy draft horses without attracting attention. At Hawk's suggestion, Lieutenant Hurst sent out scouts on wide-ranging forays so that those Indians who might have crept in close and picked the soldiers off—as they had with General Braddock's troops—would be unable to do so. The main force reached Fort Loudoun without losing a man, and instantly they began battering the walls down with the small cannons.

After one day's bombardment, Lieutenant Hurst said, "Look. Two or three more shots and we can enter. You're not obliged to make the charge, Mr. Spencer. You're only a scout, not a soldier."

"I wish you'd call me Hawk, Lieutenant."

"Why, very well. But what I say is true enough."

"I think I'll go in with your men, if you don't mind, sir."

Hurst gave a shrug, and there was relief in his gray eyes. "We need every man we can get, of course. Every gun will count."

"If you'll take my advice," Hawk said, "you'll keep blasting with that cannon and wait until tomorrow to make the attack."

"And why is that?"

"Because if you do, most of the enemy on the inside will sneak away during the night. They're afraid of the cannon, you see. Give them a chance and they'll run."

"I thought you believed Indians were courageous."

"They're courageous, but they're not stupid. They know they can't stand up against cannon—especially when you load it with shrapnel. No body of men can stand against that. An Indian will fight as long as he sees a reason, but they know their cause is lost.

If you just give them a little time, it would save lives, yours and the Indians."

Lieutenant Hurst smiled. It made him look much younger. "I'll take your advice, and I wish we had more officers like you in the service. There's a thought for you. Think it over. I believe we could get you a commission."

"No thanks, Lieutenant. I'd make a poor soldier. I don't follow orders too well."

Hurst gave Hawk an odd look. "I've never asked you why you changed your mind, but I'm curious to know, sir."

"It was Sequatchie who convinced me. He says that the Indian way of life is doomed, and he wants to unite his people and bring them under the British authority as obedient citizens."

The lieutenant's eyes flew open in surprise. "Well, I'm glad to hear it, although I didn't expect it."

"The French have always treated the Indians better than the English," Hawk said evenly. "We'll see if there's any honor in His Majesty's forces."

Hurst drew his shoulders back and looked squarely at Hawk. There was anger in his tone. "I assure you we will treat our captives with honor and dignity!"

"I'm taking your word for that, Lieutenant," Hawk said. "As a gentleman and an officer!"

———————

"All right, men! Let's go! Keep together now! Pull the cannons in line, and we'll have them!"

Sequatchie and Hawk were at the end of the line of red-clad troopers as Lieutenant Hurst gave the cry.

"I don't think we'll find many Indians in there," Sequatchie grinned. "Most of them had sense enough to sneak away last night. If the lieutenant had wanted, he could've captured most of them."

"I don't think he's really interested in that. All he wants is the fort," Hawk said. "You know, he's not a bad fellow. Well, here we go."

The two men charged forward, muskets loaded, but neither of them had a heart for killing any Cherokee. When they crashed through the broken-down barricade, they saw that the Indians who were left were, for the most part, Chickasaws.

"They've been hired by the French for this," Hawk murmured to Sequatchie.

"Look!" Sequatchie said. "There's Carter!"

Instantly a whistling sound buzzed past Hawk's ear. He flinched and saw Jack Carter drop his rifle and hurriedly begin reloading it. Hawk could have killed him right then, because his rifle was loaded. Instead he ran forward, and before the trapper could get his rifle reloaded, Hawk was upon him. Holding his musket right in front of Carter's face, he said, "Go ahead, Carter, lift that rifle and I'll send you on the longest trip you've ever had!"

Carter's face twisted with anger, but he could not face the steadiness of Hawk's gaze. "I will kill you someday, Spencer! You can be sure of that! It is only luck that has kept you alive since you left Williamsburg!"

"It was you who tried to kill me in the wilderness!"

"Yes! I thought you were dead then! I wish I'd put another bullet in your head! I knew you would be trouble for the French." At the shocked look on Hawk's face, Carter grinned smugly. "Yes, I am French. My real name is Jacques Cartier. This land belongs to us, not to you Englishmen. I have been working for my country these past years to drive all of the English back across the mountains. We were close to succeeding, but you have interfered." Cartier paused, then quietly continued, "We will still defeat you, and this land will once again be the sole property of France."

Even as Cartier stood there looking down the muzzle of Hawk's gun, a group of Chickasaws surged around the corner of a cabin. They all had tomahawks and threw themselves in a suicidal charge toward the British. One of them was almost even with Sequatchie, who was reloading his rifle. Instantly Hawk saw that his friend had no chance. Throwing his musket up, he fired, and the Indian who had raised his hatchet to strike Sequatchie fell backward. At the same instant Jacques Cartier pulled a wicked-looking knife out of his belt. With the poise of a practiced knife fighter, he whipped it in a motion that practically whistled. It was aimed at Hawk's throat, and only the lightninglike reaction of the hunter saved him. Hawk threw his head back, and the knife missed him by a hairsbreadth. Instantly, Hawk grabbed the wrist of the Frenchman, and the two of them stumbled across the parade ground, fighting for possession of the knife.

Other Chickasaws, apparently hidden, had come screaming out

of the long house, where the stores were kept, and a savage fray began to develop. For once British discipline paid off in fighting the Indians. The calm voice of Lieutenant Hurst saying, "Prepare! Load! Fire!" sounded across the parade ground with regularity. His men fired in volleys, so that when the front line fired, they stepped back and another line was ready. Some of the soldiers fell victim to the thrown tomahawks. A few of the Chickasaws had rifles, but after the first volley, many of the Indians fell under the British fire.

During all of this, Hawk was struggling with the giant Frenchman, who fought like a madman. The two of them stumbled over bodies, slipped on bloody ground, and yet neither could gain the advantage. Suddenly, Hawk felt Cartier jerk his knife hand free. In that moment Hawk knew he had lost. The knife went back and started to descend—but a shot rang out, and Cartier stiffened, his mouth opening, and he fell backward to the ground, dropping the knife.

Whirling around, Hawk saw Lieutenant Hurst standing there with a smoking pistol.

"I owe you one for that, Lieutenant."

"My pleasure, sir. Now we need to finish off the rest of them."

Recovering his musket, Hawk joined Sequatchie and the lieutenant. Soon the Chickasaws were surrounded, and most of them threw down their tomahawks. There were fewer than twenty of them left.

"That's it! Hold your fire!" Lieutenant Hurst called out. "Sergeant, put these men in irons! Doctor, see to your wounded!"

Sequatchie and Hawk came together, and Sequatchie nodded. "The lieutenant saved your life."

Hawk managed a smile. "I suppose you're going to claim he came along just like that hawk that helped you find me and the deer that saved my life from that Chickasaw. The lieutenant was sent by God to save me."

"Do not laugh. God will have His way with you."

Somehow Hawk could not joke about this. He knew that his life had hung by a thread, and if the lieutenant had not fired at the exact moment he did, Cartier's knife would have been buried in his heart. "I'm not making fun," he said.

The two of them wandered over the interior of the fort, helping get the prisoners safely locked away. It was Sequatchie who said, "The Frenchman. He is gone."

Startled, Hawk looked over to where the body of Cartier had lain and saw that his friend was right. "He was probably carried over to that shed where they're seeing to the wounded."

"We will see."

Sequatchie led the way. When they entered the shed, they looked carefully at every wounded man but found only Indians.

"Doctor, did you treat a Frenchman?"

The doctor looked up. His arms were covered with blood up to his elbows, and he said with some surprise, "A Frenchman? No. Only the savages. I haven't seen a Frenchman."

Sequatchie stepped outside, followed closely by Hawk. The two searched the fort but found no trace of Jacques Cartier.

"I thought he was dead for sure."

"He may have been carried off by some of his friends in the battle, but I think not," Sequatchie said. "He bears a charmed life, almost like your own."

"Do you think God is watching out for him like He is for me?" Hawk demanded.

Sequatchie shook his head. "There are other forces in the world besides the Jesus God. Cartier is under a dark shadow. You will see him again."

The next day, Lieutenant Hurst once again asked Hawk to join the army. "Come along as a scout. You'll be well paid," he urged.

"Thank you, Lieutenant, but it's not for me." He stuck his hand out and said, "I'm proud to have served with you. I wish all the English officers were like you."

The lieutenant's pale face flushed, and he said only, "I trust that we will learn as we gain more experience in this land. It's so unlike anything I've ever known. You would be a great help to me and, I think, to the Indians if you would stay."

Sequatchie and Hawk left the fort the next day, and as they made their way back to Sequatchie's village, the Indian said, "The French are practically defeated."

"Yes."

The two walked quietly, their eyes constantly searching ahead, and finally Hawk said, "Yes, the war will be over officially, I think."

"It will be different for our people then. The settlers will come pouring over the land into these misty mountains. They will not fear the French any longer. And the Chickasaws and the Creeks will not fight for the French unless they are paid."

"What will you do, Sequatchie?"

"I will go to my people, and I will continue to tell them that the Jesus way is our only hope." He hesitated, then asked, "Will you come with me?"

Hawk hesitated a moment. "For a while, yes." He put his hand on the shoulder of the tall Cherokee and said, "We're brothers."

Sequatchie's eyes lit up, and he put his hand over the white one that gripped his shoulder. "No matter what happens, God will be in it, my friend."

PART II

Elizabeth

April 1770 – August 1770

And Ruth said, Entreat me not to leave thee,
or to return from following after thee:
for whither thou goest, I will go;
and where thou lodgest, I will lodge:
thy people shall be my people,
and thy God my God.

Ruth 1:16

The Martins of Beacon Street

Nine

*T*he library had become the favorite room of Elizabeth Martin MacNeal, and as she sat under the beams of bright April sunshine that flooded in from the windows that filled the north end of the room, she felt a sense of comfort and belonging that always came to her there. The light illuminated her wavy blond hair with its darker tones, which, instead of being worn up as was fashionable, fell just below her shoulders. She had pale green eyes, framed by long eyelashes, and her heart-shaped face and clear complexion were the envy of women ten years younger. At the age of thirty-three, she was one of those women who managed to retain the beauty she'd had at eighteen. Her figure was only slightly fuller than it had been when she was that age, and the dress she wore augmented it.

The dress was made of a taupe-and-salmon-striped silk and had a low square neckline trimmed with a satin edging. Cinnamon-colored bows ran down the front of the bodice to the skirt, which was full and divided in front to show off an elaborate underskirt of the same color. A decoration of taupe brocade flowed from the bodice into the skirt edges. The sleeves were tight fitting and came to the elbows, which ended with salmon-colored bows and white lace frills that fell over the lower arm. It was very stylish for any woman to wear in 1770.

The only sound in the room was the ticking of the massive grandfather clock at the far end of the library and the scratching of Elizabeth's pen on the pages of the ledger that lay before her. From time to time she would stop, study the numbers, and a tiny line would appear between her slightly arched eyebrows. Once, outside the window, a pair of mockingbirds engaged in some kind of an altercation. Elizabeth lifted her head and watched as they advanced and retreated from each other, raising their tails in the swift, jerky motion typical of these birds. A smile turned the corners of her lips upward, and she put the pen down and flexed her fingers to relieve the strain. As she did, she looked around the library and thought suddenly, *I never thought I'd be living in this house after I got married. I thought I'd have a little tiny house of my own. Just Patrick and me.*

The library was a small room with a window seat beneath each of the four windows. The wallpaper was flecked with green, gold, and red, and the floor matched with a green-and-gold Persian rug. A mahogany desk with an astral oil lamp was placed by one of the four windows and was flanked by two library chairs. Near the fireplace, at the end of the room, was a small table and a walnut sofa, which was adorned in a green-and-red-striped silk damask. It was a comfortable room, lived in and enjoyed, and this aura always pleased Elizabeth.

The frown between her eyes disappeared, and she put the thought away. She had talked about this for some time with Patrick before they had married, and finally they had decided that staying with her parents might be the best thing "for a while." In the end, they stayed much longer than either of them thought, for now that Andrew was thirteen and Sarah would soon be ten, they had known no other home but the Martin mansion.

It had been a good arrangement, or so Elizabeth had always thought. The stately two-story colonial mansion had been the only home she had ever known, and Patrick had liked it well enough. It was nice to have servants, which she would not have had if she and Patrick had set up housekeeping for themselves alone. True enough, Patrick, from time to time, mentioned getting a place of their own, but so far he had not been insistent about it.

A sudden knock at the door brought Elizabeth's head around, but before she had time to answer, the door burst open and two children were shoved into the room unceremoniously.

"Andrew—Sarah! What in the world—!"

The boy with a stocky build and a head of wavy blond hair advanced slowly, propelled insistently by a young woman. His clothes were covered with sticky red mud, and his shoes left reddish streaks on the Persian carpet. Even his hair seemed to be plastered down with the mess, and he hung his head, as if too ashamed to face his mother.

"Andrew! What happened to you?"

"I . . . I fell in the ditch, Mother."

"Fell in the ditch?" Elizabeth rose and tossed the pen down on the desk. Advancing to the pair, she stopped in front of Andrew and said, "I never saw such a mess in all my life! Didn't I tell you to be careful and not get close to that muddy ditch?"

"Yes, Mother."

The answer came in a mutter, and when the boy raised his eyes, Elizabeth saw that they were filled with misery. His blue eyes usually sparkled, and now she could see that he was on the verge of tears.

"He didn't fall into the ditch. Sarah pushed him in, Mrs. MacNeal," said Rebekah, who was standing behind the children. A young woman of twenty-one, she wore the standard uniform approved by the Martins, Elizabeth's parents. It was a plain black dress made of wool, and the neckline was cut high with a large white muslin collar that came to a point in the front and covered her shoulders. The sleeves were fitted to below the elbow and ended with stiff white cuffs. Over the dress she wore a plain apron that fell to the bottom of her long skirt. She had thick, long black hair and unusual eyes, almost the color of emeralds, wide-spaced and shaded with dark lashes. She had a very pretty face, and there was a sweetness about her that, at the moment, was covered with embarrassment and confusion. She obviously was disturbed about the unkempt condition of the young boy.

"Pushed him in! Did you do that, Sarah?"

Sarah MacNeal had some of the looks of her father, but those hints of her mother's beauty were becoming more prevalent as she grew older. She had lustrous dark red hair like her father's and the same heart-shaped face and green eyes as her mother. Even now, however, those green eyes flashed with anger as she turned to the maid. "You didn't have to tell her, Rebekah!"

"Never mind that," Elizabeth said. "Rebekah is responsible for you! Now answer the question. Did you push Andrew into the mud?"

"Yes, I did!"

Elizabeth was faintly shocked at the audacity of this daughter of hers. She had long observed that it was Andrew who had the obedient spirit that one admired in children, and Sarah had a streak of obstinacy that surfaced from time to time. She was not mean or wicked, by any means, but a strong willfulness appeared in her unexpectedly that sometimes exceeded mere playfulness.

"Well, you should be ashamed of yourself! Now look what you've done to your brother's clothes! I want you to go to your room right this moment and stay there until I come up and have a talk with you! Do you hear me?"

"Yes, Mama."

"Rebekah, you go with her and make certain that she stays there until I come up."

"Yes, Mrs. MacNeal."

The two left, and as soon as the door closed, Elizabeth looked at her son with compassion. She walked over now and reached out and touched the muddy, streaked hair. "What a mess you are," she said with a smile.

"I'm sorry, Mother."

"It wasn't your fault, and it'll all wash off. I'll tell you what. You go take a good bath and put on some clean clothes. When you get all cleaned up, you come back, and you and I will read some more in that book you like so much."

The dejection seemed to fade from the boy, and the eyes regained some of their sparkle.

"Can we, Mother?"

"Of course we can. Now, you run along and let me finish my work."

"All right, Mother."

"And, Andrew . . ."

"Yes, ma'am?"

"You mustn't be upset with Sarah. She's just . . . well, a little lively."

"I know, Mother. It's all right."

Andrew turned and left the room, and Elizabeth looked down at the red muddy marks on the carpet, sighed deeply, then shook her head. "I don't know what that girl's coming to," she said almost in despair. "I'll have to ask Patrick to have a talk with her. She always listens to him more than she does to me."

Going back to the desk, Elizabeth applied herself to the leatherbound journals that were open before her. Shortly a soft knock came at the door, and Elizabeth said, "Come in."

Mrs. Martha Edwards, the housekeeper, opened the door and came in. The grandmother of Rebekah, she had been with the Martin household for many years and had been very happy when she had been able to secure a position for her granddaughter. Now approaching the desk, she asked quietly, "What shall we do about Sarah, Mrs. MacNeal?"

"Oh, we don't want to punish her too much. Take her something in on a tray and let her stay in her room for a while."

"Yes, ma'am." Mrs. Edwards hesitated and said, "Rebekah felt very bad about it."

"It wasn't her fault. She does a good job with the children." A smile came to Elizabeth's lips. "I'm so glad she's come to be with us, and I know she's a lot of comfort and company for you, Martha."

"Yes, ma'am, she is. She reminds me of George—like having him back, in a way, it is." Martha Edwards' only son and his son's wife had died at sea when Rebekah was only two. Rebekah had stayed with her grandmother all these years and had grown up in the Martin household.

"Will there be any special instructions for dinner?"

"Just follow the menu I gave you, Martha. That will be fine."

"Yes, ma'am."

When the housekeeper left, once again Elizabeth went back to her bookkeeping. The long lines of figures somehow gave her pleasure. She had always been a great reader of novels and poetry but had discovered late in life that she was gifted in bookkeeping. Since then she had been giving some of her time to help manage the accounts of the family business.

She was soon so absorbed in her work that she lost track of the hour. Looking up with surprise, the door opened and her husband entered. "Patrick!" she said. She got up at once and ran over and put her arms around him. He kissed her on the cheek, then on the lips, and she reached up and arranged a lock of thick, curly dark red hair that was, as usual, unruly. He had bright blue eyes, and though he was lean, she felt the thick muscles from the hard work that he had known for most of his life. He had a rather thin face, with patches of freckles on both cheeks, and a broken nose that gave him a disreputable look. She said suddenly without thinking of it, "You know. I think you're getting better looking as you get older."

Patrick MacNeal, a cheerful man of thirty-three, laughed and kissed her again. "Good you should think so!" he said. "I'd hate for you to be married to an ugly old man."

She traced the clean line of his jaw and said quietly, "I never told you this, but the first time I saw you unloading goods onto Father's ship, I thought you were the handsomest young man I'd ever seen."

Patrick laughed aloud. "I admire your judgment," he said. "You have fine taste in manly beauty."

"Come in and sit down. What are you doing home so early?"

Patrick threw himself into one of the mahogany armchairs and stretched his long legs out in front of him. "I just couldn't stand it anymore!" he said frankly. "Those four walls started closing in on me. I was afraid they were going to squeeze me to death!"

The line between Elizabeth's brows suddenly appeared. Feeling agitated, she started to ask, "Don't you like your work, Patrick?" but managed to bite the words off. She had been thankful she had married a man who was not a complainer. Most men would not have been content to live with his in-laws. Elizabeth knew that William and Anne Martin were not the easiest people in the world for a son-in-law to get along with—especially a son-in-law who came from a lower social position. From time to time, however, she had picked up from Patrick how he longed to do something other than work inside a warehouse.

She did not see any way that could ever happen, for the shipping business involved a fair deal of manual labor, and Patrick, she knew, could not get any other type of job. He was a hardworking man, but he was no businessman.

"Maybe we could take a vacation. Get out in the country somewhere," she said tentatively.

"Do you think so?" Patrick brightened up. "And take the children with us? That would be fine, wouldn't it? Get out and just breathe the air and run through the grass."

There was a wistfulness in his tone that said more than words. He had a gentle, agreeable spirit, but even during such moments as this, Elizabeth was aware that he was unhappy. It grieved her to think that her mother had never approved her choice of a husband. Mrs. Anne Hardwick Martin had proud English roots, and her dream had been for her only daughter to marry someone well respected and high in society. When her hope had failed to happen,

Anne Martin had accepted it, but not with a great deal of grace.

"How is Father today?"

Patrick shook his head. "Not well. I don't think that doctor's doing him any good, do you, Elizabeth?"

"We've changed doctors three times already. I think Dr. Brown is as good as any of the others." She bit her lip and said quietly, "I'm worried about Father. He's lost so much weight, and he doesn't seem to have any strength these days."

Patrick did not answer. He agreed, however, for it was obvious to him that William Martin was no longer the robust man he had been when Patrick had married Elizabeth.

"Maybe he's the one who needs the trip. Maybe a sea voyage might pick him up."

"He'd never agree to leave the business—and certainly not with Will's marriage coming up."

The two sat there for some time, talking about the affairs of life, when the door opened and Rebekah came in with a six-piece tea service on a large, ornately engraved silver tray.

"I thought you might like some tea," she said shyly.

"Why, that was thoughtful of you, Rebekah," Patrick said. He winked at his wife and said, "Now, if you could just get my wife to be as careful of my well-being as you are . . ."

Elizabeth slapped his hand. "You get treated well enough, I expect!" She smiled at the girl and said, "Thank you so much, Rebekah. I can't tell you how good it is to have you here to take care of all of us."

"Thank you very much, Mrs. MacNeal."

The two were drinking tea when they heard voices outside the library again. "Busy here today," Elizabeth remarked with surprise. She looked up and smiled when a young woman came into the room. "Why, Charlotte," she said, "please come in. You're just in time to join us for tea."

"Oh, that would be nice." Charlotte Van Dorn was the fiancée of William Martin, Jr., Elizabeth's brother. Her long pale blond hair was immaculate, and she had beautiful violet eyes. She was one of those women who was blessed with clear clean-cut features and a figure that was neither too slender nor too full. Charlotte was the daughter of Henry Van Dorn, a wealthy businessman from New York. His wife and Elizabeth's mother were distant cousins, which had led to the engagement between Charlotte and William, Jr. Both mothers had spent a considerable amount of effort on arranging the match, and Will had finally agreed.

"Is Will home yet?"

"He said he'd be along soon," Patrick said. He drank the rest of his tea and said, "I'll let you two women take up the conversation while I go get cleaned up."

Elizabeth wanted to tell him about Sarah pushing Andrew into the mud, but not with Charlotte present. Still, it seemed to her to be important. When Patrick was out of the room, she jumped up and said, "Oh, I forgot to tell Patrick something. Excuse me a moment, Charlotte." Running outside, she caught Patrick by the arm and quickly recounted the event. "I wish you'd go up and talk to her. She listens to you more than she does to me."

Humor twinkled in Patrick's eyes. "It's usually the other way around, isn't it? Big brother pushing the young sister into the mud. I'll have a talk with her."

"Good. She'll listen to you." Elizabeth turned and went back into the room, sat down, and said, "That's a new dress, isn't it?"

"This old thing? Why, I've had it for ages." This meant, in the language of the Van Dorns, Charlotte had probably had the dress for two months and had worn it twice. She looked over at the accounting books that were on the desk and asked idly, "Have you been working on those old books again?"

"Yes, a little bit."

"It would bore me to tears."

"I rather like it, Charlotte. It's odd. I like poetry, and I like adding up figures. They don't seem to go together, do they?"

"Keeping books always seemed to me a man's job." Charlotte touched her hair into place, an action not at all needed. She said, in what seemed to be an idle tone, "I wish Will could take over that part of the business. He isn't catching on to it too well, is he?"

"I think he's trying hard," Elizabeth said in defense of her brother.

"Oh yes. I know that. Still, one of these days he will be the head of the firm. I think he needs to take better hold of his responsibilities. I've been having a few talks with him about this."

I'll just bet you have! Elizabeth thought grimly. She did not know what there was about Charlotte Van Dorn that bothered her, but something about the young socialite disturbed her greatly. She could not fault the woman's manners, and yet there was some element in Charlotte's character that grated on her nerves. Charlotte had a tendency to bully Will, which irritated Elizabeth, but she supposed many fiancées did that. She even bullied Patrick from time to time, but there was a difference in it. The two sat there talking for some time, until again the door opened and William Martin, Jr., came in. He was just under six feet, with dark brown eyes and hair. He came over at once and said rather diffidently, "I hoped I might find you here, Charlotte. Hello, Elizabeth."

"Sit down, Will." Elizabeth smiled. "Tell us what you've been doing."

Will sat down and took a cup of tea. There was a nervousness—an insecurity about him—that was rather unusual for a man with his advantages. He had been born after his mother had suffered two miscarriages, and this had perhaps led to his mother's devoting too much care to her one son. More than once Elizabeth had thought, *Will would be better off if Mother kept her hands off him. She's pampered him too much. Father knows it, but he can't seem to do much about it.* Aloud she said, "There must not be much going on at the firm. Patrick came home early, and now you."

"Well, it's busy enough, I suppose," Will said listlessly. He tinkered with the cup, sipped some tea, and then looked over at Charlotte, asking, "Is that a new dress, dear?"

"Oh no! You'll see my new one at dinner tonight. How are things at the firm?"

"Oh, just fine. Father's not feeling well. I wish he'd stay home more. I've tried to get him to do that, but you know how stubborn he can be."

"You should be more firm with him, Will. You're going to take over when he—" Charlotte broke off suddenly, and a slight tinge of red came into her cheeks. Both of her listeners knew she had intended to say, "take over when he dies. . . ." but even Charlotte had enough tact not to say that. "You'll take over," she continued, "and you'll have to know all the ins and outs. Look at Elizabeth. There she is doing the bookwork. Shouldn't you be doing that?"

"Oh, I don't mind," Elizabeth said.

"I'm sure you don't, but Will needs to be an expert in every aspect of the business. Show us what you're doing. I'd like to see some of this myself."

Reluctantly, Elizabeth began to go over the accounts. It was not interesting at all, and once she asked Will, "You see these figures here?"

"Yes," Will said. "What about them?"

"Well." The line appeared between Elizabeth's eyebrows. She said, "I can't figure it out. The books show that some money is missing—that fewer goods had been delivered to a customer in Virginia than the books reported."

"Oh, I'm sure it's just a mistake."

"Who made the entries?" Charlotte asked instantly.

"Why, I think Patrick did."

Charlotte's eyebrows rose, and she laughed with a false note. "Maybe Patrick ran off with the rest of the money."

Will started and stared at his fiancée, then laughed. "That would be a joke, wouldn't it?"

However, Elizabeth sensed something more than a joke in Charlotte's words. "It's bound to be just a mistake. I'll ask Father about it when he comes home."

"Come along, Will. I want us to talk about the new furniture. After all, we only have a month to get it all picked out before the wedding."

With a groan Will rose. "I'll leave you with the books, Elizabeth," he said.

"All right. You two run along." Elizabeth sat there after they left. The line between her eyebrows grew deeper as she looked down at the entry, and she thought about the tone in Charlotte's voice. She knew full well that Charlotte Van Dorn did not like her husband, that she looked down on him for his lowly origins, and the thought angered her. Almost viciously she slammed the book shut and muttered, "Will, you're making a mistake marrying that woman!" However, she knew that there was nothing she could do about it, so she rose and left the room, trying to put the incident from her mind.

Patrick MacNeal

Ten

*D*id you have a good talk with Sarah, Patrick?"

Patrick was struggling to get his collar fastened, a skill that always seemed to elude him. He stood before the ornate oval mirror, carved in gold leaf, his thick fingers fumbling with the cravat. "I can't tie this thing!" he finally exclaimed, turning to Elizabeth.

"Here, let me do it for you."

Elizabeth had already finished dressing. She was wearing a light blue dress of embroidered silk. The neckline was square and the bodice tight with fine tucks in the front, accented with dark blue ribbon and white lace. The funnel-shaped sleeves were done with three layers of lace. A dark blue ribbon outlined the full skirt, and the underskirt was quilted of the same material. She smiled as she expertly tied Patrick's tie. "You can fix any kind of machinery on the place, but you can't tie your own tie. I never could understand it." She patted it, then rephrased her question. "What did Sarah say?"

"She said she pushed Andrew in the mud!"

"I *know* she did that, but did she say why she did it?"

Patrick picked up the silver comb-and-brush set that Elizabeth had given him for a wedding gift. He ran the brush through his thick red hair, which curled rebelliously, and he murmured, "I think she just wanted to."

"Well, you talked to her! What did you say?"

"I told her not to push Andrew in the mud again." He turned, grinned, and said, "Isn't that what you wanted me to say?"

"She's *your* daughter!"

"She's always my daughter when she does something wrong!"

"She's more like you than like me. Isn't that odd?" she said.

"What's odd about it?"

"Well, you'd think a boy would take after his father, and a girl would be like her mother, but Andrew's a lot like me, isn't he?"

"He's not as pretty as you." Patrick came over and put his arms around Elizabeth and gave her a squeeze. "You're right about Sarah, though," he said, lifting his eyebrows. "She does seem to have a willful streak in her—like me."

"You're not willful!"

"That's all you know! I just haven't let it creep out. I wanted to marry you so much, I guess I would have agreed to wear purple suits if that's what you'd wanted."

Elizabeth liked it when he talked like this. She reached up and patted his cheek, murmuring, "You *do* have your moments, Patrick MacNeal! Well, I suppose no harm is done."

"Are you ready to go down?" Patrick said, glad to be finished with the discussion. He had a soft spot in his heart for Sarah, knowing that at times she did display the same streak of stubbornness that ran in his Scotch-Irish blood. He was afraid it would get her into trouble one day, and he was happy that it did not seem to be appearing quite so prominently in Andrew.

"I suppose so." Elizabeth picked up a shawl, and as he put it around her shoulders, she said, "Oh, I forgot to tell you. There was a discrepancy in the ledger for the shipment that went to the Mc-Millan Company in Williamsburg."

"I remember that shipment," Patrick said. A puzzled look crossed his face. "Everything went as smoothly as it could. I checked it twice. The right goods were delivered."

"Well, I suppose it will all be smoothed out. As much merchandise as we ship, it's a wonder there aren't more mistakes." She saw Patrick bite his lip as he stood in the middle of the floor. There was a strength in the man that belied his wiry stature, and not just physical strength. Elizabeth had seen a firmness and depth of integrity in him that most men lacked, qualities she had grown to appreciate and lean on through their marriage.

He turned to her and said suddenly, "We'll have to get it straightened out. Your mother doesn't need another reason not to trust me."

Elizabeth gave him a quick look. She knew he was right about her mother's suspicions, but she did not like to admit it. Quickly she changed the subject. "I'm worried about Father," she said. "He's got to slow down."

"I know. I'm very fond of your father. No man could have been kinder to a son-in-law."

"I'm glad you feel that way, Patrick. He does think highly of you."

"I only wish I were better at the business. It would be better if I were as good with my head as I am with my hands."

"You're doing fine. Father was telling me just yesterday how hard you've worked, trying to take the load off of him."

"I wish I could help him with more. Oh, don't forget I'll be leaving in the morning for Virginia."

"I know. I haven't forgotten. I'll get up and help Rebekah make you a nice breakfast. I'll get the children up, too."

"It'll be too early for them."

"They can go back to bed and sleep if they want to. Andrew's asked a dozen times to go with you. Do you suppose you could take him this time?"

"Maybe the next trip. I'm afraid this one will be long and tiring." He smiled and said, "Besides, Sarah would have a fit if I took Andrew and left her home. I'll have to take both of them somewhere when I get back."

"That would be good," Elizabeth said. She reached up and patted his cheek. "Now, try to remember which fork to eat with."

"I'll watch you," he said. "That's what I always do anyhow. As long as we've been married, a fork's still a fork to me."

"Well, at least you don't still use your knife to eat the peas." Her eyes laughed at him.

He reached out and squeezed her waist. "All right," he said, "enough lessons in manners. Let's go down and eat."

––––––––––

The meal was excellent, as always in the Martin household. It was served in the large formal dining room, which was lit by silver candelabras with the light cast from the warm fire flickering in the verde marble fireplace. The green-and-gold mica wallpaper and many mirrors caught the light and gave the room a certain warmth. The aroma of turtle soup, potted fish, and beef filled the air as the family sat at the large mahogany dining table. These delicacies were brought in and placed on a gilt-edged wood serving table to one side of the room. On a large mahogany sideboard, which was placed behind Mr. Martin, were silver platters filled with artichokes with toasted cheese, assortments of cheeses, and a truffle for dessert. William asked the blessing, and as Rebekah brought a silver tureen filled with turtle soup and began serving it, he said to Patrick, "I'm sorry you have to make that run tomorrow. Lately, it seems as though I'm running your legs off—but business is picking up so much somebody has to do it."

"Those are good customers in Virginia," Patrick said. He watched his soup bowl as Rebekah spooned out the clear broth, smiled up at her, and said, "Thank you." Picking up his spoon, he sipped it carefully and said, "You tell your grandmother this is good soup, Rebekah." He received a shy smile as a reward, then turned to William and said, "Business is good in Virginia, particularly that area. More settlers are moving in all the time."

"They're mostly a rough sort, aren't they?" The question came from Charlotte, who sat across the table from Will. As Elizabeth had expected, she wore a new gown straight from the dressmaker's. The dress was an exquisite pale yellow silk of the open sack-backed style with a green bow decorating the front of it. The neckline was square and low in the back, and the tight-fitting sleeves ended with a bow and a delicate row of white lace at the elbows. A dark green brocade trimmed the edges of the neckline on down to the full skirt. The underskirt was layered with yellow pleated panels, edged with the same dark green brocade. As usual, she looked beautiful, and she followed up her question by saying, "There can't be much profit in that area. All they need are butter churns and brooms."

Patrick grinned. "They make their own brooms, I think. But it's filling up quicker than you think." He listened as the talk about Virginia went around the table.

"I heard that some people are moving across the mountains, the Appalachians. Is that right, Patrick?" Will asked.

"Yes, quite a few of them, as I understand." An excitement came into Patrick MacNeal's face, and he put his soup spoon down and began to speak of the land that lay across the Appalachians. "That's a whole new unexplored continent over there. Why, they say a squirrel could go a hundred miles jumping from tree to tree and never touch the ground! And deer are thicker than cattle!"

He was interrupted as Charlotte said, "But the king outlawed settlement in that country back in 1763, when the war ended! Isn't that right?"

"I don't know whether it was *right* or not, but he certainly did forbid it." Patrick shrugged. "A line on a piece of paper isn't going to stop people who want homes. On my last trip to Virginia, I talked to a lot of those who have gone and come back, and what I hear is that land is filling up pretty fast." Pausing, he picked up the knife on the platter of beef set close beside him and hewed off a chunk of it. He placed it on his plate, then looked up and said wistfully, "I wouldn't mind seeing that country myself. It would be something to see. I'd love to ride to the top of a mountain ridge and look out as far as the horizon and see what God has made."

Anne Martin was aghast. She gave her son-in-law a frozen look and said, "That is not much of an ambition, Patrick! Living with a bunch of savages who sit around scratching fleas!"

Elizabeth flushed, as she always did when her mother threw one of her barbed remarks at Patrick. "I'm sure it's not quite like that, Mother."

"I don't know why you should think that," Anne said spitefully. "That territory is filled with murdering savages. If you'd read your history, you'd know that! It was only the British who put a stop to that, and I think they should have gone through and driven all the savages away."

"Away where, Mrs. Martin?" Patrick said quietly. He very rarely challenged his mother-in-law, but somehow her remark had irritated him. "Would you have the militia butcher them all? I thought that's why you hated *them*—for doing that to white settlers. It is their right to live there. I just wish that everyone would realize that we are all God's children, and that there is enough land for us all to share and live together peacefully."

Anne Martin was not accustomed to being questioned. A tall, thin woman of fifty-five, her youthful beauty had faded, with lines tightly drawn around her mouth and eyes. There was a kindness in her, but it lay buried deep. She had married William for love and moved to the Colonies, but she was still bound by the traditions of English nobility. And the disappointment of Elizabeth's choice of a husband had soured her. She simply could not refrain from criticizing him in public.

"I think the less said on this subject the better, Patrick!" she pronounced firmly.

Patrick looked over at Elizabeth. He would have said more, but he saw that she was watching him with a plea in her eyes. His eyes shifted to his children, and Sarah's lips were set in a firm line. She would be ready to defend him in a moment, while Andrew looked at him hopefully, not wanting to hear a family argument. "It was only a dream," he said, putting down his fork, for the meat had suddenly become tasteless. There in the middle of a fine supper, the crux of his life had suddenly surfaced. He was a man who loved the out-of-doors, and he was doomed to work inside warehouses, running his tired eyes down lines of figures. But he loved his wife, he respected his father-in-law, and he even understood his mother-in-law's dissatisfaction with him. *I'd probably feel the same*, he thought, *if one of my children married someone I didn't like.*

Elizabeth said quickly, "This is a wonderful roast. I think the cooking gets better all the time around here."

"When we're married," Charlotte said to Will, "I've arranged to have a cook come over from France."

"From France?" Will stared at her blankly. "Why from France?"

"Why, they have the best chefs in the world!"

"I'd argue with that," Mr. Martin said. He was looking pale, and those who knew him best understood that he was in some pain. Nevertheless, he managed a smile and said, "Those times I've been in France I wasn't overwhelmed with the taste I've had of their cooking."

Charlotte smiled sweetly. "Oh, you'll learn to change your taste, Father, when I get François settled. I promise you." She suddenly glanced over at Elizabeth and said, "Did you get the problem of the missing money settled, Elizabeth?"

A silence settled around the table, and William asked abruptly, "What's that about missing money?"

"Oh, it's nothing, I'm sure," Charlotte said. "Elizabeth just found a discrepancy in the accounts." She laughed and winked at Patrick. "I told her that Patrick probably took it and donated it to himself." The joke did not go over, and Mr. Martin stared at her with an odd look. It flustered Charlotte, and she said, "It was just a joke, of course."

"I'm sure it was just a simple mistake. I will look into it with you, Elizabeth, if you'll remind me of it."

"Of course, Father. These things happen, with all the shipments we make," Elizabeth said, casting a nervous glance at her mother.

Anne Martin had taken all this in carefully. She fixed her eyes on Patrick, who seemed uncomfortable and nervous. Her eyes then went to Charlotte, who looked directly at her and nodded slightly. The two of them got along well together, and Anne thought, *Well, at least we'll have one member of the family who can keep her eye on business!*

The main parlor was cozy with a fire crackling cheerfully in the fireplace. Patrick and Elizabeth had retired to get the children in bed, saying that they had to get to sleep early since Patrick was leaving in the morning. William and Anne sat on a Queen Anne settee with Will and Charlotte across from them. They were drinking chocolate from thin, delicate Chinese cups that Rebekah had brought in. As soon as Rebekah left, Anne said rather carefully, "I was surprised to hear about that discrepancy in the figures of the ledger."

"These things happen often, Anne. I'm sure it's nothing to worry about," William said. He leaned his head back on the antimacassar and closed his eyes wearily. "As much business as we're doing, there's bound to be mistakes."

Anne hesitated, then her eyes met those of Charlotte. The two understood each other so well it was as if they had already spoken about it. Anne said rather carefully, "I know you think a lot of Patrick, but I think you should watch him more carefully."

Instantly William raised his head. "What are you speaking of?"

Anne knew this look of her husband's. He was a stubborn man, and she knew that once he got his back up, there was nothing to be done. "Oh, I simply meant that—well, he's not very good with the books, is he?"

"He does the best he can, and he's learning all the time. I'm proud of Patrick. I couldn't ask for a better son-in-law."

"Oh, I'm sure it was a mistake," Charlotte said, "but you do have to be careful, Father. My father had a Scotch-Irish worker in his employ. He told me about him. The man stole from him terribly, and Father said he'd never hire another one."

"Why, I don't think that's right!" Will said adamantly. "Some of the best men in the business are of Scotch-Irish descent."

"But you know how tight they are with a dollar, and how close they are. I just think it's better to have good honest Americans," Charlotte said.

Will rarely argued with Charlotte, but now he stared at her with some degree of distaste. "The only Americans are Indians!" he said. "Do you want us to run the business with them?"

"Oh, don't be foolish! You know I didn't mean that!" She saw that her future father-in-law was upset and said quickly, "I'm sure Patrick did nothing wrong. It's just that figures aren't one of his strengths."

"That's gracious of you to say so, but I'm not convinced he's not stealing," Anne said haughtily.

"Stealing?" Will said vigorously. "I don't believe it!"

"Neither do I," William said. He stood up suddenly and said, "I'll abide no more accusations about a member of this family. It ill behooves all of you. Especially you, Anne, and I will not have it brought up again." He turned and left the room abruptly.

The silence that fell over the room was almost palpable. Anne turned quickly to Will, saying, "Your father can never believe anything wrong about any man. He was always too trusting."

"There are worse faults than that to be found in a man."

"Don't be foolish, Will!" Charlotte said. "You're going to be running the business one day. You'll have all the responsibilities, not Patrick. You're going to have to learn to take a firm hand."

Will looked at her directly. "Do you think that Patrick was stealing?"

Charlotte knew she was walking a very fine line. Will was a placid enough young man, but there was some of his father in him, and she felt she had come dangerously close to pushing the issue too far. "Why, I don't think I meant to imply that," she said sweetly. "But as everyone knows, he's not very good with figures. Even Elizabeth has admitted that."

"He's very good with people out on the road," Will said. "None better."

"Perhaps that's his place then," Charlotte said. "What do you think, Mother Martin?"

"That might be something to think about. Once you're in charge of the business, Will, you can watch things more carefully, and Charlotte will be there to help you. Fortunately, she has a good business head as well."

Will sat there quietly as the two women talked. He was greatly disturbed by their suspicions that Patrick MacNeal was a thief, for he admired his brother-in-law greatly. Will was only mediocre as a businessman, and the thought of taking over the business made him feel uncomfortable. He had hoped that his father would take in an experienced partner, perhaps the head bookkeeper, who knew the business from the ground up, but his mother had adamantly objected to that idea, saying abruptly, "Why, you would cut your own son out of the triumph of running our business?" and that had been the end of that.

Charlotte sipped her chocolate and let the conversation flow as her mind was working quickly. She put her hand suddenly on Will's arm and said, "You mustn't worry about it, dear. I know it's a big challenge to take on a business like this, but I'll be right beside you. We'll do it all together. I'll keep the house so you won't even have to think about that, and I will study the business until we know all about it."

"I think that's a wonderful attitude, Charlotte," Anne said, smiling. "Will, sometimes I don't think you recognize how fortunate you are to have a supportive young woman like Charlotte as your bride-to-be."

"Of course I recognize that, Mother." He reached over, patted Charlotte's hand, and then rose. Walking to the sideboard, he poured himself a glass of water, drank it down thirstily, and left the room.

"Will is difficult sometimes, Charlotte," Anne said slowly. "Basically he's not as strong as his father, but I believe that can be remedied with the support of a good wife."

Charlotte smiled and answered, "I think it will go well. He just needs a firm hand, and as for Patrick, I think we can take care of that when the time comes."

"Perhaps the less said about it for now the better. My husband has a stubborn streak about that man. He's never been able to see what kind of man Patrick really is."

"Of course. You and I will have to see that it's taken care of."

They continued to sip chocolate, and the clock ticked across the room, keeping a regular cadence as the two women sat, carefully planning the lives of the Martins and the MacNeals. It was something that gave them both immense pleasure, and they were one in spirit as they set out the future for the family.

Charlotte Van Dorn

Eleven

*A*ndrew and Sarah staggered down the steps, puffy-eyed from the lack of sleep, and made their way to the kitchen, where they found their parents already sitting at the large square table under the big window. Sarah burst out, "Papa, you didn't send Rebekah to get me up early!" She ran and threw herself at him. He caught her, spun her around, and pulled her up into his lap.

"Early? Why, I couldn't get you up before dawn, could I? Look, the sun's just comin' up."

"I don't care!" Sarah pouted. She jerked at his coat and said, "You promised!"

"Well, I didn't think you wanted to get up by moonlight," Patrick said. He winked at Andrew, who was standing a few feet away, and said, "Come here, boy, and give me your best grip. Put everything you've got into it now!"

Andrew stepped forward and grasped his father's hand. He squeezed as hard as he could and looked up anxiously. His father was one of the strongest men he knew. He had seen him pick up loads at the warehouse that it took two men to pick up, and he felt worried sometimes that he would never be the man his father was. "You think I'll ever be as strong as you are, Pa?" he asked anxiously.

"As strong as me? Why, you'll be twice as strong as your old man. Here, sit down there and pitch into this breakfast that your Mother and Rebekah cooked for us now." The two sat down, and Rebekah, who had come into the kitchen after the children, smiled at them. "I made enough breakfast to get you to Virginia and back, Mr. MacNeal."

Patrick smiled at her warmly. "Put it on the table, Rebekah!

There's no cook like your mother—except yourself."

Rebekah began bringing the breakfast to the table—a yellow bowl full of scrambled eggs, a rasher of bacon covered with a spotless white cloth, a bowl of mush, freshly churned butter, and a jug of cream. And last of all, she went over to the oven and pulled out a tray full of golden brown biscuits, which filled the kitchen with a delicious aroma.

"Nobody makes biscuits like you do, Rebekah," Patrick said as she came to set the tray down. "Now, when you marry a man, if he's not good to you, you just say, 'No more biscuits for you.'"

"I wish you'd marry Uncle Will," Sarah said. "That way we could always keep you here, and you could always make biscuits for all of us."

Patrick laughed at the girl's remark and shook his head. "You're always wanting somebody to marry somebody else."

"But Rebekah likes Uncle Will, don't you, Rebekah?" Sarah insisted. "I don't see why you can't marry him instead of that snooty old Charlotte."

"Sarah!" Elizabeth said sharply. "Don't talk nonsense!"

Patrick looked up to see that Rebekah's face was pale and her lips were drawn tightly together. She whirled and left the room without another word, and Patrick's eyes sought Elizabeth's. "Well, what was that all about?"

"Oh, she just doesn't like to be teased, I think. Sarah, you ought to be more careful."

Sarah stuffed her mouth full of eggs and looked thoughtfully at the door where the young woman had disappeared. "She does like Uncle Will, though. I can tell."

"I said we'll hear no more about it, Sarah!" Elizabeth said firmly.

Elizabeth had noticed that the girl was taken with Will, but she had thought it no more than a simple devotion to the family. Now, however, she knew better, and she wondered if she should have a talk with Rebekah.

Patrick talked about his trip for a while, and as he buttered a biscuit and layered it with blackberry jam, Andrew said, "Pa, tell us more about when you were a boy."

"Not much to talk about, Andy. I got up before it was daylight and worked until the moon came up. That was about the story of my life."

"Was it really that hard, Papa?" Sarah said.

"I hope you'll never know how hard it was, Sarah." He took a bite of the biscuit, then paused for a moment, chewing on it thoughtfully. Only on a few rare occasions had he spoken of his early life, for it had been a hard one. He had come from Scotland in 1754 seeking a better life. Looking at his family, he said, "You know, the day before my good father died he said, 'Leave this place. Scotland has nothing to offer you. Go to a new country.' I asked him which one, and he said, 'Go to the Colonies. You won't have to spend the rest of your life working for an English landlord.'" He swallowed the biscuit, stared at the other portion in his hand, and said softly, "I remember he said, 'Be your own man, boy. Work your own land, and you won't have to take your hat off to anybody.'"

Elizabeth sipped her coffee slowly. She herself knew very little of Patrick's early life, except that it had not been easy for him. Now she watched the faces of the children, and somehow she felt sad that she had never met Patrick's father.

"How did you get to the Colonies?" Andrew piped up.

"When my father died, and my sister married, there was no place for me anymore. So I walked to Belfast and went aboard the first ship I saw and asked them if they were sailing for America." Patrick grinned, his handsome face and laughing eyes very attractive. "They laughed, but they were going to America—by way of South America, mind you. I persuaded the captain I could do anything, but all I did was help the cook, scrub floors, and everything else that nobody wanted to do. When I finally stepped off the boat in Boston, I didn't have a farthing, and I didn't know a soul."

"Were you scared, Pa?" Andrew asked, his eyes large.

"Well . . . yes, I was, but my mother and father had taught me to look to God. I figured He was the God of America just as much as the God of Scotland, so I put my chin in the air, and the first day I was there I got a job. Not much of one. Nearly worked myself to death, but it was a place to sleep and a bite of food to eat." He went on speaking of those hard days, then finally shook himself. "But it all turned out happily," he said, and a sly look came to his eye. "I got a job working for a wealthy businessman, and one day his daughter, who was a princess, came down to the dock. She fell so in love with a handsome young Scotch-Irishman that he had to marry her to keep her from doing away with herself. And so they got married and had two children," he said, getting up and going to squeeze them. "One, a handsome boy named Andrew, and one, a beautiful young lady named Sarah. So the princess and the dock-hand got married, and they lived happily ever after."

Elizabeth was laughing then. This red-haired husband of hers could always make her laugh. "That's the most awful story I've ever heard! There's hardly a word of truth in it."

"Well, there's one word," he said, leaving the children and coming over to Elizabeth. He bent over and kissed her, and whispered in her ear, "I've lived happily ever after since I found that princess."

The children saw their mother's face redden, and Sarah said, "Look, Ma's blushing! What did you say to her, Pa?"

"Nothing for you to hear! Now then, it's time for me to go."

There was the usual bustle as Patrick got his things together. He went outside where the coachman was waiting with the coach and handed the man his baggage. He bent over, kissed Elizabeth, and whispered, "Good-bye, my love. I'll be back before you know it." He leaned over and picked Sarah up, squeezed her, and said, "You be sweet just like me, you hear?"

"I will, Papa. Honest I will!"

Then reaching over, he took Andrew by the hand and squeezed firmly. "Keep working on that grip." He leaned over, hugged the boy, and whispered in his ear, "And you keep on thinking about that farm. Who knows, if the good Lord owns a thousand farms, He might give you and me one of them someday, and you could have a horse, and I could have a team to plow with."

He released the boy, leaped into the coach, and waved as it disappeared down the driveway.

As they turned and went into the house, Sarah said, "What did Papa say to you, Andrew?"

"Oh, nothing."

Sarah, always jealous of her father's attention, dug her elbow in his side. "You tell me or I'll shove you in the mud again!"

Andrew looked at her for a moment. "He said that God owned a thousand farms, and if I prayed, He might give us one so that I could have a horse."

Sarah stared at him, her eyes big. "Papa said that? Do you think he meant it?"

Andrew looked off in the direction of the road that led to the coast. The dust where the coach was traveling made a fine signature in the sky. Turning back to his sister, he said, "Papa always means everything he says."

———————

The day after Patrick's departure for Virginia, Will and Charlotte were in the library. Charlotte had persuaded him to spend some time going over the account ledgers, and Will had stayed home from the office under protest. The two had been working most of the morning, and finally Will said, "I can't find anything wrong with this. It must have been a simple mistake."

"It's too important to leave to chance," Charlotte insisted. She was wearing a light mint green dress, and her hair was carefully done up as if she were going to a ball. She looked at Will for one moment and then said, "I'm thirsty. Didn't I see Martha making some lemonade earlier?"

"I believe you did."

"Would you mind getting me some, dear? I'm terribly thirsty. Get us both some, and we'll take a break."

"Of course."

Will left the room, glad to be free from the tedious task. As soon as he was gone, Charlotte opened the ledger and searched for the entry that Elizabeth had questioned, but she didn't find it at once.

Right then the door opened so quietly she did not hear it. Rebekah entered the room, carrying a feather duster. Seeing Charlotte there, she started to leave. Then she remembered that Elizabeth had told her to be sure to dust off the top shelves, so she thought, *I'll be quiet about it. It won't disturb her.* As she made her way around the room, she noticed that the woman was so engrossed in the ledger that she did not even look up.

The top shelves could only be reached by climbing up on a small walnut ladder that Patrick had cleverly fixed with wheels. As soon as a person stepped on it, it pressed down so that it wouldn't move anymore. The rug was thick and Rebekah's footsteps made no sounds. She moved up on the ladder and, as quietly as she could, began dusting off the top shelf of the leather-bound volumes. She did look down and watched curiously, wondering how anyone could understand the bookkeeping, which was a mystery to her. She saw Charlotte pick up a pen and begin writing something in the ledger.

Rebekah could not be sure exactly what it was, but she admired the way the young woman was able to make such fine marks.

Rebekah coughed slightly, but even that tiny sound attracted Charlotte's attention. She whirled around and saw the girl looking down from the ladder on the open ledger. "What are you doing up there?" she demanded. "How did you get in here?"

"Why, Miss Charlotte, Miss Elizabeth told me to come and—"

"Get out of here at once!" she said. "I won't have you snooping around!"

Rebekah's face turned pale, and she instantly stepped down from the small ladder and started for the door.

"You're nothing but a snoop. I'll report you to Mrs. Martin!" she said.

Alarmed, Rebekah turned and said, "All I saw was you working on the book."

Charlotte Van Dorn's eyes narrowed. She had made a change in the ledger that would make it appear that Patrick had deliberately falsified the books, transferring money into his own account. Now she was pale with anger, and she stared at the maid. She wasn't even sure if the girl could read, but she took no chances. "Get out of here. I'm going to let you off this time, but if you ever say one *word* to anyone, I'll see that you're fired, and your grandmother also. Do you hear me?"

"Yes . . . yes, ma'am." Rebekah turned and fled from the library, tears bursting from her eyes. As soon as she left the room, however, she ran into Will, who nearly dropped the lemonade.

"Why, Rebekah," he said. "What's the matter?"

"Nothing, sir. Nothing at all." She whirled and fled down the hall.

Will, after staring at her, turned and walked into the room. "What's the matter with Rebekah?"

"Oh, she's clumsy. I told her to come back and clean when there was nobody here to bother."

"That's not like Rebekah. She's one of the most efficient maids we've ever had."

"She clomps around like an old cow," Charlotte said. "Now, sit down and let's drink our lemonade." Charlotte's nerves were on edge. She was not accustomed to intrigue, but one look at Will's face assured her that he had no suspicions about what had just taken place. As they sipped their lemonade, they talked for a while about their upcoming wedding. Charlotte's parents would be there, of course, and the wedding would be in Boston, where her maternal grandparents lived.

"I suppose it'll be a big affair," Will said.

"Why, of course it will, dear. It'll be the biggest wedding and best party Boston's ever seen. Oh, the ball will be tremendous! You won't believe the new dress that I'm having made for the occasion." She hesitated for a moment, then said, "I hope Patrick will be back so that things can be settled with the business."

"Aw, I'm sure he will be," Will said. He did not see the gleam that appeared in Charlotte's eye.

After a time the two finished the lemonade, then Charlotte said, "Let's not waste any more time on business."

"Well, that's all right with me. I think I'll go for a ride before I go back to the shop."

As soon as he was gone, Charlotte went at once to her guest room. After carefully locking the door, she went over to the small desk and pulled out stationery and a pen and began to write. She addressed the letter to her father, and quickly wrote:

> Things are going even better than I had hoped. I know we have agreed that it would be best to keep Patrick and Elizabeth away from the business. Martin Shipping is doing very well, but it will do even better without their interference. I have taken certain precautions to make sure that Patrick will be totally out of the way, and it will not be difficult to ease Elizabeth out once that happens. We'll make them a generous offer, of course, but as we have said, Elizabeth forfeited her rights when she married a rustic as she did. As soon as Will and I are married, it all will be set up. You and I will actually run the business as soon as the old man dies, and I don't think that will be very long. He's in very poor health. I do want to be safely married to Will before that happens, but surely he will last at least long enough for that to take place.

She added a few more lines, signed it, "Your loving daughter, Charlotte," then sealed it carefully. She rose, unlocked the door, and, not trusting any of the servants, had one of them drive her to town where she posted the letter herself. Afterward she had tea with some of her friends. One of them said, "You're looking especially well, Charlotte. I suppose it's the coming marriage."

Charlotte replied, "Oh yes, of course!" But actually her mind was on the day when her family would own the Martin Shipping Company completely. *Will won't be a hard man to manage*, she thought. *He's not much of a man, but then too much of a man would give Father and me problems.* Her face was impassive as she sipped her tea delicately and began speaking of the new dress that she would wear at the ball celebrating her upcoming wedding.

Dreams of a New Life

Twelve

*T*he secretary of the Martin Shipping Company sat at his desk fidgeting nervously. Hosea Simms was a tall thin man with a pair of eyes set too close together. Nevertheless, he was an astute business-man, especially about matters concerning the Martin Shipping Company. Mr. Simms liked things to go smooth and easy, and the sound of voices raised in anger coming from inside Mr. William Martin's office made him apprehensive.

"I've never heard Mr. Martin lose his temper like this," he mut-tered. He picked up a pen and tried to write, but blotted it, and with an exasperated sigh, wadded the paper up and threw it in the basket beside his walnut desk. "I knew something like this was brewing. It's been coming on ever since Mr. Patrick left for Virginia," he mut-tered. He cast a look at the door and tried to make out the voices in the next room, but the solid wood was too thick, and the carpets muffled the sounds that came from inside. Looking around the of-fice, he was tempted to go listen, putting his ear to the door, but that would be undignified. Rising from his desk, he went to stand closer, ready to move if anyone entered the outer office. He could hear the voices, but they were still muffled. The clearest voice was that of Will Martin. "Mister Will is going to have to learn to control his temper," he said with surprise. "I didn't even know he had one!"

The tension on the inside of the large office was thick, almost palpable. William sat at his desk, his face pale, and his lips drawn into a tight line. Will and Patrick faced each other, standing in front of the desk, both of them as angry as they had ever been in their lives. "Then how do you explain these figures, Patrick?" Will shouted. "Look!" He held the ledger up. "You can't explain this away, can you?"

Patrick's face flushed with anger. He did have a fiery temper, but never before had he showed it. But when he had been called into the office and accused of stealing from the company, something seemed to explode within him. He had stared at his benefactor, Mr. William Martin, to whom he owed so much, and asked quietly at first, "Do you believe this, sir?"

"Will believes it, and there's the ledger, which he claims is proof," Mr. Martin said quietly.

Even now, the older man sat there listening to his heart as it seemed to skip beats, then pound rapidly as if it were trying to catch up. He had the feeling that his heart was a very fragile instrument, and that a sudden movement could break it, shattering it like a fine crystal glass. He had been unbelieving when Will had confronted him with the accusations about Patrick, and had at first refused to listen. But Will had kept after him for several days until finally he had agreed to meet with Patrick as soon as he came back from Virginia. Now as he sat there watching the two men, he held himself stiffly upright, sadness in his heart, for he had grown to love and respect Patrick MacNeal. But he loved his son, too, making the confrontation all the more poignant and heartbreaking than if it had been two total strangers.

Patrick waited until Will stopped shouting, and then said as calmly as he could, "I realize this looks bad, and I can't account for it. But I recorded accurately what I got for the goods, and if the figures don't match, there must be an error somewhere else."

"But you're responsible for the figures," Will snapped.

"I realize that, Will," Patrick said. "Give me some time to go over it, and I'm sure we'll figure it out."

"Do you remember the delivery at all, Patrick?" Mr. Martin asked. His lips were puffy, and his face was pasty and gray.

Patrick stared at him with compassion. The last thing in the world he wanted to do was to offend this man whom he had come to respect so much. Nevertheless, he had to defend himself. "I remember it very well," he said. "In fact, it was one of the most profitable trips I ever made for the company. When I returned I went over the figures several times, and they checked perfectly against the invoices."

"Did anyone else go over them?" Will demanded.

"No. I didn't think it was necessary since they seemed all right."

"Well, they don't seem all right now!" Will said. "Look here. What about this item, and this one?"

Patrick's head was swimming—he could not think clearly.

Finally, William said quietly, "Patrick, I think it might be better if you would . . . take some time off for a while."

"Take time off? Am I being fired?" Patrick demanded.

"Just take some time off until we get this thing straightened out. I'm sure there's an answer for it. We'll find it." William stood to his feet heavily and had the impulse to go put his arm around his son-in-law's shoulder, but he knew this would infuriate Will. He sought for something to say that would make his request less hurtful, but nothing came to him. Overwhelmed by it all, he said, "If you'll please excuse me, I don't believe I'd care to continue this discussion any longer."

"Of course, Father." Will took Patrick by the arm and said, "Come along. Father's not feeling well."

Patrick shook his arm loose and walked out stiffly. He saw Simms sitting at his desk and was certain that the secretary had heard most of what had been said inside the main office. Turning to Will, he said, "Will, we've known each other for a long time. If someone came to me with a story like this about you, I wouldn't believe it."

Will flushed and lowered his eyes, unable to meet those of his brother-in-law. In all truth, he had great difficulty in accepting the story, but Charlotte, and even his mother, had kept at him until he felt there was no other course but to pursue it. "I don't want to discuss it any further, Patrick." He turned and walked away, going to his own office.

Patrick watched him go, then turned and met Simms' eyes. The secretary dropped his head and stared at the desk in front of him. He made small circles with a tip of one forefinger and said nothing. Patrick turned and started for the outer door.

"Will you be coming back today, Mr. MacNeal?" Simms called out.

Patrick stopped, whirled, and faced the secretary. His eyes seemed to have grown a darker blue and they were drawn together into mere slits as he stared in anger at Simms. "No, I won't be coming back today—or maybe ever! Perhaps that will make you happy, Mr. Simms!" He turned and slammed the door.

Simms sat there watching him. "Too bad! Too bad!" he murmured. "I hate to see things like this coming. But with in-laws, who can tell?"

"I'll tell you, Elizabeth. I feel like an absolute hypocrite!"

"You don't have to feel like that, Patrick." Elizabeth came over to where Patrick was standing. He was wearing a dark-brown suit with brown knee breeches and white stockings. His waistcoat was multicolored, and his topcoat was a dark blue velvet. He looked very handsome, but his face was clouded with worry, and he stood staring at the door as if a den of fierce animals might be on the other side. "I don't want to go to this ball," he said.

"We have to go, Patrick!"

"Why? Why do we have to go?"

"Because if you don't, it will make you look . . ."

"Look more guilty than I am? Is that what you started to say?"

"Oh, darling," Elizabeth said, coming to put her arms around him. "You know I didn't mean that. I mean, that's the way it would look to them."

Patrick had not been back to the office. Now that the ball celebrating the engagement of Will and Charlotte had come, he only wanted to leave and get as far away from the Martin household as he could. He had mentioned this to Elizabeth, but she had said, "We've got to stay here and fight this thing out. We can't run away!"

Now as they stood there listening to the music that filtered faintly to the second floor from the large ballroom downstairs, Patrick suddenly felt as alone and helpless as he had ever felt in his life. He went over and sat down on one of the fragile chairs that Anne had given them for a present and stared at Elizabeth, misery in his eyes. "You remember I told you about getting off the boat when I was just a boy without a farthing in my pocket and without knowing a soul."

"Yes, I remember."

"I wasn't afraid then. I was just a boy. But I knew everything would be all right." He glanced at the door and shook his head slowly. "But I'm pretty close to being afraid now. I feel that something's terribly wrong, and there's nothing I can do about it. If it weren't your family, I'd leave right now."

Elizabeth put her arm around his shoulder. Leaning over, she kissed his forehead and whispered, "We have to trust God. I know it looks bad, but somehow . . . somehow there'll be a way out of it."

"I don't see how."

"I know you're innocent, and once Will has calmed down, he'll believe it, too. He's always liked you."

"I thought he did, but how can a man throw a friend away on the evidence of a few scratches on paper?"

Elizabeth said slowly, "It's Charlotte, I think. She never liked you."

"No, she hasn't, but I wouldn't think she'd do a thing like this."

"I don't know. It's got to be solved, though. And we'll never solve anything by running away."

"What about your mother? Do you think she could ever change her mind? She's been looking for something like this for a long time. She always expected a poor Scotch-Irish laborer to try to steal from the company, and now I guess she's got her proof."

Elizabeth was silent. She had had a violent disagreement with her mother over the matter. For the first time in her life, she had stood up, with her eyes blazing, and told her mother that she was terribly wrong for even considering Patrick capable of such wrongdoing. It had apparently come as quite a shock to Anne Martin to be told this by her daughter, for she had wilted under the strong and courageous stand that Elizabeth made.

"She'll come around," Elizabeth whispered. "Father is too sick and confused to know what's going on."

"I know. That's the worst of it. This whole thing has made him worse," Patrick said. "And that's the last thing I want in the world."

Elizabeth saw that his hands were clasped tightly together and were trembling. She had never seen Patrick like this before, and she suddenly decided that the ball was not as important as her husband's peace of mind. Moving over, she sat down beside him, took one of his hands, and held it tightly in hers. She held it to her cheek, kissed it, and then said, "Think about it this way, dear. I know you're innocent. Sarah and Andrew know you're innocent. Even the people you work with—none of them believes it."

Patrick held her hand tightly. "You always did know how to calm me down, didn't you? Well, I guess I need a lot of calming right now." He looked out the window, for the lights from the lanterns were gleaming in a mixture of amber and yellow. They sat there silently for a long time, then finally he said, "I'm only going for you."

"I know, and I love you for it. You're an honest man, Patrick, and God will not let you down even in all this." A thought came to her, and she said, "Were you serious when you said if it wasn't for my family you'd leave Boston and leave the company?"

Patrick suddenly turned and looked at her. Her face was so sweet and gentle and yielding in the soft light. She had not mentioned this for a long time, nor had he, but it stirred a longing deep in his heart, and he whispered, "Yes, if I had my way I'd take you and the children, and we'd leave this place."

"We can do that if that's what you really want, Patrick."

Patrick was stunned. It had been difficult for him to come from what he had been into a rich and influential family. Elizabeth had always had everything she wanted, and he had learned to survive on practically nothing since he arrived from Scotland. In all these years, it had never once entered his mind to ask her to leave the luxurious home and the fine things that she was so accustomed to. Now, however, he saw that her face had an expression he had never seen before, and he asked in a whisper, "Do you mean that, Elizabeth? Do you mean that you would actually leave all of this?" He waved his arm at the ornate furniture and the spacious room. "And all the luxuries that you've enjoyed all your life?"

Elizabeth said quietly, "When we got married, do you remember what I said? That I would forsake all others and follow you. Did you think I didn't mean it, Patrick?"

Patrick shook his head. "I never thought about it. I've always been so grateful to have you for a wife that I never expected to have money and clothes and a fine home. It's been like a dream."

Silence hung in the room for a while, and they heard again the sound of violins from downstairs. Elizabeth thought of her life as she looked tenderly at her husband. She was a quick-witted woman who could think clearly and evenly, and she knew exactly what she was saying when she whispered, "I would do whatever you decide. You're my husband, and I'll go wherever you choose."

Elizabeth's eyes filled with tears at the surprised expression that came to Patrick's face. She would never forget it. She had known how hard it had been for him to make the adjustment to her kind of life, and now a grief came to her that she had never said this to him before. She did love this man with all of her heart. For a fleeting moment, a tiny voice said within her, *But could you do without all that you're used to? The fancy dresses, the rich food, having everything you want?* But she quickly quelled that thought and said, "What do you want to do, Patrick? Tell me."

For one moment, Patrick was absolutely silent, then he swallowed and said, "I met a man in Virginia from Pittsylvania County—a Jed Smith. He told me about another man who has been over the Appalachians and has already settled there with some friends. You should have heard how he talked about the land, Elizabeth. How beautiful it was . . . and free for the taking! Where men could live and make their way with their own land!"

"Who was the man who moved?"

"William Bean. He's moved his family down to a little river called the Watauga, and a great many of his friends and his family are joining him." His voice grew excited and he said, "Smith said Bean's making a fine settlement, and others are planning to join him as well." His strong hand squeezed Elizabeth's so hard that it hurt her, but she saw that he was carried away.

"What do you want to do, Patrick?" she asked again.

"Well, he asked if I would come with him, and bring you and the children." His eyes gleamed, and he said, "I've never said anything to you about this because it was asking you to give up too much. But, Elizabeth, if we could just get somewhere where I could be my own man! Where I could grow the food for my own family, and build our own house, and could teach Andrew these things. I wouldn't care if we had anything or not. It would be freedom!"

Elizabeth knew then what she had to do. She said quietly, "If this is what you think God wants you to do, I'm your wife, Patrick. The children and I will go with you."

"Have you prayed about it, Elizabeth?" Patrick asked with amazement.

"Not about this in particular . . ." Elizabeth hesitated. "But I've been praying for some time that I would be a better wife to you. And looking back over our lives together, I see how easy it's been for me—and how hard it's been for you. You've never complained, and I've loved you for it."

Patrick gnawed his lower lip and shook his head. "It would be a hard life, Elizabeth. I don't think you have any idea how hard. I don't think *I* do, though I've listened to them talk. There's danger from the Indians, hard work . . ." He went on speaking of the difficulties of the life that waited for those who crossed the misty mountains. Finally he paused and shook his head. "It's asking too much of you and the children."

"You know, Patrick," Elizabeth said slowly. "Ever since you told us how you got off the boat, just a homeless boy without a penny in your pocket, and how you were not afraid because God was with you and you knew it, I've been envious of that." Elizabeth stroked Patrick's hand and was silent for a moment. When she looked up, there were tears in her eyes. "I've never really trusted God for anything. My family gave me whatever I wanted. Once in my life," she said in a whisper, "I'd like to know that my faith is real. Not just something I talk about or hear sermons about. I'd like to trust God to take care of me when nobody else can."

"Are you afraid, Elizabeth?"

"I . . . I think I am a little . . . but if you'll love me and help me, I'll go wherever you go."

The two sat there for a long time, saying little, but something had changed and they both knew it. Patrick looked over at the door and suddenly laughed. "You know," he said quietly, "I was afraid to go through that door, but now, why, it's just a door. Come along, we've got a ball to attend, and I know who'll be the happiest couple there."

Elizabeth knew at that moment that she had made the right decision. She did not know what lay ahead of her, but she knew one thing—she and Patrick were one as they never had been before! She rose, took his arm, and the two of them passed out of the bedroom, into the hallway, and made their way down the stairs to the ballroom where the dancers had already begun.

Discovery in the Library

Thirteen

$\mathcal{T}$he architect who had designed the Martin mansion had been instructed to make the ballroom large enough to accommodate a great number of people. Taking Mrs. Martin at her word, he had made a ballroom second to none among the private mansions in Boston. It was a large rectangular room, well-lit by three cut-glass chandeliers and many gilded mirror-backed sconces placed around the entire room. The floor was an alabaster-colored marble. The walls were plain, except where they met the ceiling, and here a very ornate border of white tinplates circled the room. Large pillars placed about six feet from the outside walls formed arches at the ceiling and provided a grand entrance to the ballroom floor. Behind these pillars were many serving tables, covered with white silk damask. The tables held cut-crystal punch bowls and cups and delectable-looking food.

Silver tureens of soup, platters of cold lobster, potted meats, spit-roasted venison, beef, and goose filled the room with their aromas. Large bowls of oyster sauce, chestnut stuffing, spinach, and peach flummery filled the other tables along with a selection of cheeses expertly placed on the delicately engraved silver trays. Candied fruits, puff pastries with jams, and wafers of all sorts covered a dessert frame in the center of the dessert table.

Large floor-length windows ran along the outside wall, and each had a rich taffeta pull-up curtain in blue. Queen Anne chairs covered in blue and white silk damask stood in pairs around the room. At the end of the room, to the right, was a set of French doors that led to the gardens, and here is where the orchestra played. The ballroom had two large verde-and-marble fireplaces, and above these were large rectangular-shaped looking glasses with gilt frames that caught the flickering light from the pair of George II silver candelabra on the mantel.

Soft music filled the ballroom as Mr. and Mrs. Van Dorn stood speaking with their host. Mrs. Jane Van Dorn had some traces of her daughter's beauty. Her hair was still pale blond, and she had the same classic features that her daughter had. There was, however, a weakness in her face—and her character—that Charlotte somehow never manifested. Mrs. Van Dorn spoke very rarely, and she did not seem to have any of the more arrogant traits that many wealthy, influential ladies in high society displayed.

Her husband, Henry Van Dorn, looked more like a butcher than a successful shipping magnate. Standing no more than five feet eight, he was greatly overweight, and his brown hair had disappeared, except for a fringe around the back of his head. He compensated for this by growing a magnificent set of muttonchop whiskers, which he ran his hands through as if it gave him some pleasure.

"Magnificent ball, Mrs. Martin!" Mr. Van Dorn said, looking around at the dancers as they whirled on the ballroom floor. "I must say I've never seen such a beautiful ballroom, and it seems everybody from Boston is here."

"Well, thank you," Anne Martin said, nodding and taking the compliment as her due. She was satisfied that she could win her way over any plans that Mrs. Van Dorn might have had, and now she saw nothing in Mr. Van Dorn to stand in her way of any plans that she might make for the young couple.

They talked for some time, and then Mr. Van Dorn looked sharply at his host and said, "Sorry to hear about the trouble you've had—with your son-in-law, I mean."

"I'd rather not talk about it, if you don't mind, Mr. Van Dorn." William Martin did not look well. He was wearing a green suit with green knee britches and white stockings. His waistcoat was a green-and-tan stripe, and his topcoat was a hunter green velvet, but it hung loosely on him, and his face was drawn and tense.

Instantly Van Dorn said, "Well, of course not! Better not to talk about things like that."

The two men wandered off, and Mrs. Martin said at once, "I didn't want to say anything in front of my husband, but I never really trusted Patrick. I tried my best to prevent Elizabeth from marrying him, but she was dazzled by him. He does have a certain charm, and of course he's very good-looking."

"It must be dreadful for you," Mrs. Van Dorn said quietly.

"I'm mostly concerned about my daughter and the grandchildren. These things never seem to pass away. I just don't know what they'll do."

Mrs. Van Dorn looked across the ballroom to where Charlotte was dancing with Will. "They make a lovely couple, don't they?"

"Yes, they do. Charlotte's dress is beautiful."

Charlotte seemed aware of the gaze of those in the room. Her dress was beautiful—and should have been. The cost of it could have fed a good-sized village in Massachusetts for several weeks. She was wearing an open-robe gown made of the finest cream-colored silk. The bodice was form fitting and had overlapping rows of cream-colored lace interwoven with baby blue ribbon. The sleeves were snug and ended at the elbow with a large flounce of lace. It had a low neckline decorated with lace and ribbon that followed the edges of the robe into the skirt. The underskirt was full and had the same lace and ribbon overlapping so that the cream silk beneath was barely visible.

Looking up at Will, she said, "Look, there's Patrick and Elizabeth. I'm surprised he had the nerve to come."

Will glanced over and saw his sister and brother-in-law entering, but he said nothing. He had been stunned by the evidence against Patrick and had wished that the ball had been put off until the matter had been resolved. However, his mother and Charlotte had insisted on going on with it, since the invitations had already been sent.

Charlotte said, "Well, one good thing, we won't have to have anything to do with them. They wouldn't have the nerve to expect to keep their place in the family!"

Will suddenly turned and looked directly at Charlotte. "Elizabeth is my sister, and I love her dearly! Patrick may have done wrong, but he's still my brother-in-law and Elizabeth's husband!"

"But you're not thinking that we'll see them socially?"

William Martin Jr. was a gentle young man who disliked arguments. He had never once crossed Charlotte's will, but now something like anger came to him, and he said suddenly, with his voice biting, "It's nice that you've never done anything wrong, Charlotte! The rest of us mere mortals have to admit that we're not perfect and stumble around. We'll have to bow at your feet!"

Charlotte's face turned pale, and she could not say a word. Though she was a good dancer, she missed a step and finally managed to say, "I think I must excuse myself, Will."

"Of course." Will led her to the edge of the floor and watched her for a moment. He saw her go to her father's side, speak to him, and then the two of them left the ballroom.

"I suppose I've hurt her feelings," he muttered. "Well, I can't help that." Seeing that no one was speaking to Elizabeth and Patrick, he pulled himself up straight and walked over and stopped directly in front of them. "Hello, Patrick," he said.

"Why, good evening, Will."

Will looked at Elizabeth and said, "That's a beautiful dress you have on." She was wearing a plum-colored silk open-robe gown. The neckline was decorated with an ivory-colored lace that followed the line of the gown down the skirt, with two rows of matching lace fluttering against her lower arms. The underskirt, made of a lilac-colored silk, had four large rows of the same lace peeking from beneath the robe.

"Why, thank you, Will." Elizabeth suddenly reached out and touched his cheek. "And thank you for coming over to speak to us."

"It's nothing," Will muttered. He looked at Patrick and added gruffly, "Don't worry too much about these things, Patrick. They have a way of passing."

He turned and walked away quickly, and they stared after him. "That was nice of Will," Patrick said.

"He's a good man. He's too easily led by Charlotte, I'm afraid. He's not going to have a very happy life."

"Well, *I'm* going to have a happy life. Come on, let's show these folks what real dancing is like!" Patrick took Elizabeth in his arms, and they glided around the floor, ignoring the stares of those who wondered how they could look so happy.

On the fourth floor of the mansion where the servants' quarters were, Rebekah could hear the music faintly. She stood on the stair landing, listened to it, and moved around, pretending she was dancing. Then she went inside and saw that her grandmother had already gone to sleep. Mrs. Martin had hired caterers for the ball and had insisted that Rebekah and her grandmother were not needed for the evening. It was early, and she was not sleepy. Moving over to the desk, she picked up a book and muttered, "Oh, I've already finished this one."

Restlessly, she walked around the room, considered reading the book again, but the thought displeased her. An idea came to her, and she glanced at her grandmother, then went to the door, holding the book in her hand. Leaving the room, she went down the hall and descended to the first floor. The music floated up from the ballroom, and she longed to go look at the dancers, but she dared not. Moving to the library, she slipped inside and blinked her eyes. Only one small candle was lit in a sconce on the wall, and it had nearly guttered out. Quickly she crossed the room, moving carefully to avoid stumbling over the desk. She reached the spot where the two corners of the bookcases met and, groping around, felt for the gap from where the book she held had been taken. She knew the book to the right of it was the second in the series. Replacing the one, she reached for the other. She had no sooner pulled it down when suddenly the door to the library opened, allowing the light to flood in, then it closed again.

Rebekah was terrified. She felt like an intruder and wanted to flee, but there was no way out. Whoever had entered was standing just inside the door, and she could not slip by unnoticed. She suspected it was a young couple who had come to have a moment alone in the darkness, but then when they spoke, she recognized Charlotte's voice immediately.

Can that be Mr. Will? Rebekah thought. But she did not recognize the voice that came. Then she heard Charlotte whisper, "Father, it's all going to work out fine." And she knew that it was Mr. Van Dorn, Charlotte's father, whom she had seen once already.

"We must be careful." The voice came in a secretive whisper. "If we're found out, it would be terrible, Charlotte."

"We're not going to be found out. I've taken care of that."

"How can you be sure of it?"

"Because I've changed the ledgers so that they think Patrick has stolen the money. How will they ever know any different?"

"That's what you said in your letter, but it's very dangerous. A study of the books might—"

"Nobody's going to study the books!" Charlotte said. "It's all done, and all we have to do is wait and be careful. You did destroy the letter, didn't you? The one I wrote you?"

There was a silence, and Mr. Van Dorn whispered, "No, I didn't."

"Father, you're a fool! If anyone saw that letter—!"

"They won't see it! I promise you!"

"Is it at home? One of the servants might see it!"

"No, it's in my suitcase in my guest room."

"Then, as soon as this party's over, go up and destroy it!"

"All right. I will."

Rebekah stood there listening, and suddenly it all clearly fell into place. She remembered how she had seen Charlotte changing the books the day she was dusting in the library, and how angry the woman had become and had driven her out of this very room. Now she knew the truth, but what could she do about it? She was terrified lest they find her there, so she crouched down and listened as they continued to whisper.

"If you hadn't lost most of our money in that foolish investment, we wouldn't have to be doing things like this!" Charlotte snapped.

"It was a sure thing! I did it for the family."

"You have almost made paupers out of us, and now the only hope that we have is to take over the Martin Shipping Company. If they ever found out how close to bankruptcy we are, Anne Martin would call the wedding off. That's the reason I've been pushing for an early wedding."

"I . . . I wish we didn't have to do this."

"We'll be doing them a favor. Will's a fool! He could never run the business. As for Patrick, he's a nobody! Who cares what happens to him?"

"I suppose so," Mr. Van Dorn said, his voice tired. "We'd better get back to the party before they miss us."

"Don't forget. Burn that letter as soon as the party's over."

"All right, Charlotte."

The door opened again, and Rebekah blinked against the light, then it closed. Her heart was beating fast, and she waited only long enough to give the pair time to move away. Then she quickly left the library. No one was in the hallway, so she ran to the stairs and hurried to the second floor. *They'd never believe me. It would be my word against theirs. I've got to have that letter. . . !*

She went to the room that the Van Dorns were occupying and tried the door. It was unlocked. She stepped inside quickly, and by the light of the lamp on the bedside, she scanned the room. There were three bags beside the bed, and she opened two of them, finding them filled with Mrs. Van Dorn's things. The last one was obviously Mr. Van Dorn's. She went through the contents with trembling hands, thinking, *If someone comes in, they'll think I'm a thief. I'll be put in jail.* But she had to go on. Finally she found a thin package of letters next to his shaving kit. With hands trembling so badly she could hardly handle the papers, she went through them until she found the one signed by Charlotte in which she told her father how she had changed the books. Quickly she replaced the things in the suitcase, put it down, and left the room. Fear made her knees tremble, and she stopped to take a deep breath, for she felt faint.

"I've got to tell Elizabeth and Patrick, but they're at the ball now. I'll wait until morning, then I'll give them the letter."

Conspiracy Unveiled

Fourteen

*W*hat's that? Did you hear something, Patrick?"

Elizabeth slept very lightly. She had heard what she thought was a faint scratching at the door and sat upright in bed. Reaching over, she shook Patrick, saying urgently, "Wake up! There's somebody at the door!"

"Uuuhh! What's that you say?" Patrick's voice was fuzzy with sleep, but when Elizabeth repeated her insistent statement, he awakened fully and got up at once. "Who could it be at this hour?" he muttered. He walked over to the door, put his hand on it, and opened it. "Who is it?"

Elizabeth could not hear what he said, but he shut the door, then came back and said, "Put your robe on, Elizabeth."

"Who is it? Is one of the children sick?"

"No, it's Rebekah. She seems quite urgent about something." Patrick pulled a light wool robe out of the clothespress and put it on as Elizabeth slipped into the blue silk one she kept next to the bed.

"What can she want at this hour? It must be one of the children!"

"We'll soon find out."

Elizabeth waited nervously as Patrick moved across the room, stopping to light a lamp from a candle they left burning. He turned the wick up so that the room was illuminated. His hair was wild and ruffled, and concern lined his face as he opened the door quietly. "Come in, Rebekah," he said. He stood back, and the young woman stepped inside. She was fully dressed, and her eyes were wide, the hollows of her cheeks highlighted by the lamplight.

"Is Sarah sick?" Elizabeth asked quickly. "Or Andrew?"

"Oh no, ma'am. They're all right. It's not that."

They waited for her to speak, and when she did not, Patrick said kindly, "Are you sick, Rebekah? Or is it your grandmother?"

"No, nobody is sick, sir. It's just—well, I don't know how to say it."

Seeing that the girl was terrified, Elizabeth walked over and said, "Don't be afraid, Rebekah. Whatever it is, it's all right. Here, sit down and tell us about it." Seating herself beside the frightened girl, she asked, "Is something wrong with you, Rebekah?"

Rebekah's cheeks flushed, and she reached up and touched one of them nervously. "Oh no, ma'am. It's not me. It's just something I thought you and Mr. Patrick ought to know about."

Patrick pulled a chair closer and said quietly, "I can see you're troubled. Just take your time." He reached over and patted her shoulder and gave her a warm smile. "Don't worry. Whatever it is, we'll help you."

His reassurance warmed Rebekah at once. She twisted her hands nervously and looked down at them. She knew she had to tell them what she had discovered, but now that she had come, it all seemed dangerous somehow. The world of the servant was so far removed from that which these two occupied. They could have no possible way of knowing how difficult it was for her to step across the invisible line. For a servant to meddle in the affairs of those who ruled the big house—well, it was something she had never heard of—certainly something she had never thought she herself would do. Looking up and seeing the concern on their faces, she gathered her courage and began, "I . . . was in the library last night while the party was going on."

"Were you, Rebekah?" Elizabeth said quietly. "You went to get a book, I suppose?"

"Yes, ma'am. I couldn't sleep . . . and usually I don't go into the library. Mr. Will, he usually gets books for me, or sometimes his father does. But I read the last of the ones he gave me, so I thought I'd just go down and get another one. I didn't think there'd be any wrong in it."

"Of course not! I've heard Father say many times he's proud of the way you've picked up on your reading so much."

"Did he say that, ma'am?"

"He surely did. So I don't think you have to worry about borrowing another book. It wasn't such an awful thing, going into the library like that."

"Oh, but that wasn't it, Miss Elizabeth," Rebekah said quickly. She took a deep breath and said, "I . . . I know about the trouble you've had—you and Mr. Patrick. About the money being missing, and how you . . . well, you've been blamed for it." She looked straight at Patrick, and there was a fierceness, almost, in her mild sweet face. "I know you didn't do it, sir. You wouldn't do a thing like that. Never in a million years!"

Patrick reached over and took her hand and squeezed it. "I appreciate your saying that, Rebekah. It's good to hear."

"I'm saying no more than what anyone thinks who knows you, Mr. Patrick. It's not right."

"But what does all this have to do with your going into the library?" Elizabeth asked, somewhat bewildered. She felt a warm feeling for the young servant girl and determined if there was any way to help her in the future, she would do it. Not that there would be any way with her and Patrick out on their own resources, but she knew many people who would be glad to have a good servant like Rebekah.

Rebekah swallowed hard, looked at the two, and then said, "Well, I was in the library—over in the corner, you see. It was real dark, and only one candle was lit. I'd just reached up to get a book, and I opened it and was looking at it to see if it was the right one— and then the door opened."

The girl halted abruptly, and a frightened look crossed her face. "Who came in, Rebekah?" Patrick asked.

"It was Miss Charlotte and her father, Mr. Van Dorn."

"Did they see you?"

"Oh no. They didn't see me. It was like, ma'am . . . they just came in to talk, kind of. And they whispered like they were afraid someone would hear them. I was over in the dark corner, and I crouched down so they wouldn't see me. Oh, I was so afraid! All I thought was they would catch me there, and they would report me to your mother. She wouldn't like it, Miss Elizabeth."

"Did you hear what they were saying?" Patrick inquired.

"Yes, sir, I did." She looked at him fully in the face and said, "They were talking about the company, Mr. William's shipping company, and about you."

A warning alarm went off in Elizabeth's head. Something seemed sinister about Charlotte and her father creeping into the library to find a secret place for a meeting while the party was going on downstairs. "What did they say, Rebekah?" she asked quietly. "Tell me every word of it."

"Well, I didn't hear it all, ma'am, but what I did hear was that Miss Charlotte had written a letter to her father, and she had told him in the letter how she had changed those business books that you're always working in to make it look as though Mr. Patrick had taken the money."

Patrick stared at the young woman, unable to believe what he was hearing. "Are you sure you heard them right, Rebekah?"

"Oh yes, sir! They were whispering, but I've got very good hearing. Miss Charlotte said, 'You didn't keep the letter, did you?' And he said, 'Yes, but it's in a safe place.' And then she said, 'You didn't leave it at home? One of the servants might find it.' And then Mr. Van Dorn said, 'No, it's in my suitcase.' Then that's when Miss Charlotte told him to burn it, and they said a lot of things about how it would be better if you and Miss Elizabeth weren't in the business anymore, and how when your father died, Miss Elizabeth, they could take it all."

"I see. Did they say anything else?" Elizabeth asked calmly. Fury was rising in her, but she hid it from Rebekah.

Rebekah thought hard for a moment, then said, "They said how it would be better if you and Mr. Patrick were out of the house. That she would always be able to make Mr. Will do whatever she wanted him to. And I almost forgot—that Mr. Van Dorn has lost his money somehow, and that the new business would save them as soon as Mr. Will and Miss Charlotte got married."

Patrick reached over and hugged the girl's shoulders. "It took a lot of courage for you to tell us this. I think, though, we'll have to have the letter. No one would believe you. It would be your word against the Van Dorns'."

"Oh, I've already got the letter," Rebekah said. She reached into her pocket and pulled it out. "I went up right away, into the room, and I took it." She looked very frightened and pulled her shoulders together. "Would they put me in jail for stealing it, sir? I couldn't bear to leave my grandmother."

"Of course they won't. Now don't you worry. You did the right thing. Now that I have this letter," Patrick said, his jaw growing tense, "it's all I need."

Elizabeth reached over and hugged the young woman. "You'll never know how much this means to me and Patrick. Now Patrick won't have to go around with a blot on his name."

"That's right. You just about saved my life, Rebekah." Patrick smiled. "I'll have to find some way of making it up to you."

"Oh, it was nothing. You and Miss Elizabeth have been so kind to me and to my grandmother. I hope this will all come out right for you." She hesitated, then asked, "Do you still think Mr. Will will marry Miss Charlotte?"

"I doubt it," Elizabeth said dryly. "Once he finds out about her deceit in this, I hardly think he'll want her for a wife."

An odd look appeared in Rebekah's eyes, and for the first time she smiled. "I think that would be good. She wouldn't make him a very good wife, I don't think." She rose suddenly and said, "I've got to get back to my room."

"Thank you again, Rebekah," Patrick said, walking to the door with her. He patted her shoulder as she went outside and said, "I'd kiss you, but my wife is a jealous woman. She won't let me kiss any good-looking young girls, you know."

As soon as the door closed, Patrick turned to his wife, and for a moment they stood there, both thinking about the fraud that had to be exposed. Patrick took a deep breath and said, "It's going to be like a blast of gunpowder going off. Are you sure you want to let your parents know about this?"

Elizabeth stared at Patrick. "What are you talking about? Of course we'll let them know about this. You don't think I'd let Will marry a . . . a vixen like that, do you?"

"It'll hurt your mother terribly."

"Not as bad as if Will married the minx and they found out what she was later. Besides, Mother is very protective of Father. When she finds out what they've tried to do to him . . ."

"Well, maybe we can stop her from scalping the Van Dorns. Really, I think I see the hand of God in this. That young girl has saved our good name, Elizabeth. We really don't have to leave here now, you know."

"Yes, we do!" Elizabeth said firmly. "Ever since we've talked, I've been praying, and God has showed me more and more clearly that we need to leave and be on our own. Just you and me and the children. Sometimes," she added, "I think it would be best if all young married couples would get a thousand miles away from every in-law and relative. Far enough away so that they'd only have each other to cling to."

Patrick grinned suddenly, looking very young in the amber lamplight. "Not a bad idea," he said. "We'll do the best we can. We're starting a little late, but it looks like the time has come."

"When will we tell my parents?"

"Today. As soon as possible." He paused and thought about it. "Without this letter, it would never have worked. Do you know Charlotte's handwriting?"

"Yes." Elizabeth took the letter and nodded. "This is it, and she's signed it. It's enough evidence to hang her if this were a hanging offense."

"I doubt if we'd go that far, but the Van Dorns are going to have to find other victims to restore their lost fortune. Well, let's go back to bed, but I doubt if I can sleep."

They went back to bed, and for a long time lay there quietly. Finally, Elizabeth reached over and put her hand on his arm. "It's going to be good, isn't it? Just you and me and the children."

"Yes, it will be very good, wife." He reached over and pulled her toward him. She moved against him and felt like a bride again, even after all those years.

Later in the morning, Elizabeth went to her parents first, and without revealing the secret, she said, "We must have a family meeting at once."

"About what?" her mother asked, eyeing Elizabeth sharply.

"I won't tell you now, but it's something important that we need to handle as a family."

After Elizabeth left, having asked her parents to bring the Van Dorns and Charlotte and Will to the library as quickly as possible, Anne said, "I think I know what it is."

Her husband looked at her cautiously. "What do you think it is?"

"I think they've finally realized there's no hope, so Patrick's decided to make a clean break of it and throw himself on our mercy."

"If he does, he'll certainly have it!" William said.

"Well, of course, we'll have to be forgiving. The Scriptures teach us that. But at the same time, a certain amount of retribution should accompany wrongdoing of this nature."

"What are you thinking of, Anne?" William said wearily. "I think he's had punishment enough just having to bear the awful gossip that's gone around about him. I can't imagine how he must have felt at Charlotte and Will's engagement ball, knowing everyone was talking about him."

"We'll talk about it later. In the meanwhile, I'll go down and get the Van Dorns and Charlotte and Will. You go on to the library."

Fifteen minutes later, the library seemed very small. Will was there, standing beside Charlotte; Anne and William were ranked on the other side of the room; and Mr. and Mrs. Van Dorn stood slightly back toward the line of books against the far wall. Patrick and Elizabeth came in last, and Anne said at once, "Very well! What's this all about, Elizabeth?"

"I'll let my husband tell you," Elizabeth said calmly. She looked at Patrick, nodded slightly, and then held his arm, squeezing it to give him assurance.

"I never desired to be the bearer of ill tidings," Patrick said slowly. "When I tell you what I've discovered, you're going to think that it's because I've been mistreated, that I'm angry and want revenge. I assure you that's not the case."

"What do you mean *discovered?*" Will said. "What are you talking about, Patrick?"

Patrick looked over at Will and felt a great wave of pity. He was about to shake this man's life to the very foundation, and it was not pleasant. "Will, I've loved you like a brother, and the news I've got is going to be most unpleasant for you."

Will's face paled. "What are you talking about, Patrick? Get down to it! You've called us all in here. I assumed you wanted to tell us you were guilty and ask for pardon."

"No. I'm not guilty. I never have been, Will. But there are guilty people in this room."

Anne Martin had a sudden feeling of fear—something about her son-in-law's face frightened her. Although she had always looked down on him, she had been well aware of a steadiness and a strength to his character that was a rare find. She had never admitted it to him or to Elizabeth or to the grandchildren, but now as she watched him, his firm lips drawn into a tight line, she suddenly knew that he had some awful news to deliver. In a voice not entirely steady, she asked, "What are you talking about, Patrick?"

"There's been a conspiracy to take over the Martin Shipping Company," Patrick said in an even voice. "I might as well state the accusations right now. Mr. Van Dorn, you and your daughter have been involved in a scheme to blacken my name, and you plan to take over my father-in-law's company. You've played on his ill health, upon your relationship with my mother-in-law, and you've been completely dishonest. In fact," he said, his voice getting stronger, "you're nothing but a pair of crooks and thieves!"

Charlotte cried something incoherent. Her face went suddenly pale, and she grasped Will's arm strongly. "Will, don't let him talk to me like that!"

Stepping forward, Will clenched his fist. "I won't have you talking about my fiancée or her family that way!"

"I'd think less of you, Will, if you felt any differently," Patrick said. "I know what I'd feel like if someone accused my wife of being dishonest, but I have hard evidence of what I'm saying. Charlotte, I have a witness who heard everything that you and your father said in the library last night."

Mr. Van Dorn's face turned ashen. He tried to speak, but his throat seemed to be clogged. Finally he managed to wheeze, "I . . . I don't know what you're talking about!"

"Who is your witness, Patrick?" William asked. He seemed to have gathered strength and was now staring at his son-in-law with a strange light in his eyes. He gave the Van Dorns one look and did not like what he saw. Mrs. Van Dorn looked merely shocked, but guilt was written plainly across the faces of Charlotte and her father. "Who is this witness?"

"I'll bring her in, Father."

Elizabeth stepped to the door, opened it, and said, "Will you come in, Rebekah?"

As Rebekah came in, Elizabeth said quietly, "It was very difficult for Rebekah to come to us with what she had discovered. I hoped to keep her out of it, but she insisted on telling what she heard. She's been a faithful servant in this household, and she's hated every lie and bit of evil gossip that's been spread about Patrick."

"That girl hates me because I have not tolerated her!" Charlotte cried out at once.

"Be quiet, Charlotte!" William spoke with authority, and his strength seemed to have returned. He came over and stood before the servant, who looked back at him fearfully but with her chin held high. "What is it that you've seen, Rebekah?" he asked quietly. "Don't be afraid. Just tell the truth."

Rebekah began to speak, falteringly at first, but when she saw the encouragement on the faces of Patrick and Elizabeth, and the kindness in Mr. Martin's eyes, she grew steadily stronger. She told the story from beginning to end—how she had seen the two and heard the secret conversation in the library.

When she had finished, William Martin turned to say, "What do you two have to say for yourselves?"

"It's all a lie," Mr. Van Dorn blustered. "You're not going to take the word of a servant girl over that of a gentleman, are you? Why, she's nothing but a maid!"

Patrick spoke up. "I knew that her word would not be enough. However, I think this will be. You know Charlotte's handwriting, do you not, sir?" He handed the letter to his father-in-law.

The room grew absolutely still, and the sound of the clock ticking sounded very loud as he calmly read it. Finally, he raised his eyes and put them on Charlotte. "I'm ashamed of you, Charlotte! And for you, sir," he said, turning his eyes on Mr. Van Dorn. "If I were a younger man, I would call you out for this. As it is, I will tell you to take yourself, and your family, out of my house and never be seen here again!"

Mrs. Van Dorn's face was as pale as paper. She evidently knew nothing of all of this, and Elizabeth felt a great compassion for her. She went to the woman at once, saying, "I'm so sorry, Mrs. Van Dorn. Could I get you a glass of water? You look faint."

"No," Mrs. Van Dorn whispered. "I . . . I really don't understand any of this."

Charlotte was watching Will's face. She did not take her eyes off of him. He had lost his color also, and there was a trembling in his lip for a moment. "Will," she said, "what about . . . what about us?"

Will reached over and took the paper from his father's hand. He scanned it, then handed it back to his father. "There is no *us*," he said briefly. "I hope I never lay eyes on you as long as I live!"

It was a terrible moment, and it was Elizabeth who said, "Mr. Van Dorn, I think it would be best if you'd take your family away from here immediately. If you'll come with me, Mrs. Van Dorn, I'll take you to your room. Will, would you see that the carriage is called for the Van Dorns while they get ready to leave?"

"Certainly," Will said and left the room without another word.

The Van Dorns shuffled toward the door, all of them moving as if they were in a daze. As soon as they were gone, Anne turned to her husband, her knees very weak, and whispered, "William, it can't be true!"

"Here's the letter."

Anne took the letter and tried to read it, but she could not seem to focus. She stood there and looked very helpless. Patrick, who had moved slightly away as if disassociating himself from the pair, started to leave the room, but then he came over and stood before his mother-in-law. "I know this is hard for you, Anne," he said, calling her by her first name, which he had not done since he had been married to Elizabeth. "It's always hard to be disillusioned, but believe me, it's better for you and far better for Will that this came about before they were married."

Anne raised her eyes to look into the face of the young man that she had so despised. She expected to see hatred and triumph in his countenance, but instead she only saw compassion. Her eyes filled with tears and she whispered, "Patrick, I'm . . . I'm so *sorry!*"

He interrupted her and put his hand out. When she groped for it blindly, he took her hand with both of his and said, "I don't want you to feel any guilt about this. We've all been deceived by people at one time or another. You have a good heart. You just put it in the wrong place."

"Patrick—" William had come to stand in front of his son-in-law. "I can't think of what to say," he said lamely. "No, don't interrupt me. All my life I've prided myself on being faithful to my friends. Even if you had done what you were accused of, my behavior has been unforgivable." He put his hand out and said, "I'm sorry. That's little enough, but that's all that a man can say."

"Thank you, sir. We'll say no more about it," Patrick said. "I'm just happy the real tragedy has been averted."

Patrick turned and left the room, and instantly Anne turned to her husband. "How could we have been so wrong?"

"Nobody ever knows how he makes a fool of himself. We'll look back, and for a long time we'll be remembering that there were signs that we were headed the wrong way."

"How can Patrick and Elizabeth ever forgive us?" Anne moaned.

"It's not that. They've already done it, I think. But how can we forgive ourselves?" William said. "That's the hard part. It always is."

———

For two days after the Van Dorns hastily departed, the Martin household was strangely quiet. People seemed to speak in a whisper until Sarah and Andrew finally looked at each other and Andrew said, "It's like somebody died. I don't see what everybody's so sad about."

"I don't either. Now Will doesn't have to marry that old Charlotte woman!" Sarah said.

The adults seemed oblivious to their conversation, as the Martins were still struggling through the difficult time. The marriage was off, which meant that Anne Martin would have to spend a great deal of time explaining the reasons to her friends. "We can never tell the truth," she said to her husband.

"I think we should. Patrick deserves it."

Anne shook her head. "I mentioned it to him. He said there was no point in harming that family anymore. I think he feels sorry for Mrs. Van Dorn. I don't think she knew anything about any of this."

"No, she seems to be a sweet woman. I feel sorry for her, with that scoundrel she's married to and that daughter of hers. I fear it will be hard on Patrick too. People will always remember that he was accused. And they'll think that Charlotte broke her engagement because there were thieves in the family."

"I doubt if she'll be saying a great deal. From what I understand, the Van Dorns are pretty well broke."

"How'd you find that out?"

"I've made some discreet inquiries of a few of my business friends in New York. It seems the Van Dorns are in debt over their heads and have borrowed from everybody they could."

"Why didn't we hear any word of this before it all happened?"

"Would we have believed it?" William said. "In any case, I think Patrick is right. It's hard now, but think how it would have been if

Will had married Charlotte. They would never have known a moment's happiness."

That evening at supper, everyone's spirits seemed to be somewhat better. At least Elizabeth and Patrick were almost boisterous, and their ease and apparent happiness brought Will out of his depression. Finally, at the end of the meal, Will spoke up. "I don't know how to say this, Patrick. No man likes to admit he was a fool, but I was. I was wrong about you, and I'm sorry."

Patrick was embarrassed. "Enough apologies. It's all over, Will. I say let the past be buried."

"One thing is going to change." Everyone looked at William and he smiled at Patrick. "You're coming back to the firm, but this time as a full partner." He waited for Patrick to leap at the invitation, but when the tall red-headed man said nothing, William glanced at Elizabeth and saw a slight smile on her lips. "Well, aren't you happy to hear this news, daughter?"

"Well . . . yes, but we have news of our own. Tell them, Patrick."

Patrick leaned forward and said, "I know this is going to come as a shock to you. I know you've had more than your share of difficult news lately, but, well, Elizabeth and the children and I"—he looked across at Andrew and Sarah who were listening intently—"will be leaving this house."

"Are you going to get a place of your own?" Anne asked, surprised.

"Well, more than that. We're leaving Boston. We're starting a new life."

"You're going to work for another shipping firm?" Mr. Martin asked, incredulous. "But that's not wise. Whatever you could do with them, you won't be a partner."

"I won't be having any partners in my new venture," Patrick said. He hesitated, then said, "You're going to think we've lost our minds, but we've decided to move over the mountains. We're going to be pioneers."

The silence lasted for about three full seconds, and then Andrew let out a whoop that any wild Indian would have been proud of. "Pa, can I have a horse when we get across the mountains?"

"Sure you can, son. And, Sarah, you can have a spinning wheel and learn how to make your own clothes."

"No, I want a horse, too. Just like Andrew."

"And you'll have one," Elizabeth said.

For the next thirty minutes, the conversation was rather one-sided. The older Martins tried desperately to dissuade the couple from throwing themselves into such a venture, but William soon saw that his son-in-law's mind was made up, and he knew well the steadfastness of Elizabeth. Finally he said gently, "I know you two are followers of the Lord. I assume you've prayed about this."

"Yes, we have, Father, and I know it seems very unwise, leaving everything, but we're trusting in God, and we believe it's what He would have for our family."

"In that case, I will say no more. It will be grievous to lose you, Elizabeth, and you too, Patrick, and these grandchildren. But a man and a woman must make their own way. I want to pray for your safety." He bowed his head, and the thought came to him as he was praying, *Once they leave, I will never see them again.* He knew that his heart condition was worse than anyone suspected. He also knew that the journey would be long, and once they left they could not come back for years, perhaps. In any case, he was saying a final farewell to them.

There were tears on his cheeks as he concluded his prayer. ". . . And I ask, O gracious God and Father of all, protect Patrick and Elizabeth from the dangers of the wilderness, the frontier. From the Indians, from sickness, from disease. Protect these two children, Lord. Help them, and give them courage to meet whatever danger arises, and we know that whatever they have is in your hands, and when we put our lives in your hands, all things will be very well. I ask you to watch over them, to build a fence around them so that evil cannot come in, and I ask it in the powerful name of Jesus Christ."

Everyone at the table said "Amen"—even Anne Martin. She was perhaps even more grieved than her husband, for she realized that for years she had almost daily belittled her son-in-law. Now that he was lost to her, in effect, she knew it was too late. She said her own prayer, asking for forgiveness, and when they arose, Patrick came to her, and she whispered, "Forgive me, Patrick."

"All's forgiven, Mother," he said, calling her such for the first time. "Now it's put away forever."

Will took Elizabeth aside and said quietly, "I hate to see you two leave. You'll be so far away."

"You'll have to take care of Father. He needs all the help he can get."

"I know." A slight shudder ran through his frame, and he said, "Think what an awful mess I almost made. I almost married that horrible woman!"

"You'll have to be more careful."

"I will, but how's a man to know what a woman's like? Every society woman in Boston has trotted in front of me for years, and finally when I did say yes, look what I would have gotten."

Elizabeth wanted to say a great deal, but she simply put her hand on her brother's cheek and said quietly, "The next time, look closer to home for a wife."

"What? What does that mean?" Will asked in a puzzled voice.

"You will figure it out, Will. Remember, look closer to home, and you'll find a wife." Elizabeth said no more, and Will stared at her with a strange look.

Later that night Elizabeth said, "Will's going to fall in love, Patrick."

"I assume so—but when? And with whom?"

Elizabeth smiled mysteriously, then said, "You wouldn't believe me if I told you!"

A Mended Heart

Fifteen

*W*ill Martin was sitting in his father's chair in the library with a book propped before him. He had been staring blindly at the printed pages for an hour without turning a single page. His mind seemed to be elsewhere, and time and again he would shake his shoulders together, grit his teeth, and force himself to follow the lines on the page. A week had passed since the traumatic experience of losing the woman who was to be his wife, and Will had not endured it well. His life until this point had been easy and without great strife, but the pain of what had occurred had made a deeper impact on him than most of the family realized—perhaps because he was not outwardly emotional as a rule, and he kept a wall between himself and the rest of the world.

But even now as the birds sang outside the library window, and he heard the voices of two of the servants laughing and joking as they cut the grass, he was going over and over in his mind how badly he had failed as a man. *What's wrong with me?* he thought in agony. *Don't I have any sense at all? Couldn't I see what kind of a woman she was? Of course, I knew she was domineering . . . but who could've known she was absolutely wicked?*

He shifted in the chair, fixed his eyes on the page, and tried to read again, but his mind drifted away. *And poor Patrick! I can't understand why he doesn't hate me. We've been friends for years, and without giving him a chance, I jumped on him with all the rest.* Shame flooded over him, and he suddenly threw the book down, shoving it away. Putting his head on the desk, he shut his eyes, trying to forget the past. But it would not go away—every scene and every word came trooping before him, especially that which he had done to Patrick. A slight sound attracted his attention, and he looked up to see Rebekah, who had stepped inside the door.

She gave him a startled glance and said, "Oh, I'm sorry, Mr. Will!" then turned to go.

"No, don't go, Rebekah!" Will straightened up in the chair and passed his hand in front of his face. Making an effort he said, "Come in. I won't be in your way."

Rebekah hesitated for a moment, then stepped inside and said quietly, "I just came to straighten up a little bit."

Will looked at her for a moment and said, "Rebekah, I've got to talk to someone. Shut the door, will you, please?"

"Why, of course, Mr. Will." Closing the door, she came across the room and stood before the desk. "What is it, sir?"

"Oh, Rebekah, forget *sir* and *Mr. Will.* We've known each other for years." Will suddenly slammed the desk with his fist in an unusual show of anger. His mouth twisted and he said, "Rebekah, do you despise me?"

Startled at his sudden outburst, Rebekah's eyes flew open. She had lovely eyes that were wide-spaced and almost an emerald green. "Why . . . why in the world would you say a thing like that?" She could not bring herself to call the man by his first name. Servanthood was too deeply ingrained in her. She saw, however, that he was profoundly disturbed, and she knew what was on his mind. For the past week she had watched him, and because she cared for him, she understood the agony of his spirit. She longed to go to him and take his hand and comfort him, but she dared not do that. However, she knew she had to make some effort to ease his suffering. Quietly she said, "We all make mistakes, Mr. Will. Every one of us. I've made about a thousand, I guess. It wasn't your fault."

"It was my fault!" he said. "I should've known better!"

"She's a very lovely woman."

"I'm not talking about her!" Will said, shaking his head almost violently. "Oh, I was stupid about Charlotte. I knew she was too bossy, but I don't know any way a man can look inside a person's heart and see evil when it's there." A sudden thought came to him and he said, "What did you think of her? Before all this happened, I mean."

"Oh, I don't like to say," Rebekah protested.

"No, you wouldn't. You never say anything bad about anybody, do you, Rebekah?" He realized suddenly that he had known this girl for years, but her quietness and shyness had never allowed him past the gentle exterior. Aside from the fact that he knew her grandmother, he knew little about her. Suddenly he grew curious. "You never say anything about yourself. Not to me, I mean."

Rebekah did not know how to answer. She glanced down at the floor, unable to meet his intense gaze, and then she looked up and smiled. "It's not for servants to tell the young master of the house about themselves."

"Well, you can tell this young master." He suddenly said, "What about your suitors? I don't know anything about that. Are you seeing any young men?"

"No, sir, not really."

"Well, are they all blind around here? A pretty girl like you?" He smiled, saying, "I'll have to see about that. Maybe I'll become your marriage broker."

"Oh no, sir! You mustn't do that!"

"Oh, I was only joking, Rebekah. You don't need a marriage broker. Not with those beautiful eyes of yours." He saw that he was embarrassing her, and he got up from his chair. "I'm sorry. I don't seem to know how to talk to anybody. I'm just a bumbling fool!" He stood beside her and shook his head. "I can't get over it—what I did to Patrick. I must've been crazy and blind at the same time."

"He doesn't hold it against you, sir."

"Will you stop calling me sir! You make me feel like I'm a thousand years old!"

"Why, I have to call you *sir*. That's the way it is in a big house. You wouldn't like it if James the gardener didn't call you *sir*."

"You're not James the gardener. Right now I don't care what James would call me. If he called me an idiot, he'd be just about right."

Suddenly Rebekah felt she knew what to say, and a strange comfort came to her, and an ease that she had never felt in Will Martin's presence. "You know," she said, "it's much easier to forgive others than it is to forgive ourselves. But when God forgives our sins, we mustn't go back and dig them up again."

"What do you mean by that, Rebekah?"

"I mean when we're Christians, if we sin against God, the Bible says if we confess our sins, He's faithful and just to forgive us our sins. And He cleanses us from all unrighteousness. Say we tell a lie, and we go to God and say, 'God, I lied. Forgive me.' Then we go back again the next day and say, 'Oh, God, forgive me for that lie.' " She smiled and two dimples appeared in her cheeks. "I think God would say, 'What lie?' "

The charm of the girl took Will Martin, and he had to smile. "You mean we shouldn't keep on asking for forgiveness once we've received it?"

"I think it would be an insult to God. I mean, if I had done something wrong to you and you forgave me, and I came back the next day and asked you again, and then the day after that . . . don't you see? It would hurt your feelings. Sooner or later you would say, 'Don't you believe me? I've already forgiven you!' "

The girl's simple wisdom impressed Will greatly, and he impulsively reached out and took her hands. "You're a very wise young woman, Rebekah. If I'd had a keeper like you from the beginning, I might not have made such a horrible mistake."

Rebekah was very aware of his hands on hers. They were large and strong, and they held hers firmly, and a flush crept up her neck to her cheeks. "Really, you mustn't hold my hands, sir."

Will did not let go of her hands. "Why, that's the way of it. Didn't you know? Young masters of houses always flirt with pretty maids."

"Oh, really you mustn't, sir!"

Instantly Will released her hands. "Of course not. I was only teasing, Rebekah. Come and sit down. I'm going crazy. I read the last page of this book a hundred times."

"I . . . I must be about my work."

"I'm the master of this house—at least while my father's gone," Will joked. "Now, tell me about yourself." He looked around. "What books do you like to read?"

He had touched on a good subject, for Rebekah loved to read. She said, "Oh, I like every kind of book. I like history and poetry and novels and books about foreign countries."

"Have you ever read this one?" He rose and took a book down off the shelf and said, "It's all about Africa."

"No, I haven't."

"Let me show you this portion. It's like nothing I've ever read before." He opened the book and began to read to her. He read steadily for a few moments, then looked up and saw that Rebekah's lips were open and her eyes were dreamy.

"Oh, do go on! Read some more!"

"No, ma'am! I'm saving it for later. Come along. Let's take a walk and see what James is doing with the garden."

"But I have my work!"

"Remember, I'm the master of Martin Hall, and you have to obey me. Come along now. Do you ever play games?" he asked, a smile turning his mouth upward.

"Why, I did when I was a little girl."

"But I mean now. When you're grown up."

She remembered suddenly dancing on the stairs and pretending he was her partner. "Well, sir, yes I do."

"Look. When nobody's around, you can call me Will. Rebekah, I need a friend right now. It's a hard time for me."

"I know, W-Will," she said, pronouncing the name with difficulty. "But you're going to be all right. God's going to be with you. Just look to Him."

"Come along then, and here's the game we'll play. We'll pretend that I'm a young man who's come calling on you. This is your house, and you're showing me around. Now, show me the garden, Rebekah." He took her arm, and they walked to the door and left the house. The sun was shining, and they waved at the men who were cutting the grass. "Show me the garden as if I'd never seen it before."

Suddenly she felt relieved and almost playfully she said, "All right. Let me show you the flowers. My favorite flowers are roses. We have four varieties here. I'll show you my favorite, and then you can tell me yours."

The couple moved among the flowers of the garden, smelling this blossom and that, with Rebekah exclaiming over the beauty of particular blooms. And as Will Martin watched her, taking in the trim figure and the clear, unblemished skin, he remembered suddenly what Elizabeth had said. *Next time, look closer to home for a wife.* The words seemed to echo in his mind, and the quiet strength of the girl and the excitement of her face brought peace to his troubled spirit. An hour later he realized that he had forgotten his problems entirely. Her charm and words of faith had driven them completely from his mind. *Well,* he said to himself after she had finally excused herself and disappeared into the house, *there are women in this world with beauty and honesty in their hearts.* The thought stayed with him as he continued to walk slowly along the garden, smelling the flowers, and thinking of how much better a flower looked in Rebekah's slender hand.

Appalachian Destiny

Sixteen

$\mathcal{M}$ ay had turned to June, then June to the heat of July, and now August of 1770 made its appearance, and on the first day of that month, Elizabeth and Patrick awakened in their room in Boston as the bright sunshine shone through the windows. Patrick sat up and said, "Elizabeth!" She was already awake, he saw, and when she sat up and stared at him, he said, "Well, it's time. We've had our last day in this house. You've spent all your life here, and now you're leaving it. Are you a little sad?"

Elizabeth looked around the room and thought of the graciousness of the mansion, of the grounds, and of the years she had lived here. But she shook her head, her hair cascading down her back, and smiled. "I'll always remember they've been good years. But the best of our life is before us. God has promised me that." She reached over and pulled his head toward her, kissed him soundly, and said, "Now, get up and get dressed. I'll bet the children have been awake since daybreak."

They made their way downstairs and found William already moving around the room, dressed in a gray suit and wearing a fresh white shirt. He looked somewhat better, which was probably attributed to the fact that Will and Patrick had practically forced him to take a lengthy two-week sea voyage vacation. The time away from work and the rest had seemed to work wonders with him. He looked at them now and said quietly, "Well, I'm trying not to be sad, but it's hard."

Elizabeth went to him and put her arms around him. This man had guided her throughout childhood and her adult life with his strength and words of wisdom. Next to Patrick, he had been the most important man in her life. Tears came to her eyes, but she was determined not to let him see them. Blinking them away she said, "Well, have you seen the lovebirds this morning?"

A wry smile touched the lips of William Martin. "Oh yes! They've already been around. They can't seem to take their eyes off of each other."

Elizabeth said tentatively, "I've been worried about Mother. She wanted Will to marry somebody high on the social scale."

"I think we've had enough of that sort of thing. Your mother has learned a hard lesson in that regard. Rebekah will make a good wife for him. Did I tell you we've decided to send her to school for a while? Maybe for even a year. Oh, not that she needs it, but she loves reading, and she told me that she'd feel better about meeting our friends and William's if she had a little more grace and charm."

"She doesn't need any of that," Patrick said. It had pleased him when Will had fallen in love with the young woman who had helped spare him from making a grave mistake. He had been afraid that Anne Martin would raise the roof with her son marrying a maid of her own house. But somehow the shock of the Van Dorn scandal had done something to Anne Hardwick Martin. She had had a painful reminder of what high society could do to a person's values. After she had accepted the shock of Will's announcement that he was in love with Rebekah and intended to marry her, she had gone out of her way to be friendly to the young woman.

"I can't believe how she's blossomed. Rebekah, I mean. She just needed some love and attention, and I'm glad she's going away to school. It will give her and Will a time apart. He can do some mooning around. A young man needs to suffer a little bit before he gets married," Elizabeth said.

"I think it is a good thing," William said. "And I'm proud of Will, and of you, too, Patrick. You two have brought the business along so that it's better now than it ever was. I've decided to leave it completely in Will's hands. He will have Mr. Simms to help him, if he needs it."

"I think that's a wise move. You deserve to enjoy yourself."

"I'll miss you two," he said, "and the grandchildren."

Elizabeth could say nothing. She knew that the mails were unreliable, and almost nonexistent, for the most part, beyond the mountains. She knew, also, that this was probably the last time that she would ever see her father on this earth, but she had deliberately purposed not to dim the last day with sad thoughts. "Let's have a good breakfast," she said, grabbing her father's arm and moving into the dining room where Anne was working with Martha, putting the breakfast on the table.

"It's all set," Anne said. "Come and sit down."

"What about Will and Rebekah?"

"I'll get them," Sarah said. "They're out kissing in the garden."

Everyone laughed, but no one rebuked the young girl. She dashed out the door, and soon the young couple came back, Will holding Rebekah's hands despite the dictates of decorum. It had taken some persuasion to get Rebekah to sit at the table with the family she had served so long, and now her grandmother looked at her proudly without saying a word. Her heart was full as she recognized that this granddaughter of hers was now going to have a life that was better than she had ever dreamed of for her.

They sat down, but most of them discovered that despite the succulent food and the abundance of it, none of them could eat much. They did the best they could, but everyone's mind was on the events of the day—a mixture of melancholy and anticipation. Finally, the time came when Patrick said, "Well, we've got a long way to go. I expect the carriage is waiting."

Everyone looked at William, and he dropped his head for a moment. His face was filled with emotion, and choking back tears, he looked up and said, "You'll have to forgive an old man for being overcome. The only thing that sustains me is that I know that God is in this."

Anne Martin reached over and put her hand on her husband's, holding it tightly. The pain of losing part of her family was harder on her than she had expected. She had gotten to know Patrick better in the last three months than in all the years before. From the many talks they shared in the garden, she had discovered him to be a better man than she had ever thought. "We'll miss you, but you'll be in our prayers every day—every day of our lives, I promise you. We love you very much."

They all joined hands and bowed their heads then, and William said the final prayer, asking God to bless them on their journey.

The entire family made the trip to the wharves in Boston where the ship was set to sail for Virginia. With the final bustle of excitement, Andrew and Sarah became practically frantic, and Patrick had to corral them. Holding them by the back of their necks, he said, "Be still now and say good-bye to your grandmother and grandfather."

The tears could not be contained then, for they all knew that this could well be a final farewell. When William put his arms around Elizabeth, he said huskily, "Christians never say good-bye, you know."

Elizabeth swallowed hard, sobbed for moment, then clung to him and nodded. "That's right, Father. So I won't say good-bye. Thank you for all you've been to me." After kissing her mother and clinging to her, she turned and hugged Will and Rebekah and Mrs. Edwards. Then climbing on board the ship, they stood on the deck as the bell sounded. The huge craft began to move, slowly at first, then picked up speed as the sails filled with the stiff breeze. None of them said anything; even the children were subdued. Finally the ship cleared the harbor, and the figures at the dock faded away.

Patrick said huskily, "Well, we're on our own now. Just the four of us."

Andrew looked up and said, "No, there are five of us."

Patrick looked down at his son. "What do you mean, five?"

"Don't you remember the story of the three men and the fiery furnace? The king said, 'I see four men in the furnace, and one of them is likened to the Son of God.'"

Elizabeth suddenly knelt down, grabbed her son, and held him. She squeezed him tightly and then stood up and looked at her family. "That's right. We're not four—we're *five*. Now, we're going over the misty mountains, and who knows what great things God has for us there. . . ."

PART III

Westward Journey

August 1770 – September 1770

Thou shalt bring them in, and plant them
in the mountain of thine inheritance, in the place,
O Lord, which thou hast made for thee to dwell in,
in the Sanctuary, O Lord,
which thy hands have established.

Exodus 15:17

Watauga

Seventeen

*H*awk and Sequatchie had been hunting deer, walking in a large circle through the western range of mountains, and for days they had not seen a living soul. Unless they caught sight of an Indian, it was unlikely they would see another human being, much less a white man, this far west in the wilderness. Leading their packhorses out of a small valley walled on both sides with dense evergreens, a rider suddenly appeared out of the thick growth ahead. Both men threw their rifles up. Hawk's finger was on the trigger, for he had learned to be cautious. Yet, his keen eyes had identified the man, and now he slipped off his horse and tied the animal to a tree as the long hunter came forward.

"Well, I declare! I never expected to see you, Daniel."

Boone had a scraggly beard, which made him look somewhat older. His pale blue eyes lit up with pleasure at the sight of his friends, and he put out his hand, saying, "Spencer, good to see you." He turned and winked at the Indian, shaking hands with him, too, and saying, "Sequatchie, you still running around with this old coot? I'd think you could find better company to keep."

Sequatchie's eyes showed a trace of humor. "Someone has to watch Hawk to keep him straight, Boone," he said.

"I reckon that's gospel." Boone looked at the heavily laden pack animals and grinned. "Seems like you found a deerskin or two."

"Hunting's been good out this way," Hawk said. He noticed that Boone's pack animal was carrying only the minimum of equipment that a long hunter took with him on his hunts. "Are you just starting out?"

"I'm meeting up with a bunch. We need to get a heap of pelts,

Hawk. Times are a little bit hard, and it looks like they might get harder."

"What's happening back across the mountains?" Hawk asked.

"Oh, the British are still having it out with Sam Adams. I reckon there's going to be trouble with the Redcoats one of these days." He gave Hawk a curious look. "What would you do if Sam Adams stirred everybody up, and we got into a shootin' war with the British? We been fightin' on their side for a long time now. It'd be a bit hard to draw a bead on fellers that you fought with."

"I hope it won't come to that." Hawk leaned on his rifle. His thick jet black hair caught the sun as he pulled his coonskin cap off and ran his hand through it. He was thirty-five years old but still retained the vigor he'd had when he was eighteen. He studied the ground for a moment and then looked up and met Boone's eyes. "I guess we'll have to do whatever comes, Daniel. It would go hard, though, as you say."

"What about my people? How do the settlers feel about them?" Sequatchie asked.

Boone shifted uneasily. "Well, I guess you know how I feel, Sequatchie. I reckon there's room for everybody, but not everybody feels that way."

"No, there never will be enough room for everybody," Sequatchie said. A gloomy expression crossed his face. He had made up his mind that if the Cherokee were to survive, they would have to surrender and seek a new way of life. "It will be hard for my people to change their ways . . . but they must do it. There is no other way for us."

Boone and Hawk exchanged knowing glances. Both of them felt pity for the Indians that were caught in a part of history that baffled them. For hundreds of years the Cherokees had hunted in these lands without interference, and now suddenly there was this invasion of white settlers, pushing them farther and farther to the west. All three men knew there was only one end to that, but there was nothing that could be said about it that would change the situation.

"Let's bait up," Daniel said. He nodded to his horse, where a quarter of a deer was draped across the saddle horn. "Real fresh meat."

"Good," Hawk said. "I could use a good meal. We've traveled a ways today, and I'm starved."

All three men tied their pack animals and horses out to graze. Then they gathered wood, and soon the smell of roasting meat filled the air. Their arduous travels required a tremendous amount of energy, so there was no spare flesh on any of them. They were all lean and hearty, and their muscles were strong, for they lived on meat, for the most part. They ate without ceremony, and when they were through, they all sat back.

"How's your family, Daniel?" Hawk asked.

"Fine as froghair!" Boone spoke of his family for a while, and then finally inquired, "Did you hear about the new treaty with the Cherokees?"

"No," Sequatchie spoke up at once, his eyes alert. "What sort of treaty?"

"Well, this fall at Lochaber—that's in South Carolina—a fellow named Stuart negotiated a treaty with your people. You remember the one called the Hard Labor Line that gave the settlers rights to the upper Holsten valley?"

"Yes, I thought it was a fair treaty, but I thought that would end it. We've given up so much land already."

Boone reached out and circled his knees with his arms, placing his chin on them. He stared off at the woods, studying the movement of the trees, listening intently—a habit of his. "Well, this time they gave the settlers a triangle of territory west of that land. It's about seventy miles from Fort Chiswell to a new point six miles west of Long Island—Long Island of the Holsten."

"The Long Island," Sequatchie murmured. His eyes grew dreamy and he said, "It is the holy place of my people. They will never give up the Long Island."

"I hope they won't have to," Boone nodded. "But there'll be new settlers moving in there before long. It's rich land. I crossed the Blue Ridge back in 1760."

"I saw your sign there," Sequatchie said.

"My sign?" Boone looked up.

"Yes, I found a tree with your carving, 'D. Boone cilled a bar.'"

Boone smiled. "I'd forgotten about that. That was some bar, too! Big as a house he was, almost, and fat as a possum. Anyway, that's good country there. It's on the Watauga River. Traders been goin' in and out of there a little bit, but nothin' like we're going to see."

"I would like to see that place again," Sequatchie said. "I grew up there as a boy. My father taught me many things there."

"I'm headin' that way to meet the other hunters," Boone said. "Why don't you two tag along? It'd pleasure me to have your company."

"Well, we've got plenty of deer hides. I don't reckon it'd set us back none," Hawk said. He enjoyed Daniel Boone's company, for the man was already a local legend and held a fascination for him. There was something about Boone that drew Hawk, and he made up his mind instantly. "Sequatchie, let's go along. Maybe we'll find a way to get rid of these deer hides, if we can find a trader there."

"Might be you'd find one," Boone agreed. "Well, if you've baited up enough, why don't we start out now?"

Hawk and Sequatchie agreed to go, and so the three men packed up their gear and mounted. As they made their way down the trail, they listened intently while Boone talked of the vast lands that lay to the west. He had an almost poetic gift of making things come alive, and both Sequatchie and Hawk marveled at the man's knowledge of the wilderness.

"Men, let me make you known to William Bean," Boone said. The three men had ridden into a settlement, consisting of half a dozen cabins, and had been met by a tall, lanky individual who had come out with a musket in his hands. He put it down at once and greeted Boone cheerfully, then turned to look at the visitors.

"This here's William Bean. William, this fella here, he's got a fancy name—Jehoshaphat Spencer. But he prefers to be called Hawk. And this here is Sequatchie. I reckon as how you may have heard of him."

William Bean studied the two visitors. He was a typical frontiersman, lanky and strong, with a pair of alert brown eyes, and a patch of brown hair. He nodded, stepped forward, and put his hand out. When it closed down on Hawk's, it was like a vise. "Glad to know you, Hawk," he said. He shook hands with Sequatchie and spoke to him in Cherokee, and the two grinned.

"Looks like you'uns nabbed every deer in the forest," Bean said, looking at the heavily laden pack animals.

"We had a good hunt," Hawk nodded. "We're lookin' to trade some now."

"I'd suspect so," Bean said. "And I reckon you're in luck. There's a trader come in just two days ago. He had his pack animals loaded down with everything a fella could want. Lookin' to haul back deerskins."

"Where is he?" Hawk asked quickly.

"Oh, not more'n a few miles down the trail there. He ain't had much luck so far, so he'll likely be right glad to see your pelts."

"That sounds good," Boone said. "I'm takin' a bunch out myself. Maybe we could make a quick hunt and do some tradin' with him."

Bean was studying Hawk with a careful glance. "Likely you know your way around if you been able to get this many hides."

"Sequatchie does." Hawk smiled. "He's taught me a little bit."

"If it ain't unmannerly, what you aim to do after you trade your hides for goods?"

Hawk nodded toward Sequatchie. "We'll take most of the goods to Sequatchie's village."

"How far is that?"

"Two—three days," Sequatchie said.

Bean pulled his hat off, turned it around in his hands, then he suddenly said, "Oh, I plumb forgot to introduce my family. This here's my wife, Lydia." Lydia Bean was a small woman with reddish hair and blue eyes. She was holding a newborn infant, and she smiled and nodded to the two hunters.

"That's my youngest son, Russell, my wife's holdin'. My other kids are off runnin' around."

"Looks like he's fresh out of the shell," Daniel said.

"I reckon he is. Probably the first white child born in this territory. Maybe they'll name it after him, Russellville or something like that."

Bean stood there, talking and drawing circles in the dirt with his moccasin. It was apparent that something was on his mind, and he said finally, "You say two days and you might be back to your village?"

Sequatchie nodded. "Yes, I think so."

"I got me kind of a problem," Bean said. "The settlement here is small. We got more folks that want to come, but they're on the other side of the mountains. I'd go get 'em myself, but I'd be afeered, what with a new baby and all." He looked at the two men and said,

"Might be you'd be willin' to go and guide 'em over the mountains to the settlement here?"

Boone said instantly, "I'd take it as a personal favor, Hawk, if you and Sequatchie could help out here. William needs all the help he can get to put in corn and make this settlement go."

Hawk had already decided not to go, but when Daniel Boone asked a personal favor, well, that made things different. At once he said, "Be glad to go bring your people in, Bean, if that's all right with you, Sequatchie."

"I will go after we trade and take the supplies to my people."

"Well now, that's right neighborly of you," Bean said. A look of relief washed across his face, and he went to his wife and put his arm around her. "Now, you're going to have company to show that new baby of yourn off to!"

Lydia Bean smiled. "Dinner's almost ready. Y'all tie your animals up and come on in."

The men went inside, and Lydia Bean quickly prepared a meal. It was simple food, but she had killed one of the pigs, and Bean had barbecued it. It was a treat for the men, for they had eaten nothing but wild game for weeks.

"Where are your people located, Bean?" Hawk asked.

"They are gathering at Williamsburg."

Hawk had started to lift a portion of rib to his lips. He halted abruptly, and Sequatchie, who knew his friend well, saw the dark look that clouded Hawk's face.

Bean noticed it also, as did Boone, and said, "You know Williamsburg, don't you?"

"Oh yes. I know Williamsburg," Hawk said. He bit into the succulent meat and chewed it thoughtfully. A reluctance had risen in him suddenly. He had done all he could to put Williamsburg and all that had happened there out of his mind, and now it was back again. For years he had steadfastly refused to return—and the thoughts of his son and his parents had become dim.

Sequatchie, however, said, "It will not take long. We will leave as soon as we take the goods to my people."

Bean was relieved, for he had seen Hawk's face darken and noted the displeasure at the mention of Williamsburg. Something had disturbed the tall hunter, but Bean decided not to question Hawk further. He would ask Boone later.

Three days had passed, and now that the two men had delivered the trade goods to Sequatchie's village, Hawk felt even more reluctant about returning to Williamsburg. He squatted beside the fire inside Sequatchie's hut and talked with Awenasa in Cherokee. She had become rather feeble in her old age, but her mind was clear. He liked to speak to her in the Cherokee tongue. Though there would always be more to learn, he had become quite fluent in the guttural language. He listened as she smiled and told him about the babies that had been born, the fights the young men had had, and the various disagreements that had taken place in their absence.

Awenasa set a bowl of stew before him, and he ate it slowly, for it was very hot. "Good," he said and patted his stomach. He remembered the first time he had eaten puppy dog stew, but he knew this was a fish stew. The Cherokee were expert fishermen with their white oak baskets, and Awenasa was the best of cooks.

"You will leave again soon?"

"Yes, we will, but I do not like it."

The old woman turned from the fire and looked at him. "Why will you go, then?"

"I do it as a favor to a friend."

"That is good. Friends are hard to make."

"Yes, they are, and I reckon, apart from Sequatchie, Daniel Boone's about the best friend I have."

"How long will you be gone?"

Hawk moved his shoulders restlessly and said, "I do not know. It depends on how many settlers are traveling west."

Awenasa nodded, and as soon as Hawk finished the stew, he rolled up in his blanket and fell into a restless sleep.

The next morning Sequatchie found Hawk and said, "Let us go to Williamsburg."

Hawk was standing beside a tall alder that had been left in the clearing among the Cherokees' cabins. He stripped the bark off of it, pulled out his knife, and began whittling at it, not answering. Finally Hawk said, "Sequatchie, I don't want to go back to Williamsburg."

"You said to Boone that you'd go."

"I know what I said, but you know the way to Williamsburg.

You can go bring those settlers back to Watauga."

Sequatchie shook his head. "They are white people who do not know this country. They've heard many stories, I think, of how evil the red man is, and how they butcher people and scalp. They would not trust themselves to me. You must go with me."

Hawk stopped whittling on the tree. He shoved the knife back in his belt and turned to face his friend, saying frankly, "I know I promised Daniel I'd go, but it grates on me, Sequatchie."

"Why do you hold back? What is there that frightens you?"

Hawk was offended. "I'm not frightened! It's just that—well, it was not a good time for me in Williamsburg."

Sequatchie knew that Hawk had grown up in Williamsburg, although the tall hunter had spoken very little of his life there. Now he said, "Is there a woman there that you left behind?" He saw the pain leap into Hawk's eyes and knew that he had struck a nerve. He reached out and touched his friend's arm. "I do not want to cause you grief, my friend."

"That's all right, Sequatchie." Hawk stood silently for a moment, then said finally, "There was a woman there. My wife. Her name was Faith. . . ." The words would not come, and suddenly a picture of Faith's features came to him as they had before, but had not for a long time. Without his willing it, the loss and the grief that her death had brought struck a fresh blow. His lips tightened, and he turned his face away from Sequatchie, saying nothing for a while.

Sequatchie studied his friend, and being a man of great intuition, he said, "She died, this wife of yours?"

"Yes, she died." The words were short and clipped.

"There were no children in your lodge?"

Hawk suddenly gave his friend a harsh look. He did not answer directly but said, "All right, I will go with you, and we will bring them back. After that, I never want to see Williamsburg again!"

That morning, the two men left, and for several days they rode their animals steadily. As they headed eastward, they began to see more and more cabins and settlements. Hawk rode side by side with Sequatchie, saying almost nothing. Finally, one night, after they had made camp and sat around the small fire staring at the fiery sparks that floated up toward the heavens, Sequatchie said quietly, "You left a child in Williamsburg."

Hawk looked up, startled. His mind had been on Faith and his son ever since they'd ridden out of Bean's settlement. He knew, however, he could not deceive his friend. "Yes, I did. My wife had a baby, and she died having him. That is why I left. I couldn't face living without her."

"Who has the boy?"

"My parents."

Neither of them was a man of many words. Finally, out of the silence, Sequatchie said, "A boy needs a father to teach him what is right."

"My parents can do that. My father's a better man than I am."

"But you are his father." He hesitated, then said, "I think God is leading you back to that place."

"Don't talk to me about God!" Hawk snapped.

Sequatchie had already learned how hardened Hawk was against any mention of God. Nevertheless, now he said, "You are foolish to deny God! Look up there!" He waved his hands to the stars that spangled the dark heavens. "Do you think they made themselves?" He held up his hand and made it into a fist. "Look at these fingers that know how to trap and hunt and live off the land. Look at all a man can do. Do you think he made himself? No, God has made all things. You have read over and over how God made man, and He saw that it was good. And He made woman, and He saw that was good. And when they came together and had a child, that was good."

"It wasn't good that God killed my wife!"

"I cannot answer all of these things. Men live and die, but God is always the same. Jehovah, God in the Bible, and the Lord Jesus. You have read, He changes not."

"You're the one who believes the Bible! Not me! I just read it to you!"

Sequatchie knew that arguing was useless. He stared into the fire, praying for his friend for a long time. He had listened along with his people as Hawk had read the Bible through. It had been wonderful. He looked across the fire to where Hawk was staring out into the darkness. Sequatchie admired the strength of the man. Hawk had already surpassed most of the Cherokees in many of their native skills. He could run faster, was stronger, and was absolutely unerring with a rifle. He was fearless, too, Sequatchie knew, which all the Indians of the village admired. But for some reason Hawk was destroying himself, and it grieved Sequatchie. He prayed, *Oh, God, my friend needs to know you! You must speak to him. He has read your words out of your book, but it has not touched his heart. Oh, God, I pray that his heart might be broken so that he might hear the voice of his God. . . !*

Hawk's Son

Eighteen

A cold snap had gripped Williamsburg in August of 1770, making everyone expect a cold winter was on the way. Mr. and Mrs. Spencer were sitting inside the parlor, sharing the warmth of a crackling fire. The pleasant smell of burning wood came faintly into the room, and the yellow and red flames danced in the hearth, sending sparks flying up the huge chimney.

Esther Spencer was knitting, and from time to time she looked outside the mullioned windows and watched the white clouds as they scudded across a dark blue sky. The brisk wind stripped the leaves from the oak trees in the front yard, then sent them tumbling madly through the air until they hit the streets, where they piled themselves into small mountains, only to be scattered again when another gust of wind came.

"Going to be cold. Never saw August so cool," Mr. Spencer said. He was sitting across from his wife in a Regency style beechwood fauteuil, which had an arched, padded back and carvings of foliage and shells and was covered in a chocolate brown woolen moreen. Looking up from reading his Bible, he shook his head. "It seems like the times are changing. The next thing you know we'll be having snow in the middle of August."

Jacob Spencer, sitting across the room on a cushion, looked up at his grandfather. He was fourteen years old and had thick dark hair and the darkest blue eyes James had ever seen. He was a sturdy boy, tall and lean, but he would fill out one day to be a strong man. "Snow in August? That's not possible, Grandfather!"

James Spencer laughed. "Anything's possible, I guess, Jake. Not very likely, though, I will admit." He looked over fondly at his grandson and said, "What are you reading now?"

"The *Odyssey*."

"You're getting to be quite a scholar."

"Not really. I'm reading the English translation. I'd like to learn Greek, though."

"Would you?" James Spencer cocked one eyebrow and looked at the boy thoughtfully. "I suppose we can arrange for a tutor if that's what you really want."

"I think it would be fun."

"Well, you did like Latin . . . and you did well in it, too," he said rather proudly. He winked at his wife and said, "What would you think if we had a lawyer on our hands, Esther?"

Esther looked across at the boy, her knitting needles clicking faintly in the room. "Would you like to be a lawyer, Jacob?" she asked.

"I don't think so."

"What would you like to be? We've talked about this before. Pretty soon you're going to have to make up your mind. You're growing up fast."

Jacob Spencer did not answer for a time. He was not a young man who spoke a great deal. There was a quietness about him, although sometimes with young people he would throw his reticence aside and join in with the frivolity of his peers. Now, however, in the quietness of the room, he thought of the question and shook his head. "I don't know, but I'll think about it, and as soon as I decide I'll let you know."

Again James winked at his wife and said, "Well, that will be good—" He broke off, interrupted by a knock on the front door.

The door opened, and Ellen, the maid, entered and said, in her quiet voice, "There's a gentleman to see you, sir."

"Who is it?" asked James.

"He doesn't say. Shall I show him in?"

"Is he a tradesman?"

"I . . . I don't think so, Mr. Spencer," Ellen said.

Spencer studied the puzzled look in the maid's eyes and said, "Well, have him come in, then. Bring him into the parlor where it's warm."

"Yes, sir."

"I wonder who that can be? Ellen knows everybody in town, I think," Esther said calmly.

"I can't imagine." He looked over at Jake, who had lost interest and was buried again in the book that he held on his knees. *It would take a blast of black powder to jolt that boy out of a book when he gets into it,* James thought. He had no time to think more, for he glanced up and his heart seemed to skip a beat. He stood up at once and found that his knees were not quite steady. Glancing over, he saw that Esther had risen also, then both of them moved forward at the same time.

"Josh!" James Spencer cried, and he heard his wife's sobs coming quickly as they moved across the room. It had been almost fifteen years since they had seen their son, and this tall tanned man wearing buckskins could have passed them on the street unnoticed, but in this house, even though the years had thickened the wide body of their son and brought some creases into his brown face, they recognized him immediately.

Jacob looked up with astonishment, seeing his grandparents run across the room. The tall stranger opened his arms and put them around the two. He towered over them both, and Jacob suddenly found himself, for some reason, afraid. From the reactions of his grandparents, he realized that this man must be his father. The years of loneliness when he had not seen him swept over Jacob. It was a strange feeling for him. There was a longing to rush forward and join the little group, but he merely stood to his feet and held the book tightly in one hand, staring at the three. A hardness gripped him, and he remembered the years when he was a small child and he had wept silently in his bed night after night, longing for his father. And now he suddenly appeared—yet the man standing before him was a total stranger.

Hawk felt strange and uncomfortable. It had been a long time since he had been to Williamsburg. His parents, he saw, had grown almost totally gray, and as he held them, they seemed very frail to him. And then he looked over at the boy who was staring at him. *He looks exactly as I did at his age.* He detached himself from his parents and walked over to the boy. "Well, Jacob, look at you. Almost a man," he said quietly.

Jake swallowed hard. He did not move but stood there stiffly. He could not think of a thing to say, and he could not bring himself to embrace his father. The only people he had ever embraced were his grandparents. Finally he said, "Good day, sir."

Hawk blinked at the terseness he heard in his son's voice, but the thought came, *We're strangers, not father and son.* And that brought another streak of pain, for despite the strong resemblance to himself, he saw many of Faith's features in the boy. Memories flooded back of that night Faith had died and he had walked out.

"Come and sit down. Tell us where you've been—what you've been doing." Esther came and took Hawk's arm. "Josh, you look so *brown.*"

"A man gets that way when he stays outdoors in the woods all the time."

"When did you get in?" James asked.

"Just late last night. My friend Sequatchie is waiting outside."

"Waiting outside? Well, go bring him in!"

"All right, but not everybody wants an Indian in their home."

"I'm surprised you would say a thing like that!" James said. "Any friend of yours is welcome here. Go bring him in this instant!"

Hawk rose, opened the door, and went outside. "Come on in, Sequatchie."

Sequatchie entered hesitantly, for it was he who had insisted on remaining outside. He was wearing his usual dress of fringed buckskins and moccasins. His single scalp-lock hung down his back, and he looked smooth and polished without lines in his face.

"This is my friend Sequatchie. Sequatchie, this is my father and mother, and this is my son, Jacob."

Sequatchie greeted the family and said, "It is good to be in your home." He looked over toward Jacob and studied the boy carefully. Turning to Hawk, he said, "You have a fine son. He looks like you."

There was a moment's embarrassed silence, and then Esther Spencer began at once, saying, "I must fix you something to eat. You must be hungry."

Hawk protested, but he could tell that she really wanted to make him and Sequatchie feel welcome. They all sat down in front of the fire, and after his mother came back from instructing Ellen about the food, he said, "I'm sorry that I've been gone so long. Time just seems to have slipped by." He wanted desperately to apologize, to tell them how hard it was for him to come back to this house. It was like a knife piercing his heart. The night that Faith had died here was still painfully vivid in his memory after all these years.

"We're just glad you've come now, and we're glad that you're here, too, Sequatchie," Esther said. "Have you known our son a long time?"

"Yes, we are brothers."

"Sequatchie saved my life," Hawk said, then he began to tell them how he had met Sequatchie, and how his Cherokee friend had given him a new name. "My name is Hawk on the other side of the mountains. I'm more comfortable with that, but it probably won't be easy for you."

"Hawk ... well, that's a strong name," James Spencer said. "Now, tell us what you've been doing out there."

Awkwardly Hawk began to speak of his life over the mountains. Sequatchie sat back, and finally when the food was brought in on a tray, he tasted it with interest. It was a fine white cake, and he did not wait for a spoon but picked it up in his hand and ate it.

Across the room, Jacob suddenly grinned, the first sign of life that he had shown. Sequatchie caught it and smiled at the boy. "Good," he said. "You eat, too."

Jacob had kept himself back out of the group, but now he reached out and took the plate that his grandmother had offered. Ignoring the fork, he picked up the cake with his hand and stuffed it into his mouth. "Good," he said to Sequatchie, smiling.

Hawk saw instantly that the boy had a sense of humor, and he was glad that Jacob had made the gesture of friendship toward the Indian.

Time seemed to drag very slowly, and if it had not been for James, who had skillfully drawn Sequatchie out by entertaining them with his stories of Indian life, it would have been even more awkward.

Finally, James sensed that it might be okay to leave Hawk and Jacob alone, and he said, "Sequatchie, you come with me. Mrs. Spencer and I will show you how we live here. Then someday maybe I'll come across the mountains and you can show me your home."

The three left the room, and after a long silence in which neither spoke, Hawk finally said, "How have you been?"

"Very well, sir."

Another long silence filled the room and Hawk thought, *This is not going to be easy. We have nothing to talk about.* "Do you like your studies?"

"Yes, sir."

Politeness—that was all. There was a coldness in the boy's tone, and Hawk desperately wanted to break through it, but the harder he tried, the more difficult the one-sided conversation became. He got up finally and looked out the window, saying, "Fine day outside. I could go around and see some of the places where I used to go when I was a boy. Maybe you could come with me."

Jake was staring at his father, his eyes hooded. Abruptly he asked, "Why did you run off and leave me?"

There was such anger and pain in the tone of his son that Hawk could have taken an arrow in the back with less of a shock. When he'd first left, he had gone over this in his own mind many times, trying hard to come up with a good answer. Now, he went over to where the boy was standing and reached out and placed his hand on his shoulder. "I nearly lost my mind when your mother died, son," he said quietly. He tried to explain how the loss of his wife had brought such pain that he could not bear to think of it. He related how he had fled, almost like a madman. "I . . . I know I was wrong to leave you," he said. "But I was almost crazy. I would've been no man for a young boy to be around," he said lamely.

"You didn't have to leave!" Jacob said.

"Your grandfather and your grandmother have done a better job of raising you than I could have."

Jacob's eyes burned with bitterness, and he said, "You left me! Do you know what it's like to be without anybody?"

"You have your grandparents."

"I didn't have a mother, and I didn't have a father!"

Hawk had never felt exactly as he did at that moment. Guilt welled up in him. He knew he had been wrong, and finally he said, "Son, try to understand. I . . . I can't live in a town. I have to be out-of-doors. I have to be moving or I'll go crazy."

"You could've taken me with you!"

Hawk felt the boy's shoulder tense under his hand and he said quietly, "I couldn't have taken a baby with me into the woods! I nearly died myself. The first few years I was out there, it was just a matter of trying to stay alive every day. I couldn't have taken care of you!"

Jacob looked up, and his lips trembled as he said, "How . . . how long are you going to stay? A long time?"

Hawk cleared his throat. "Well . . . no. We're leaving tomorrow to take a group of settlers back over the mountains—"

"Go on! See if I care!" Jacob slapped his father's hand away and ran out of the room, his eyes bleared with tears. He almost ran into his grandmother. Dodging by her, he ran out of the house.

Esther came in at once and walked straight up to her son. "What's the matter with Jacob?"

Hawk turned to her, his eyes glazed with pain and frustration. "There's nothing the matter with him," he whispered. "But there's something the matter with me."

"Are you going to stay for a while?"

"No, I've got to get away, Mother."

"Josh, you've just arrived—and it's been so long. You . . . you can't leave—not now. Jacob needs a father."

"He needs a better one than I am! Father can take care of him!"

"It's not the same thing," Esther said, her eyes pleading with her son.

"He's a better father than I could ever be."

"He's getting old now, and he's not well. Jacob needs you, Jehoshaphat." She pronounced his old name, all of it, and the sound of it brought back many memories. Hawk turned away blindly and went to the window. He stared out but saw nothing. Seeing his parents and his son after all these years had deeply stirred feelings in him that he had tried so hard to avoid. His mother came over and put her arm around him. "You can't run away forever, son," she said.

Early the next morning Hawk and Sequatchie were preparing to leave. Hawk had tossed and turned all night. The previous afternoon and evening he had tried to get close to Jacob, but the boy had merely stared at him harshly, his lips drawn into a tight line.

Sequatchie had wisely said nothing. But he had seen the pain in the boy, and the longing to have his father stay. Desperately, he wanted to do something to bring Hawk to his senses. He had prayed, but he knew that Hawk did not want to hear about God. When they rose that morning and went down to breakfast, Jacob was not there.

After they sat down, Mr. Spencer asked the blessing, and Hawk asked, "Is Jacob sick?"

"No," Esther said simply. She tried to think of some way to soften what the boy had told her, which was, "I never want to see him again! He doesn't care anything about me!" Looking at her son, tears threatening to spill over, she simply said, "Jacob does not want to see you."

Hawk started to say something but stopped. He felt miserable and ate only a few bites. He pushed the food around on his plate, and finally when the meal was over, he stood up and said, "Well, they'll be waiting for us. We've got to get them over the mountains safely." He moved to the front door, accompanied by Sequatchie, then he turned. His mother embraced him, and tears ran down her cheeks.

"Come back safe. Your father and I, we pray for you every day."

"I . . . I know you do, Mother."

James Spencer embraced his son also. His heart was breaking at the thought of Josh leaving so soon. He wanted to hold him tightly and keep him from going. His voice choking with emotion, James muttered, "We love you here, Josh. We always will. Remember that."

Upstairs, Jacob was in his room. He was crying, and as he looked out of the window, keeping well back, he saw his father and Sequatchie step outside and move around to the side of the house where the stable was located. Soon they came out, mounted, and rode away. The sounds of the horses' hooves rang on the stone pavement, and Jacob's eyes blurred so that he could not see clearly. He watched until his father and Sequatchie disappeared, and then with a choking sob, threw himself on the bed and stuffed the bedclothes against his face so that he made no sound as he lay there weeping.

The Journey Begins

Nineteen

*A*s the two long hunters made their way down through the busy streets of Williamsburg, Sequatchie's eyes ran over the assorted shops and townspeople in bewilderment. Several times he stopped and asked, "What is this place?" At one of them he insisted that Hawk go inside. It was a wigmaker's establishment, and Sequatchie had never seen anything like it. Because of France's King Louis XIII, wigs were all the rage. As rumor had it, the young French king was going bald at twenty-three. He became depressed and put on a wig, and soon all his courtiers followed suit. Soon women followed, adorning their wigs with jewels and fresh flowers. European wigs were quite colorful, and some even dared to wear blue or pink ones. The colonists were more reserved and stayed with the natural colors, though there was a preference for white powdered wigs.

Sequatchie prowled around the store, and the diminutive wigmaker's eyes never left him. The man's hands were trembling, and Hawk grinned, for he saw that the wigmaker expected to be scalped.

Hawk was amused by Sequatchie's curiosity, and he said, "How about if I buy one of these for you, Sequatchie?" He picked up a large wig with masses of curls and stuck it on the Indian's head.

Sequatchie glanced at the mirror in front of him and was startled at his strange reflection. Jerking the wig off, he threw it at Hawk and said, "White men are foolish!"

"I expect you're right about that, Sequatchie. At least where wigs are concerned."

Sequatchie stomped out of the shop, and the wigmaker gave an audible sigh of relief. As they made their way farther, Sequatchie asked many questions about Williamsburg and the ways of the people who lived there. Finally, turning to face Hawk, he ventured, "Maybe sometime soon we come back and visit your son."

"Maybe," Hawk grunted.

Encouraged by even this much response, Sequatchie said quietly, "A boy is like a piece of pottery. You've seen the squaws make them. When they're soft, they can mold the clay into any shape they like, but when the clay gets hard, it's too late. What's done is done." He paused and glanced at his friend. "Boys are like that. Your boy's already almost a man, but he needs you still."

Hawk shook his head. He did not want to talk about it and quickly changed the subject. "I've got a friend I want you to meet. We'll pick up some supplies at his place and then go meet these folks we're supposed to guide back to Bean's settlement."

———

Jacques Cartier entered *The Brown Stag* and ran his eyes across the room. At once he saw Rhoda Harper, who had her back to him as she stood behind the short bar, putting glasses on a shelf. Stealthily the big man advanced and without warning threw his arms around the woman, squeezing her. "Ah," he said. "You little pigeon! I am back!"

Rhoda was accustomed to being grabbed and mauled by those who frequented the place. It went with being a tavern girl. When she turned around, however, and saw the face of the man who held her, she gasped. "Jacques!"

Cartier grinned and kissed her noisily. "Yes, little pigeon. It's been a long time. Too long! But now I am back, as you see." He looked carefully and saw that she had aged somewhat. Her smooth face had a few lines that were not there the last time he saw her. But her figure was better than ever, fuller and rounder. "Come," he said. "We must talk."

Rhoda did not protest as he led her out of the tavern to the single door at the back. She followed him inside the small room with a table and four chairs used for card games and meals. She sat down in the chair, leaned over, and put her chin in her palm. "I didn't expect to see you ever come back here, Jacques. As a matter of fact, I heard you were dead!"

"I am in good health, for a dead man," Cartier said.

He was lolling in the chair, and she saw a scar across his neck and down to his chest that had not been there before. He looked tired and worn, but Rhoda knew how strong he was. The buckskins were molded to his muscles, which were large and heavy. "What are you doing in Williamsburg? I thought the French had all left this country."

"No, we have not all left. There's still a few of us here, and we have some big plans."

"Frenchmen aren't too popular around Williamsburg," Rhoda said.

"Ah, what does it matter what they think of Jacques Cartier? Let them say so, and I'll slit their throat."

"You haven't changed, Jacques."

"You have not changed either. Still the beautiful Rhoda!"

He sat there boasting about his exploits, and Rhoda wondered why he had come back to the Colonies. Since the Line of Demarcation, most of the French had left the country. Finally she said, "I know you, Jacques. You're not here for nothing."

"That is right, my Rhoda. I have come to do you a big favor."

Rhoda laughed without humor. She ran her hand through her hair and shook it free, saying, "You never did a favor for anyone in your life!"

"Maybe I am a changed man."

"And maybe the moon's made out of buttermilk! What are you up to, Jacques?"

"I have a little job that I want you to do for me, and I will pay you well. Look." He pulled out a leather thong around his neck and extracted a heavy deerskin bag suspended on it. Tossing it into the air, he caught it, and it made a musical clinking sound. "Gold," he grinned. "Lots of gold, and some for you if you do this little job for me."

"What kind of a job would I do for you?"

Cartier leaned forward and whispered, "There is a party of settlers that will be leaving Williamsburg soon. They are going to a place called the Watauga. I want you to join up with them."

"Why should I go there? Where is it?"

"Very far away. Across the mountains."

"I don't want to go there. I'm afraid of the Indians."

"As long as Jacques is around, no Indian will harm you. But that doesn't matter, you will not actually go to the mountains."

"Stop talking in riddles, Jacques. What do you want?"

"All right. Listen to me. I want you to join this group. They'll be glad to take you. They need new people at the settlement." He grinned at her, tossed the bag up, and listened to the coins jingle inside.

"And why would you want me to do that?" Rhoda demanded.

"I do not want them to reach their destination. I want them to turn back before they get to the Watauga."

"What can I do about that?"

"I will tell you what you can do. These are soft people," he said contemptuously. "It will not be hard to frighten them. Things like their cattle pulling loose and running away in the night, their food getting something in it perhaps, or their water, a wheel breaking down. It will not be hard to discourage them and turn them back."

Rhoda sat there thinking of her life. It wasn't much of an existence. Her mother had died the previous year; her brothers and sisters had all moved away. She had no reason to stay around, and she was growing older and knew that no decent man in Williamsburg would have anything to do with her. The thought of getting away, even for a while, attracted her. Finally, she looked at Cartier and said, "I'll do it . . . if no one gets hurt."

"Why should anyone get hurt? All I want them to do is come back. It will be better for them anyway. If they keep on going, those Cherokees will have their scalps. No one will get hurt. I promise you. You will do it then?"

"All right. I'll do it."

"That's my good girl. Here!" He opened the bag, poured out a few coins, and put them in her hand. "This is for you now. When you get back after the settlers return, I will give you that many more."

In Rhoda's hand was more money than she had seen in a long time. *If I can just get the rest of it, it'll be enough to leave this place,* she thought desperately. *I can start over again somewhere.*

"When do I go?" she asked.

Jacques grinned as he said, "Let's get you ready. Your new life begins now."

Rhoda could not stop herself from shuddering as she walked out the front door of *The Brown Stag* with Jacques Cartier.

———

"Josh!"

Paul Anderson had seen Hawk come in along with the Indian, but he had not recognized him. The two had walked right up to him, the Indian remaining in the background, and only when they were less than five feet away did Paul finally recognize his old friend. He moved forward and put his hands out, pleasure spreading across his face. "Josh, when did you get here? Where have you been? Look at you! A long hunter!"

"Hello, Paul. It's been quite a while. It's good to see you again." One of the pleasant things Hawk remembered about Williamsburg was being with Paul. "This is Sequatchie, my Indian brother."

"I'm happy to see you. Both of you. Come along and sit down."

"Well, we actually came to buy some supplies."

"We can take care of that later. In the meanwhile, I want to know all about what you've been doing. Come, sit down!" He practically dragged them to a table and set some apple cider down in front of them, which they drank with evident pleasure. Sequatchie had never tasted it before and finally picked up the jug, ignoring the glass.

"Help yourself, Sequatchie," Paul grinned. "Plenty more where that came from."

"You're looking well, Paul. I guess you're an old married man by now."

"No, just an old bachelor. Have you been by your folks' house yet?"

"Yes, we just came from there."

"That boy of yours. Isn't he something? Fine-looking lad! Better looking than you, I think." He expected a smile, but Hawk's face clouded and he looked down at the table.

Paul knew the loneliness of Jacob Spencer. Since Josh had left, he had become a friend to the boy and had tried to be as much of a father as possible. Once Jacob had opened up and said what was on his heart. *I wish I had a father, Mr. Anderson.*

Paul remembered the boy's words now and could almost see the boy's loneliness as it had spread across his face. Seeing his friend's reaction, Paul knew it was not the time to pursue the subject, so he said, "Let me tell you what's been going on here."

Hawk listened halfheartedly as Paul related the events happening in the Colonies. He was not really interested in Williamsburg, or Virginia, or anything except getting away from there. The town depressed him, and he wanted to return to the wilderness he now called home. But when Paul continued to press him, he told how he had become a long hunter, and then nodded to Sequatchie. "He's taught me how to be a hunter. I feel more like an Indian than a white man now. They even gave me another name—Hawk."

Sequatchie said suddenly, "He reads the Bible to my people. I tell him how to live in the wilderness. I think we have the best of it."

Paul Anderson stared first at the Indian's bronze face, and then at Hawk. "Why, I think that's wonderful," he said. "Do your people like to hear the Bible?"

"Many of them are Christians. I have been baptized myself, and so have many of my people."

He repeated the story of how a missionary had converted many of the Cherokees, and Paul Anderson's eyes grew wide. When Sequatchie finished, Anderson hesitated. He swallowed hard, then said, "You won't believe this, but God has been speaking to me. He's been calling me to go across the Appalachian Mountains as a missionary, but I've never felt the time was right, but now I feel strongly that He wants me to go to your people, Sequatchie, to the Cherokee."

Sequatchie instantly sat up straight, and his eyes gleamed. "You would come and preach to my people the gospel of Jesus?"

"God has been putting it on my heart for several years now, but I didn't see any way. I don't speak the language, and I don't know the territory."

Sequatchie shook his head. "You come! I will be the servant of the servant of God."

"Wait a minute," Hawk said. "You don't know what you're getting into! It's rough out there, Paul. A lot of men are lying in shallow graves, killed by animals, by Indians, and some by renegade whites."

"God is calling me to do it," Paul said simply. "I must go. And I take your coming at this time as a sign that it's time to go now. Sequatchie, shall we shake hands, or how do your people agree on a thing?"

Sequatchie said, "As Christians we give our word." He put his sinewy hand out, took the hand of the white man, and a broad smile spread across his face. "It will be good to have a preacher to explain the Book. Hawk reads it, but much of it we do not understand."

"Well, much of it I don't understand either, brother, but I'll do the best I can," Paul said with excitement. His eyes sparkled, and he pumped the two men with questions, finally saying, "Well, I've got plenty of money, but I don't know what to buy. Are you two going back?"

"Yes," Hawk said slowly. "We're leading a group of settlers to William Bean's little community."

"Is that far from your people, Sequatchie?"

"No, it's very close. You can come with us now."

"What all will I need?"

"Well, you'll need a gun, for one thing—a rifle," Hawk said.

"I haven't hunted since we were boys."

"Every man in the woods needs a rifle, Paul," Hawk said. "At least, I can remind you how to use it—perhaps teach you a little more." Actually the more he thought about the idea, the more he liked it. He had always liked Paul Anderson, and the thought of seeing him in his own territory pleased him. "Now," he said, "let's get you outfitted. We've got to buy you a horse, a pack animal, and quite a few other things."

"You pick it all out," Paul swept his hand. "My father will give it to me as a going-away present. Pick out some things for yourself, too."

The two long hunters began at once, and soon the counter was piled with equipment and supplies. Even as they were adding more to it, Hawk looked up to see a red-headed man walk through the door with his wife and two children.

Paul walked up to the man and said, "Good day. May I help you?"

"I think you might, sir. My name is Patrick MacNeal. This is my wife, Elizabeth, and these are my children, Andrew and Sarah."

"I'm Paul Anderson. Happy to make your acquaintance. How can I help you?"

"Well," the man said, taking off his hat and running his fingers through his red hair. "I'm putting myself at your mercy, Mr. Anderson. We're headed out over the mountains. We're going to settle out there. We've just come in from Boston, and we need just about everything."

Anderson stared at the couple. They were wearing clothes that would have been suitable in Boston, and though they looked hale and strong, neither of them looked like the pioneer type. He asked quietly, "Have you ever been over the mountains or spent a lot of time in the woods, Mr. MacNeal?"

"Hardly any. Oh, I've hunted some, but I must say my wife and I know very little. I've worked for a shipping firm, but we want to have a place of our own."

"Have you chosen a spot yet?"

"A friend of ours invited us to come along on an expedition west. Perhaps you know him—Jed Smith?"

"Well, what a coincidence!" He turned and said, "This is Hawk Spencer and his friend Sequatchie. They've come in from over the mountains to lead that same party to the settlement established by a man called William Bean."

Patrick asked excitedly, "The settlement at Watauga? Wonderful. That is where we were planning on settling."

"Will you tell us about it, Mr. Spencer?" Elizabeth said. She was fascinated by the rugged look of the tall hunter. Her eyes took in the buckskin hunting shirt, the leggings, and the coonskin cap, and her eyes brightened. "What's it like living on the other side of the mountains?"

"Well, you'd have to ask Sequatchie, here. He's been there all of his life."

Sequatchie was studying the small group closely. He said at once, "Hard place, but a good place."

"It sounds like what I've heard," Patrick MacNeal said. "I wonder if you could give us any advice, Mr. Anderson."

"Well, as it happens, I'm going out myself. God's called me to be a missionary to the Cherokee, and I'm about as green as you are." He grinned and said, "Sequatchie is going to make sure that I do the right thing. I'm sure the group going out would be glad to include you."

"Isn't that wonderful, Elizabeth? We made it in time to join the wagon train." The man turned to his wife, then to his son and daughter, saying, "Do you hear that? We're going to join some other settlers and start our own farm."

"Can I have a horse, Pa?" the boy asked.

"Well, I would think we'd all need animals, wouldn't we, Mr. Anderson?"

"Oh yes, and pack animals, too. Several of them. You'll need farming equipment, and it'll be rather expensive, I'm afraid."

"We have plenty of money to get us started. Is this your store?"

"It belongs to my father. My brothers run it mostly, but for new folks like you, I can get whatever you need at good, honest prices."

"We'd be very grateful to you," Elizabeth said. "It must be God's will, for we don't know a soul."

Hawk replied, "I don't know if God's in it or not, but Sequatchie can tell you everything you need to know about that country. Daniel Boone's out there, and he'll be a help, too."

"Do you know Daniel Boone?" Andrew MacNeal gasped. "I heard about him!"

"I guess a lot of people have heard about Boone," Hawk said. "How old are you, boy?"

"Thirteen. Going on fourteen, though."

"Well, you can't go in those clothes. They wouldn't last an hour on the trail. You'll have to have something tougher than that."

"What should I wear, Mr. Hawk?"

"Just Hawk is fine. I guess Mr. Anderson can help you get outfitted. I'll be glad to introduce you to the settlers who are going, but there'll be no problem with you joining up with them."

That settled the matter. It took the rest of the day to find four horses and pack animals for the group. By the time they paid for all their goods it was late afternoon. Hawk led the little procession out of town, and Paul Anderson kept pace with him. "I don't know any of these settlers," he said. "But I know Bean. He's a good fellow." He looked cautiously back and studied the faces of the MacNeals. "I don't know about those people. They're mighty soft, Paul."

"Yes, they are, but a fine-looking family, aren't they?"

"They won't be fine looking if they get scalped."

"Is there much of that going on?"

"Always possible for a war party of Creeks to come marauding through," Hawk said rather gloomily. "No way to guard against it. Men like Boone, and well, like myself, we live every day in danger, and we're always ready for it. But settlers . . . they forget how dangerous it is."

They made their way out of town, and without trouble found

the small group of settlers exactly where Bean had said they would be. As Hawk looked around, he was surprised to see at least thirty or forty people, including children, gathered with their wagons.

A tall man came forward at once and said, "My name's Smith. Jed Smith."

"I'm Hawk Spencer. This is Sequatchie. Here's a letter from William Bean. He asked me to guide you folks over the mountains to Watauga."

A look of relief passed over Jed Smith's face. "Well, we been waitin' long enough. We was about ready to start out without a guide."

"Not too good an idea," Hawk said. "Would you be willing to have some more folks join your party?"

Jed Smith looked at the others and said, "Always glad to have good folks."

Hawk introduced Paul Anderson, and Anderson in turn introduced the MacNeals. Jed recognized Patrick MacNeal from a trip Patrick had made earlier from Boston. In fact, he was the one who had encouraged Patrick to bring his family and head west. Patrick then introduced his family to Jed Smith. Quite a crowd had gathered then, and there was a hubbub of talk as the newcomers were welcomed.

Jed Smith said, "We just took up a bait of supper. Y'all come on, and we'll see what the women have got cooked up."

Hawk showed the MacNeals how to care for their stock, and how to unload the packs, which took some time. He found out that the boy, Andrew, was underfoot all the time, curious about everything. It bothered him, somewhat, but he did not let it show. And he was careful to answer the boy's questions. Actually he did not want to get too attached to the boy. With the dangers of the journey that lay ahead, Hawk knew it was a real possibility that some of them would not make it. Young and old alike had died trying to cross over the mountains through Indian territory.

As they were getting ready to eat, another rider galloped down the dusty road, into the group of wagons.

Jed Smith said, "Who's that? It's not one of our party."

His wife, Mary, said, "Maybe she's going west over the mountains. She's got a pack animal."

"Anybody know her?" Jed Smith said, staring at the woman as

she rode up, loaded down with supplies.

Two members of the party knew her. Hawk was standing back in the shadows, and he recognized Rhoda instantly. He said nothing as she rode up and inquired for the leader.

When Jed Smith introduced himself, she said, "My name is Rhoda Harper. I heard about your group traveling west. I'd like to go with you."

"Well now," Jed said, scratching his whiskers. "Have you got a man?"

"No, I'm alone."

"Hard for a woman to travel alone," Mary said. But she was a friendly woman and added at once, "Well, you get off that horse, Miss Rhoda Harper. If you ain't got a man, we'll find you one when we get to the Watauga."

Rhoda dismounted, and several hands were ready, especially among the younger men, to help her. Finally the food was set out, and the meal began. Rhoda sat apprehensively and was startled when a man dropped down beside her, saying quietly, "Hello, Rhoda."

She turned to him quickly, but in the fading darkness she did not recognize him. "You know me?"

"You know me, too, but it's been quite a while. My name was Josh Spencer, but people just call me Hawk now."

Rhoda stared at the tanned face of the man who had seemingly appeared from nowhere. She had heard rumors from some of the men at the tavern that he had become a long hunter, like Daniel Boone, and a wanderer. From time to time she'd thought of him, but she felt strange now, seeing him after so many years. Memories came of the time when they had gone to school together as children, but she was certain he still did not remember her as a schoolgirl. To him she was nothing more than a tavern girl. "Hello, Josh," she said quietly.

"Better make it Hawk," he suggested. "If it's all the same to you."

Rhoda nervously looked around. She had hoped to escape her past, but now she felt there was no hope at all. She felt somehow that she needed to explain to this tall man what she was doing, and she said quietly, "I haven't seen you for a long time . . . but I've had a pretty bad life, Hawk. I wanted some way to get out of it."

"It's pretty hard where we're headed, Rhoda." He smiled then, and his teeth flashed in the firelight. "But I'll help you all I can."

Rhoda felt better then. Her heart lifted for a moment, and she nodded. "Thank you, Hawk," she said and then ducked her head so that he could not see her face.

Sabotage!

Twenty

$\mathcal{F}$ine weather favored the small band as they wound their way out of Williamsburg and headed west. By dawn, the procession of wagons and horses had left Williamsburg behind them. Hawk had roused them all while the stars were still winking faintly in the sky, and the women had quickly prepared a hot meal for their families. "We won't have time to stop and cook at midday," Hawk had informed them. "We'll take cold vittles, and then you can cook again at night."

By noon they were on a road that was mostly barren, except for a few scattered farms. Hawk drew up his hand, and the procession stopped. "There's a stream down there where we'll water the stock. It will be a good time to let them have a rest. I reckon some of you could use a little rest yourself."

He spoke the truth for Elizabeth MacNeal, who was accustomed to padded coaches and carriages. The hard seat of the wagon had become an absolute agony for her. She had said nothing to Patrick, but she resolved to gather something to make a cushion to sit on for the rest of the day's journey. Climbing down stiffly, she stretched and watched as Sarah and Andrew leaped to the ground and ran about, quickly finding the other young people.

"They make friends so fast, don't they, Patrick?"

"Yes, they do," Patrick said. He watched fondly as the young people talked and moved out to explore the forest that surrounded the small winding road. "I think we ought to offer to share what we have with some of the others." A frown crossed his face, and he shook his head. "We have so much more than some of them do. I don't see how they're going to make it."

Some of the settlers had practically nothing, while the MacNeals had filled their wagon to capacity with an abundance of goods and food.

"I think I'll go over and see if Mary and I can share the meal. I like the Smiths so much."

Elizabeth took some of their supplies to the Smith wagon, and soon the two women had a meal going. The group broke off into smaller ones, and the food was shared all around.

Hawk sat down beside Sequatchie, the two of them keeping a watch ahead. "I don't expect any trouble this soon," Hawk said, "but it doesn't hurt to keep a lookout. I think you'd better ride ahead when we start again and scout for a good place to camp for the night."

"Yes, that would be good." Sequatchie watched the people as they laughed and talked. "By the time we get there, some of that laughter will be out of them. It's going to be a hard trip. They have no idea how cruel the wilderness can be sometimes." His eyes fell on the young woman Rhoda Harper, who sat off by herself. He had observed Hawk speaking to her the previous day and asked, "You know the woman? The one who came alone?"

"I met her years ago back in Williamsburg."

"Pretty woman. Maybe she will make a fine wife for you."

"I don't think so," Hawk said. Nevertheless, his eyes went to Rhoda, who was sitting in the shade of a group of tall hickory trees. She was eating something and drinking out of a jug, and he wondered aloud, "I can't figure out what she's doing. Not quite right for a woman to travel alone into the wilderness."

"She will find a man there. She's a good strong woman and will make some man a fine wife."

Hawk gave Sequatchie a quick look, but there was an impassive expression on the Cherokee's face that revealed nothing. "You'd make a good poker player, Sequatchie," he said. "When you put on that poker face of yours I can't tell what you're thinking." Hawk rose and walked around, checking the stock. He came to one of the families that he was concerned about. He hadn't met the people yet, but something about them had disturbed him. Their equipment was falling apart, and he knew it would never make it through the rough terrain all the way to the Watauga. The man was leaning up against the wagon wheel, and he rose as Hawk came up. "My name's Hawk Spencer," he said.

"I'm Zeke Taylor. This is my wife, Iris, and my girl, Amanda." Zeke Taylor was not a tall man, standing under five nine. He was unkempt, with dark brown hair and a scraggly beard. His eyes were dark brown but appeared almost black, and he was overweight, with a paunch that came from too much eating and not enough hard work. Still, he appeared to be strong, for he had thick shoulders and a deep chest.

"Glad to know you, Taylor." Hawk took off his cap and bowed to Iris Taylor, who was not over five two. She appeared rather frail, and her blue eyes were dull. She glanced at her husband, and Hawk saw the fear in her look, although Taylor had said nothing.

Amanda Taylor was already as tall as her mother, although she was no more than eleven. She had her mother's dark hair, long and straight, and her father's brown eyes, and was far too slender. She glanced shyly at Hawk, then dropped her eyes.

"I'm afraid that team of yours isn't going to make it all the way to Watauga, Taylor," Hawk said. He walked around and put his hand on the lean withers of the sorry-looking animal and shook his head. "I think you better trade for a better team before we get too far into the wilderness."

"I reckon I can handle my own business, Spencer."

Hawk turned quickly, and his eyes narrowed. There was an arrogance in the man that he had spotted earlier. He saw also that Mrs. Taylor and the child were terrified. Hawk did not like pressure from any man, but he was in no mood for a fight. He knew from the defiant look on Taylor's face that he would be told nothing. Hawk started to say something else, but once again the frightened look of the woman and child deterred him. "If I can be of any help to you, let me know," he said pleasantly, then turned and walked away.

As he moved along, he stopped at Jed Smith's wagon, and Smith said, "I don't think you met these two fellers—William Bean's brothers-in-law. This is George, and this is John." George Russell was a tall, handsome man with dark hair and eyes and a ready grin.

"Glad to know you, Hawk," he said.

"Glad to know you, George. Have you been in the woods a lot?"

"Quite a bit," George said. "I've been kind of a wanderin' man."

"He stayed home," John Russell said, "until his wife passed, and then he just took off to the woods."

Hawk's eyes went at once to George Russell. "I reckon I know what that's like," he said quietly. "We can use good woodsmen, though."

John Russell was forty-two, thickset, with brown eyes and hair. He nodded shortly and said, "This here is my wife, Leah."

Leah was John Russell's second wife, as Hawk discovered later. She looked half his age, which she was, at twenty-one. She had hazel eyes that contrasted sharply with her black hair. She was a very pretty girl, and somewhat of a flirt, as Hawk discerned almost at once. "How do you do, Mr. Hawk," she said, smiling at him and turning her head to one side. "We're glad to have an experienced scout like you to get us safe where we're goin'."

John said, "These are my young'uns. That's Tom. He's fifteen, and Dake is thirteen. Lelah there, she's ten, and Morene, she's three."

All of the children were blond and had blue eyes, completely unlike John Russell. Quickly Hawk decided they must have looked like their mother. "Fine-looking family you got here, John," he said. "How long do you think it'll take before we get to the Watauga?"

"Hard to say. If there were just men on horseback it wouldn't take too long, but with wagons and some of the stock in pretty poor condition"—his eyes ran over to the Taylor outfit—"and then, of course, we're tied to the slowest in the train. We'll just have to take it as it comes."

"I've done a little scoutin', in my day," George Russell said. "Maybe I can be a little help there."

"That'd be right good, George. As a matter of fact, you can ride ahead with Sequatchie. He's going to scout out a good spot for tonight."

"Are you expectin' trouble?" Russell asked.

"No, not this close to the settlements. Still, you never can tell. Don't let the children wander away from the train. All it takes is one lone Indian to bring a lot of grief."

Hawk walked away and George Russell said, "You know, I think he's a pretty talented fella."

"I believe you're right, George," John Russell agreed. He turned to Leah, and his eyes narrowed, for she was still staring at the tall man as he walked away. "Why don't you feed those kids, Leah?"

Quickly Leah Russell turned and said, "Come along. We'll finish eating, and you can help me reload the wagon."

Soon the wagons were rolling again. It was a long day, and when the sun cast shadows across the road, Hawk rode back and signaled for everyone to pull up and make camp. Those who were not used to such methods of travel were exhausted, and Hawk said to George Russell and Sequatchie, "Well, they'll settle down to business now."

"How many miles did we make today?"

"About twelve or fifteen, maybe. Not too bad with this big of a train. But it'll slow down when we leave this good road."

George looked at the rutted road and grinned. "You call this a good road?"

"The best you'll see." Hawk nodded. "When we get to no road at all, we'll have to leave the wagons behind and pack in what we can. Some of these wagons won't even make it that far."

The smoke of cooking fires soon filled the camp, but Rhoda had pulled some cold beef out of the sack that she had on her packhorse. She was about to begin to eat when a woman came over to her and spoke. Rhoda had noticed her before—her clothes were fine and new—and Rhoda felt wary.

"My name is Elizabeth MacNeal. I know your name—it's Rhoda Harper. I was there when you came in."

"I'm glad to know you," Rhoda said shortly.

"We've got a long way to go, haven't we, Rhoda?"

"I guess so. A fair piece."

"I've got supper started, but I wish you'd come over and help me. I'm not much of a cook, you see. I'd take it as a favor."

Rhoda knew instantly that this was an overture of friendship, that the woman probably didn't actually need help.

"I wouldn't want to put you out," she said.

"Oh, I'm serious." Elizabeth smiled and added, "I might as well tell you the truth. I think before this trip is over, we're all going to be better acquainted. But the truth is, well, I come from a well-to-do family. I've not done that much cooking in my life." She laughed and held her hands out. "Look."

Rhoda reached out in the twilight and touched the woman's palms. They were indeed soft and smooth, and Rhoda looked up with astonishment. "They're so soft! You *ain't* done much work, have you?"

"No! I tried to cook this morning, and all I did was burn everything or serve it raw. Can you cook, Rhoda?"

"Yes, I'm a good cook."

"Please come over and help us then. I want you to meet my family. I need a friend, you see. We all do. None of us know much about the wilderness."

Rhoda hesitated. The woman obviously did not know about her background. *If she knew what I was, then she wouldn't be asking me.* Nevertheless, remembering Elizabeth had said, *I'd take it as a great favor,* she nodded and walked over to the MacNeals' wagon.

"Patrick, this is Rhoda Harper. You remember, she rode in yesterday? She's going to teach me how to cook! Isn't that fine?"

"Well, Miss Harper. I'd be indebted to you forever." He winked at Rhoda broadly, saying, "If somebody doesn't teach Elizabeth how to cook, I'm afraid we'll all die of starvation."

Rhoda took an instant liking to the tall red-haired man. "I really don't know much, but I've cooked a heap." She turned and said, "Are these your young'uns?"

"Yes. This is Sarah, and this is Andrew."

Sarah, always bold, came up and asked at once, "Have you got any children, Miss Rhoda?"

"No." Rhoda shook her head. "Haven't even been able to catch a husband."

Sarah reached up and took her hand confidently. "You will." She turned and said, "Mama, you can tell her how to catch a husband. You caught Papa, didn't you?"

"I certainly did," Elizabeth said, laughing. "And I'll be glad to give you all the tips I can, Rhoda. Come on now and give me my first cooking lesson."

It was an unusual experience for Rhoda Harper. She was shocked that the family accepted her so readily. They were, indeed, ignorant of the wilderness, she saw, and knew absolutely nothing about rough living. She herself was used to such hardship, and she quickly organized the meal and found Elizabeth to be an attentive student, despite the fact that she obviously knew little about cooking.

"Oh, I'll never learn!" Elizabeth said as she dropped the frying pan into the fire.

"Oh yes, you'll learn!" Rhoda said with encouragement. Finally the meal was finished and they sat down, and Rhoda started to eat. However, she stopped abruptly when the family all joined hands.

Sarah was sitting next to her, and she reached out her hand for Rhoda's. Rhoda took it, not knowing what was happening. Then she saw them all bow their heads as Patrick MacNeal started to pray.

"Our Father, we thank you for your mercies, for your goodness, for this food. Thank you for this guest, and we pray that you would bless her life. And we ask it in the name of Jesus. Amen."

Somehow, those few simple words went straight to Rhoda's heart. The confident grasp of Sarah's hand on hers brought a warmth to her, and for the first time in a long while tears came to her eyes. She lowered her head quickly, then turned to one side and dashed the tears away, hoping that no one saw.

The children chattered away, and Rhoda kept waiting for one of the MacNeals to ask her about herself, but they did not. Finally, it was time to go to bed, and Rhoda cleaned up the dishes while Elizabeth put the children into the wagon.

When Elizabeth came back and sat down, she took some of the coffee that Rhoda had made and sighed. "I'm so tired. I don't think I can stand up, and this is just the first day. Rhoda, I wish I were as hearty as you."

Rhoda knew then that she had to tell the truth. She held the coffee mug in her hand and listened to the murmuring of voices from the other campfires. "I guess you don't know about me," she said.

Both the MacNeals looked at her, and Elizabeth said, "Why, no. Except you're a good cook, and we're glad to have you with us."

"You won't be when I tell you who I am." Rhoda saw surprise come to the eyes of the couple, and she said, "I've been a tavern girl most of my life. I reckon you know what that means?" She waved her hand at the others. "Two or three of them know already what I am . . . and the way people talk, before we get very far, everybody will know." She put the coffee cup down and said, "I thank you for the food, but I don't suppose you'd better be havin' anything to do with the likes of me." She shook her head and said, "It won't help your reputation."

Instantly Elizabeth came to her feet. She crossed to where Rhoda stood and—to the woman's absolute astonishment—put her arms around her, kissed her, and said, "You sit right down there, Rhoda Harper!" Forcing Rhoda to sit, she took a position beside her and said, "I don't ever want to hear anything like that again from you!

Whatever you've been is not our business. I can see you're kind, and that's what counts. I want us to be friends."

"I'd take it kindly if you would be a friend to my wife, Rhoda," Patrick said. "A woman needs a friend. I've taken Elizabeth out of all she knew, and it's going to be hard for her. She's going to need all the encouragement she can get."

Once again tears stung Rhoda's eyes. She dropped her head and stared at the fire. It crackled, and a log broke and sent showers of red and orange sparks into the air. Far off an owl hooted its haunting cry. Rhoda lifted her eyes. The MacNeals watched her with a kindness in their expression that she hadn't thought possible.

After a moment Rhoda said, "I'd be pleased to have you for friends, but folks won't think the more of you for it. I'm nothing but a tavern wench, and that's the truth of it."

"No more of that!" Elizabeth said. "Now, you come over and make your bed close to us. You're traveling with us all the way to the Watauga."

Once again, Hawk roused the train while stars still spangled the skies. They cooked a quick breakfast, and Hawk and Sequatchie were invited to breakfast with the MacNeals. The two men sat down and ate, and Hawk said nothing about the presence of Rhoda Harper. As he sipped his coffee, he said, "You're a good cook, Mrs. MacNeal."

"Oh, call me Elizabeth . . . and I'm not a good cook at all. Rhoda cooked this. All I do is burn my fingers and drop the meat in the fire!"

Sarah giggled and said, "That's right, Hawk, but Rhoda's going to teach Mama to cook, and Mama's gonna teach Rhoda how to catch a husband."

Rhoda flushed, and Elizabeth said, "Sarah! Will you hush and never say anything like that again! I'm sorry, Rhoda," she said, "but Sarah's just impossible!"

"It's all right, Elizabeth," Rhoda said. She looked up and met Hawk's smiling eyes, and a look of understanding passed between them. She wondered how a godly family like the MacNeals could take in a woman like herself, with her reputation.

Hawk looked at Patrick and said, "How'd you decide to go across the mountains?" he asked.

Patrick spoke with enthusiasm, giving him an abbreviated version of the family history. He ended by saying, "I know this doesn't sound sensible, but as I told you before, I think God has led us on this trip."

"Well, Paul Anderson agrees with you." Rhoda's ears perked up. She had heard that Paul was part of the entourage, but she hadn't had an opportunity to speak with him.

"It's good to have a minister on the train. I haven't met him yet."

"He's going to preach tonight," Sequatchie said. "Preach the gospel from the Bible."

"Oh, that'll be wonderful!" Elizabeth said. She saw that Rhoda looked downcast, then added brightly, "Is it a Christian community, Hawk?"

"Like every place else," Hawk said. "Some are Christians, and some aren't."

"What about yourself, Hawk? Are you a Christian man?"

Sequatchie glanced covertly at his friend and listened for his answer. It came about as he expected. "My parents are the best Christians I've ever known," Hawk said quietly. "But I don't reckon I can say that I have faith, even though I once did." He did not speak for a while, and then he said, "I suppose I'm a lot like that brother-in-law of William Bean's, George Russell. He lost his wife and did about what I did—just left and went out to the woods."

"Well, I'm sorry about your wife," Elizabeth said. "It's hard to lose one we love. But you know the last thing my father said to me when I left?" She grew meditative and said, "He's not in good health, and it's unlikely that we'll ever meet again in this world. That was so painful for me." She reached out and took Patrick's hand and squeezed it. She continued softly, her voice barely audible. "He said, 'Christians never say good-bye.' Isn't that wonderful?"

"That is good," Sequatchie said. "We all go to be with our people. That is what the Bible says, isn't it, Hawk? Read me that part!"

"Not now, Sequatchie!"

"Yes!" Sequatchie said. "About when Abraham died."

"It says Abraham died and was gathered to his people." Hawk knew that verse well because Sequatchie loved it. "Isaac died and was gathered to his people, then Jacob died and was gathered to his people."

Sequatchie was squatted on the ground, staring at the face of his friend. "I will be gathered to my people one day, and with the Great Jesus God. Death is not the evil that we think."

Hawk looked up suddenly, knowing that Sequatchie said this for his benefit. But, still, the bitterness in him brought him to his feet. He walked away without another word.

Rhoda said, "He's a bitter man, isn't he, Sequatchie?"

"Yes, he thinks God took his wife. He's mad at God. But he will learn better one day." The Indian nodded. "I have asked the Great God to help Hawk."

Shortly the train pulled out, but they had not gone more than two miles when the heavily rutted road tossed the wagons around. A cry came from somewhere in the back, and Hawk turned his horse and moved to where John Russell's wagon was turned at a cockeyed angle. "What's the matter, John?"

"Axle broke," Russell grunted. He crawled out from under it, and said angrily, "It didn't break by no accident either."

"These are pretty rough roads," Hawk said.

"Crawl down there and look at it!"

Hawk stepped off of his horse and slipped under the wagon. He looked at where Russell, who had joined him, pointed and said, "Look! That axle's been tampered with, Hawk."

Reaching out, Hawk touched the axle. It was splintered, but half of it was sawn through cleanly. Alarm ran through Hawk and he said, "You're right, John. That axle didn't saw itself through. You got any enemies on this train, John?"

"Nary a one that I know of, but I must have! Like you say, that axle didn't saw itself."

The two men crawled out and stood there thoughtfully. "This is going to set us back. We're going to have to send back to Williamsburg for an axle."

"No, I've got a spare," John said. "If you'll jist let me get some men together and jack this wagon up it won't take too long."

Hawk nodded, and soon a crew was busy replacing the broken axle. When they had finished the repair, Hawk was walking along thinking hard. He turned to John who had joined him and said, "I don't like the looks of this, John."

"I can't figure it out! Why would anybody want to saw an axle only halfway? Why didn't they saw it all the way in two? That's the way I'd do it if I wanted it to break down on the journey. But why would anybody want that? Must've been some kid just being mischievous."

"I don't think so," Hawk said. "I looked for some trouble on this trip, but not this kind." His eyes narrowed and he said, "Keep your eyes open, John. If a thing like that can happen, no tellin' what will come next. I don't like it."

Rhoda moved around the wagons as they were drawn up for the night. Everyone was in bed. She had seen Hawk moving silently along earlier, but now no one seemed to be awake. Overhead, a sliver of a moon was falling down in the sky, and it seemed to be dragging some stars with it. Taking a deep breath, she continued to walk, for she could not sleep. It had been a wonder and a puzzlement to her how she had been taken in with such wholeheartedness and warmth by the MacNeals. As she had known it would happen, some word had gotten out that she had been a prostitute at a tavern, and some of the men had already been pestering her. It was then that she had been most thankful to be with the MacNeals, because she stayed very close to them, and those men did not have the nerve to bother her when Patrick MacNeal was close by.

Suddenly, a shooting star lit the heavens overhead. Rhoda looked up and admired the fiery track of light as it scored the blackness of the heavens. She never saw one that didn't make her heart beat faster. She thought, *It's the most beautiful sight that earth's got to offer.* Somehow the pains and griefs and discomforts of her life seemed to be a little bit less. "They say, make a wish when you see a shootin' star," she whispered. She stood there in the darkness, looking up as the light from the fiery finger of flame seemed to fade, and she whispered, "I wish I could be better, somehow, than I am."

It was a special moment for her in the silence of the forest, and she hated to go back. Suddenly a voice called her name, and she started violently.

"Rhoda!"

She knew that voice and said at once, "Jacques, is that you?"

"Yes!" Cartier seemed to simply materialize out of the darkness. For all his size, he could move as quietly as a cloud through the woods. He held her arm and said, "I see you kept your part of the deal and joined the train, and that's good."

Rhoda said, "That wagon wheel. I heard Patrick say it was tampered with."

"Yes, and it was I, Jacques Cartier, who did the tampering." He frowned and said, "I didn't intend for it to break so soon, and I didn't think he'd have a spare. But there are other ways."

"What do you want, Jacques?"

"I have decided to let these people wear themselves down before we make life really hard for them. I will meet you two weeks from tonight. Once the sun sets, you go outside of camp and I will be there."

"Why didn't you come along on this train yourself, instead of sending me?"

"Because Spencer and that Indian friend of his would recognize me. They think I'm dead, and I want them to keep thinking that." He touched the scar on his neck and said, "Someday, I will have the scalps of both of them dangling from my belt."

Rhoda suddenly knew fear, for there was no mercy in the big man. She wished somehow that he would go away and never come back, but she knew full well he would never do that. "Why do you want to do all this? Why not let these people go on?" she asked. "They're good people, Jacques."

"As I told you before, that is not for you to ask. You just be ready, and meet me in two weeks."

"Ready for what?"

But Cartier had faded back into the darkness. Rhoda stared, trying to catch sight of him, and for one wild moment she had the impulse to go to Hawk and tell him what was happening. *But if I told him that, he would know that I'm part of it, and he would hate me. And so would everyone else.* She found it odd that she desired their acceptance so deeply, but she couldn't deny that she did. Wearily she moved back, thinking of the wish she had made—that she might be better. "I'll never be any better," she said grimly. "No matter how hard I try." Sadness came to her, and her shoulders slumped. She went back to her bed and lay awake for a long time. Just as she dropped off, somehow she thought of two things at once—the beauty of the shooting star and the words of Elizabeth MacNeal—*I want to be friends with you, Rhoda. We can help each other*—and then she plunged into sleep.

Amanda

Twenty-One

he exodus of the small group from civilization to the wilderness had lasted for one week. During that time, the road had practically disappeared, so that now what the pioneers followed was little more than a path. At times the men would have to get out and chop away the thick growth that had overgrown the path so that the wagons could squeeze through. It was difficult to keep the packhorses on the trail, for they would wander away and nibble at the grass among the trees. Day after day they forded creeks, some of which were so deep midstream that the wagons were washed sideways as the teams struggled to pull them through. Once, one of the packhorses was caught by the strong current when he missed his footing and was dragged to his death by the heavy load of supplies on his back. The men salvaged the supplies but watched with apprehension as the dead animal floated off, for there were no extra pack animals.

"This old path was used by my people before the white men came," Sequatchie said. He looked down at the faint ruts that wagons had made where traders had taken goods to cabins farther on, and he shook his head. "One day there will be a big road through here, and the white people will come like the locust."

"I suppose you're right," Paul said.

He had, as a single man, moved around from family to family, getting to know people better. He was always sharing food from his supplies to those in need.

Late Saturday evening as they were all sitting around the campfire, Elizabeth said, "Reverend Anderson, wouldn't it be good if we had a service tomorrow? It's the Sabbath."

"I think it would," Paul said. He looked up and saw Hawk passing by and called out, "Hawk! Could you come over here a moment?" When Hawk came to stand beside them, holding his rifle in his hand as he generally did, Anderson said, "Elizabeth thinks it might be a good idea if we held services tomorrow."

"I'd like it mighty well," Patrick agreed. "I've always felt that a man can do more in six days than he can in seven. At least that's what my father always taught me."

Hawk rubbed the barrel of his musket and nodded. "I think a rest might do us all good. Some of the folks are just about worn down. It will be all right with me, Reverend."

Rhoda said nothing, but afterward Paul joined her, saying, "Let me help do a little of the clean-up work." They took the tin dishes down to the small creek, which had a sandy bottom, and scoured them. "This water's cold," Paul said.

"Yes. It'll be frozen over in a few months." Rhoda paused, and a thoughtful look came into her eyes. "I've always hated winter."

"I always liked it myself. I used to ice-skate when I was a boy. I don't guess I'll be doing any of that out here."

Rhoda smiled at him and continued washing the dishes. It was quiet, with only the murmuring of the creek as it bubbled over the rounded stones. There was a peacefulness during this late hour. Overhead the skies were milky, and the moon hung low in the sky.

Paul asked, "Do you ever think of those days when you and I and Hawk were in school together? Of course, he was Josh then."

Rhoda cast a quick glance at him and said, "Sometimes."

Something in the tone of her voice caught at Anderson. He was a thoughtful young man, and now he quickly contemplated her age. He was thirty-five, and he remembered that she was two years younger. "I think of them a lot," he said. "I remember you had a braid that went way down past the middle of your back."

"You pulled it one day," Rhoda replied. "And I picked up a stick and hit you with it."

Anderson's white teeth gleamed as he smiled at her. "I remember that," he said. "It's a good thing you didn't hit me in the head or my face, or you might have left a scar."

"I've forgotten where I hit you," Rhoda confessed.

"Right across the bottom! It left a welt that my mother saw. She wanted to know how I got it."

"What did you tell her?" Rhoda smiled.

"I lied to her, of course."

"I didn't think preachers lied."

"Well, I wasn't a preacher in those days, but I think even today if I had a welt there that you'd given me, and Hawk or somebody asked me about it, I believe I'd have to use a little imagination rather than tell the exact truth."

"Then I'd better not hit you with a stick."

They laughed and Rhoda found herself enjoying the man's company. She had expected that he would launch out at her with a fiery sermon as several ministers had done back in Williamsburg. So far on the trail, he had not even mentioned God to her, and it puzzled her. The dishes were all done, and she turned to him now and said, "Paul, why don't you preach at me? You know what my life's been."

Anderson was surprised at her straightforwardness. He turned to face her, and in the darkness he could barely make out her features. "Well, to tell the truth, Rhoda, I've had the temptation, but it just seemed that the time hadn't come."

"It surprised me a little bit," she admitted. "You know what I've been—nothing but a Jezebel!"

"Well"—Paul was flabbergasted at the bluntness of her words—"no matter what you have been, it's not too late to change, Rhoda."

"It's too late for me," she said. "And some of the men on the train have been after me. You'd be surprised. Some of them are married men."

"I know. I've been watching, and I've been proud of you. You've stayed with the MacNeals, and that's good."

"But I can't stay with them forever!"

"Maybe I will preach at you a little bit, if you don't mind, Rhoda."

She suddenly felt a warmth with this man. She knew men very well, and Paul Anderson was different. There was a goodness in him that most other men did not have. "All right. Go ahead," she said.

"It won't be much preaching. It's just that you only need one thing in your life to make you happy and complete, Rhoda—and that's Jesus."

"I believe in Jesus," she said. "But it's too late for me to do anything about it."

"No, it's not too late. Jesus said, 'Come unto me all ye that labor, and are heavy laden, and I will give you rest.'"

"The Bible says that?"

"Jesus said that. Yes, it's recorded in the Bible. It's one of my favorite Scriptures," Anderson said slowly. "I think it's one of those Scriptures that sounds so simple, yet it means so much. Can you imagine," he said thoughtfully, "any other human being who ever lived promising that? Anybody can come and get rest."

"What does it mean, Paul?"

"I think Jesus knows our hearts better than we can ever know them, and most of us get tired and worn out. We suffer failure, and we do wrong things. We're sorry, but then we do them again."

"I know all about that," Rhoda said bleakly. "A few times I tried to change the way I lived, but I never was able to. After a while I always went back."

"That's because you didn't go to Jesus."

"What does that mean, Paul? Go to Jesus? I mean, He lived a long time ago. I've never even seen Him."

Paul had found it difficult to explain salvation to those who had no concept of who Jesus was. He said, "Well, let me try to explain as best I can. Sit down on the bank here, Rhoda." The two sat down, and Paul began. "God created man, but then man sinned against God, thinking he knew what was best for his own life. He soon learned he was wrong, and from that point on, man has been lost and wicked and sinful. But there was no way for man to change," Paul said finally. "So God did the only thing that could help. He sent His only Son as a sacrifice for man's sins. He died on the cross so men and women and children might be free from sin."

"How can my sins be taken away from me because He died?"

"Nobody can explain that, Rhoda. It's the great mystery of salvation, but it's true. Let me tell you another story. Back in the Old Testament, the children of Israel were wandering in the desert. They disobeyed God, and God sent a curse. He sent fiery serpents—snakes with a venomous bite. Everyone who was bitten was dying, and many people were bitten. They came to Moses and begged him to go to God for them to take the snakes away."

"And did God do that?"

"No, the Bible doesn't say He took the snakes away," Paul said. "He told Moses, 'You take a piece of brass and make a brass snake out of it. Then set it on a pole, high up in the air, so everybody in the camp can see it, no matter where they are.' There were about a million people in that camp, Rhoda, so it must've been quite a pole. Then God said, 'If anyone is bitten, let him look at the brass snake up on that pole, and as soon as he does, he'll be healed of his snake-bite.' "

Rhoda listened to the murmuring of the brook and the breeze that was rustling the autumn leaves overhead. She had never heard of anything like this. "What happened, Paul?"

"Every time anybody got bit, they looked at that brass snake. Just imagine a man out in the field, and suddenly he feels a bite. He looks down and sees that awful serpent with its fangs in his leg. He shakes him off, but he feels the poison running through him, and he knows that everybody that's ever been bitten by one of those snakes has died. He feels himself growing weak. His eyes become unfocused. Pain courses through him as the poison begins to kill him, and then he remembers what God had said. 'If anyone is bitten, let him look at the brass snake, and he'll be healed.' And, Rhoda, imagine that even as he falls to the ground with the last bit of strength he has, he looks up at the pole and the sun catches the brass snake and makes it glitter there in the desert. And the minute that he looks, suddenly the pain is gone!" Anderson exclaimed. "The poison is gone! He's healed, and he knows that he's alive. His eyesight clears up, and strength rushes through his body."

Rhoda was enthralled. "How can just looking at a brass snake do that? How could that help a man who was dying?"

"Well, later, in the New Testament," Paul said, "Jesus was asked one time about how He was going to help the world. And He said this, 'Even as Moses lifted up the serpent in the wilderness. Even so, must the Son of Man be lifted up.' " Anderson paused and said, "Jesus was lifted up on the cross, just like that serpent. Now, no matter that it's seventeen hundred years later, God says, 'If we'll just look to Jesus in faith, all of our sins will be forgiven, and God will take them because of Jesus.'

For a long time the two talked, and finally Rhoda said, "I never heard anything like this."

She rose quickly, and Paul rose with her. "I haven't offended you, have I?"

"No, I feel real good, Paul." She reached out and touched his arm. It was the first time she had touched a man with any affection for a long time, and she said quietly, "Thanks for talking to me. I'll think about what you said." As she turned and walked back and the darkness seemed to wrap about her like a shroud, she thought about the serpent on a pole and about all she had ever heard about Jesus Christ, and her heart was strangely warmed.

Another service was held a week later, and more people attended that one. Hawk stayed on the outskirts, supposedly guarding the group. He noticed that Zeke Taylor did not attend the services. As he kept his eye on the man, Hawk saw that Taylor was drinking heavily. Immediately after the service was over, he walked by and said, "Taylor, we're getting into more dangerous territory now. Not unlikely we might find ourselves in trouble with the Indians."

"What you tellin' me this fer?" Taylor demanded. His face was flushed, and he stared belligerently at the tall frontiersman.

"I'm telling you because a man can't shoot when he's drunk, and you're drunk, Taylor!"

"Spencer, you been puttin' your nose in my business enough! I'm tellin' you now. It ain't none of your business what I do! Now get away from here, and don't come around to me with more of your talk!"

"Taylor, you don't understand this country. I won't argue with you, but I won't put up with any disorderly behavior. You give me any trouble, and I'll lay you out!" Hawk turned his back and walked away. He could feel the burning gaze of Taylor and knew that sooner or later he would have trouble with the man.

It was the day of rest, but not for Hawk, who still left the camp and circled the surrounding territory with Sequatchie and John Russell. They were alert but saw no signs of Indians.

Back in the camp, Zeke Taylor continued to drink. He finally had drunk himself practically into a stupor, and late that afternoon he yelled at Amanda, "Bring me some of that stew, girl!"

Amanda, terrified of her father, quickly ran to get the meat. She hurried to bring the stew, and as she approached him, she tripped and spilled the stew right down the front of Zeke Taylor's dirty shirt. Yelling, Taylor reached up and grabbed her. "I'll teach you to spill food!" He grabbed a strap of leather and began to beat the girl. When she didn't cry out, he grew angrier and slashed at her almost in a frenzy. His wife came and tried to stop him, but he slashed her across the face with the leather strap, too. She yelped and fell backward, hiding her face from him.

All this, of course, did not escape the attention of the others. George Russell started across the camp to help the woman, but John Russell reached out and grabbed George, saying, "That's family business," he said. "A man could get hisself killed messin' around with another man's business."

Finally, the savage beating stopped, and the camp grew quiet.

Elizabeth had not seen the beating, but she heard about it from Leah Russell. When she saw Amanda, she was shocked at the child's puffy face and its red welts. She could only guess at the girl's body, and she said to Patrick, "Something's got to be done!"

"I'll speak to the man," Patrick said.

"No, wait! That's Hawk's job," Elizabeth said. "Wait until he gets back!"

Hawk and Sequatchie returned less than an hour later and were met by Patrick and Elizabeth. Hawk listened as they told him the story, and he saw that Elizabeth had been crying.

"That poor child, Amanda. Her face is—well, I can't describe it! I can't imagine what her body looks like! That man is a beast!" she cried indignantly.

"Can't you do something about it, Hawk?" Patrick said. "I know a man's got a right to run his own family, but—"

Hawk said briefly, "I'll have a word with Taylor."

"He's drunk," Patrick warned him. "Be careful. He's a vicious man, and he's dangerous."

Hawk, who had faced many men more dangerous than Zeke Taylor, said quietly, "I'll be careful."

"Do you think he could get hurt?" Patrick asked Sequatchie as Hawk turned and walked away.

"I think Zeke Taylor could get hurt," Sequatchie said. "He's never met a man like Hawk."

Hawk approached the wagon, and Zeke Taylor had sobered up to some degree. When he saw Hawk coming, he turned and pulled a knife out of the wagon and stuck it into his belt. "What's your business, Spencer?" he demanded, his voice still thick with alcohol.

"My business is the dirty skunk who beats a woman and child," Hawk said calmly.

"It ain't none of your affair, or nobody else's."

"You may be right about that as far as this train is concerned. I was asked to guide you people to the settlement, and I'm not your judge. However, I am telling you this man to man—if you *are* a man. If you lay your hand on your wife or daughter one more time and I see it or even hear about it, I'm gonna take a bullwhip and take the hide right off of you! Do you understand that, Taylor?"

Whipping out the knife, Taylor yelled mindlessly and threw himself at Hawk. Hawk simply allowed the knife to come within a few inches of his chest, then reached out and pushed it aside. He grabbed Zeke Taylor by the neck, and his iron grip closed around the man's wrist. He started to squeeze, and Taylor began to cry out. He was much smaller than Hawk, although strong, but his strength did him no good at all. "I'm gonna turn you loose, Taylor," Hawk said. "And I'm giving you a chance to act like a man. If you come at me again with that knife, I'll put you down!"

He shoved Taylor away and stood waiting. An unholy fire burned in Zeke Taylor's eyes. He cursed and began to come forward, waving the knife in the gesture of an experienced knife fighter. This time he moved carefully. Hawk had left his rifle with his gear, but he would not have used it in any case. He poised himself on the balls of his feet, with his hands out slightly.

Those who were close enough to observe saw that he was smiling. It was not a very attractive smile, however, and John Russell whispered to Sequatchie, who had come to watch, "What's going to happen?"

"Taylor's a dead man unless Hawk decides to show a little mercy," Sequatchie said.

Zeke Taylor lunged forward once again, and the blade shot out. Again, Taylor was much too slow. With a lightning motion, Hawk grabbed the wrist, turned his back slightly, and flipped Taylor over, so that he struck the ground with a thumping noise. Hawk stamped down on the man's wrist, grinding it into the dirt. Taylor shrieked in pain, but Hawk continued to grind until the knife fell to the ground. Reaching over, Hawk picked it up and pressed the knife to Taylor's throat. With his other hand he lifted Taylor's hair and said, "I've heard of folks being scalped alive, and it would pleasure me right now to do that to you." He pressed the knife close.

"Don't kill me!" Taylor began to moan.

Hawk said, "I'm giving you one more chance. You get out of line one more time, and I *will* scalp you after I get done beating you with that whip! That's a promise—and I always keep my word, Taylor."

As Hawk walked away, Zeke Taylor's eyes burned with resentment. Getting to his feet, Zeke cast a baleful look at those who had gathered to watch. "What are you all starin' at?" he said. "Get away from here!" He looked at his wife, wanting to beat her, but the feel of the cold steel on his throat was still too strong. He went to the wagon, found a bottle, and began to drink again.

"He'll be more trouble before we get there."

"I'm not his keeper," Hawk said to Sequatchie. "But if he touches his wife or child again, I'll put a crimp in him. I can't stand to see a woman or a child mistreated!"

While the altercation between the two men had been taking place, Rhoda had left the camp. It had been two weeks ago to the day when she had spoken with Jacques, and she knew that she had no choice but to meet him. She had walked no farther than a few feet out into the darkness when she heard his voice call her name. He appeared suddenly and handed her a sack.

"What's this?" she said.

"Put some of it in the water. It will make folks sick."

"It's poison!"

"Not bad. It won't kill them. It'll just make them sick."

"What is it?" she demanded.

Instantly Cartier's arm shot out and he grabbed Rhoda by the neck. "You do what I tell you! I have given you half the gold. These people get sick enough, they will go back. You mind what I say! Put some in the water!"

Rhoda took the bag, and Cartier disappeared.

"What am I going to do?" she moaned. She looked with horror at the bag. "How can I poison people who have been so kind to me?" She knew, however, that if she did not, Cartier would kill her. When she got back to camp, the people were still gathered around talking about the fight between Hawk and Taylor. Each wagon had its own large cask of drinking water, and she managed to put some of the poison in several of these before she decided it was too dangerous.

The sickness had come on so suddenly that it was frightening. The day after the fight between Hawk and Zeke Taylor, the train had started up, but by supper that night several people were complaining about terrible stomachaches. They were vomiting and breaking out into fever and sweat.

Several had such high fevers that it was questionable whether they would live. Now, three days later, there was talk of turning back.

"I don't know what's making people so sick!" said Paul Anderson, his face twisted with pain. "I never saw such bellyaches! What do you think it is, Hawk?"

"I'm no doctor, but it came on real sudden like," Hawk said.

"Could it be cholera?" Elizabeth asked with fear in her eyes.

"No, it's not at all like cholera," Paul said. "I've seen that. I don't know what it is . . . but we've got to do something."

Hawk looked at the group that had come to ask him if it would be best to return to Williamsburg. Hawk did not say anything about the broken axle or the other accidents that had happened. Most of them were to be expected. However, he and Sequatchie had been conscious that there was something strange about many of them. Now, this sickness coming on so unexpectedly alerted him.

"I don't want to alarm you, but I think this is more than just a sickness. I think it's something in the food—or more likely in the water."

"What makes you think that, Hawk?" John Russell asked. All of his children were down sick, and so was his wife. "Half the people in the train have got it."

"But it's all in families. Some got the sickness and some don't."

"Most of it is in your family." And Hawk named off four others. "You're the sickest of all, and everybody in the family's got it. I don't think sickness works like that."

"What do you think it is, then?" Patrick asked in despair. He and his family had had no sickness at all, nor had Rhoda.

Hawk said slowly, "I think somebody's put something in the drinking water. Since we each carry our own, it would make sense to me that somebody put poison in some of the water barrels, but not in others. That's why your whole family's sick. You've all been drinking out of the same keg, John." He named off other families, then paused and said, "And as for me, I never drink out of the kegs myself, and neither does Sequatchie, so I think it's in the water."

"But who would do a thing like that?" Patrick asked.

"Who would saw my axle halfway through so that it would break down?" John Russell said suddenly. "I think you may be right, Hawk."

"Get rid of all the water in every keg," Hawk said. "Keep a close watch on the food. Anybody that'd poison water could get to the food."

Hawk and George chose some men to go around and empty and refill the water casks, since some of the people were too sick to move. It was three days before they finally all recovered, and Elizabeth said to Patrick, "I'm so thankful they've all gotten well. Who could've done such a terrible thing?"

"I have no idea. Taylor's mean enough to do it. He'd kill Hawk in a minute. Have you seen how he looks at him? But I don't think he'd put poison in our water. Besides, his own family was sick. I thought his wife was going to die."

Rhoda, who was cooking at the fire, did not look up. She had been in total misery since the sickness came. She had kept busy nursing those who were ill, until she had lost weight. And now her heart was as heavy as a stone.

Elizabeth came over and put her hand on Rhoda's arm. "I'll finish this, Rhoda. You've worn yourself out, taking care of sick folks. Go on to bed. God knows you've been good to the sick in our company."

Elizabeth's words went like an arrow straight through Rhoda's heart. She did not look up but turned and left at once. As she walked away, she gazed upward, saying, "Oh, God! Why did I ever do such a thing?" But it was done, and it was one more proof to her of the wickedness of her heart. She had thought much about Paul Anderson's words about Jesus and looking to Him, but now how could she ever think to look to Jesus after what she had done?

Through Storm and Flood

Twenty-Two

I don't like it much!" Hawk shook his head slightly as he stared down at the line of wagons and pack animals. "Here it is the middle of September, and we've still got a ways to go."

"Some of the outfits have slowed us up," George Russell said. "Especially Zeke Taylor." He stared at Taylor's wagon as it wobbled by, the poor animals straining with all their might. "We ought to shoot those horses and make him pull the wagon himself."

"I would if I thought he could," Hawk muttered.

"Has he given you any more trouble since you put the run on him, Hawk?"

"No, but if looks could kill I'd be a dead man."

The caravan had passed over some rough, hilly country that had wearied them all. Hawk and Sequatchie had killed game fairly regularly, including two wild turkeys the day before that had been a welcome change from the monotony of the diet.

"The food is running low, and I'm worried about the settlers making it through the winter," Hawk said to Russell.

"We'll make it somehow. As long as there's bear and deer in the woods, we won't starve to death. I'm getting awful hungry for vegetables, though," Russell said.

"You can raise you a garden next year." Hawk grinned. He had come to like the young man a great deal, and as the two men turned and made their way to the head of the column, they spoke of the difficulties that lay before them.

Following the trail slowly, the travelers crawled across a rocky, flinty mountain ridge where a wheel from the Suttons' wagon came off. There were no more wheels to spare, so they had to wait all night, patch the wheel together, and struggle on the next day.

In the morning, as Elizabeth stirred meal into a wooden bowl and mixed up a johnnycake, she looked down at her blistered hands. She frowned at how dirty her dress was and remembered how in Boston she'd send the children to bathe and change clothes for the least smudge. Shaking her head, Elizabeth reached up and touched her hair, which was gritty. Looking over at Patrick, who was watching her, she said, "I'm as dirty as a pig, Patrick. Wouldn't it be nice to get into a steaming hot bath, and wash your hair, and put on nice fresh clean underthings, and a fresh dress?"

"I don't know as I'd care for it," Patrick said.

"You like being dirty?" she said in amazement.

"No, I don't like being dirty, but I don't think I'd want to put on a dress."

"Oh, you!" She stirred the batter again and put some of it out to bake in the large frying pan. The food in their wagon had gone down alarmingly, and she knew if it had not been for the game that Sequatchie and Hawk brought in day by day, they would have been hungry long before this.

"Are you sorry that we came, sweetheart?" Patrick came over and sat beside her, put his arm around her, squatting before the fire.

"No, I'm not. It's been the hardest time I've ever known physically, but—oh, it's so exciting, Patrick!"

"I hope you'll always feel that way. It's been good for the kids, hasn't it?"

"Yes, look how brown they are. Just like little Indians, almost."

"I'm proud of both of them. I'm proud of you, too," he said, and reached over and kissed her soundly.

By the time they finished their meal and packed up, Hawk came by saying it was time for the train to pull out again.

They were moving at a very slow pace now. One day differed from another only by the nature of the disasters. Once Sequatchie's horse mired in a stream, and it took half a day to drag him free of the mud, and he was unable to go on for another two hours. They crossed the same stream, it seemed, numberless times, for it wound around in their way. More than once, rainstorms swept over them. Though they were all wet to the skin, they forged on as best they could. Sometimes they made only a mile a day when wagons bogged down almost to their hubs in the red claylike mud.

Sequatchie was extremely quiet one Saturday morning. He kept looking up at the sky, and finally Hawk asked, "What's the matter? Something wrong?"

Sequatchie sniffed the air almost like a hound dog. He shook his head and said, "Storm coming."

Hawk shrugged his broad shoulders. "We've had about a dozen. I guess we can take one more." He turned in his saddle to look over the stragglers and shook his head. "I'll be glad to get there. I'd rather try to herd a hive of bees across a desert than do this again, Sequatchie."

Sequatchie did not answer. He kept twisting in the saddle, turning his head to one side, and finally he said, "*Bad* storm coming. Very bad."

Hawk knew Sequatchie's almost uncanny ability to foretell weather. He could not understand it, nor explain it, nor could the Cherokee. Sometimes as long as a week before a storm hit, Sequatchie would begin to grow edgy, and grow more so until finally it would come.

"Maybe we better find some shelter and get out of it," Hawk said.

"Good," Sequatchie replied. "I'll go tell preacher Anderson to pray."

They had not had the wagons and animals secured long before huge black clouds began rolling out of the north. Inside of them, lightning bolts flickered back and forth, reaching down with long jagged blades to stab the earth.

"How far away is that storm, Papa?" Sarah MacNeal asked her father. She was holding his hand and watching the dark clouds.

"Well, I'll tell you how you can tell how far a storm is. Now, wait until the next lightning bolt, and as soon it comes, you start counting slowly like this. One—two—three. Like that. See?"

"All right, Papa."

The pair watched the dark clouds, and almost immediately a monstrous finger of lightning scratched the sky and lit up the whole horizon. At once Sarah began counting, "One . . . two . . . three . . . four . . . five . . ." When she said twenty-five, the air was filled with a loud rumble of thunder.

"There—the storm is five miles away. It took twenty-five seconds for the sound to get here."

"Five miles?" Sarah's eyes grew wide. "That's not very far, is it?"

"Not really. It's going to be a bad storm, I think. I want you and Andrew and your mother to get into the wagon."

"What are you going to do, Papa?"

"The horses might get real jumpy with that lightning flashing around. I'll tend to them."

Hawk galloped his horse down the train, saying, "Tie everything down! This is going to be a bad blow!" He stopped to say to the Russells, "As a matter of fact, if we had time, I wouldn't mind tying the wagons to trees."

"You think it's a tornado?" John Russell asked with alarm.

"I don't know what it is, but if Sequatchie says it's a bad one—well, you can count on it being a bad one!"

Within minutes the wind struck with a gale force that was almost unbelievable. The canvas tied across the wagon ends ripped loose of several wagons at once, and the tremendous deluge poured in, half drowning the occupants and soaking everything. It was futile to try to tie the canvas down, and those who lost the tops simply huddled together, shaking from the cold rain.

Hawk and Sequatchie had tied their horses down securely, and now Hawk ran from wagon to wagon shouting, "Get under the wagon! You could get hit by lightning!"

When he got to the Taylor wagon, he saw that Taylor was almost paralyzed with fear.

"We're all gonna die," Taylor said, sitting with his head buried in his hands.

"We're not going to die! Get out here and unhitch this team! We've got to get them tied off! They might run away! You should've already done that!"

But Taylor was beyond helping himself, so Hawk and George Russell unhitched the team and tied them. Then they helped Mrs. Taylor and Amanda get under the wagon.

"What about him?" Russell asked Hawk, nodding to Taylor, who shook at each peal of thunder.

"I don't care if he does get hit by lightning," Hawk murmured.

"It's a bad one, ain't it?" Russell muttered. The water was running off of his hat in a cascade, and he, like all the others, was as wet as if he'd been thrown into a river.

"Yes, it's going to get worse, I reckon." Hawk said.

The winds howled with a tornadolike force, although the travelers saw no funnels, which they all dreaded. Hawk leaned against the wind and made his way to the MacNeal wagon, where he found them all huddled underneath except Patrick. "Are you all right under there?" he yelled against the screaming of the wind.

"We're all right," Elizabeth said. "Come on under here."

"No, I'll help Patrick with the horses." He looked over and saw Rhoda, who was holding Sarah MacNeal. The girl had buried her face against the woman. Andrew was watching with enormous eyes, and Hawk reached over and gently punched him. "It'll be all right, Andy. Just another storm. It'll pass by, and tomorrow the sun will be out shining."

The words immediately drove the fear out of the boy, and he said, "Can I come out and help you and Pa with the horses?"

"No, you stay here and take care of your mother, son. A woman needs a man with her at a time like this."

At once Andrew said, "Sure, Hawk," and moved over and put his arm around his mother.

Elizabeth winked at Hawk and said, "You're right about that. Andrew will take care of me."

Finally the wind began to lessen, and Sequatchie wiped the water from his face. He wore no hat and rivulets ran down his face and neck. "Good," he said. "It's over now."

Thirty minutes later, the rains slacked off and then stopped completely. Paul Anderson came struggling out, covered with mud, from where he had been lying under the wagon.

Hawk reached down and helped him to his feet. "Well, preacher. You look like one of those mud cats we used to catch out of the river, except you're uglier!"

Anderson grinned, his teeth white against his muddy face. "I guess I am," he said. "It was bad, wasn't it?"

"It was one of the worst I've seen, but I think the wagons are all intact." He looked at Paul and said, "Did you do your praying like Sequatchie asked?"

"Yes, I did. I know you don't believe, but I believe in praying about everything—including storms."

"I hope you always believe like that, Paul," Hawk said simply. He slapped his friend on the shoulder and said, "I'll tell you what. I think we ought to get some fires going and dry everything out before we go any farther. Everybody's had a bad drenching."

Hawk wisely decided that the morale of the train had deteriorated to such an extent that they needed a few days to rest. He amazed them by going around to each wagon and starting a fire, though every stick of wood in the forest seemed drenched. Finally, he showed them how to make racks out of saplings to dry their clothes. He and the men cut down trees and brought in enough firewood to make huge bonfires. He directed the women in cooking what food was left, then he and Sequatchie went out and an hour later came back with the carcass of a huge bear!

"Nothing like bear meat to put some spizzerinctum in ya!" He grinned as he and Sequatchie dressed out the huge animal.

"What are you going to do with the skin, Hawk?" Andrew asked.

"I'm going to give it to you, if you want it. It will make you a nice rug on the floor of your new home, Andrew."

"Do you really mean it, Hawk?"

Hawk reached out and rubbed the boy's head. "Of course I mean it. It'll be pretty smelly for a while, but I'll show you how to scrape it. We'll fix a rack for it, and you'll have the best bearskin rug in the whole country."

Elizabeth squeezed Patrick's arm and whispered, "That's wonderful. He looks up to Hawk."

"Yes, he does. I'm glad of it, but I wish Hawk would turn back to God. We need to help Hawk find his way back to God."

Sequatchie, who had been skinning the bear, waited until he was alone with Hawk, and then he said, "That was good. What you did for the boy."

"Ah, it's just a bearskin. There are lots of other bears in this woods."

Sequatchie wanted to say, "Your own son could use something like this," but he did not. He kept his lips closed firmly together, but later he went to have a long talk with Paul Anderson.

Anderson listened intently, even though he already knew most of what was eating at Hawk Spencer. "He's wrong about Jake," Paul said. "He's lost the best part of raising him, and now the boy's how old, fourteen? And it's killing Hawk. You know a man can get killed as surely from something like this as he can from a bullet in a brain."

"Yes, he is a bitter man. Bitter at himself." Sequatchie nodded sadly.

As Sequatchie moved away, Anderson watched him go, thinking, *That Cherokee has more wisdom than most graduates of William and Mary.*

————————

The next day they reached a swollen creek that was more like a river. Hawk stood looking down at the muddy brown waters that rolled past, measuring the distance to the other side. The men all came to stand with him, and the women stayed behind, some holding the children, their eyes filled with consternation.

"That's a mighty bad river," John Russell muttered.

"Too bad," another settler said. "Ain't no way to get across that."

"What do you think, Hawk?" Paul Anderson said.

"It is a bad river. I think we're going to have to wait, but the trouble is it's been raining over there." He pointed to the east. "Up in those mountains. They're all full of water, and it's still raining."

Sequatchie, who was standing nearby said, "Yes, there is still rain over there."

"What does that mean, Hawk?" John Russell asked.

"It means this creek's going to be up for a long time. Maybe a week, or even two."

A groan rose from the group, and they began complaining and muttering. "Now—what are you going to do about it?" one of the men, a tall, lanky individual named Simmons, asked Hawk. He was truculent and always seemed to argue about everything.

"Well, I think I'll just wave my staff over it like Moses did, then we can cross like the Israelites did the Red Sea," Hawk said. "Would that suit you, Simmons?"

"You don't have to be makin' fun of the Bible!" Simmons snapped.

"Then you don't have to be asking me what we're going to do! I can't control that river!" Hawk snapped back.

"Hawk's right," George Russell said. "We'll just have to wait it out."

The men went back to their wagons and set up camp. They waited for five days, and during that time, the river did not go down one inch. Day after day, the strong current scoured the banks, sometimes pulling trees down, tearing them out by their roots and rolling and tossing them upside down.

Hawk kept to himself. Hunting was hard, and he stayed out in the dense forest, looking for game. They had run out of salt. What little they had had been spoiled by the first storm, and those not accustomed to going without complained about the blandness of the meat.

When the river finally went down, Simmons and a few others came to Hawk and said, "We can cross that river now. I've crossed worse streams."

Hawk looked at the water carefully. Though it appeared smooth enough, Hawk shook his head. "That river's still treacherous. If the animals step in a hole that's been gouged out by the current, they could disappear."

But Simmons was insistent. "We can send a rider across—or you can go. And if a horse can make it, a team and a wagon can surely make it."

Hawk refused at first, but after another day the river did seem calm enough. "What do you think, Sequatchie?" he asked.

"May be safe now."

Hawk hesitated, then said, "All right." He looked at the men who were waiting and said, "Get hitched up. I think we can try it." Instantly everyone flew into action, and soon all the pack animals and wagons were ready. "I'll let you try it, Sequatchie." Hawk grinned. He slapped his friend on the shoulder and said, "Don't let anything happen to you. You hear me?"

"It is not my time."

Hawk looked with surprise at the Indian. "What do you mean, not your time? You don't know when you're going to die."

"I know it will not be today. The good Lord Jesus has given me peace."

Hawk looked at his friend grimly and muttered, "I wish He'd give me some." Then, as if ashamed of uttering the words, he said, "All right. Go ahead and see how safe the bottom of that river is."

Sequatchie mounted his horse, and everyone gathered to watch as he made his way across. The horse, a sturdy buckskin, moved slowly, held back by Sequatchie's hands. The water came up to his stomach, and then a little higher. They all held their breath—but then he reached shallower water, and Sequatchie's mount climbed out on the other side. He turned and waved. "If you come exactly as I have come, it will be all right."

"Let's go," Hawk said. "We'll cross one at a time." He rode across with the first team, determined to take every precaution. George Russell was mounted on the opposite side. He felt the power of the current as it moved the wagon sideways more than five feet. Hawk's horse was nearly caught and momentarily floundered, but he tugged at the bridle and yelled to the team, as did Russell on the other side, and the animals' hooves found safe footing.

When they reached the other bank, Russell looked at Hawk and said, "I didn't like the feel of that. That current's still mighty strong."

"You're right about that," Hawk said. "We'll have to go ahead now. We can't be on both sides of this creek."

The next three wagons went over with little difficulty, for Russell and Hawk were aware of the power of the current now, and they had directed the others to the solid bottom. Sarah sat in the wagon seat between her father and mother when their turn came. She was frightened and reached out and grasped for her father's hand. He took it and looked down at her. "Why, you're not afraid, are you, Sarah?"

"I am scared," Sarah whispered, her face so pale that her freckles stood out.

Her manner of speaking brought concern to the face of Patrick MacNeal. "Why, you don't have to worry. You've seen those other wagons go over safely."

"I'm afraid of water, Papa!" Sarah cried out.

Her parents glanced at each other. They knew her fear was real. Sarah, unlike Andrew who loved the water, could never be enticed to go swimming or do anything but get her feet wet on the banks of lakes or creeks. "It'll be all right," Elizabeth assured her. "We'll be on the other side soon. You'll see."

Rhoda was riding her horse beside the wagon, and she too saw the fright in the girl's face. She called out, "Don't worry, Sarah, it'll be all right!" The child, trying to smile, looked at her and waved.

They started across with Hawk and Russell leading the team, and at first everything went well. But then, without warning, a sunken log struck the rear wheels of the wagon. Elizabeth made a grab for the seat, almost slipping into the murky waters below. Then she saw Sarah, who had lost her white-knuckled grip, thrown off balance. She watched in horror as Sarah suddenly fell out into the muddy waters.

"Sarah!" Elizabeth screamed, and would have gone after her, but Patrick reached out and grabbed her.

"Here, you hold the team. I'll get her!" Patrick said, handing the lines to Elizabeth.

Hawk had already seen the child fall. Seeing her pale face disappear as she tried to scream, he drove his horse forward. When the horse stumbled and went down, he swam with strong strokes. For the first time in years, he prayed, although he was not fully aware of doing so. *Oh, God, let me find her. Let her come up again, so I can see her. . . !*

Even as he prayed, the child surfaced only a few feet in front of him, struggling to keep her head up. With two powerful strokes, he lunged and reached for her, catching her hair in his hands. He pulled her up, rolled over on his back, and whispered, "It's all right now, Sarah. Don't be afraid!"

Hawk could hear the yells of the others from the riverbank, and the power of the current had him, but he was a strong swimmer. He held Sarah's head high in the air as he swam on his back with one arm. Soon his feet touched bottom, and he turned and put both arms under Sarah. The mud sucked at his feet, but he climbed out onto the bank, and when he was clear of the river, he sat down and held the trembling girl.

"Are you all right, sweetheart?"

Sarah buried her face in his chest, sobbing. He put his arms around her and held her, feeling her body tremble in violent spasms. "You're all right, aren't you, honey?" he asked anxiously.

"Y-yes, but I was so afraid!"

Hawk felt a wash of relief. He suddenly thought, *Well, that's one prayer that God answered. . . .* Looking over to where Russell was helping the team ashore, he saw Elizabeth standing up and holding her hand over her bosom. Patrick was urging the team forward like a maniac, his face pale.

"It's all right! It's all right!" Hawk yelled. "She's fine!"

Finally, Hawk got up and walked down the side of the river, carrying the girl. She seemed so very small and fragile to him. By the time he got to the wagons, Elizabeth had leaped down, and she and Patrick had come to take the child. Hawk surrendered her to them and turned and walked away.

Rhoda came over at once. She got off her horse and said, "It's a good thing you were there or she would've drowned."

"She might have," Hawk said, wiping the water from his face.

Rhoda looked at the river, and then back at the couple holding the weeping child. Andrew had come now and stood beside them, reaching out to pat his sister on the back. "It would have killed them if that girl had died."

"I think you're right," Hawk nodded.

"I know what preacher Anderson will say," Rhoda said suddenly.

"What?"

"He'll say that God was in it. That He had you in that place, at that time, just to save that child."

"That's what Sequatchie will say, too." Hawk nodded, a grin pulling the corners of his lips upward.

"You know, I never thought about God much before this trip."

Surprised, Hawk looked down at the woman. "Are you afraid of death, Rhoda?"

"Sure I am! Aren't you?"

Hawk considered the question. "I put it out of my mind. That's a foolish thing to do, I guess. My father and mother taught me better. You haven't been converted, have you?"

"The likes of me? What kind of a Christian would I make? You know what I've been!"

Hawk put his hand on the girl's shoulder. Her honesty touched him. He knew she had had a hard life, and now he remembered many things about her. "Don't listen to people like me," he said. "You listen to Paul and to the MacNeals and to Sequatchie. They've got the right of it."

"Well, what about you? You won't listen to them."

Hawk stared at the girl. His black hair was plastered against his face, and he looked at her strangely. "I'm a fool," he said, "but that's no reason for you to be one. You listen to the preacher." He turned and walked away, and Rhoda looked after him wonderingly.

Living Water

Twenty-Three

$\mathcal{A}$fter the traumatic crossing of the river, Hawk decided it would be best for the group to stop for the rest of the day. It would also give the horses time to rest after fighting the strong current. The MacNeals were still shaken over the ordeal. Elizabeth had quickly taken Sarah to change her clothes while Patrick started a fire.

Paul Anderson, at once, went to Hawk and said, "I think it would be good to hold a service to thank God for sparing our lives."

"Go ahead, preacher," Hawk said. "You don't have to ask my permission."

At once Anderson moved among the travelers, announcing the service. After they had set up camp, almost the entire group gathered together beside the river. The skies were clear, but there was a bite in the air, a reminder that winter would soon be upon them. The wind was blowing, but the men removed their hats, which they rarely did for any occasion, and the breeze stirred their hair.

Paul Anderson stood upon a small rise and looked out over his small congregation. He paused for a moment, then said, "Patrick, would you lead us in a few hymns?"

Patrick, who had a fine tenor voice, began to sing, and soon the voices of the others joined him. As he led them in the hymn, "O God, Our Help in Ages Past," by Isaac Watts, the words of the first stanza took on new and added meaning to all who were singing:

> O God, our help in ages past,
> Our hope for years to come,
> Our shelter from the stormy blast,
> And our eternal home!

At first the service seemed rather feeble, for there was a sense of loneliness in the great wilderness. The trees swayed about them like giants, and already the leaves were beginning to turn colors. But there was something about the young minister that spoke of hope. After the singing was over, he read his text, which came from Matthew 5:6. "Blessed are they which do hunger and thirst after righteousness: for they shall be filled."

He turned the pages of his Bible and said, "Let me read another verse." He read the verse aloud in a clear voice, " 'As the hart panteth after the water brooks, so panteth my soul after thee, O God.' And let me add to these one more verse to tie all things together. In the fourth chapter of the book of John, Jesus met a woman. He was tired and thirsty, so He asked her for a drink of water. She was surprised by His request, because men did not speak to women, especially Jewish men to Samaritan women. Jesus said, 'If thou knewest the gift of God, and who it is that saith to thee, Give me to drink; thou wouldest have asked of him, and he would have given thee living water.' "

Hawk had posted himself at the rear of the crowd, as was his custom. He never put himself any place close to the front and usually kept completely out of sight. Sometimes he left rather than listen to the preaching. Yet there was something in the particular Scriptures that Paul had read that seemed to reach out and touch him. He could not help but recall his encounter with the deer a few years ago and what Sequatchie had said about it. Curious, he decided to listen to what Paul had to say.

Rhoda Harper, however, was at the front of the crowd. She stood there wearing a simple butternut dress. Her hair, tied with a dark blue ribbon, hung down her back like a cascade, fine and shining in the sun. She looked up at Anderson, her lips slightly parted, as he continued to speak.

"I think all of us have been on this journey long enough to clearly understand what the writer of the Psalms meant when he said, 'As the hart, or deer, gets thirsty for water, so I get thirsty for God.' Right now we've been through rainstorms, so there's water everywhere, but I'm sure that Sequatchie or Hawk could tell us about those times of drought when all of the creeks dry up, when the trees begin to shrivel from the heat, and when the ordinary sources that furnish drink for the wild beast begin to disappear. It isn't too hard to imagine a deer that has wandered long in the forest, kicking up dust, his tongue swollen, his eyes glazed with thirst as he stumbles desperately through the forest. Finally he comes onto a little creek, perhaps only a foot wide. But we can imagine how his ears might be raised, his eyes would brighten, and he would begin to run. And we can think how it would be when he would bow his head and lower his nose to drink of the cooling water. What a relief!"

Looking around at the men, women, and children gathered, Anderson said, "I reached that point in my life, in my search for God, when I was a very young man. Oh, how I longed for God! Very much like that deer longed for water, you see. I attended the house of God. I heard sermons. I read the Bible, and all the time I grew drier and drier until my spirit shriveled up within me. . . ."

Anderson went on to describe his search for God as being a hopeless thing, and then he lifted his voice and a smile came to his lips. He raised his Bible over his head and called with a powerful voice, "But then one day I found the water that I had sought for. Like the hart found that brook in the forest, so my *heart* found God! I discovered, as the woman at the well did, that Jesus is the water that we all thirst for. He's what keeps our spirit from drying up and burning to a crisp. Blessed be God who satisfies the thirst of His people!"

Hawk had been listening carefully. He had seen deer during periods of drought in exactly the condition that Anderson described. He had seen them when they died for lack of water, their carcasses shrunken in the arid wilderness, and he himself had suffered the pangs of thirst, and knew well what it was to come upon a small pool or stream when his tongue was parched and his lips cracked. He remembered more than once throwing himself down, burying his face in a small stream after nearly dying for lack of moisture. He shifted his weight, and his bronze face grew still. He realized there was a truth in all of this that he was missing in his life, and as Anderson went on, speaking of men who hunger and thirst after righteousness being filled, a longing began to grow in him. Hawk had thought his spirit was dead to the things of God. Standing there, holding his musket as usual, he looked down with shock and saw that his hands were actually shaking. *I didn't think anything in the world could make me do that!* he thought. Clamping his jaw shut, he shook his shoulders and was tempted to turn and go away, but something about the words of the preacher held him as tightly as if his moccasins were fastened to the ground with thongs.

Hawk was not the only one stirred. Rhoda Harper was shaking too, and as the sermon came to an end, Anderson said, "If there is one of you out there who is thirsty for God, let me tell you that the water of life is still flowing. Jesus still says, 'Come and drink of my waters! Oh, do not turn away from God and die thirsty and arid and dry. Come to the fountain and drink of the water!' The prophet cried out, 'Ho, everyone that thirsteth. Come and drink and be filled.' I want you this morning to come and to taste of that water. Jesus said to that woman at the well years ago, 'If you drink of the water that I give you, you will never thirst again,' and I promise you it's true. You may say, I'm not worthy. I've sinned too greatly." Anderson's voice rose with emotion. "Jesus is the Friend of sinners. If you're a sinner, He's your friend. Won't you come to that Friend and let us pray that you might find forgiveness and life itself?"

Without being told, Patrick MacNeal began to sing a new hymn written by William Cowper, "There is a fountain filled with blood. . . ." And as he did, Rhoda Harper wanted desperately to move forward, but somehow she could not. Hawk was watching her, and he also was stirred, but the hardness of his heart was as yet unbroken.

One person began to weep and go forward—Iris Taylor, the wife of the brutal Zeke Taylor. She fell on her knees, and at once Elizabeth went to her and began to pray with her. She prayed quietly as she held her arms around the sobbing woman. After a few words, Elizabeth led Iris Taylor through a simple prayer.

Looking up at Anderson with tears running down her face, Elizabeth said, "Thank God. She's found the Lord Jesus."

As soon as Anderson dismissed the group, the families went back to their wagons to prepare the meal. There was considerable rejoicing among the fervent Christians of the wagon train. Elizabeth and Paul stayed to talk to Iris for a few moments. The usual fear that had clouded the poor woman's face for so long was now gone. Though filled with tears, there was a peace about the woman's eyes.

"I feel like I'm not alone in this anymore," she said, wiping her face with the handkerchief Elizabeth handed her.

Paul looked at Elizabeth, then turned back to Iris and said, "Iris, we all know it has not been easy for you with your husband. If you ever feel a need to pray, I'm sure Elizabeth would be happy to pray with you."

"Thank you. I . . . I'm not sure what's going to happen now, but I know it's going to be better."

"God has accepted you, Mrs. Taylor," Paul assured her. "And He will guide you and help you." As Iris walked back to her wagon, Paul wondered how things would go for her.

Zeke Taylor, however, was taken aback when he saw his wife approach. The look on her face was something he had never seen in his married life. His wife had tearstains on her face, but a new light shone in her eyes.

Iris looked at her husband and said quietly, "Ezekiel, you've been a hard man, and you've made my life miserable. I've been afraid of you almost since the day we got married. I want to tell you something. I'm going to be a good wife to you—but I'm not afraid of you anymore." She smiled and tears appeared in her eyes. "I'm going to pray that you will find Jesus as I have, then you won't be miserable, and you won't have to drink no more."

Zeke Taylor was shocked down to his boots. He stared at his wife, unable to think of a word to say. Amanda came and put her arms around her mother, holding tightly to her. The two watched the face of the husband and father. Each of them expected him to go into a rage, but instead a puzzled expression came across his face, and to the shock of both, he scratched his head and said, "Well, if you've got religion, I'm glad of it. Maybe it will make you a better wife." He gnawed his lip and seemed about to say something else but turned away.

Amanda said, "Mama, is he going to be better to us?"

"Yes, he is. We're going to obey Jesus, and he's going to be saved, too. You'll see."

Andrew MacNeal had been listening to Paul Anderson's sermons since the train had left Williamsburg. He had not been particularly impressed—not until he had seen Iris Taylor fall to her knees. Somehow when she did, he began to feel afraid. He had listened to the sermon, but he had heard sermons before. All afternoon he tried to put the thing out of his mind. He played with the other boys, laughing and shouting. They found the trail of a deer in the forest, and although they were forbidden to go far, it was exciting to imagine a day when they would become long hunters like Hawk, who had become their idol.

But despite this outward hilarity, Andrew grew steadily more thoughtful. This disturbed him, and finally he left the group and sat down by himself. Taking out the new knife that his father had bought for him at the Anderson store back in Williamsburg, he began whittling listlessly on a stick. Finally, he just sat there and stared at the stick.

"Well, I don't see you this still very often, son."

Andrew looked up to see his father, who had come and was standing beside him. "Don't you feel well?"

Andrew hesitated. "I guess so," he said.

Instantly Patrick read something unusual in the boy's face. He sat down beside him, and for a time the two spoke of the things they'd do when they reached the settlement of Watauga. Finally Patrick turned and said, "I think I know you pretty well, Andy. What's wrong? You worried about something? Young fellows worry about things. I did when I was your age."

"I don't know, Pa. I just feel funny."

"You mean you're sick to your stomach?"

"No, it's something about what happened to Mrs. Taylor."

"Oh, I see." Patrick became thoughtful and looked down at Andrew. *He looks so much like his mother and her grandfather.* He admired the wavy blond hair and the blue eyes that were now quiet and thoughtful. He said kindly, "I guess all of us think about God sometimes. Maybe it's your time, son."

"My time for what?"

"Well, everybody has to make up their mind about the Lord. Most things don't matter too much, but the most important thing for any of us is what we will do with Jesus Christ."

Andrew grew very still. The name seemed to have power over him. "What . . . what do I have to do to get rid of this feeling?"

"I think the feeling comes from God, so don't be afraid. Everybody feels that way at some time or other. It's God trying to catch our attention. It's kind of like fear, isn't it?"

"Yes, it is, Pa. I . . . I do feel a little bit afraid," he confessed. "If I was to die, I don't know where I'd go."

"Well, let's talk about this, son." Patrick MacNeal began to speak quietly. For a long time he spoke of God's love and His law, putting them in very simple terms. He stressed how everybody needed God, because everybody has sinned against God. Then he spoke of the death of Jesus, and finally he said, "I think this might be your time, Andrew. Some people wait until they're old before they let God come into their lives, but the older you get the harder it is, I think."

"Mrs. Taylor got saved."

"Yes, she did, and I thank God for it. But it would have been easier for her if she'd been saved when she was your age."

"I don't know. It scares me to think about it."

"Well, you know, son, I'm glad you are afraid. That means you're serious about it. But Jesus died for you, and that means He loves you. Anybody who would die for you has to love you. You know, I've heard you memorize the Scriptures that your grandfather taught you. You know a lot of them already. I'll bet I know your favorite."

"Yes, sir, John three, sixteen. It's always been my favorite."

"My favorite, too, and it's so simple."

"But, Pa, how do I become a Christian?"

"The Scriptures say you have to be born again. You were born my son by flesh and blood, and that's not going to change. You're always going to be my son. But you need to be born of the Spirit. It's very simple. You just call on God and tell Him that you need Him, that you've done wrong things, and you want to live for Him. You tell Him that you believe in Jesus, and you want Him as your Savior."

"I don't know how to say all that, Pa!"

"You just talk to God the best way you know, and He'll understand. I'll tell you what, son. Why don't I just say a prayer, and while I'm praying out loud, you just call on God in your heart. Tell Him you're sorry for what you've done, and that you want Jesus to come into your heart."

"Do you think He'd do it for me?"

"He said, 'Whosoever will, may come.' You trust Him, and you'll see." Patrick MacNeal began to pray for his son. His heart was full, but he prayed simply for God to make himself known to the boy who sat beside him. When he finished the prayer, he turned and saw that Andrew was trembling. "Did you ask God to do something for you, son?"

"Yes, sir, I did."

Patrick hesitated. It was so easy to lead young people to say things that they didn't feel. He waited for some time, and finally Andrew went on.

"I asked him to make me a Christian, and"—he looked up at his father and there were tears glimmering in his eyes—"I don't know how it's supposed to feel, but I just feel—well, like I did something right. And that fear that was in my stomach, it's all gone."

"Jesus always takes away the fear," Patrick said. "I want you to remember this spot, Andrew. Look at it. This very log. Put it in your mind. I want you to sit here for a while, and I'll stay with you. Don't ever forget it. Look at those trees, at that river there, and the wagons."

"Why do you want me to remember this spot, Pa? It's just like a lot of other spots."

"No it's not. It's like no other spot in the world. We'll leave here tomorrow, and maybe tomorrow night, or the night after, or a week from now you'll begin to think, 'Ah, there was nothing to that stuff about God! I'm not really a Christian.' That'll be the devil putting that in your heart, and you tell him, 'Yes, I am saved. I can take you back to the place. It was beside a group of walnut trees, and there's a log down there my dad and I sat on, and that's when I asked Jesus into my heart.' You tell the devil that and he'll flee."

Andrew brightened up. "Is that right, Pa?"

"That's right. This will always be the place where you can go in your mind and say, 'I remember that day on September 16, 1770, I asked God to save me, and He did it.'"

———

Rhoda Harper was an emotional wreck. The sermon had torn her to pieces, and as soon as the meeting was over, she turned and walked quickly away, not wishing to speak to anyone. She wanted to get away from the train and put her hands over her ears, for it seemed she could still hear the voice of Paul Anderson saying, "Blessed are they which do hunger and thirst after righteousness."

"Why can't I do what Iris Taylor did?" she whispered in despair. Still, something in her would not turn loose, and for a long time she walked, hoping the misery that weighted her down would go away.

She was startled when a figure moved in beside her, and she gasped when she saw Jacques Cartier.

"What are you doing out here, little pigeon?"

"Don't call me that anymore! I never liked it!"

Jacques Cartier was surprised. He scowled and his eyes grew small. "You're getting hard to handle. Why haven't you done more to get this wagon train to turn back?"

"I couldn't do anything. Besides, it was wrong to poison that water. Some of these people nearly died!"

"If you would have put a little more in, maybe two or three of them would have died, then they would have turned back!"

"I'm not going to do anything like that again!" she said and started to head back down the trail to the wagons.

Cartier grabbed her by the arm and said, "Shut your mouth or I will close it for you! Maybe for good!"

Rhoda had always been frightened of the man, but now, somehow, it didn't seem to matter. She looked up fearlessly into his face. "Why are you doing all this, Jacques? What do you care whether this little group of settlers finds a home in the wilderness?"

"All right. I will tell you. I work for the French government. We French have lost the war, yes, but we still want a colony here in this part of the world. France must have a presence in this country, and the more English settlers that come, the less France's chance of re-taking the territory. Me, and a few others, we are paid to stop the settlers from coming this way."

"You can't stop people from coming! It would be like trying to stop a river from flowing."

Cartier gritted his teeth. "There is one way they can be stopped!"

Something in the large man's tone caught at Rhoda, and fear shot through her. "What are you talking about?"

"Since you've botched your job, we will have to try something else."

"Something else? Like what?"

"There's going to be an attack. The Indians are going to attack this train. I've come to get you out of it. You've failed, but I don't want you to die with the rest. You're going to be my woman."

Rhoda stared at him in disbelief. "You . . . you can't mean that, Jacques! You can't kill innocent people—what about the women and children on this train!"

Cartier shook his head. "Maybe we just kill a few, and they will go back. But the train will be stopped."

"Please, Jacques, don't do it!" Rhoda began to beg. She held her hands tightly together and squeezed them until they cramped.

Finally Cartier said, "Come and go with me. If you don't, you'll be dead, Rhoda."

Rhoda had not even one instant's temptation. "I won't go with you, Jacques."

For some time Cartier tried to convince her, then angrily he grabbed her and shook her. "You little fool!" he said. "You think the Indians will spare you when I turn them loose to attack the whites? They might take you and make you a plaything for a while, but you would be their slave, and you would die after that. You'd better come now. It's your last chance."

Rhoda did not doubt Cartier's words or his intention, but she said, "No, I won't go with you."

Cartier stared at her, then he shoved her away so that she staggered. "Very well! Be a fool and die with the rest!"

As Cartier turned and disappeared into the forest, Rhoda stared after him and turned slowly. She walked back toward the wagons, and all the rest of the afternoon, she stayed by herself.

A few noticed she was being exceptionally quiet, and it was Elizabeth who said, "I think Rhoda's under conviction, Patrick."

Patrick, who had shared the good news of Andrew's conversion with the family, said, "The Spirit of God is working. We'll have to pray much for that woman. She really needs Jesus Christ."

Rhoda said nothing of Cartier's threat. She was stunned by his words and purposed more than once to say something to Hawk. She did determine she would tell Hawk the next day about the dangers that lay ahead from the impending Indian attack, no matter what they would do to her after finding out that she had helped Cartier. Finally she went to bed and drifted into a restless sleep, tossing and turning. Overhead the skies were dark, for it was not the time of the full moon. A few tattered skeins of clouds drifted across the heavens, and the people in the wagons slept.

Another Loss

Twenty-Four

*P*atrick MacNeal awoke early. He climbed out of his blankets and discovered that Elizabeth was already up and had started breakfast, even though Hawk had not sounded his usual wake-up call for the camp. "What are you doing up so early?" Patrick said, going over and putting his arms around her.

"I couldn't sleep," she said. Looking up from the fire she was kindling, she said, "I'm so happy about Andrew, I didn't sleep much last night. I kept waking up and thinking how wonderful it was that you were able to bring him to Jesus."

"I didn't sleep much myself," Patrick said. He was tired and sleepy, but there was a peace on his face, and he said, "I think it was the best day of my life, expect maybe for the day I married you." He kissed her cheek and said, "God is good, isn't He?"

"Yes, He is." She continued to work, and as he built up the fire, she pulled together the fixings for a simple breakfast. When it was cooking, the smell of meat soon drew the children out of the wagon.

Andrew looked at his father and mother and said shyly, "I still feel good." He pointed over to the spot among the walnuts and said, "I remember what you said, Pa. I'll never forget that place as long as I live. That's where I asked Jesus to come into my heart."

Elizabeth's heart was full, and she smiled at this tall young son of hers and said, "I'm happy for you, Andrew, and I'm more happy that it was your father who led you to the Lord. You'll never forget that. We never forget the ones who lead us to Jesus."

"Who led you to Jesus, Mama?" Sarah asked.

"It was my own father, and I was just about your age."

Sarah was quiet for a time, and Elizabeth saw the expression on her daughter's face. "Maybe you and I ought to have a talk about Jesus."

"I'd like that, Mama," Sarah said quickly.

"All right. We'll do it then."

Dawn came quickly, and the family sat around the fire, eating their breakfast. Up and down the line, other fires were being started as families climbed out of their wagons. Sequatchie and Hawk walked by, acting like sentinels, as always.

"Don't those two ever sleep?" Patrick said. He looked down to where Rhoda was sleeping under the wagon and said, "Rhoda's sleeping late this morning."

"I heard her tossing all night. I don't think she went to sleep 'til a few hours before dawn. I think she's very troubled about something."

Patrick stared at the sleeping woman and nodded slightly. "We'll have to pray much for her," he said. "I wonder—" He never completed his sentence, for suddenly a wild scream rent the air and froze Elizabeth's blood. She was holding a frying pan and dropped it, whirling to look where the sound had come from. Three war-painted Indians burst out of the woods and fell upon the Simmons family. Elizabeth and Patrick and the children watched in horror as tomahawks rose and fell, and all four of the Simmonses lay dead.

At once, Patrick cried out, "Indian attack!" and made a wild leap for his musket. It was leaning against the wagon wheel, as Hawk had taught them all to keep their weapons at hand. He leveled it and fired. One of the charging Indians fell and lay motionless twenty feet away. At once, Patrick groped for his powder horn and began reloading his rifle.

Wild screams filled the air from all around the camp. Hawk and Sequatchie were crying out the alarm. And as Elizabeth gathered the children and hurried them into the wagon, she saw Hawk kill one painted brave with his rifle, then run directly at two others. He and Sequatchie were soon engaged in a fierce hand-to-hand struggle with the screaming Indians.

Patrick had gotten his rifle loaded, and he ran forward to join the men who had collected their muskets and now had formed a little group. Musket fire was coming from outside now, from the woods, and Patrick saw Jed Smith go down clutching his leg, which spurted bright red blood. He turned and stared into the forest but could see nothing. Quickly he ran and joined the line of men.

Hawk had retrieved his rifle and was putting a bloody knife back in his belt. "Get under cover!" he shouted. "Make a circle! Sooner or later they'll charge us. When they try a rush, hold your fire until they're no more than ten feet away! We'll get one shot apiece! Make every one count!"

The gunfire from the Indians was erratic. Ten minutes after the settlers had formed a circle there was a volley from the woods, and then someone screamed a command. Hawk shouted, "Here they come!" He held his rifle steady until a half-naked brave came charging directly into the center of camp. When the Indian was no more than ten feet away, Hawk shot him through the heart. With no time to reload, he grabbed up the Indian's tomahawk and met the wave of attackers head on. Sequatchie was right beside him, and John and George Russell formed a little line that courageously fought against the attackers. The Russells were using their muskets as clubs, which proved very effective.

Patrick had saved his shot as Hawk commanded. When it was gone, he stood there momentarily confused. He started to reload, and then he saw a man, not an Indian, appear. He was a big man dressed in buckskins, and he had a musket that he was swinging up, aimed directly at Hawk. Without thought, Patrick leaped up and dashed wildly ahead, crying, "Hawk—look out!"

Hawk turned at the warning and saw Patrick MacNeal come between him and a large figure in buckskins. A shot rang out, and Patrick crumpled to the ground.

Hawk leaped forward and rolled Patrick over and saw that he had taken a bullet in the chest. Through the smoke of the black powder that scored the air, Hawk looked up and caught a fleeting glimpse of a big man turning and leaving the battle.

Hawk never remembered much about the rest of the battle. He fought like a madman, and finally he saw that the Indians were retreating. Quickly he yelled, "Load up! They may come back!"

The Indians, however, seemed to have been beaten. At least a dozen of their braves lay dead, and many more were groaning with wounds that would probably prove fatal. Hawk looked around and saw some of the settlers lying dead, too. He shook his head at the sight of the Simmons family, who had been the first killed in the attack.

Many others were wounded, including Jed Smith, but most would recover. Hawk's thoughts went immediately to Patrick. He ran over to where Elizabeth was kneeling beside her husband. He looked at Paul Anderson, who was kneeling on the other side, and Anderson gave him a shake of his head, and Hawk knew that there was no hope for Patrick.

All around the circle of wagons could be heard the groans of the wounded, but Hawk stood there. He had grown fond of Patrick MacNeal, and suddenly he felt a tremendous guilt, for he knew Patrick had died saving his life.

Elizabeth was weeping, and the children were gathered around their father.

"Oh, Patrick!" Elizabeth cried. "You can't die! You just can't!"

The children were sobbing, too, and then Patrick opened his eyes. The front of his shirt was covered with blood, but for the moment his eyes were clear. He looked at his family, then his eyes fell on Hawk. He lifted a hand and made a motion.

Hawk quickly knelt down and took the dying man's hand. "What is it, Patrick?" he whispered huskily.

"Hawk—" Patrick gasped and blood stained his lips. Elizabeth wiped it away and Patrick said, "Take care . . . of my family. Will you do that?"

Hawk nodded and said, "I'll do that. I give you my word. I'll care for them like they were my own."

A peace flooded Patrick MacNeal's face then. Elizabeth was supporting him. He reached up and touched her face and whispered, "I've always loved you, Elizabeth."

"Oh, Patrick—"

"Never grieve for me. I've loved you, and you've been the best wife . . . a man can have."

He reached out then and touched the faces of his children, and he said in a faint voice, "I want you all . . . to promise me." He saw that they were watching, and his eyelids began to droop. He pulled them open, gathering his strength. "Don't grieve for me, and never feel angry at God. I'm going to be with Him—my Father. I will . . . see you . . . in the morning."

Patrick simply closed his eyes, his chest heaved twice, and then he was gone. Elizabeth cradled his head and wept. Outside the circle, others watched silently. One of them was Rhoda Harper. She had felt a deep affection for this man who had welcomed her into his family. As she watched, something seemed to die within her as Patrick MacNeal breathed his last. She turned away and began weeping bitterly. Hawk rose and walked blindly away with a hardened look on his face.

The service for those who were killed was brief. Paul read the First Psalm before the open graves. The bodies wrapped in blankets were lowered, and then Paul said a short prayer. The survivors were led away where they would not have to hear the clods of dirt falling into the open graves.

Elizabeth stayed by her children that day, but at twilight she went back to the grave. She was standing there looking at the raw red mound when she felt as if someone was watching her. Turning, she saw Hawk standing there holding his musket and staring at her, his face impassive.

Elizabeth looked down at her husband's grave, and for a time silence reigned over the scene. Neither of them said anything, then she turned and said, "Everyone has been so kind."

Hawk seemed unable to speak, but finally he said in a strained voice, "The train will have to go ahead and get to Bean's settlement to beat the winter, but I'll take you and the children back to Williamsburg. We'll have time for that."

Elizabeth listened to his words. Her face was drawn, and for a while she said nothing at all. Then she turned to face him. "Thank you, Hawk, but I won't be going back to Williamsburg."

Hawk stared at her as if he had not heard correctly. "But you won't want to go on now without . . . without your husband." He did not seem able to pronounce Patrick's name, and he shook his head. "It wouldn't be the same."

"If I went back to Williamsburg," Elizabeth said, "it would be like saying that Patrick's dream was wrong. That was his dream, you know? To have a home. Not just for himself, but for the children."

"But that dream is over now with Patrick gone."

"As long as I'm alive, that dream is alive, Hawk."

Hawk wanted to argue. He knew the difficulties and dangers that would await a lone woman in a frontier settlement. "You'll have to go back, Elizabeth," he said. "There's no place for a widow with two children."

"There'll be a place for us," Elizabeth said. "God led us this far, and He won't fail us now."

Suddenly anger twisted Hawk's lips into an ugly line. "How can you talk about God when He's done this to you? He's taken your husband!"

Elizabeth thought of all she had heard of Hawk's past and knew that she had to speak very carefully. "God is all wise, Hawk. I can't explain why He chose to call Patrick home and leave the children and me alone, but I believe that God is good. I believe that He loves us, and He will be with me and with Sarah and Andrew, no matter what the future holds." She pulled herself up straight and said, "I will miss Patrick terribly, but Jesus said, 'I will be with you always. I will never leave you nor forsake you.'" She watched his face and saw unbelief there, and a great pity rose in her for him. "I wish you could believe this, Hawk. You're missing so much."

Elizabeth turned and walked away. Hawk stood there watching her, and for a moment a blinding fear came to him—fear or anger, he could not tell which, for he knew that she had found some secret to go on and face life that he had missed. A final burden of guilt ate at him—he knew full well that Patrick had taken a bullet meant for him. The thought burned in his spirit, and he whispered huskily, "Reckon he died for me, Patrick did." He thought of trying to go home and making things right with his son but quickly cast the thought away.

"It's too late," he muttered. "Too late for me." He remembered, however, Patrick MacNeal's last words. "I promised to look after them," Hawk said to himself. Looking up, he said, "God, I don't believe in you anymore. If you *are* there, you're not kind and good as Paul Anderson and Elizabeth say you are. But I made a promise to a friend, and I'm going to keep that promise!"

He turned and walked slowly toward the train, his jaw set and his eyes cloudy with the prophetic dream of what lay ahead.

PART IV

As the Deer...

October 1770 – October 1771

As the hart panteth after the water brooks,
so panteth my soul after thee, O God.

Psalm 42:1

New Homes, New Lives

Twenty-Five

*W*ell, you done good, Hawk."

William Bean looked over the settlement, gazing at the spots where new cabins were going up. Some were too far away to see, but at least five cabins near him were in the process of having their walls raised. Bean ran his hand through his hair, and a warm light appeared in his brown eyes. "It makes a feller feel good to see more folk comin' in. First thing you know, we'll have a real town here!"

Hawk was standing with an ax in his hand. He had been helping cut down trees all day, and now he pulled his coonskin cap off and wiped his brow. "A sight too many people for me, I reckon, William. But we all have to play it the way we see it."

"Fellers like you and Daniel Boone—seems like you don't like to live in too close. Daniel, he always says it's too close to him if he sees the smoke from a cabin nearby. I reckon he'll leave here one day and go out into Kaintuck."

"I reckon he probably will."

Hawk cast his eyes around the settlement, noting the new cabins. "They did better than I expected, William, and it's a good thing, too. It's gonna turn cold soon."

Already, the late October wind had a biting edge to it, and both men knew that one day the winter that lurked over the hills would descend and touch everything with a deadly finger, turning the green grass dry and brown, and freezing the earth. The newcomers had all been made welcome by those of Bean's original settlement. They all willingly pitched in to help their new neighbors. One by one, each family had taken a little time to choose their homesites, and now around the Watauga the ring of axes could be heard as trees for new homes were being felled.

Hawk hefted the ax, testing the blade. "Ax is dull," he murmured. "I'll have to use your grindstone to put an edge on it."

"Shore. Come along," William Bean said. "We'll give her a lick and a promise."

The two went over to the grindstone that William had hauled all the way from Virginia. William began to pump on the pedal, and Hawk touched the edge of the double-bitted ax to the wheel. The sparks flew, making a yellow shower, and Hawk steadily ground until he had finished one side, then turned it over and sharpened the other. Touching it with his finger, he looked up and grinned. "A feller could shave with this. Want to try it, William?"

"No thanks. I'll jist keep these here whiskers. Don't see no sense in shavin'. Of course, a bachelor like you . . ." William grinned. "I can see a little bit of sense in that. My wife, she tells me gettin' kissed by me is like gettin' kissed by a bar. And I always ask her, 'How many bars you been kissed by, Lydia?' "

Hawk grinned slightly, then remarked, "Don't reckon I'll grow a beard myself. Tried one once, and I spent all my time scratchin' at it."

"Sequatchie tells me he's goin' to light out sometime soon. I asked him if you wuz going with him, and he said he didn't know."

Hawk ran his fingers along the ax handle and appeared to be thinking deeply. Finally he shook his head. "Reckon I'll stay on for a while, William."

William Bean was an astute man—one of those who are called "country smart" by some. With only a smattering of education, he possessed an ingrained sense of how to do the right thing with people. There was something about him that men trusted, and he had a special ability of understanding people's ways. He was especially interested in Hawk Spencer. Glancing up at the big man, he said, "I reckon you'll be helpin' the widow MacNeal."

Quickly Hawk shot a glance at Bean's face but saw nothing there but simple interest. "Guess I will," he said slowly. "I'd like to go with Sequatchie, but I promised her husband just before he died that I'd help his family. A promise like that is pretty strong."

"I'd say so," William agreed. "She don't talk none about goin' back to Boston? She's got people there. She comes from a rich family, I hear."

"Yes, she does—but she won't hear a word of it."

"I wonder why not," Bean said, pulling his beard.

Hawk set the ax down and sat on the bench beside the grinder. He reached over, picked up a stick, and began tracing a design in the dirt. It was a way he had fallen into throughout his long years of wandering. He was slow to speak, thinking often for long periods before he would answer. He looked up, and his dark eyes looked almost black. Finally he spoke up slowly. "She says that God told them to come here. And the way she makes it out, William, if she goes back home, it means her husband died for nothing. She just plain can't stand to think about that."

Bean scratched his head. "Not a bad way of thinkin', I'd say. A fine woman, and those young'uns, why, they're handsome as young deer! Smart, too—both of them. Still, it'll be mighty hard for her to make a go of it. I don't know of any that have ever filed a claim without a man to help them. Of course," he said, "there are plenty of bachelors around Watauga looking for a good wife. There's Sy Hawkins. He lost his wife, you know, last spring. A little bit old for Elizabeth. He's over fifty now, but he's a good man and has those three young'uns that need a mama."

Hawk gave Bean an odd look. "Too soon for that, William."

"Yeah, of course it is! What am I thinking about?" Bean slapped his hands together with a loud crack and said, "Well I, for one, am glad you ain't going with Sequatchie. We need all the men and rifles we can get around here."

"Any trouble that you know of stirring up?" Hawk asked.

"There's always trouble stirrin' up. You know that, Hawk. Most of the Cherokee are listenin' to Little Carpenter, but some of the Creeks are just spoilin' for a fight. The Chickasaw have been passin' through, and you know what they're like."

"I know," Hawk said grimly. "I think they're the worst." He thought about Elizabeth and the two children, alone and unprotected, and shook his head.

"We'll get everybody to pitch in and help Mrs. MacNeal. And that other young woman, too, Rhoda. I wonder if she'll stay with the MacNeals."

"Might be," Hawk said. "I wish she would. It would be good for all of them."

Even as the two men spoke, Elizabeth stepped out of William Bean's cabin and saw them. Walking quickly she came toward them and spoke cheerfully. "William, Lydia and I have decided we've got to plant some flax next spring."

"Oh, she's been at you about that, has she?" Bean grinned. "That woman would rather weave on a loom than eat. I declare! She was after me until I finally brought a spinning wheel all the way from Williamsburg, and now I'm working on the loom."

"Yes, but it's gonna take flax and wool to make the clothing."

"I'd just as soon have buckskin," Hawk said. He was studying Elizabeth, who was looking very well indeed. She was wearing a simple dress made of a dark brown wool. The dress had a high neckline, long sleeves, and a full skirt covered with a white apron. Her bonnet was a light brown muslin that was full in back, with a wide brim that was tied underneath her chin and a matching ribbon framing her face. Her cheeks were flushed because she had been helping with the work inside, and she smiled at Bean.

"Lydia wants you. I think she needs some help moving some furniture around."

Bean shook his head. "Seems like she could make up her mind about that! We've had that furniture in every spot of that cabin, and it seems we change it every day," he grumbled but went inside.

Hawk said, "Elizabeth, I know I get tiresome talking about this—"

"Now, Hawk, you're not going to try to talk me into going back to Boston."

"It'd be best," he said. "You don't have any idea how hard it can be out here on the frontier!"

"But everybody's offered to help, and I can't go back now." She did not speak of her vow to God, for she knew Hawk would be resentful about that.

"Well, if you've made up your mind, I think we need to get started on a cabin."

"But I thought you were going with Sequatchie and Paul to the village."

"They can go on ahead without me, but this cabin won't wait."

"I . . . I hate to be a burden to you, Hawk."

He grinned and suddenly looked much younger. "I reckon I can put up with it. And I've got a surprise for you."

"What is it?" she said, thinking perhaps he had shot a deer and had a quarter of venison.

"I've got a spot I want to show you. I think it'd make a good place for your homesite—if you're determined to stay, that is."

"Oh, Hawk, how wonderful! I wish the children were here, but they've gone out with Amanda Taylor and the Bean children fishing."

"Well, if you like it we'll take them back later. Are you ready now?"

"Yes!"

"I think we'd better ride out," Hawk said. "It's a pretty fair walk."

"All right."

Thirty minutes later the two of them were clear of the settlement. Hawk had observed her mount easily and had watched her ride sidesaddle all the way. Now as they moved at a brisk trot through a patch of woods turning orange and yellow and red, he said, "I don't see how in the world anybody ever rides a horse like that! I'd fall off and break my neck!"

"I do envy men a little bit, being able to ride astride. But this is such a nice mare that it's not really hard."

"All right, see if you can keep up." He kicked his horse's flanks and laughed as Elizabeth tried to get her mount to speed up. The animal was obstinate, however, and only when Hawk fell back and slapped the mare's rump hard did the pace increase. "You need a stick to beat that animal with," he said, grinning. "You can't argue with a female." He laughed at her indignant look, then added, "She's got an easy gallop, but trotting is hard on anyone."

The sun was hot, and they stopped once to water the horses under the shade of some towering hickory trees. The small brook gurgled over the smooth stones, and it was Elizabeth who remarked, "That brook's been here a long time, I suppose. If it could talk, it could tell us some fine tales."

Somewhat surprised by the remark, Hawk turned to study Elizabeth's face. She was a woman of a strong spirit, and from time to time she revealed the inner world that made up her life. "I suppose it could," he said finally. "It would be mostly about Indians, mostly about their wars."

"Not only wars," Elizabeth responded quickly. "I don't know much about Indians, but they must be like us in many ways."

"Most of the settlers wouldn't agree. They think of them only as savages who need to be brushed aside so they can have the land."

"You don't believe that!"

"Well, I did once, pretty much. But no more." A slight sound behind him pulled his head around, his body stiffening. He half lifted the musket he held loosely in his left hand, every sense alert as his eyes searched the brush. Finally he relaxed, saying, "Rabbit."

Elizabeth had seen this side of Hawk before. "You're so tense," she observed. "You never seem completely relaxed."

"Living in the woods does that to a man—if there are Indians around, or even bears." He pulled his horse's head up, then added, "Trouble—it's always there. Your hair gets to standing on end, and it just won't lay down." He spoke to his horse, and as he moved out of the creek, he said, "Hope you won't be disappointed in the spot I picked out. Don't like to make decisions for other people."

"I'll like it, Hawk!"

The assurance in her voice caught at him. "Pretty sure of that, are you?"

"Yes."

He smiled suddenly, then nudged his horse into a fast gallop. Elizabeth kept up with him, and when he pulled up short and swung his arm forward in an abrupt gesture, she lifted her head—and then caught her breath.

"It's beautiful!"

"Don't know about that—but it's good ground for planting crops."

Elizabeth was stunned by the panorama that lay in front of them. A line of ragged mountains lifted to the east, green and rolling as they filled the horizon. To the west a series of short, choppy hills spilled out, and directly in front of them a third line of hogback ranges formed a valley.

She turned and whispered, "I know where I want the house."

"Where?"

"Down there, in that space where the brook bends. You see? If we build it there, it'll be as though the brook has thrown its arm around the house."

Again Hawk was taken by the swift imagination of Elizabeth's mind, but he said practically, "That's the best spot, I'm thinking."

She turned and smiled brillantly. "Did you really pick just that spot?"

"Sure did. Seems like we have the same tastes in cabins. Come along and we'll see what's to be done. . . .

———————

In the days that followed, Elizabeth learned a great deal about building a log cabin. She was impatient to begin and would have begun hacking at the trees back of the meadow, but the first day of actual work, Hawk said, "Can't build a cabin on dirt. Doesn't the Bible say somewhere that a wise man doesn't build his house on sand?"

"Yes, but this is dirt."

"All the same. Now, the first thing we do is haul rocks from the creek for a foundation. You're going to be sick of stones and rocks before this is over!"

Elizabeth denied this vehemently, but by the end of the day, his word proved prophetic. She wore blisters on her hands very quickly, and Hawk forbad her to do any more work. She drove the horses, pulling the sled that Hawk had built, while he loaded and unloaded the rocks.

"Now—for the sills," Hawk said after the outline of the cabin was plainly marked with flat stones.

"What's a sill?" Elizabeth asked.

"Beams or logs that rest on the foundation," Hawk grinned, adding, "Then we can cut the sleepers."

"Sleepers? What in the world is *that*?"

"The floor beams of the cabin. Then we put hewn boards on top of them."

"Most of the cabins I've seen have dirt floors," Elizabeth said. "Wouldn't it be quicker that way?"

"Don't want you to get your feet dirty," Hawk said mildly. He had taken an interest in the cabin, and for some reason he wanted it to be the finest he was capable of raising. "After we get the floor in, I'll plane it down nice and smooth. You'll have the best cabin in the territory!"

Elizabeth turned to meet his gaze, and there were tears in her eyes. Her voice was not quite steady when she said, "It'll be the house Patrick dreamed of, Hawk."

Hawk had to bite his lips to keep back the words that almost jumped out: *But he'll never see it, Elizabeth.* . . . He was rather mystified by her attitude. He knew that she grieved over her husband, although she never said so. She had lost weight since his death, and Andrew had once told him very confidentially, "My mom cries at night when she thinks we won't hear her." Then Andrew had added, "I do too . . . cry that is—sometimes."

Hawk had said, "It's all right to cry."

"Do *you* ever cry, Hawk?" the boy had asked.

"I want to sometimes," Hawk had told the boy. "Maybe I ought to. You loved your pa, so it's all right."

Now as he stood beside Elizabeth, he was reminded of the scene and wondered if Andrew still wept for his father. But aloud he said only, "Well, I'll haul the stones for the fireplace tomorrow."

"I'll help you."

"No, your hands are blistered already. You make a good dinner, and we'll call that a bargain."

The next morning he hauled more stones, and again Elizabeth drove the team back and forth from the creek to the cabin site. Andrew had insisted on helping with the stones, and once Elizabeth said quietly to Hawk, "He's having such a good time. I . . . I've been worried about him."

"He misses his father, doesn't he?"

"Of course." Elizabeth bit her lower lip, then said quietly, "So does Sarah—and I think sometimes I can't go on without Patrick."

Hawk had nothing to say to that, so he turned and walked down to the creek for more stones. The cabin raising gave him as much pleasure as hunting—which puzzled him. Finally he thought, *I guess I'm building something that will last. When a man kills a deer, he eats it and that's the end of it. But there's something eternal about building a house.*

When Elizabeth called out that lunch was ready, they all sat down on the ground and ate hungrily. She had broiled steaks over an open fire, and Hawk said, "These are fine—but wait until you get in your new house and have a fine new fireplace."

"I'll show you some cooking, indeed," Elizabeth smiled. She looked at the huge pile of stones that waited to be fitted into a fireplace, then asked, "Is it hard to build a fireplace?"

"Hardest part of building a cabin. If your foundation is wrong," Hawk said, "the whole thing will fall down. If the throat isn't done right, it won't draw, and you'll cough the rest of your life from the smoke."

"When will we start cutting trees?" Andy piped up.

"I'd say right after dinner." Hawk remarked. "But don't be in a hurry."

"I can't help it," Andy protested. "I want to get it done so we can move in."

Hawk grinned and ruffled the boy's hair. "I guess I'd like to be sitting down in this cabin myself. But it takes time to do things that count."

"Will I have a room of my own?" Sarah piped up.

"You and Andrew will sleep in the loft," Elizabeth said. "You'll have to climb up a ladder to go to bed. Won't that be fun?"

Sarah thought it over, then slowly nodded. "Yes, it will be fun. Will I have my own bed?"

"Sure you will," Hawk spoke up. "I'll make it myself—but it won't have but one leg."

"One leg! It'll fall down!"

"No it won't, Sarah," Hawk promised. "It'll be fastened on three corners to the wall, and one leg will hold up the other corner."

"Oh, that's nice!" Sarah exclaimed. "When will you make it?"

"Got to have a cabin to put it in first." Rising to his feet he said, "I guess we can go cut down our first tree. Anyone in here want to go?"

Hawk had no troubled getting volunteers. Indeed, the two youngsters were so anxious, they protested when he took time to sharpen his ax. But finally they all walked across the meadow to the fine grove of straight trees that Hawk had decided to use.

The rest of the morning was a pure delight to the MacNeals. Hawk was a good man with an ax, and the three stood around and watched as he measured the first tree with his eye, then began cutting. The chips flew, and as the notch in the tall walnut tree grew, Andy said, "Which way will it fall, Hawk?"

"Over there—so don't stand in that direction."

Quickly the three moved away, and the chips seemed to fly as Hawk swung with machine-like precision, the blows of his ax echoing down the valley. Once he stopped to wipe his face and grinned at them. "A beaver could do a better job than this—but I don't know how a man could train a beaver to cut down trees."

Finally the tree seemed to shiver, and Hawk called out sharply,

"Stand back, now!" The tree swayed, then fell to the earth with a crash.

"I wish I could chop down a tree like that!" Andrew said.

"Well, here's your ax. I made the handle a little smaller just to fit you. Come along. I'll mark the end, and you can cut it off."

Elizabeth watched anxiously. Andy, as she had begun to call him because Hawk did, had not had any training with tools, but she saw Hawk show him exactly how to hold the ax, how to swing it, then how to cut at a different angle. Hawk stayed right with him until the boy grew tired.

"Now, let's look at those hands." He looked at Andy's hands and said, "Well, they still got some blisters from haulin' rock. You do a little today, a little tomorrow, and first thing you know they'll look like mine." He held out his hard, callused hands, and Andy ran his over them.

"I want to work today!" he protested.

"Be plenty of time, boy," he said. "We've got lots of trees to cut down."

At midafternoon, Hawk hitched up his horse to one of the logs. Handing the lines to Andrew, he said, "All right. Let's see you drive him."

A frightened look came over Andrew's face. "Well, what'll I do?"

"Slap those lines on his rear and say, 'Get up, Easy!' That's his name. Easy."

"But what if he runs away?"

Hawk laughed. "Then you say, 'Whoa, Easy!' and haul back on those lines. He's a pretty smart horse, though. He knows what we're doin'." He had borrowed this particular animal from William. It was a heavy iron-colored horse, very large and strong with powerful legs and bulky shoulders.

Tentatively Andrew slapped the reins and said in a rather feeble voice, "Get up, Easy!"

Instantly the animal moved forward, and Andrew said in a panic, "What do I do now?"

"If you want him to go left, pull that left rein. If you want him to go right, pull the right line. That's all there is to it." Elizabeth and Hawk followed along. Hawk stayed in close reach so he could leap forward and grab the lines if necessary.

"I've never seen him so happy," Elizabeth said.

"The boy likes to learn to do things. He'll be a good man."

Hawk's words pleased Elizabeth, and she wanted to say how much she appreciated his sacrifice in working for them, but she had already learned that he did not like her to thank him.

When they got to the site of the cabin, Andrew hauled back on the lines and said, "Whoa, Easy!" Instantly the big horse halted, and Andrew looked around with triumph brightening his eyes. "I did it! I did it!"

"You sure did. I don't know any man who could've done it better," Hawk said, smiling at the boy.

The simple praise brought a flush to Andrew's eyes, and he dropped his head for a moment. Looking at his mother, he saw her smiling at him, then he turned and said, "Can we go get another one, Hawk?"

"I reckon so, but first, let's eat. Why don't you fix up that bait of food, Elizabeth? After we get these logs hauled, I'll be ready to eat like a bear!"

As Elizabeth and Sarah cooked the supper over an open fire, Sarah said jealously, "Andy gets to have all the fun, Mama! He gets to drive the horses and everything!"

"We'll have fun, too. As we build the cabin, you'll have to help me decide where to put the furniture and where to put the beds. It'll be fun." She reached over and squeezed the girl and said, "Oh, we're going to have a wonderful home here!"

"I wish—" Sarah started to speak, then broke off suddenly.

Elizabeth looked down and read the child's mind. "I know," she said. "I wish your daddy were here, too. But we promised him we wouldn't worry and grieve."

"I know, but sometimes I can't help it. I miss him so much."

Elizabeth hugged her, and Sarah grabbed her mother and held on with all of her might. "We'll be all right, Sarah."

"I'm glad Hawk is here to help us. I don't know what we'd do without him."

Elizabeth nodded and whispered, "I don't know either. I think God gave him to us to get us through this time."

Rhoda Harper was staying with the family of John Russell. She liked John and his wife, Leah, very much, but with four children, the small cabin was already overcrowded. Actually she would have preferred to sleep outdoors, but that would have seemed ungrateful.

She had watched Hawk and Elizabeth ride out along with the children early in the morning, and she was glad for Elizabeth. She knew of the promise Hawk had made to Patrick MacNeal and was aware of how dependent the family had already become on the tall frontiersman.

Needing to escape from the crowded cabin for a while, Rhoda strolled along the outskirts of the settlement. She heard the sound of axes and cheerful voices ringing everywhere over the cool October air. She took a deep breath, thinking how much better it was here in the clean freshness of the open country than in the stale dark interior of *The Brown Stag*. For a time she had grieved over the deaths of the Simmons family and of Patrick MacNeal. She had known Patrick the best, of course, and even the thought of him now ran like a sharp knife into her heart as she considered how she might have prevented it. The attack had come early, but no matter how many times she told herself that, she knew she should've gone to Hawk at once and warned him.

Her mood grew somber, and she wondered when Jacques Cartier would appear again. Somehow she knew she had not seen the last of the man, and she muttered, "I wish he had gotten killed in that attack! He deserves it!"

Walking along the bank of a creek where most of the settlers drew their water, she heard her name being called. She turned to see Paul Anderson dismounting from his horse and waving.

"Rhoda!" he cried. "Let me tie my horse."

Rhoda stood there and waited, and he came up to her, a smile on his face. He wore better clothing than most of the settlers—a white shirt with a string tie and a pair of black wool trousers topped off by a light green coat.

"Hello, Paul," Rhoda greeted him. "Where have you been?"

"I've been talking with Sequatchie. We'll be leaving in a few days to go to his village."

Rhoda was disappointed, for his kindness to her was part of what made her feel secure. "I know you're anxious to go," she said quietly, "but I'll miss you."

Anderson blinked with surprise. "Will you?"

"Why, of course I will! What did you think?"

Anderson had pulled his hat off, and now he twirled it around in his hands. It was a low-crown brown felt hat, and he studied it before looking at her. "I don't know what I thought."

She laughed at him. "I thought preachers always knew everything."

"You don't know much about preachers. Where you going?" he asked.

"Just out walking."

"Mind if I join you?"

"No, let's walk along the creek here." They turned and moved slowly along the bank. The creek was no more than ten feet wide, but there were deep holes in it that contained panfish, and soon they passed a group of youngsters who were fishing. Rhoda said, "You know, I've never caught a fish in my whole life."

"You haven't?" Paul looked at her with astonishment. "Well, that's easily fixed. I hate to boast, but I'm rated as one of the best fishermen in my part of the world. Of course, there're different kinds of fish here, I guess. But"—he smiled and looked very young as the October sunlight framed his face in its yellow beams—"a fish is a fish."

They walked a little farther, noticing a large turtle that was sleeping on a log. When they got close, it plunged off and Paul said, "He'd make a good soup."

"You can eat turtles? Those ugly things?"

"I don't know about that one, but I've had some good turtle soup." As they continued to stroll along the bank, Paul said, "Rhoda, what are you going to do? Are you going to continue staying with the Russells?"

"I don't have much choice, Paul."

"You said something about preachers knowing everything. Well, they don't. Half the time I don't know what to do. Sometimes I think God is telling me to do something . . . and then it turns out it was just my own head making up the thing. But sometimes, Rhoda, I get an idea or a thought, and it comes over and over and over again. And when that happens, I always have to at least consider that God is trying to get something through my thick head."

"You mean God actually talks to you?"

"Oh, not with a literal voice. Not like your voice that I'm hearing now. It's in the spirit. Someday you'll understand." She did not respond, and he said quickly, "I think you ought to have your own little cabin, Rhoda."

"Why, I couldn't build a cabin!"

"Well, I can. Well . . . I guess that's a little boastful. I've been watching them cut down trees and make log cabins." He laughed ruefully and said, "That's not the same thing. Like watching a chicken lay an egg—I don't think I could accomplish that!"

"Oh, that's foolish!" she laughed. The smile left her face, and she stopped and turned to face him. "Why would you want to do a thing like that for me?"

Paul looked embarrassed. He kicked a stone with his boot and watched it sail into the creek, then shrugged. "It's not so much that I *want* to—although, I would like to learn to do things like that. I won't need a cabin, because I'll be on the move. But I think God is telling me to help you." He saw the unbelief on her face and said, "I know you don't believe in God, but I do. Would you let me help you with this?"

"You need your own cabin, Paul."

"No, I'll be going to Sequatchie's Cherokee village after the cabins are all built."

"I wouldn't want to be a burden. I couldn't let you do it."

"You know, Rhoda," Paul said, raising one eyebrow. "There's one thing you don't know about me."

"What's that?"

"I'm a very stubborn fellow, and right now I've got my mind made up that God wants me to help you build a little cabin. Not a big one, and I'm not foolish enough to think that I could do it all myself. But haven't you noticed how everyone chips in around here? How they help each other?"

"They wouldn't want to help me."

"Sure they would—at least some of them. Some of them wouldn't help anybody, but the others are good people, Rhoda."

"They know what I—what I was back in Williamsburg. Some of the men still come, trying to get me to go with them."

"You haven't, though."

Rhoda instantly looked up. "How do you know that?"

"I don't know it, but I don't think so."

She studied his face carefully. Men had been in her life since she was only a young girl. Most of them had been hard and had used her for their own pleasure. But now as she looked up into Paul Anderson's face, she knew he was a good man whom she could trust. She liked his green eyes and his straight nose. He was not a handsome man, nor large and powerful like Hawk, but there was an honesty about him and a spirit of fun that she was drawn to.

Finally she whispered, "I just don't know what to say."

He reached out suddenly and took her hand and said, "Let's shake hands. That's what people do when they make an agreement." He took her hand firmly in his own and smiled. "You'll just agree that I'm a stubborn preacher with a crazy idea. Maybe we'll get the cabin half built, and I'll leave you and go off on another wild-goose chase. No telling what I might do. But maybe we'll get it built, and maybe you'll have a home of your own, and then we can get someone to plant some corn for you. I want you to have a good life, Rhoda," he said simply.

Rhoda Harper felt a sudden wrenching in her heart, and for some ridiculous reason she wanted to burst out crying. She struggled against this, turning away from him to look out at the trees that were swaying in the brisk wind. Finally she turned again, and her eyes were slightly misty, but her full lips turned upward in a smile. "All right, Paul. If you want to be a stubborn preacher, I guess I'll have to let you do it!"

The Settlers of Appalachia

Twenty-Six

The house raising was an exciting time for Elizabeth, unlike anything she had ever experienced. She watched with delight as the men worked smoothly in crews. Some notched the logs, others split cedar shakes expertly, and another crew worked on the fireplace. Nothing had ever thrilled her so much as the sight of her new home as it rose from the earth, log by log—and her eyes shone so that Hawk smiled at the sight of her pleasure. She seemed to be reaching out and becoming part of the cabin in some mysterious way, and it puzzled him how a cabin could mean so much. But then he was a man—a man of the open country who could not read a woman's heart.

"We still have to do the roof poles, and the rafters have to be set in place," Hawk said. "Then after that, the roof can be put on, and the chinking can go between the logs. Got to lay the floor, and finally build the fireplace and chimney. That's a pretty big job in itself."

"I don't care," Elizabeth said, walking around inside the cabin, her eyes filled with wonder. She ran her hands over the logs and then turned to face him. "Just think. These were trees just a few days ago, and now they're a home for us."

Hawk looked up to the open sky above. It was November, and the heavens were gray. There was even a hint of snow in the air. "Be a little bit drafty," he said wryly, "living in here without a roof."

"We'll get a roof," Elizabeth said. "Won't we, Hawk?"

For that moment the two of them felt completely united. They had both worked so hard, throwing themselves into the building of the cabin, and now as they stood there alone, listening as the voices of the children outside came faintly from the creek, there was a strong bond of friendship between them.

Suddenly Hawk shook himself and dropped his head. "We'll get the roof on. It won't take long. If you've got the money to hire a few hands, it'll go quicker."

"Oh yes. I still have the money." She reached into her pocket and pulled out her purse and handed it to him. "Take what you need."

Hawk stared at the fine leather purse with the solid brass snap. It was a fine reticule that only a woman from a rich family would carry.

"You're mighty trusting with your money, Elizabeth."

"Not with everyone." Elizabeth smiled at him. Then she whirled around the cabin, saying, "If we had music, we could have a dance in here!"

"I haven't done that in a long time," Hawk mused.

"Come on!" Elizabeth said. "Let's celebrate. Just one dance. I'll sing, and it'll be the celebration for my new home."

Hawk put his arm around her waist, took her hand, and the two of them spun around the floor as she sang. She was light and easy to lead, and her hair had a good smell of perfumed soap. Suddenly vaguely familiar feelings stirred in Hawk. He had never thought he could feel so alive again, and somehow Elizabeth brought that out in him. Smiling broadly, he looked deep into Elizabeth's eyes.

Elizabeth read a change in his eyes and stopped abruptly. She laughed self-consciously and smoothed her hair down. "Well, there," she said. "We've had the celebration for the new house."

"We'll get the roof on as soon as I can get some men together," Hawk said. He turned and left so quickly that Elizabeth was surprised.

"Well, for one moment there I thought he was going to be human!" It was the first time a man had touched her since Patrick had died, and somehow it made her feel guilty. *That was a foolish thing to do!* she thought. *I'll have to be more careful. . . .*

Elizabeth came every day to watch the roof go on. Hawk hired three men, and the roof almost built itself, it seemed, with the ridge-poles going up quickly. It went so fast that Hawk said, "We'll put a loft in while we're here. Then when you have company, you'll have a place for them to sleep."

The sky had been dark with winter clouds. Hawk feared its impending delivery and hired two more men to help with the chimney. They hauled stones from the creek and mortared them together with mud, grass, and sticks. It was a large chimney, spanning an enormous length of wall, and when it was finished Hawk looked pleased. He was hot and sweaty from putting the last rocks on the top, and he said, "Well, here's your house, Elizabeth."

"It's beautiful, Hawk!" She looked around and smiled at him. She remembered the dance that they had had together, and somehow it embarrassed her.

"Not much furniture, but we can put a few things together if you're ready to move in."

"Oh yes! As quick as we can! I brought blankets and plenty of cookware."

"You'll need a bed and a mattress and a lot of other things."

"I'll make out." Elizabeth hesitated and said, "Are you going to be leaving now?"

"I thought I might. This is the longest I've stayed in one place."

Andrew and Sarah had come in and heard him say this, and they stared at each other. Sarah came over and took his hand. Looking up at him, she said, "Please don't leave, Hawk!"

Andrew said nothing, but there was a worried look on his face.

Elizabeth said quickly, "Now, don't you pester Hawk! He's done more for us than anyone had a right to expect!"

Hawk said slowly, "Tell you what. Let's make the first fire in the fireplace. I'll go out and shoot something, and we'll cook it right here. Your first meal."

"Oh, could we really?" Elizabeth wondered, pleased at the thought.

"Won't be very fancy, but we can do it. Come along, Andy. Let's see what we can put on the table—even though we don't have a table."

While Hawk and Andrew went to the woods in search of game, Elizabeth walked around the corner, hugging herself and smiling from time to time at Sarah. She had strong feelings of pleasure and pride at having her own place. She had never felt this way about the mansion she had grown up in. Now every log, every shake, every piece of this cabin somehow was hers in a way that the mansion in Boston never had been.

She and Sarah gathered firewood and started a fire, and soon Hawk and Andrew came back with two rabbits.

"Look, Ma! He shot 'em right through the head, and they were runnin', too!"

"Good thing rabbits don't shoot back." Hawk grinned. "Come on. I'll skin one, and then you can skin the other."

Forty-five minutes later, the four of them were seated on the dirt floor, eating the rabbit they had roasted on wooden spits over a hickory fire.

Elizabeth thought of the white tablecloth, the fine heavy silver, and the crystal goblets of her home back in Boston, and a smile trembled on her lips.

"Sequatchie's going back to his people day after tomorrow," Hawk said suddenly.

"Yes, there's been talk of a service before he goes. Everybody's planning to attend. Will you be there?"

"I guess I will." He looked up and said, "It's getting cold. You're going to need a lot of firewood to get through the winter, Elizabeth. And in the spring you'll have to have someone plow your land."

"I can't ask you to do that, Hawk."

Andrew's eyes, however, were on the tall hunter, and they lit up at Hawk's words.

"I don't guess it would kill me to do a little firewood cutting and plowing. Think I'll build a shack, a lean-to, in that little hollow about a quarter of a mile from here. That way I'll be able to keep an eye on you to be sure you're all right."

Elizabeth's heart leaped. She hugged Sarah and said, "I'd feel so much better if you were near—but it's asking a lot."

Hawk got up and tossed his stick into the fire. "That's a good fireplace," he said. "It draws well. There will be a lot of meals cooked over it, Elizabeth." He looked around the cabin and said, "I had doubts, but now I see that this is what you want, so I'm glad you have it."

Elizabeth rose, and soon they were on their way back to the main part of the settlement. "I'll see you at the service next Sunday."

"Guess so," Hawk said reluctantly.

Elizabeth was glad and said with a smile, "We'll hear some good preaching. Paul's getting better all the time."

———————

The service conducted by Reverend Paul Anderson was attended by the closest thing to celebrities that the wilderness in the Holston area could boast of. Aside from William Bean and his wife, who had begun the settlement, Hawk met perhaps the most influential man in these parts. His name was James Robertson.

Hawk remembered that he had heard how Robertson, mounted on a good horse, had come to the Watauga alone and followed Boone's trails along the mountains. The twenty-eight-year-old had been inspired by the vastness of the wilderness, and at Sycamore Shoals he had cleared land and planted crops. After he had lain by his corn crop early, he headed back home through the mountains, but his horse could not navigate the heavy thickets. Robertson had not been able to keep his gunpowder dry and had wandered for days, lost and desperate, surviving on berries and roots, and might have died except for the chance encounter with two hunters.

Hawk said to William Bean, "I think that Robertson's quite a fella, isn't he?"

"You're right, he is. He's gonna be a man of influence in this part of the world. And you see that fella over there? That's Evan Shelby."

"Who's he?"

"He's a Marylander," Bean said. "He was a scout with General Braddock. Afterward he became a fur trader among the Indians. I don't know what he's doin' here, but he's gonna settle somewhere, and you can count on a man like Shelby. If we get enough folks like that around here, this country will be tamed in a hurry."

Sequatchie stood close to Little Carpenter, the most influential of the Cherokee leaders. He was, as his name suggested, a small man, wizened by many years of living. When Sequatchie introduced him to Hawk, the chief studied the tall hunter and nodded, saying in Cherokee, "A good man."

Hawk replied, "Thanks, chief. I appreciate your kind words."

"You speak our language?"

"Sequatchie taught me."

The three men stood there, and finally the service started. It was a relatively brief service, with more singing than preaching, and Paul Anderson, after his sermon, called upon William Bean to introduce the strangers. Bean introduced Daniel Boone, John Sevier, Valentine Sevier, Little Carpenter, James and Charlotte Robertson, and Evan Shelby.

After the service was over, Hawk spoke for a while with Elizabeth. "It looks like this place is gettin' to be important," he said. "I wish they'd all stay and help us plant corn next spring."

Elizabeth had enjoyed the preaching. It had given her comfort, for she had been very lonely these days. Now that the cabin was finished, she had more time to think about what the future held for her and the children.

Hawk looked at her, noting the strange expression, and asked at once, "What's the matter?"

"Nothing. Nothing at all." She smiled at Hawk and asked, "Can I help you cut firewood tomorrow?"

"You better start thinking about making some mattresses. I'll make a bed for you first, and you can move into the cabin tomorrow."

Elizabeth smiled. "That'll be wonderful."

Elizabeth had a peace and inner serenity about her that was a puzzle to the long hunter. He could not understand how she could accept the death of her husband so bravely. Hawk recalled a conversation he had had with Rhoda when he had visited her at her new cabin home. He asked Rhoda, "Do you think she didn't love Patrick?"

"Oh, she loved him all right!" Rhoda said instantly.

Hawk looked at her strangely, then asked, "Then why doesn't she show it?"

"Women don't always show things, Hawk," Rhoda said. "Inside she's still hurting. There'll always be a part of her that will belong to Patrick. She's that kind of a woman."

As Hawk thought about that conversation, he said simply, "It's not a bad kind of woman to be."

A Frontier Christmas

Twenty-Seven

By mid-December, Elizabeth's cabin was well furnished. Hawk had taken some pleasure in cutting and stacking a great pile of firewood up against the south side of the cabin. Then he had turned his hand to making chairs, baskets, pails and tubs for washing, and noggins, piggins, and keelers to hold drink. He had fashioned cups from wood and shaped baskets from hickory splits. The bed downstairs had one support that touched the floor. The two thick saplings joined there were fastened at right angles to the cabin. Hawk threaded rawhide thongs through it, and Elizabeth placed a mattress on it filled with dried shucks that Lydia Bean had saved for just such a purpose.

One day Hawk was too tired to work on the cabin, so he located Andrew and said, "Let's you and me go hunting today, Andy."

Nothing, of course, could have pleased the boy better. Whatever Hawk suggested was exactly what Andrew wanted, so the two left at dawn, and by ten o'clock they had a sack full of rabbits.

On the way back Andrew said idly, "I almost forgot. Christmas is just about here."

Hawk looked down at Andrew, who was wearing warm woolen clothing purchased at the store back in Williamsburg. The boy was now, he guessed, about five-foot-seven, and though he was lean, there was a promise of future strength in his limbs. He had his father's sparkling blue eyes and had gained much confidence over the past months.

"What was Christmas like back at your place?" Hawk asked.

Andrew thought for a moment and said, "Oh, we had a big Christmas tree with presents under it. Grandma always had a lot of special dinners with plenty of food. We sang carols and went for sleigh rides if there was any snow."

Andrew continued to babble on, and Hawk listened with some amusement. It came to him, however, as they walked back, *This will be a bad Christmas for them. Elizabeth and probably the kids, too, will be thinking about the finer things they had in Boston. They're away from their family, and it's the first Christmas since the death of Patrick.*

"I've been proud of the way you've taken care of your mother and sister, Andy," Hawk said aloud. "Your father would have been very proud of you, too."

A pleased flush touched Andy's face and he said, "I couldn't have done it if it wasn't for you."

As they approached the cabin, Hawk admired the neatness of it, especially the tightly joined logs and the solid chimney, out of which curled a wreath of white smoke.

I'll have to do something. They've got to have some kind of a Christmas. I owe it to Patrick.

———

A light snow had begun to fall on December twenty-fourth. At about three o'clock Sarah and Andrew were out in it, trying to make snowballs, but it was a fluffy snow and sent only puffballs into the wind. However, two hours later it began to pick up again and cover the ground. Elizabeth stood at the door and watched the children outside, thinking of Patrick and their last Christmas together. He had given her the gold chain that she wore every day of her life hidden beneath her dress, for it would have seemed ostentatious to flaunt it. She had given him a new set of razors that she still kept carefully concealed in a trunk with other special mementos of their life together. Going back inside, she began to prepare the evening meal.

The children finally came in, banging open the door. "I'm hungry, Ma!" Andy said.

"Me, too!" Sarah said. "Can't we eat early?"

"I don't think we need to do that," Elizabeth said. She would have said more, but as she went to the door to shut it, she glanced across the meadow and saw something that startled her. She said nothing, but the two children saw her looking and came to join her.

The three stood there for a moment staring at the man coming across the meadow.

"It's Hawk, and he's got a tree! A Christmas tree!"

Hawk was riding his horse and pulling the sled he had used to haul the rocks from the creek. The snow was falling heavier now and frosted his coonskin cap. When he approached the cabin, he slid off the horse and said, "Merry Christmas!"

"Merry Christmas! Merry Christmas!" the children said.

"What in the world are you doing with that tree?" Elizabeth asked.

Hawk went back to the sled. "I haven't had a Christmas tree in fifteen years. I thought it was about time." He walked straight past her, brushing them all aside with the tree and placed it on a little stand he had made. Turning around, he looked at their astonished faces and said, "We'll pop popcorn, and string it, and drape it around the tree. Maybe even put two or three candles on there. It's Christmas, woman! Wait until you see what else I've got!"

He went outside and came back in carrying the carcass of a huge turkey. "Stir up the fire! It'll take until tomorrow noon to cook this big fellow." He looked at the bird fondly. "He just plumb asked to be shot."

Tears came to Elizabeth's eyes at Hawk's kindness. Turning, she busied herself with finishing cooking a quick supper. After the meal was eaten and the table cleared, the children began popping corn, and Elizabeth helped them string it together with needle and thread. Hawk sat on one of the stools he had made, balancing backward and watching it all with an amused smile.

He stayed until long after dark, only returning to the lean-to that he had made after promising to return the next day for Christmas dinner.

On Christmas morning, Hawk returned with a sack over his shoulders. When Elizabeth opened the door and the children grabbed at him, he said, "I guess St. Nicholas missed this place, but he dropped this sack, so let's see what's in it."

Elizabeth and the children watched as Hawk reached down into the sack and pulled out a package. "I reckon this is for you, Sarah."

Sarah grabbed the package and tore it open. When she had the

THE SPIRIT OF APPALACHIA

paper ripped off, she held up a beautifully designed fur coat. "One of the finest squaws in the Cherokee nation made that for you. I trapped those furs myself. They're martins."

Sarah slipped her arms inside the coat and preened, "Isn't it *beautiful*, Mama?"

"Yes, it is. Why, that would cost a fortune in a shop in Boston."

He reached down into the sack again and brought out another package. "This is for you, Elizabeth."

"Well . . . we didn't get you anything," Elizabeth said.

"I guess I'm a man who doesn't need anything. Hard to buy for, you might say."

Elizabeth undid the package and discovered a pair of beautifully designed fur-lined deerskin boots.

"That ought to keep your feet warm," Hawk said.

"Oh, let me put them on!" Elizabeth said. She kicked her shoes off and slipped on the supple deerskin. "They fit perfectly," she said, "and they're so *warm*."

"They'll shed water, too. Those squaws know how to fix 'em. I don't know how they do it."

He turned to Andrew and said, "Couldn't get your present in this sack. It's just right outside. You close your eyes and hold your hands out like this, palms up." He pulled Andrew's hands up, stepped through the door, and was back in a moment. He winked at Elizabeth and then moved forward, holding a shiny new rifle. He placed it in Andrew's hands and said, "Merry Christmas."

Andrew's eyes flew open and he gasped. "It's a musket!" he said. "A brand-new one!"

"I traded a few beaver skins for that some time back. It's a bit undersized for a full-grown man, but just about right for you. Well-made weapon, too."

While the three MacNeals admired their unexpected gifts, Hawk sat down at the table. It gave him a feeling of well-being to see the happiness that his small gifts had brought.

Later that afternoon they had the turkey and the fresh bread Elizabeth had baked. They all ate until they could hold no more. Elizabeth had used dried berries to make a cobbler, and Hawk spooned one final portion in his mouth and groaned, "I'll die if I eat another bite!"

After the Christmas dinner, they went out and walked, making tracks in the blanket of snow that covered everything. It was three or four inches deep and glistened under the sun. There was a quietness on the land that a gentle snowfall always seemed to bring. Finally, they went back into the house, and Elizabeth said, "The one thing we always do at Christmas is read the Christmas story."

The children sat down at once, and Hawk stirred rather uneasily. He listened as Elizabeth read the Christmas story from the book of Luke, how the Christ child was born. When she was finished, Andrew and Sarah asked if they could go out for one more time, and she agreed.

When the children were outside, Elizabeth turned to Hawk. "It seems," she said, with a smile, "I spend my life thanking you. Someday I'll do something for you, and you can thank me."

"Why, it was nothing. I wanted you and the children to have a good Christmas."

"It *was* a good Christmas. At first I thought it would be very bad, but you've made it very special." Elizabeth sat down in front of the fire on a stool and clasped her knees. "Patrick always loved Christmas. It was the best day of the year for him. Because of that, he made it the best day for everyone around him, and so I hated to see Christmas come, Hawk." She looked up at him, and there was a strange expression of contentment on her face. "But somehow this has been so good!"

Hawk sat there watching her, and they listened to the wood crack in the fire. "A man gets lonesome at Christmas," he said finally. "Most of the time, all these years, I didn't even notice. But every time Christmas came around, I'd think back to the days when I was a boy. It was kind of like the Christmases you had. Christmas is fine if you've got people around you, but when a man's all alone, it can get pretty bad."

Their eyes met, and they shared a smile, and somehow each understood the loneliness that was in the other. Elizabeth said, "It's good to have a friend, and you've been a good friend to us, Hawk. To Andrew, especially, and to Sarah, too."

Hawk said nothing. He sat there as the fire sputtered, and he felt a sense of contentment that was so alien to him that he could barely identify it. Suddenly he realized that he had not felt a peace like this for many years.

"I wish," he said slowly, "that folks could take moments and days like this and bottle them up, and then every once in a while when they get lonesome and get to feeling down, they could open the bottle and take a sip of it."

"That's what memories are," Elizabeth whispered. "We live our lives, and we have to build as many good things into them as we can so that as we grow older we can look back and draw on those memories."

Soon the children came in, and after a time of storytelling, Elizabeth sent them to bed. Hawk said good-night and made his way back to his lean-to. The moon overhead looked down on him and seemed to smile, and Hawk looked up momentarily. "What are you smiling at?" Then he laughed at his own foolishness. "It was a good Christmas," he said aloud, then he continued to his home.

Spring Returns

Twenty-Eight

*T*he winter passed slowly from the little settlement. The snow that covered the ground melted, and by late March, there was a hint of a warm spring that fell across the land. The newcomers to the Holston area had survived their first winter in the wilderness.

Smoke rose from the cabin that had become a new home to Elizabeth MacNeal. Hawk had come to eat an early breakfast and spend the day plowing a small area that would be her garden. She had just set a bowl of mush and fresh bread on the table, when Hawk suddenly looked up from where he was lolling in his chair, his eyes narrowing. "Someone's coming," he said.

"I didn't hear anything," Elizabeth said. But she went to the door and opened it, crying out at once, "It's Sequatchie and Paul!"

Immediately Hawk got to his feet and went outside. The two men were stained with travel, and their horses were muddy almost to their bellies. They pulled up and stepped to the ground.

"Well, Preacher, you're back. And you, Sequatchie," Hawk greeted his friends.

Sequatchie grunted. It was difficult to read the face of the Cherokee, but pleasure showed in his dark eyes as he greeted Hawk. "It is good to see you, my brother."

"Hawk, it seems like it's been a long time."

Elizabeth came up to greet both men, and taking Paul by the arm, she pulled him toward the cabin. "You two come in right now. You can sit and eat and tell us all about what you've been doing."

The breakfast had to be stretched thin, for Elizabeth had not planned for two very hungry men to be added to their company. She kept their plates filled, however, as Paul told about traveling to many Cherokee villages.

"It was like nothing I've ever experienced," Paul said around a mouthful of bacon and mush. His eyes were sparkling, and his face was withered from the hard winter. "We must've gone to—oh, I don't know how many Cherokee villages, and everywhere we went, I preached the gospel." He looked over at Sequatchie and grinned. "I don't trust this fellow, though, as an interpreter."

"What do you mean by that?" Elizabeth asked, her eyes alight with interest.

"Oh, I mean I don't know enough Cherokee to preach in it yet, although I try a little. So I preach in English and Sequatchie translates for me. But I think sometimes he's not happy with my theology, so he changes my sermon to fit his own viewpoints."

Humor again glinted in the eyes of Sequatchie, but he said nothing.

Paul looked around the cabin and smiled with satisfaction. Leaning back in his chair, he shook his head. "I can't believe how beautiful you made your house," he said.

Elizabeth had worked hard at it, and she was tremendously proud of how warm and welcome the cabin was. "Well, it was mostly Hawk," she said, "and the neighbors. Everyone was so good, but it's been fun to decorate it."

"A little bit different from your house in Boston, I would think," Paul said.

Elizabeth smiled and nodded. "I feel differently about this place. It's mine. Mine and the children's. I never did a bit of work on the house at home."

"You've made a wonderful adjustment, Elizabeth. You and these two young'uns here. They look like they were born on the frontier."

As they sat there talking, Paul listened while Elizabeth and Hawk told him the news of the growing community. After a moment, he asked with some diffidence, "How about Rhoda?"

Elizabeth gave him a peculiar look. There was something in his tone that piqued her interest. "Rhoda has done wonderfully well. She stays with us a lot, and visits, and helps with the work here . . . but her own house is finished now. It was so good of you, Paul, to see that she got a place of her own to live in."

"I expect she's married by this time. A single woman, and a nice-looking one, too."

"No, she's not married, though she's had several offers. As a matter of fact, some of the men have pestered her to death to marry them."

"They don't mind her past?" Paul asked. "I was afraid she'd have a hard time about that."

"They don't seem to mind—at least some of them don't. Of course, a few still throw it up to her, but she's gotten along well."

"What are you going to be doing now, Preacher?" Hawk asked. He leaned forward and rested his elbows on the table and studied the face of his friend with interest. He had half expected that Anderson would not be able to bear the rigors of the frontier and would give it up, but apparently Paul had thrived on the hard winter travel.

"I'm going to stay around here if you can put up with me," Paul said. "I think the folks here might be able to listen to my preaching for a while."

"That would be so fine!" Elizabeth said, clapping her hands. "We're going to start a little school for the children, and you can help with that."

"What about you, Sequatchie? Are you going back with your people?"

"Yes," he nodded. "I will go soon."

Hawk hesitated, then said, "Why don't you help me get this land plowed and put Elizabeth's garden in, then I'll go back with you."

"Good, you have not been with us for a long time."

A shadow passed Elizabeth's face as Hawk spoke of leaving, and Hawk himself, Paul noticed, seemed somewhat unhappy over it. *Those two seem to have an odd effect on each other*, Paul thought as he sat there listening to the talk go around the table.

Soon after breakfast Paul excused himself and hurried away, saying that he had to visit the other families. Sequatchie stayed to help plow the land, and Paul waved as he mounted his horse and rode away. He went at once to Rhoda's cabin and was pleased that she was outside getting ready to plant a garden. Hawk had broken the ground for her already. It was a small plot. As Paul rode up, he saw her face turn toward him, and he was pleased when she instantly smiled, waved, dropped her spade, and came forward to meet him.

"Paul!" she said. "When did you get in? I'm so glad to see you!" Her eyes glowed with a warm welcome, and when she took Paul's hands, a thrill went through him.

"Well, Sequatchie and I just got in this morning. We had breakfast with Elizabeth, and I rode right over."

"Come and sit down. I've got some sassafras tea. You can tell me all about your trip."

It was a pleasant hour for Paul. He had indeed undergone some hardships during the winter. He had slept on the cold ground and traveled when the snow was deep. There had been some danger, although Sequatchie had not told him this very often. He had faced real disappointments, too, which he spoke of freely to Rhoda.

"It's very difficult to preach to the Indians. You just can't tell what they're thinking," Paul said as he sat across the table from her. The cabin was snug and well chinked, and light was streaming in through the window. Rhoda had taken the covering off, and now as a fire burned cheerfully in the fireplace, he felt very much at home. "I preach as well as I can, and sometimes they sit there and listen and then get up and leave without a word."

"That must be very discouraging," Rhoda said. She was somewhat shocked at her emotions, for she had not known how much she had missed the minister. She knew well that his kindness to her had come at a time when she needed it, and though she had fared through the winter without great difficulty, there had been days when she felt lonely. She had stayed alone for much of the time, and now his cheerful smile and his laughter seemed to fill the cabin. She listened as he continued to speak with enthusiasm about his ministry.

Finally he said, "You'll have to put up with me for a little while."

"You're staying here?"

"Yes, for several months, I think."

"Oh, Paul, that's wonderful! I'm so glad."

"You are?" Paul said, lifting his eyebrows with some surprise. "That's good to hear."

Rhoda was wearing a simple brown dress, but she had just washed her dark brown hair, and there was a peace about her that had not been there the previous fall. True enough, she still seemed tense and there was something in her that he wished he could reach out and touch and heal, but he could not identify it.

They sat for over an hour in the cabin, and then Rhoda took him outside and gave him a tour around her place. "Hawk and the others showed me how to make the claim. It'll be mine one day," she said. "If you build a cabin and stay on it for a year, the land belongs to you."

"I'm glad, Rhoda. You've got a fine place here."

"Of course, a woman can't do as much as a man, but I've been finding out something, Paul."

"What's that?"

"There are good men in this world. For a long time I didn't think so, you know. I was even suspicious of you. I guess I saw the worst side of men for so long, I built a wall around myself, but coming here and getting to know good people has changed all that."

He turned to her and suddenly reached out his hands. She took them without thinking, and he held them for a moment. There was a sudden understanding that came to her as she realized, *Why, this man truly cares for me!* It was different from what she had seen in other men. She looked up at him as he smiled at her.

"How about if I come by and help you some," Paul said.

"Why . . . why, thank you, Paul," Rhoda stammered, feeling a strange flush on her cheeks.

She smiled, and the warmth of his hands felt good on her own. He had strong hands, browned by the sun now, and when he squeezed hers she had a feeling that she had not felt for many years. *Maybe it's going to be all right,* she thought. He took her hand then, and they walked for some time around the place, and Rhoda Harper felt like a young girl again.

———————

By early April, Hawk and Sequatchie had done most of the work on the garden. Sequatchie had gone off to hunt, and Elizabeth and the children helped Hawk as he worked putting in more rows of corn. Every day Elizabeth felt more and more satisfied with her new home. She was sleeping better now, and although she thought of Patrick every day, the passage of time had done much to heal the immediacy of her grief. She had to remind herself that she had promised Patrick not to grieve, and somehow she had managed to find peace in her heart. She knew it came from God, and now as she watched the tall man hoeing in the field, she realized how much she owed to Hawk.

"Mama, look! Somebody's coming!"

Hawk had heard the sound of a horse approaching, too, and at once turned, his eyes ever vigilant. The rider was a tall man with a pair of steady gray eyes.

"Hello," he said, not dismounting. "My name's James Robertson."

"I know. I met you at the meeting last fall when Preacher Anderson spoke."

"Yes, I remember you. You're Hawk Spencer."

"Get down and rest yourself, Mr. Robertson. I'm Elizabeth MacNeal, and these are my children, Sarah and Andrew."

Robertson got off his horse stiffly and stretched. "Well, I've had a long journey," he said.

"Have you breakfasted yet?"

"No, I haven't, as a matter of fact."

"There's plenty left," Elizabeth said. "Please come inside."

Hawk left the field and came inside to sit down. He had been hearing much about James Robertson and wanted to know more about the man. He sat there not eating, but watching as the tall man put away a fine breakfast. He knew the country well, and the politics also.

Elizabeth finally said, "It seems like you've met everybody in Holston country, Mr. Robertson."

"Well, I've tried to." A frown came to him and he turned to Hawk. "I've really come to see you, Hawk."

"Me? Why is that?"

"Do you know anything about what's going on back in North Carolina?"

"No. Not a thing. What is it?"

Robertson's lips grew grim. "There's some mighty fine folks there who are in considerable difficulty. Some very rich landowners in the eastern part of the colony are making it hard on these folks."

"Why don't they just sell out and leave?"

"That's exactly what they want to do," Robertson shot back. "I've been talking to William Bean and some of the other leaders, and every one of them suggests that you might be the man to hire."

"Well, I don't hire out much, Mr. Robertson. And I'm about done with Mrs. MacNeal's garden, so I'm headed back for the Cherokee village where I'm a little overdue. I've got to go get some deerskins, too. I'm behind on my hunting."

"I thought you might say that, but just hear me out." Robertson was a persuasive man, and he sat there talking for some time. Finally, after he had presented his case, he said, "So you see I need someone to go bring those folks here. They need to get away, and I'd be willing to pay you well to be their guide. More than you would make hunting deer and trading skins and furs."

Hawk did not really want to go and said, "Well, I've been helping Mrs. MacNeal around here."

"I really think we can handle it now that you got the garden in, Hawk, and Paul will be here. It would be nice to have more neighbors," Elizabeth said.

Hawk thought quickly, then said, "How long do you think it would take them to clear up their affairs?"

"They're ready to go now if someone would come and guide them over the mountains."

He named his sum and Hawk was surprised at the wages that Robertson offered. Calculating quickly, he knew he would have to work a long time to shoot enough deer, and dress hides, and then trade them to earn the equivalent.

Seeing Hawk's surprise, Robertson said, "And this would be in hard money. Not in trade goods."

Hawk said slowly, "Well, I'll do it. Maybe Sequatchie would like to go with me. He's anxious to go home, but two of us could do better than one on this job."

After Robertson left, Andrew came to Hawk and said, "Do you have to go?"

"I'm afraid I do, Andy, and that'll mean you'll have to be the man of the house." He put his arm on the boy's shoulder and squeezed it. Smiling down he said, "You can handle it, can't you?"

Andrew MacNeal looked up into Hawk's eyes, and there was love in his face and trust, and he nodded proudly. "Yes, sir. I'll do the best I know how."

"That's all any man can do, Andy."

The Regulators

Twenty-Nine

*H*awk and Sequatchie made the trip to North Carolina quickly, and on the first week of May, they arrived. The first people they met were a family named Stevens. George Stevens, who welcomed them, was a tall man, well over six feet, with gray eyes and reddish brown hair turning gray at the temples. George had lost his first wife several years before, and now introduced his second wife, Deborah.

Deborah Stevens invited the two men inside the cabin, and now she said, "We have a meal ready. Let's all sit down and eat." She was a pretty woman with thick, long, sandy brown hair.

A young girl joined them and was introduced as their daughter Abigail. She was tall for a fourteen-year-old and was very shy.

As they ate, Hawk listened while Stevens sketched the problems that had driven him and others to seek their futures farther west.

"Most people call this the Regulator movement. We got that name because we have asked local officials to meet with us and regulate taxes around here, but they refuse. All we want is to be treated fairly. The royal governor of North Carolina, William Tryon, has decided he must have a "palace" built in New Bern that will be our capital building as well as his home. He has ordered fifteen thousand pounds in taxes to be levied on the citizens of the colony. Well, we western frontiersmen are not as wealthy as the landowners on the eastern seaboard, yet we pay the same amount in taxes. We can't get it changed because they have more representatives in the government. We hoped for a peaceful solution, but folks around here are getting madder and madder. Many are doing what we are doing and leaving for lands over the mountains so they can live their lives in peace. It's come to the point where we can't take it anymore, Mr. Spencer."

Hawk was enjoying his meal, eating biscuits with honey poured over them. "I'm not much on being called mister. Just Hawk will do."

"That's good. I like first names better," Stevens said.

Deborah Stevens was pouring coffee into their mugs and spoke up. "Most of the county officials were appointed by the governor and his council. When these western counties were organized, sheriffs, lawyers, clerks—they all came down on us like buzzards!" she exclaimed, her eyes flashing.

"We've just got to get out of here, Hawk! There's not anything else to do," George added.

Hawk shrugged. "Well, there's plenty of room in the Holston country, but it'll be slow traveling."

"We're ready to go. Well . . . some of us are. We'll have to get everybody together. Some people are going to sell out, and that takes a little time."

"I'd just as soon go as quick as you can make it," Hawk said. He looked over at Sequatchie, who seemed to be eating biscuits without chewing them, just swallowing them whole. Hawk shuddered. "Sequatchie, you never taste anything! You just ram those biscuits into your mouth and swallow them! You look like a snake swallowing a rabbit!"

Sequatchie's only reply was a grunt. He reached out, poured honey all over the biscuit and swallowed it as he had done before, then licked his hands and grinned at Mrs. Stevens. "Good," he said. "Honey is good."

"Well, the quicker you get started the better, I say," George Stevens said.

Abigail Stevens, called Abby by her parents, spoke for the first time. She had her mother's gray-green eyes, and it was obvious she was going to be a beautiful young woman. "Are there many young people in the valley?"

"Lots of them," Hawk said. "And I'll tell you what. I know about the best-lookin' young fella your age there, and I'm gonna tell him to start courtin' you right away. Why, those young fellas will be swarmin' around you like bees!"

Everyone at the table laughed, and Abby flushed.

"I don't care anything about boys," she said.

"Ho, that's not the way I see it!" her father crowed. "What about when you went mooning around after Asa Stanfill? I thought we were gonna have to call the doctor, you were so moonstruck."

"Papa!" Abby protested. "I did not!"

"Don't tease her, George," Deborah said. She went over and put her arm around Abigail and said, "Tell us about the people there."

"Good people," Sequatchie said quickly. "Many are fine Christians."

"Well, that's good news," George said quickly. "We're not actually going out in the wilderness."

"It's pretty wild," Hawk said. "Not like the first pioneers, but it's not settled like around here either."

"I don't care, as long as we can have some peace from these confounded courts! You know there's a line from Shakespeare that I always liked." He grinned and said, "It goes, 'First we kill all the lawyers.' "

Hawk laughed outright. "That's a bit strong, but I can understand the feeling. Well, Sequatchie and I are ready when you can get your people ready."

Stevens had a determined look on his face. "I'll get the word out today. Hopefully we can leave in a week."

It actually took two weeks, but on May the sixteenth, the settlers from North Carolina were all ready. There had been some who had changed their mind at the last minute, but still a goodly number had sold all their possessions, packed their wagons, and now they were lined up and eager to head west.

Hawk had enjoyed the Stevens family, and he was sitting with Abby, telling her about the young people at Watauga. "There're lots of fine young folks there, but I'll have to put in my recommendation for Andrew MacNeal."

"Is he your kin?" Abby asked.

"Not really. His father was killed as the family was traveling out to the Holston valley, and I've tried to help them along. You'll like Andy, though. He's just your age. You two ought to hit it off."

"What does he look like?"

"Well, he's not as good-looking as I am, of course," Hawk said with a straight face.

Abby looked up startled, for she did not like men who bragged. When she saw Hawk's eyes twinkling at her, she said, "Oh, you! Tell me. What does he look like?"

"Well, he's got wavy blond hair and sparkly blue eyes. He comes about up to here on me, and all in all, he's a fine young man."

Hawk would've told more, but suddenly the door burst open and George Stevens rushed in.

"The militia's been called out!"

Deborah, who had been over at the fireplace cleaning up, turned pale. "What's the matter, George?"

"It's the governor. He's called out the militia, and they're on their way right now. Some of the men are saying we ought to stop and fight 'em."

"Oh, please, George, let's not do that!"

"Oh, I'm against it—but I have to stand with my friends. They stood with us."

Hawk watched but said nothing. He knew little of the situation. He and Sequatchie mounted up and joined the men who had armed themselves and now were ready to head out.

"Where are they located?" George, who seemed to be sort of a military commander, asked.

"They're coming on the Hillsboro road," one man said.

Stevens tried to appease the crowd one more time, saying, "Look, men, we're leaving the country. Let's just let them do what they please." But there was anger in the crowd and he was yelled down, and finally he said, "All right. We'll go take a stand."

The Battle of Alamance took place late that afternoon. Governor Tryon's men were well trained and well armed. The Regulators were not. They were merely farmers who stood as well as they could against the troops of the governor. But nine men were killed on each side, and many were wounded. The governor immediately demanded that they take an oath that they would stay in the country. Of course, Stevens and his people would not sign it and finally said, "Governor, we're leaving."

"Good riddance!" the governor said. "See that you don't come back to North Carolina!"

The next day, as the procession of Regulators moved west,

George Stevens shook his head. He spoke to Hawk and Sequatchie as he rode alongside them at the head of the column. "Nine of our men dead . . . and all for nothing!"

"It wasn't totally for nothing," Hawk said. "You stood up to oppressive governing and now you have your freedom." He turned and moved his horse back to where Deborah Stevens and Abby were driving a heavily loaded wagon. "It'll take a while to get there, ladies," he said. "But you'll see some mighty pretty country." He winked at Deborah and said, "Abby's already got her cap set for a young friend of mine named Andy MacNeal." He laughed when Abby sputtered in protest. Wheeling his horse, he then rode back to the head of the column.

Hawk and Elizabeth

Thirty

*L*ook out! You've got a bite there!"

Abigail Stevens had put her pole down and lain back on the fresh, soft green grass. Andrew's yell sounded almost in her ear. She jumped up and looked around wildly, crying with fear, "What?" She had been asleep and for a moment didn't know where she was.

"Look!" Andrew MacNeal shouted. "You've got a fish! He's getting away with your pole."

The two had been fishing on the creek late in the June afternoon with white fleecy clouds high in the sky. Ever since the Stevenses had arrived at Watauga, the two had been almost inseparable. At first, Abby had been shy because Hawk had teased her about Andrew. She had found, however, that Andrew was even shyer than she was. It all worked out very well, and soon the two of them spent every available moment together.

Abby glanced at her pole floating downstream and said, "Well, it's just an old stick. You can cut another one."

Andrew MacNeal stared at the girl in disgust. Pulling his own line in, he ran downstream, waded out, and grabbed the pole, then hauled a thumping pumpkin-seed perch out and said, "Look at that! The biggest one we caught, and we almost missed him!"

Abby watched as he removed the fish and put it on a stringer.

Handing her the pole, he said, "Now you can put another worm on there." He grinned, knowing that she would not.

"I won't do it!" Abby snapped stubbornly. "We've got enough fish, anyway."

"There's never enough fish!" Andrew said. He picked up the string filled with perch and bass, all good sized, for they had thrown back the smaller ones. The sun caught their scales, and the weight dragged Andrew's arm down. "The only thing I hate is cleaning them, but I'll let you do that. I know how you love to gut a fish and pull the insides out."

Abby stared at him indignantly. "I'm not going to touch those ugly things! I'd rather eat nothing but corn bread the rest of my life than do that!"

Laying the stringer aside, Andrew baited her hook, handed her the pole, and sat down beside her. He put his own pole back out and told Abby what kind of fish he planned to catch next.

Abby turned to him and said, "You know. I was afraid to come here. To Watauga, I mean."

"Afraid? You mean of the Indians?"

"No, I mean I lived in North Carolina all my life in the same house, and we had to leave all of my friends and everything I knew. And I didn't know who would be here. Whether I'd have any friends or not."

Andrew watched his cork, which was bobbing gently, and muttered, "Come on! Get on there, you sucker!"

He turned then and looked at Abby, admiring her long, thick sandy brown hair. She was the prettiest girl he had ever seen, and at first he had been stunned by her and had kept away from her. Not because he didn't like her, but because he liked her too much. He remembered she had finally confronted him, asking, "What's the matter? Don't you like me, Andy?"

He had muttered something and finally said, "Sure I like you, but you're so pretty, and I'm just afraid of pretty girls, I guess." It had been exactly the right thing to say.

Just then Andrew's thoughts were interrupted when his cork disappeared with a resounding plop. "Hey! I got another one!" he yelled.

Abby watched as he wrestled the fish, noting that he always kept his mouth open for some reason when he was landing a fish or when he got excited. "Someday a bug is going to fly into your mouth if you don't shut it, Andy," she said sweetly and laughed at his look of indignation.

After he got the fish on the bank, he looked regretfully at the creek and said, "I guess we'll have to go back. It's getting late."

The two gathered their fish and poles and the little lunch that was left over and walked back to the cabin that had been thrown up with almost miraculous speed for the Stevens. When the settlers from North Carolina had arrived, everyone pitched in to build the cabins. Many of the earlier settlers had helped as well. Hawk and Sequatchie and Andrew had helped the Stevenses build their cabin, which was very close to the MacNeals.

Andrew and Abby walked up to Hawk and Elizabeth, who were sitting under a tree. Hawk took in the long, heavy string of fish and nodded, "Well, it looks like you two have found where they were hiding."

"I wish you'd been there, Hawk," Abby said quickly. "It was so pretty out there by the creek."

Andrew gave her a look of disgust. "We didn't go out to see pretty scenes. We went to catch fish! Girls don't know anything about fishing!"

"I think that's right." Hawk winked at Elizabeth. "Next time, let's leave all the girls at home, and you and I can go fishing. Who wants to take an old girl anyway?"

Andrew was speechless, and trapped, then he saw his mother break out laughing. He grunted and turned red. "Oh, I don't want to listen to that, Hawk. I'm going out and clean the fish."

"I'll come and watch you," Abby said. "But I'm not going to touch their old insides. . . ."

After the two had left, Hawk and Elizabeth sat out for a time, waiting for supper to finish cooking. The Stevenses had invited Hawk and the MacNeals to supper and were now outside walking around, looking at their new place. By the time they came back, the fish were cleaned and the smell of cooking fish filled the air. When they sat down, they had fresh corn bread, fish, and even some greens that had sprung up early.

"Sure will be glad when the vegetables all get big enough to eat," George Stevens said. "I could eat tomatoes raw and live on nothing else."

"I'll remember that," Deborah giggled. "When the tomatoes get ripe, I'll just quit cooking, and you can live on tomatoes."

Hawk smiled and sat calmly, watching the family around him. There was a peace and a harmony in the Stevens household that he liked. He had been amused by Andrew's obvious infatuation with Abby Stevens. He whispered to Elizabeth, "I think Andy's going to stick his fork in his ear if he's not careful. He can't take his eyes off of that girl."

"Hush! It's sweet," Elizabeth said, reaching over and squeezing his arm. She smiled at him then and said, "It's been so good to have new neighbors, and such good ones, too."

Deborah Stevens was a faithful Methodist and had been working on Paul to get him to liven up his preaching a little. Now she said to Rhoda, "Has Reverend Anderson said anything about a brush arbor meeting?"

Sarah MacNeal looked at her with an odd expression. "What's a brush arbor meeting?"

"Oh, we just make a big covering out of saplings, and we have preaching sometimes for a week or a month between the time we lay the crops by and wait for harvest," Deborah said. "It's about the best preachin' there is. We go early in the morning and hear preaching, and then we eat at noon, and go back for the afternoon and get more. Then we eat supper, and sometimes the preachin' goes on until midnight. Sometimes people shout and holler." Her eyes lit up. "I've done so myself many a time."

George made a face. "She tries to get me to do the same, and I tell her the Spirit don't move me in that direction."

"I think the Spirit moves you that way. You're just too stuck up and stubborn and proud!" Deborah said.

Hawk listened as the talk went around, and finally when a silence fell, he said, "I remember going to those meetings when I was just a boy. They were Methodist meetings, too. It seems like the Methodists and the Baptists could always shout louder, jump higher, and fall down to the ground more than anybody I ever saw. I'm not sure all that's of the Lord, but I saw some real good folks who believe in it."

Deborah smiled at him. "Why, thank you, Hawk. I'm glad to hear there's one other person here who's got a little judgment about things like that."

Elizabeth smiled but covered it up. "It seems like Paul's torn between this settlement and the Indians. When he goes back to the village, we don't see him sometimes for months."

"That's right. I think we need a permanent preacher here," George said. "I wonder if Brother Anderson would consider it."

"I doubt it." Hawk shook his head. "He's mighty given to returning with Sequatchie and preaching to those Cherokees, and they love him, too. I never saw them take to a white man the way they take to him."

"Why is that, do you suppose?" Elizabeth asked.

"Well, for one thing, he loves those Indians and they know it. You can't fool an Indian about a thing like that."

"I don't think you can fool anybody about that," Elizabeth said quietly.

"Well, *I* been fooled a few times," Hawk grinned. "But anyway, I don't think you'll ever nail Paul Anderson down to one place. He's not as much a wanderin' man like me. I go sometimes just to see what's on the other side of the mountains. Paul, he goes to find a heathen to preach to." He tasted another bit of the cake that Elizabeth had made and nodded at Andy, who had heard very little of this, for he was whispering to Abby. Then Hawk turned and said, "But as long as he's got a heathen like me to work with, I guess he won't have to go too far."

After the meal, Hawk and Elizabeth moved outside, and he walked her home to her cabin. The children were staying all night with the Stevenses, which suited both Andrew and Sarah. They had begged so hard that Elizabeth couldn't say no. They always stayed up in the loft.

When they got to the cabin door, Elizabeth looked over in the direction of Hawk's lean-to and said, "It's a shame you don't have your own cabin and have to live in that old shack. Don't you get tired of it?"

"It's the most house I've had for fifteen years," he said. "Most of the time in the woods I just roll up in a blanket."

"And when it rains do you get wet?"

"That's what happens when you get out in the rain," Hawk said. The two stood there talking. It had grown darker, and now the stars were out.

Elizabeth looked up at the sky and said, "I wish I knew their names. We all have names."

"I guess a fella could learn them, but who's got time for that?"

"I think we ought to make time for things like that." She pointed and said, "That's the Dipper, the Big Dipper. I know that."

"That's right, and there's the Little Dipper."

"Where?"

"Look right there at the top of the Dipper, the big one. It makes a line. Just follow it." She could not see it, so he got behind her and said, "Okay," putting his hand over her shoulder and pointing. "Now, look right along my finger." He moved his head down so that it was right next to hers. Her hair brushed against him, and he could smell the fresh scent of soap and, very faintly, some sort of lilac perfume.

"I still don't see it," she said with one eye closed. Then suddenly she was conscious of how close he was. She turned around slowly, and his arm was still over her shoulder. Without thinking, he pulled her close and kissed her. It was a kiss that stirred Elizabeth MacNeal to the very fiber of her being. Except for a few innocent pecks before she married, Elizabeth had kissed no man in her life except Patrick. It took her off guard, and she felt so strange being touched and held and kissed by a man. His lips were firm on hers, but his hold was gentle. If he had grabbed her, she would have been offended at once and shoved herself away, but he held her tenderly, and she gave herself to his embrace.

Hawk felt the soft curves of her body, and they stirred the hungers that a man, especially a lonely man, feels for a woman. He had always considered her one of the most beautiful women he had ever seen, and now as he held her, savoring the wild sweetness of her kiss, everything else seemed to fade away. He forgot the forest, and he forgot about all of the trials and difficulties of his life. There was nothing but this woman in his arms, yielding herself to his embrace.

Then Elizabeth stepped back. Her lips were trembling, and she turned away from him.

Hawk thought she was angry. "I'm sorry, Elizabeth. I didn't plan to do that," he apologized.

"It's all right," she said, still turned away. She could not face him, for the kiss had shaken her more than she could have imagined. She had never once thought of loving any other man, but now with the touch of his lips still so near, she knew she would think of this moment and be disturbed for weeks to come. Taking a deep breath, she turned to face him. Her expression was serious and she said, "You're the first man I ever kissed, except for Patrick."

Hawk looked down at her. "He was a good man. You'll never find another one like him."

"No, I never will," Elizabeth said. "But then I don't want to. He was who he was. God made him exactly the way He wanted. He makes other men in other ways. He made you what you are."

Hawk was quiet for a moment. "Well, I made pretty much of a mess of what God made," he said. There was a heaviness in his voice, and he looked at her. "I'm sorry about the kiss. Good-night."

He turned and walked away, but Elizabeth called after him and ran and caught him. "I'm not angry," she said. "And you mustn't think so. I think about you so much, Hawk. You don't know how I feel. If it hadn't been for you we wouldn't have a home. I don't know what would've become of us," she said quietly. "And the children dote on you. I think there's something in you that wants to get out. People love you, but you've built a wall around yourself."

Hawk listened as she continued to speak. He, too, had been stirred by the embrace, and he knew that this woman had wisdom beyond most women. He could not answer her for a while, then finally he said, "In all that, you may be right, but I'm still pretty much of a lost man." He thought for a moment and said, "Someone asked Daniel Boone if he was ever lost, and he said, 'Nope, I got confused once for a couple of weeks, but I'm never lost. Not in the woods.'"

Overhead, the wind sighed in the trees, and an owl made a soft call, and Hawk said, "I think I'm lost, Elizabeth. Not in the woods, but somewhere in my own heart." He turned quickly without another word and disappeared into the darkness.

Rhoda and the Preacher

Thirty-One

*I*t had been almost a ritual—Paul's coming and having supper with Rhoda Harper. Hawk had warned him, "I'm not one to gossip, but some around here are. You keep on seeing Rhoda like you have, and there's bound to be talk."

Paul Anderson thought of Hawk's words now as he sat with Rhoda in front of her cabin. He had come over, eaten supper, then the two had washed up the dishes, and gone out to sit on the bench backed against the logs of the small cabin. Paul had been telling her of the meetings that he'd been having in the area. "It seems like the settlers want more church services. They've asked me to be a regular minister here."

"Will you do it, Paul?"

"No, I can't. I've still got to go to the Indians."

"What will happen if they get a regular preacher? Will you come back here?"

"Well, not a great deal. There wouldn't be any need for me then."

Rhoda was troubled over this and tried to picture life without the good humor and the many helpful things that Paul Anderson found to do for her. She finally said, "I'm sorry for all the trouble I've caused you."

"What trouble? I've enjoyed all of it. It was fun building the cabin, and we've had fun with the garden, too." He grinned ruefully and looked at her. The moon was coming up now clearly in the sky, a huge disc. It was a harvest moon, for mid-September had come in the year 1771. "I'm not much of a gardener, but we did get a fair crop for a couple of amateurs, didn't we?"

"We didn't know one end of a row from the other, did we, Paul?

You remember I wanted to plant some crops under the trees so I could work in the shade, and everybody laughed at me?"

"That wasn't as foolish as some of the things I did, but it's a good garden, and I've enjoyed it more than anything I've done in a long time." He turned to her and said, "I've never told you how much I admire you, Rhoda."

Accustomed to men using sweet words as a ploy for physical intimacy, Rhoda turned to Paul and studied his face carefully. The silver light of the moon highlighted his cheekbones, and she noticed that his jaw, which was very prominent, gave him a stubborn appearance. But there was an honesty in his eyes, as always, and she knew that he meant nothing indecent by the remark.

"What's the matter?" he asked, seeing her drop her head and become silent.

"I don't know. I just feel like there's something in me that can never be cleaned out." She looked at him suddenly and said, "I don't want you to come here anymore, Paul. It's not right for a preacher to spend time with a bad woman like me."

"Rhoda," Paul said quietly, "if you're bad, it's the same way that I'm bad. The Scriptures say that there is none that doeth good and sinneth not."

"You haven't sinned as much as I have," she said stubbornly.

"It doesn't matter. The Bible says that all sin is bad. The things I've done wrong may be different from the things you've done, but we both have one thing in common. Like everybody else, we need God's forgiveness, and I want you to find it, Rhoda."

There was a long silence, and suddenly Rhoda was surprised to feel two tears roll down her cheeks. The simple trust and obvious admiration of Paul Anderson had long been a mystery to her. He knew many of the terrible things that she had done. She had mentioned it to him more than once, and now she whispered again, "You can't know the awful life I've led, Paul. You think you do, but you don't. All the men—all the drunkenness—you just can't know!"

Paul Anderson suddenly knew that God had softened Rhoda's heart. At once he began speaking gently but very insistently. He quoted Scripture after Scripture, and finally he said, "Rhoda." He turned her around to face him. Tears ran down her cheeks, making silver trails as they caught the reflection of the moon. "I know you feel terrible. I know your life was bad, but I don't think you understand. We can never shock God."

Rhoda stared at him. "What do you mean by that?"

"Well, I would be disappointed if you told me you'd do something and then you didn't do it. Or if you did something wrong—but God knows everything that's in our hearts. He knows the hairs of our head. They're numbered. He knows all about us, Rhoda. He knows every sin you ever committed, and He isn't shocked." Paul thought about how to say it better. "God is grieved with our sins, but never shocked. So the things that you would be ashamed to tell me, you can tell God. He already knows them."

Rhoda had never thought of this. She was silent for a long time, and finally she whispered, "Do you think I could become like you, and like Elizabeth?"

"Why, of course you could!" Paul said at once, and exultation filled him. "God's just been waiting for you to ask that question."

Paul continued to quote Scriptures concerning salvation. As Paul watched, he was amazed at the change he saw on Rhoda's face. Whenever she spoke of her past life, the guilt and shame of it all would cloud her face like a dark veil. As she listened to the promises of cleansing, Paul could see the hope and deep longing begin to dawn in her troubled eyes. The tears that ran down her face were no longer ones of despair and of a life thrown away, but of honest repentance. She cried out as Paul prayed for her, confessing her sins aloud. Paul never admitted it afterward, but he was shocked at some of the things she confessed. She was not confessing to him, but to the One who had promised to make her white as snow. She began to shake and weep so hard that Paul reached over and held her.

"Oh, God," he prayed, "you've heard this woman's cry of her heart. You've promised that if we confess our sins, you are faithful to forgive us *all* of our sins. Forgive her and save her in the name of Jesus."

"Oh, Paul, I feel so . . . so *different*."

"You *are* different, Rhoda. You no longer are what you were. That's gone forever, and God has made you His daughter. God has come into your spirit. I can see it in your eyes. The wildness and the fear and the anger, it's all gone."

Rhoda stood up and took several quick paces. She was still trembling, but her tear-streaked face beamed with peace and joy. "Will it go away? What I feel now?"

"No." Paul stood up and took her hands. "That's what brothers and sisters and the Lord are for. To help those who come into the kingdom of God."

"Will you help me, Paul?" Rhoda asked simply.

"Yes, I'll help you, Rhoda." He held her hands tightly and said, "Come along. Let's walk and I'll tell you what it's like to begin the Christian life."

For two days Rhoda stayed in her cabin, reading the Scriptures. Paul had given her a Bible, and she was shocked, and pleased, and rejoiced at how it spoke to her. He put her to reading the book of John, and she read it every moment she was not working. Paul came by, and soon the word spread through the whole settlement that Rhoda Harper had been converted. She knew some sneered, but many came by to wish her happiness. Elizabeth, of course, was rapturous, and Deborah Stevens had come at once to throw her arms around Rhoda and tell her that she was on the Glory Road now, and she could start shouting anytime she pleased.

Rhoda had not shouted, but she had wept a great deal. Not out of misery, but out of a newfound joy.

Paul left to go preach to a group of settlers located several miles to the north, and Rhoda missed him. She ate supper alone that night and afterward picked up her Bible and began to read. The candle flickered suddenly and the door opened. When she turned, shock ran through her as she saw Jacques Cartier standing there.

"What's the matter? You surprised to see me?" he sneered.

Rhoda could not answer for a moment. "What . . . what are you doing here, Jacques?" she stammered.

"Watching you, for one thing. A man's been coming here. Is he one of your customers?"

"He's a minister—and a better man than you'll ever be! I don't have anything to do with men anymore. And I'm not going to help you anymore, Jacques. I've turned away from my old ways."

Cartier stared at her with cynicism in his eyes. "I do not think this is the way it will be."

"Yes, it is. I won't help you. Now get out of here!"

"And what if I tell your minister and the others what you did on the trail? Aye, what then? You think they will like that?"

Suddenly, for the first time since her conversion, Rhoda knew fear. *They'll hate me*, she thought. She was yet a new Christian and was not firmly founded in the knowledge that she could trust her fellow Christians. She began to tremble, and Cartier came over and took her arm. "You will do what I tell you one more time, and then we will call it even. Aye?"

"What . . . what do you want me to do?"

"I want you to have that preacher hold a service out in the woods. They do that sometimes—I've seen them. I want him to have everybody there. As soon as you know when it will be, you come and tell me where it will be."

"How do you know about the services?"

"Oh, a little bird told me." He laughed loudly and said, "You do this one thing for me, and you won't have to do nothing else. If you don't, I'll tell everybody what kind of a woman you really are. A cheat, and a liar, and how you tried to kill them all by putting poison in their water. I think you will do as I say."

The door slammed, and Rhoda slumped into her chair in despair. She put her head down on the table and began to weep. She cried out to God, "Oh, Jesus, help me!" Over and over again she cried this. All thought of food or sleep fled, and she walked the floor all through the night praying. When dawn finally came, she walked to the door and watched the sun come up. Lines of weariness etched her face, but a light of determination shone in her eyes, and she said, "Lord, I don't know how to serve you, but I'll do the best I can!"

Mercy and Grace

Thirty-Two

*P*aul Anderson stared at his reflection in the tiny mirror that he had fastened to the wall of a small cabin he had built—with the help of many others—and then carefully raised the straight razor. Drawing it down, he blinked with pain as it grabbed at his whiskers. The rasping sound grated on his nerves. Tears came to his eyes as he continued to rake away at the tough beard. Then he laughed aloud at himself and shook his head. "I guess it'd be easier to grow whiskers, but they make me look like a wild man, all woolly and going in every direction." Leaning down, he washed his face in the basin and straightened up to reach for a towel, when suddenly an urgent knock came to the door. "All right. I'm coming!" he said. He tossed the towel down on the small table under the mirror, moved across the room, and when he opened the door, he was shocked to see Rhoda standing there. "Rhoda?" he said with surprise.

"Paul, I've got to come in."

Rhoda practically shoved past Paul. It was hot outside, and the one window in the cabin was open, allowing light to filter through. Paul quickly pulled his shirt off of a peg, put it on, buttoned it, and then said, "I wasn't expecting visitors." He studied her face only for an instant and knew she was troubled. "What's wrong, Rhoda?"

Rhoda was winding her fingers together in an agonized gesture. "Paul, after you left, something happened last night. I . . . I don't want to tell you about it. I don't want to tell anyone, but I have to!"

"All right. Come and sit down." Paul pulled a chair out for the trembling woman, and when she sat down, he seated himself across from her. He saw her indecision and fear, and he said, "Most trouble isn't as bad as we think it is, but I'm glad you came to me with it, whatever it is."

"Paul, I'm so ashamed!"

Paul suddenly felt a stab of fear. It sounded very much as if Rhoda had fallen badly out of her Christian walk, but he allowed none of this to show on his face. "It doesn't matter what it is. Just tell me about it, and we'll work it out."

"Paul, there's a man called Jacques Cartier—he's a wicked, evil man, Paul!" She hesitated, then said, "He's the reason I'm here in Watauga." When she saw the surprise on his face, she said, "He came to me when I was working at the tavern, and he paid me to travel with the train that Hawk brought out, the one that we all came on." Rhoda sighed and continued, "Things that happened to slow the train down—Paul, I was the one who put the poison in that water. Jacques paid me to do it."

Paul stared at her wordlessly for a moment, taken off guard. "Why would he do a terrible thing like that?"

"He's being paid by the French. They want to keep as many English settlers out of the valley as they can. They think somehow the French can regain control of the territory. And that's not the worst of it, Paul." Tears came to her eyes and she said, "He came to me the night before the Indian attack. I could've saved Patrick's life! I was going to tell Hawk in the morning, but the attack came before I woke up!"

Paul Anderson sat quietly, listening as Rhoda told the story. It was sordid enough, but when she was finished, he said, "Nothing has changed in your heart, Rhoda. When you became a Christian, the past was cleansed away."

"Patrick's still dead," she said almost bitterly. "*That* won't go away!"

"No, that's true enough, but the wrong in your heart has gone away." He thought for a moment and said, "We've got to go tell Elizabeth, and we've got to tell Hawk, too. What did the man want?" He sat there listening as she told him what Cartier had said, and he became alarmed. "Come along. We don't have a moment to lose!"

The rifle cracked, and black smoke emerged from the barrel. Fifty yards away, a rock that had been placed on a post suddenly burst into pieces and Hawk said, "Now that's shootin', Andy!"

Andrew MacNeal tried to look innocent. The men that he admired the most made little of their accomplishments, so although he was delighted with the shot, he said, "I guess I'll get the hang of it someday."

"Well, I guess you will. If that had been a squirrel, we'd have squirrel stew for supper."

"Can we go out and maybe shoot squirrels today, Hawk?"

"I don't know. We'll have to see what your mother says about that." Hawk looked up and saw Paul and Rhoda approaching on horses. They were coming so fast that he said quickly, "Go call your mother. I think something's wrong."

Hawk stood there while Andrew ducked inside, and when Paul and Rhoda pulled up, he asked, "What's wrong? Has there been an Indian attack?"

"No, but we've got trouble," Paul said. He reached up and helped Rhoda down, and by the time she was on the ground, Elizabeth and Sarah had come outside, accompanied by Andrew. "What is it? Is someone sick?"

Rhoda had prepared for this moment. She set her jaw and said, "I've got to talk to you, Elizabeth . . . privately."

"Why, of course. Come in the house. The rest of you, wait out here."

"No, Hawk needs to hear it, too."

"I'll stay out here with the children," Paul said at once.

Elizabeth turned, and as soon as they were in the cabin, Rhoda faced Elizabeth as if she were facing a firing squad. Without preamble she said, "A man called Jacques Cartier hired me to put poison in the water." She went ahead and told the whole story again. Her voice quivered as she got to the point of the Indian attack, and she said, "If I'd only gone to Hawk that night, things would have been so different."

Suddenly Rhoda began to weep. She held her hands tightly to her side, her eyes closed. She tried to hold the sobs back, but she could not. At once Elizabeth and Hawk exchanged glances. Then Elizabeth went over and put her arms around her. "You mustn't carry guilt. There was no way you could've stopped the attack, and men would have been killed anyway, so you can't hold yourself responsible for that."

Hawk stood there listening to Elizabeth comfort the woman and thought, *If everybody in the world were as forgiving as Elizabeth*

MacNeal, it would be a good world. Any other woman would be so angry with Rhoda for getting her husband killed that she'd want to claw her eyes out.

Finally Rhoda stopped weeping and sat down. Elizabeth said, "We won't tell the children about this. They might not understand."

Rhoda looked up with gratitude in her tear-filled eyes. "I'll tell them if you want."

"Maybe someday, but not now. Hawk, you can go ask Paul to come in now. I know something's got to be done." Hawk walked to the door and called Anderson.

When the four were inside, Paul asked, "Did you tell him what Cartier wanted you to do?"

"Cartier? What's he up to now?" Hawk demanded.

"He came to my cabin last night. He wanted me to get Paul to have a meeting with as many settlers as possible. He knows we have meetings outside, and as soon as I can arrange it and get Paul to agree, he wanted me to tell him where it would be."

"I reckon we know what he wants that for if he's leading those renegade Indians."

"What do we do, Hawk?" Elizabeth asked in alarm.

Hawk stood there thinking. "We're going to be attacked. There's no way out of that. Cartier's made that pretty plain." He stood as still as a statue, and then suddenly he looked at Paul and said, "Would you be willing to have a meeting?"

"I'm always willing to have a meeting, but wouldn't that give Cartier a good chance at us?"

"I think it might give us a good chance to turn the tables on that fellow." He smiled grimly and said, "If Cartier wants to attend one of your meetings, I think a few of us can provide a welcome reception for him and his Indian friends."

Jacques Cartier

Thirty-Three

*C*artier studied the face of the woman carefully. He was devious to the heart and suspected every human being that drew breath. He had come to her after dark, and she had admitted him to her cabin. Now he stood looking down at her from his great height. "What is it you have to say, Rhoda?"

Rhoda's face was drawn, and she looked tired. "There's going to be a meeting the day after tomorrow. Everybody in the valley will be there. Word's gone out. You've probably heard about it."

"No, I did not hear. Where will this meeting be, and why will everyone be there?"

"You know the big walnut grove down by the bend in the river?"

"Yes, I know that place."

"That's where it will be. In the big open clearing there."

"And why is everyone coming to such a meeting?"

"Reverend Anderson has called for a revival meeting, just like you told me to suggest. Everyone should be there, I expect."

Cartier stood looking at the woman and said finally, "If you are lying to me, Rhoda, it will not go well for you."

"I'm not lying. That's what Paul said."

Cartier stood looking for a moment, and then nodded. "Very well." He hesitated, then said, "It's better you go with me, Rhoda. This will not be a good place for you to stay."

"No, I'm not leaving here."

He reached forward and twisted a lock of her hair around his large finger, then shrugged with a fatalistic gesture. He turned and, as always, moved silently as a cat and left the cabin without another word.

As soon as the door closed, Rhoda took a deep breath and walked over to the chair at the small table and sat down. She clasped her hands together in front of her and sat silently for a while, then she bowed her head and began to pray.

———————

"What do you think, Hawk?" William Bean asked.

Hawk looked over the crowd that had gathered in the space by the bend of the river and said, "I think our plan has got a good chance of succeeding, William. But one thing bothers me."

Rhoda had told Bean all about Cartier's visit, and it was obvious that the Frenchman was planning a raid against the settlers. So the men had gotten together and planned to ambush Cartier and his Indians. They would have them all in one place at one time. Bean looked over the crowd and thought hard. "It looks like a good meeting to me."

Now Bean scratched his head and said, "What's wrong with it?"

"If scouts get close enough, they'll notice something peculiar about this crowd."

Again Bean studied the milling mass before him and said, "It looks ordinary to me."

Hawk shook his head and said, "There're no children."

Bean's jaw suddenly dropped and said, "That's right! I hadn't thought about that. But we couldn't have the children there." He grinned and said, "Nor the women either."

Hawk returned his grin. "I'll do almost anything for the settlement, but I downright refuse to put on a dress!" He looked over and said, "Look at Jed Smith." Grinning, he continued, "He looks mighty pretty, doesn't he?"

The plan that had finally evolved was to secure the women and children in a safe place. Someone said that if Jacques and his band of Indians saw a crowd of people with no women, they would know something was wrong. After much coercion, ten of the men finally agreed to put on dresses and bonnets and stay on the inside of the crowd.

Bean smiled faintly, but then his brow clouded. "It ought to work, but we don't know how many will be coming at us."

"I reckon we'll know pretty soon," Hawk said.

He looked over the terrain they had deliberately chosen and said,

"Look. They can't come across the river. We could wipe 'em out, and they know that. So they've got to come from that direction." He turned and pointed to the west, where the thick woods gathered and towered on a massive rise.

"You're right," Bean said. "And I've got a hunch those woods are filled with Indians wanting to scalp us."

"Well, when they do come, they'll have quite a surprise."

"We got the men in place. They didn't like taking orders from a Cherokee, but he knows Indian ways best." At Hawk's insistence, Sequatchie had been put in charge of the men that lay hidden in the forest. The plan was simple. When Cartier and his Indians attacked through the woods, the crowd, serving as bait, would turn and form a battle line. They would retreat as far as the river, and hopefully Cartier and his band would follow them. Then out of the woods, Sequatchie would lead the bulk of the settlers, and the attackers would be caught as if in a vice.

"It's a good plan," William said. He looked over and nodded at Hawk. "You should've been a general."

"Not me. I just wish this thing were over."

"I reckon all of us wish that."

The two men stood talking, and then they walked over to where Paul Anderson was standing.

"I reckon it's about time for the charade, Paul. Why don't you get up on that little rise and start preaching a sermon to us."

Paul Anderson was wearing his usual dark suit and white shirt and tie. This time, however, something was different. He held a rifle in his hands. He looked at the two men and said, "No sense wasting a congregation. I stayed up last night asking God for a good sermon. Some of you need it!"

"I reckon that's gospel," William Bean grinned. "All right. Go to it, preacher, and let her fly!"

Anderson nodded, walked to the rise of ground, and laid his rifle down at his feet. He took out his Bible, opened it, and lifted his voice, which rose above the hubbub. "All right! Gather around! We're ready to begin the service."

Hawk kept on the outskirts of the crowd. He had posted George and John Russell on the other side, and the three of them turned their backs to the speaker, their eyes searching the woods for the first sign of trouble. He heard the preacher's voice, and the words came to him. "The subject this morning is on repentance. The Scripture says, 'Repent or you shall perish. . . . ' "

The sermon went on for some time, and Hawk's eyes never left the massive front of huge trees. Still, at the same time, he was taking in the words of the speaker. Paul Anderson spoke powerfully, repeating the phrase, " 'Except you repent, you shall all likewise perish!' " over and over again. Anderson had the habit in his preaching of repeating his text at least ten, sometimes twenty times. When a person heard one of his sermons, the Scripture would go through his mind over and over after he left.

I reckon he's preaching to me, Hawk thought. He was not afraid. He had been living close to death for too long to be afraid, but he well knew that within the next few minutes he might be lying dead with an Indian tomahawk in his skull or a bullet in his heart. His thoughts moved past that, and he wondered about eternity. *No heaven for me,* he thought, and a sadness came over him. He envied men like Paul, and women like Elizabeth and Rhoda, who had settled the matter of eternity. His thoughts went back to Williamsburg as he waited. He thought of his parents and his son. As always, when the face of Jacob came before him, his heart grew heavy, and he said, "I deserve eternity in hell—if for no other reason than for the way I've abandoned my boy!"

The sadness lasted for only a moment, for a sudden movement caught his eyes. He straightened up and grasped his musket. It was only a flash, but he recognized that someone was moving over to the left of the grove. His eyes swept the edge of the tree line, and he began to see other movements. *They're coming,* he thought. He raised his voice and said, "Don't turn around, but get your muskets handy. They'll be here soon."

"I see 'em," George Russell's voice came calmly. "They're massing over here on this side, too."

Anderson never faltered. His voice continued to rise and fall, but then suddenly out of the trees a line of half-naked Indians broke, and the quietness of the air was suddenly rent by the screech of war cries.

"Here they come!" Hawk said. "Break up and form a line of battle. Don't mass! Form two lines so we can give 'em volleys!"

It was Hawk's idea to put the men in two lines. All of the men were experts with the muskets and could reload in less than thirty seconds. Now instantly they broke into two lines with ten yards between them. The first line knelt down to where they could brace themselves and not miss. The Indians began to fire when they were a hundred yards away, and the whistling of a musket ball came so close that Hawk flinched. He was on the left flank of the front line with John Russell on the other flank. When the Indians closed to within fifty yards, Hawk yelled, "Fire!"

A thunderous crash of muskets broke out, and it seemed that every shot hit its target. Indians fell kicking, some of them lay still, others struggled to their feet, wounded, but there were many others behind them that rushed on. Hawk said, "Go back and reload!" The men who had just fired quickly arose, and the line behind them moved forward. While the first were reloading, the cry came to fire, and again the thunder of musketry broke the air. The sound of dying men and the screams of rage from the Indians filled the field. Up and down the line of settlers, men began to drop, for the Indians had stopped to take better aim.

Hawk fell in to fire his second volley, and he looked around and saw Anderson standing beside him. "Preacher, you better get out of here!"

Anderson shook his head grimly and lifted his musket. Hawk saw the mass of Indians coming and said, "I think there's too many of them. I never saw so many Indians in one place in my life."

Hawk gave the command to fire, and the battle continued more fiercely than anything Hawk had ever seen. Scores of Indians came boiling out of the woods. Hawk searched them for Jacques Cartier but caught no sight of the big Frenchman.

Step by step, foot by foot, the settlers were forced back to the river. His face grimy with smoke, Anderson said, "We can't go any farther than this." He looked back; the river was right behind them.

"No, but look over there, and there—and there!" Hawk cried out.

From their hiding places in two small groves that flanked the open field, the groups of riflemen suddenly appeared. They were led by Sequatchie, and they hit the attacking Indians like twin blows. Screams of rage rent the air as the Indians realized they had walked into a trap.

"All right! We've got them! Move forward!" Hawk shouted.

The battle was really over then, for the Indians were caught in the middle. Some of the settlers dropped, but the attacking Indians could not fight against the barrage of fire that came against them from three sides. They lost their courage immediately and began to flee.

Cartier was frantic with rage. He saw that he had been outmaneuvered and shouted for the Indians to retreat. He himself turned and, knowing the ground better than the others, took a shortcut. He had not gone far when he saw movement ahead. He threw up his rifle and pulled the trigger, but his powder had gotten wet, and his rifle did not fire. Flipping out his knife, he leaped and grabbed a woman who had tried to hide herself.

Rhoda had been with the rest of the women in the hiding place, but when she had heard the sound of battle begin, she had decided to move forward and try to see what was going on in the open space. Now she knew she had made a terrible mistake. Cartier grabbed her and pressed his large knife against her throat. "You betrayed me! I will kill you!"

"Go ahead," Rhoda said calmly. "You're through, Jacques. The Indians will never follow you again. They'll probably kill you themselves if they catch you for leading them into a trap and getting so many of them killed!"

Cartier gritted his teeth. "Aye, it would be too easy to kill you now!" he said. "I will take you with me. I will make you wish you had never been born. A little at a time you will die!"

She tried to run, but he grabbed her and dragged her through the forest.

Cartier did not see that another woman had appeared. Elizabeth had seen Rhoda leave and had grown worried. She had followed after her to persuade her to come back to safety but had stopped when Cartier had suddenly appeared.

"I've got to tell Hawk!" she whispered, then turned and ran as hard as she could toward the battle.

———————

As soon as Elizabeth got to Hawk and told him what had happened, he said instantly, "I'll go fetch her back." His face was blackened with powder smoke, and he glanced over the field that was littered with dead and wounded settlers and Indians. "Show me where you saw him."

Sequatchie came at once and said, "What is this?"

"Cartier's taken Rhoda."

Paul Anderson and William Bean were standing close and came over when they saw Elizabeth. "We'll form a party and follow them," Bean said.

"No," Hawk said. "You'll just get in the way." His eyes met Elizabeth's, and he did something he had not done before in his life that he could remember. He said slowly, "You stay and pray. All of you. Sequatchie and I will go, but I want you to pray for Rhoda."

"For Rhoda, and for you and Sequatchie," Paul Anderson said. Elizabeth reached out and touched Hawk's chest. "God will watch over you," she said simply.

A sudden quietness fell over the scene. Everyone there knew Hawk was not a man who believed in prayer, but he had asked for it!

Hawk turned suddenly and said, "Give me plenty of powder and ammunition." He filled his powder horn and his bullet pouch, and Sequatchie did the same. Then he said, "Come, Elizabeth. Show me where you saw them."

"He cannot travel fast with the woman," Sequatchie said. "And he makes no attempt to hide his trail."

The two had followed hard after Jacques and Rhoda. He had gotten a considerable head start, but he was slowed down by Rhoda. If he had been alone, he could have probably escaped, for he knew the woods as well as Hawk.

"It will not go well for the woman. He knows she betrayed him," Sequatchie said. "God"—he looked up—"protect this woman's life."

The two were walking along, and Hawk did not lift his eyes from the ground, but he said softly, "Amen."

Sequatchie was surprised. It was the second voluntary thing that Hawk had ever said concerning God. "Maybe something good will come out of this," he muttered to himself. "My friend is seeing that he needs God—maybe more than ever."

The eyes of the two saw signs that most people would have missed. A tiny indention in a soft spot of ground, a broken twig, a vine torn from a tree. Following the man's trail was simple, for they had lived for years by being vigilant and careful and watching their surroundings.

"They are not far ahead, I think," Sequatchie said.

"No." Hawk pointed to a clear footprint beside a soft spot. The edges of it were crumbling. "Not more than a few minutes."

The two men were now moving at a fast trot, their heads down, and as they swung out into a small meadow, no more than twenty feet across, a shot suddenly rang out. Hawk flinched as a musket ball grazed his neck, just where it joined his shoulder. He looked up and saw a movement in the brush across the clearing, but he dared not fire for fear of hitting Rhoda. He said, "Come on! He can't shoot again. He doesn't have time to reload." Both men raced across the opening. They were halfway across when Jacques Cartier stepped out into the open. He had lost his hat, and anger and rage twisted and contorted his face. His left hand gripped Rhoda by the neck, holding her with his powerful grasp as if she were a child. In his right hand he had a long wicked-looking knife held across her throat.

"Stop where you are!" he said. "Or I will slit the neck of the woman!"

Instantly Hawk and Sequatchie stopped. Both knew that the man had nothing to lose.

"Let the woman go!" Hawk said. His neck was bleeding, but he ignored the burning pain.

"And then you will kill me, eh?"

"No, you can go, Cartier. If you let her go."

"Why do you think I would believe you, Spencer? You think I trust your word?"

"My word's always been good, Cartier. If you knew me, you would know that."

Cartier advanced, holding the knife against Rhoda's throat. Rhoda's eyes were fixed on Hawk, and she made no outcry. There was no fear in her eyes, Hawk saw. He wondered at this, yet somehow he knew that it had something to do with her newfound faith in God. It was not a natural courage.

When Jacques Cartier was ten feet away, he said, "Now, you have two loaded muskets. You can kill me if you wish, but one move and I slit her throat. I will do that before I die."

"What do you want, Cartier?" Hawk demanded.

"Lay your muskets down and back away. I will let you have the woman, but not as long as you have those muskets."

"Do as he says, Sequatchie." Hawk laid his musket on the ground, and Sequatchie did the same. He straightened up and said, "Now, let the woman go."

"First you back away!"

Hawk and Sequatchie took several steps backward.

Hawk knew there was no goodness in the man and he did not trust him. The thought jumped into his mind, *As soon as he gets the muskets, he'll kill us both, and then he'll kill Rhoda.*

"That's right. Back up!"

When the men were five feet away from the muskets, Cartier moved forward until he stood over the muskets. He had the knife in one hand and Rhoda in the other, and for a moment he hesitated. He could not seem to decide whether to sheathe the knife or loose his hold on Rhoda. Finally he said, "You stay right there, Rhoda!" He let go of her and bent down to pick up one of the muskets.

Rhoda had understood from the beginning that death waited for all of them if Cartier got his hand on one of those muskets. As soon as he bent over, she threw herself at him with all of her strength. Her fingernails sank into his face, and the huge man flinched in pain. With a roar he knocked her backward with his powerful arm, but it had put him off balance. He quickly grabbed the musket, but he had no time to level it and fire. Hawk was on him like a cat.

It would not be a matter of muskets now, but a fight of brute strength. He did have time to swing the butt, which caught Hawk high on the head, and for a moment Hawk could see nothing but flashing blinding lights.

As Hawk fell to the ground, Sequatchie threw himself forward. Sequatchie landed several blows on the large man, but Cartier stopped him in his tracks with one blow of his powerful fist. Rhoda screamed as Cartier saw his chance, picked up the musket, and leveled it at Hawk, an evil light in his eyes.

"Now, this will be the last time I will have you to think about!"

In that brief moment, it was as if time froze. Hawk knew he was a dead man, and great regret washed over him as he thought of his life. A wave of remorse suddenly overwhelmed him. It was not fear, but a deep sadness that he had wasted his life so foolishly. The night

Faith had died, and how he had run away, abandoning his son, suddenly flashed before him.

At the same time, as memories filled his heart and mind, his hand went to his belt. In one smooth lightning motion, Hawk pulled the knife and threw it. He had only a split second, for Cartier had aimed the gun at his heart.

The blade sailed through the air and bit into Cartier's heart. At the same instant his finger tightened, and the musket exploded. *At least*, he thought as he fell backward dying, *I've killed him.*

But the bullet passed over Hawk's head, and Hawk slowly rose to his feet.

Rhoda ran to him at once. They looked at the Frenchman, whose eyes were glazed with death. "It's all over, Rhoda. You're all right."

Sequatchie came and looked down at the man who had been responsible for so much pain. "He was an evil man. I wish he had known Jesus."

Hawk shot his friend a glance. He remembered now, more clearly than ever, the remorse that had come when he was staring death in the face—and it was still there. He knew now that those feelings of regret would *never* go away.

Never Thirst Again

Thirty-Four

*T*he fruitful season of harvest finally had come. Elizabeth and Hawk walked along the rows of the garden that both of them had taken so much pleasure in planting, and Hawk remarked, "I've never seen a better garden."

"It has been good, hasn't it? I'm looking forward to the harvest celebration. We'll have pumpkins and plenty of fresh vegetables."

Overhead, the skies were a hard blue, and a wisp of clouds scampered across the horizon as the cool October wind rustled through the trees.

"What do you think about Paul and Rhoda? I didn't think a preacher knew so much about courting," Hawk said, a slight smile turning the corners of his lips upward.

"I think it's wonderful," Elizabeth said. She was wearing a dark blue woolen dress with a high collar and long sleeves and red ribbon along the edges. Her hair was ruffled by the cool wind, and she put her hand up to smooth it down, then said, "If I ever had any doubts about Paul Anderson, I lost them after the way he's helped Rhoda. She's a new woman in every way, isn't she?"

"Yes, she is," Hawk said.

"She'll make a wonderful wife for Paul, and she loves the Scriptures and going on trips to the Indians as much as he does."

"She's got some kind of a gift for languages," Hawk remarked. His eyes searched the horizon in his customary fashion as he added, "She's learned more of the Cherokee language in a month than I learned in a year. Chatters like a magpie."

"They'll be happy. And Sequatchie is happy, too. Paul's been able to help him do a lot to convince the Indians to accept that times are changing."

"The work they're doing with the Cherokees is good. I think the school they started is going to go very well."

"God's done a very wonderful thing in the lives of those two."

They walked slowly down the rows of corn, stopping to admire the healthy stalks, and when they got to the end of the row, Hawk turned to her and said, "Elizabeth—"

When he said no more, but stood there looking at her, Elizabeth was mystified. "What is it, Hawk?"

"Let's get out of the sun." He turned and walked slowly toward a towering maple tree at the edge of the tree line. The maple had been left at Elizabeth's request. It made such a magnificent spectacle, beautifully shaped and towering, and offered shade now, although the leaves were curling and falling.

When they reached the tree, Hawk turned and after a moment's hesitation said, "I know it's only been a little over a year since Patrick died. . . ."

Not knowing what to make of this, Elizabeth said quietly, "Yes, that's right."

"You still grieve for him, I know."

"He asked me not to, and God's given me a peace about that. I think of him often, every day. But the grief and pain are mostly gone now, and I think God's done a miracle in the children, too. I still miss him, but I have a peace in my heart knowing he is with God." They had left Sarah and Andrew at the Stevenses' for the day, and now Elizabeth smiled as she thought of them. "You've been a father to them, Hawk."

Her words stirred him. He kept his dark eyes fastened on hers and said abruptly, "Have you ever thought of me as a man you might marry?"

Elizabeth was taken completely aback. She stared at Hawk, and when he took her hands suddenly and held them, she was absolutely speechless.

He saw the surprise that leaped into her eyes and quickly said, "I never thought that I'd ever feel this way again, Elizabeth. When my wife died so many years ago, something in me died—love, or whatever it is that ties a man to a woman. All these years I haven't ever thought of sharing my life with another woman, but I love you, and I'd like you to consider marrying me."

Suddenly tears came to Elizabeth's eyes. His hands were warm on hers as he held them tightly, and she knew what it had cost this man to say what he had just said. She prayed silently for a moment, for wisdom to say exactly the right thing, and finally when she spoke there was gentleness in her voice. "I think you know how very fond I am of you, Hawk. Oh, I'm grateful, of course, for all you've done for me and the children, but it goes further than that." He still held her hands and she said, "I've been surprised that I could come to care for someone after losing Patrick."

"You do care for me then?" Hawk asked quickly.

Instead of answering directly, Elizabeth withdrew her hands, clasped them together, and for a moment looked down at the ground. When she looked up, there was determination on her face. "The man that I marry, Hawk, if I ever marry again, must have one quality."

Hawk instantly knew what she was speaking of, but said nothing for a moment. When she did not speak again he said, "It has something to do with God, doesn't it?"

"Yes. I want to share the rest of my life with a man who loves God more than he loves me. Everyone has to have God in their life, and I could not bear living with a man who loved me more than he loved the God who created him. That was the way it was with Patrick and me. As much as we loved each other, we both loved God first."

Hawk was silent, for this was unusual and strange to him. He looked off to the distant hills, swaying slightly as if indeterminate, and then he looked back at her.

Elizabeth continued, "If you had loved God more than you loved your wife, you wouldn't have lived as you have all these years. When she died giving you a son, anger became your god, Hawk. Only God can have first place in a person's life if there's to be real peace. The man I marry must love God more than he loves me."

"I don't understand that."

"When Patrick died, I was heartbroken. We had shared so much together, and it was a great loss not to have him around. But I had God to draw strength from because He was first in my life. I learned a long time ago that nothing is permanent in this life. Money, possessions, people—they are all temporary. We should not depend on anything that is of this world because it will not last. If Patrick had held first place in my life, I would have been devastated by his death. But since God is first, and He will never leave me, He was there when

I needed Him the most. He is all that is truly permanent in this world. Somehow, Hawk, you have to lose yourself to God in order to be found . . . in order to have any peace in this life."

"I don't understand that either," he frowned.

"Jesus said, 'Whosoever will come after me, let him lose his life and he will find it.' You've read that many times in the Scriptures."

"I never could understand it. It seems that a man has to do what he can for himself."

"If you hold fragile things too tightly, what happens?"

"Why . . . they break."

Elizabeth struggled to explain her feelings. She spoke quietly for a long time, and finally he interrupted and said, "I don't know how you can love a God who takes things away from people—like He took my wife and your husband."

"If you believe one thing, that won't be hard for you."

"What's that?"

"That God loves you. You know, I think you love Andrew. You two have become very close."

"I do. I'm closer to him than I am to my own son, I'm afraid. If anything happened to Andrew—"

"But you see, God loves you more than you love Andrew, if you could accept that. Think of it like this. Would you do anything to hurt Andrew? No, of course you wouldn't. But some things you would take away from him if they put him in danger. You wouldn't have given him a gun if he was only three or four years old. He would have hurt himself with it no matter how much he wanted it. We have to trust that God works for the good in all people who love Him, no matter how hard the problems we face. Patrick certainly did that. He loved God more than anything."

"We're a million miles apart then, I guess, Elizabeth. I don't understand a God like that." Hawk looked at her and said, "I love you, but I can't believe in a God who takes things away and hurts people."

Finally Elizabeth knew just what to say. "Hawk," she said, putting her hand on his arm. "Patrick was a gift. God gave him to me, and I had him for many years. What if I'd never had him at all? Then I wouldn't have Andrew and Sarah. So, I have my memories of Patrick, and he is alive in them. It was time, in God's judgment, for Patrick to go, but I still have him in a way. It would discredit his memory and the wonderful gift he was if I didn't trust God and accept that."

When he did not speak, she said, "You could've had your wife in that way, and your son, Jacob, if you had just looked to God. Faith was a gift from God. She belonged to Him, not to you. You should be thankful for the time you had together, and for the precious gift of your son."

Her words cut Hawk like a knife. He stared at her for a moment, and his heart was filled with confusion. He shook his head and said, "I'm sorry I troubled you. Forget what I said."

He turned and walked away, leaving her standing alone. She hurried to catch up with him, but he did not look back at her. Finally, he turned off into a side path that led into the woods, and she stood watching him and wanted to weep. "Oh, God," she whispered, "don't let him lose himself!"

———————

Hawk found Paul and Sequatchie at Rhoda's cabin. They were seated around the table, and Paul greeted him warmly, but as soon as Sequatchie saw his friend's face, he knew something was wrong.

Hawk listened as Paul and Rhoda spoke for some time, and he saw the happiness they shared, and he envied it. He was still stung by Elizabeth's hard words, but he said nothing of them. Finally Sequatchie said, "What is troubling you, my friend?"

Knowing that he could not deceive the sharp eyes of Sequatchie for long, Hawk said, "I'm leaving for a while."

"Are you going hunting? I will go with you."

"No, not this time, Sequatchie." He saw the hurt in the other's eyes and said, "I'll be gone a long time. You won't want to leave your people."

"Why . . . where are you going, Hawk?" Paul asked with surprise. "It's almost winter. You'll be back before then?"

"I doubt it."

Rhoda asked gently, "What is it, Hawk? Something's wrong. Can't you tell us about it?"

"Nothing's wrong!" Hawk said sharply. "I just want to go hunting. I've been cooped up here for more than a year now, and that's a long time!"

"Where will you go?" Sequatchie asked quietly.

Up until that moment, Hawk had not thought of it. Now he said impulsively, "I think I'll go up northwest of here."

"I wish you would let me go with you," Sequatchie insisted.

"No, I think you would not be happy up there. I may never come back."

Paul, Rhoda, and Sequatchie all had intuition into this man. They had all prayed for him, and now it was obvious that he was disturbed. Paul finally said, "Hawk, you have people who love you here. You have a place, a home. You could have a good life." He did not mention Elizabeth, but he was well aware of Hawk's feelings for her. "Don't go. Stay here and make a life for yourself."

"I'm going, and this is good-bye."

"You can't run from God always," Paul said quietly.

Hawk started to say something, then stopped. He did not want to mar another farewell. He shook his head and said, "You're a good friend, Paul." He shook hands with him, then smiled faintly at Rhoda and took her hand. "You got a good man, and he's getting a good wife. Be happy." Then turning to Sequatchie he said, "Good-bye, old friend."

"Elizabeth told me once," Sequatchie said, "Christians never say good-bye. They gather to their people. I want you to be one of God's people, but I see you must find your own way. Good-bye, my friend."

Hawk turned immediately and left the cabin. As soon as he was out of sight, Paul said, "I want us to join our hands, and I want us to pray that God would break that man. He thinks he's stronger than life and stronger than death, but he's wrong. He's got to be brought to his knees."

The three joined hands and prayed fervently that Hawk would realize his error and see his desperate need for God. When they ceased praying, Sequatchie said, "I think God is on the trail of Hawk as a man on the hunt for a deer, and we will pray that God will find him."

———

For weeks Hawk traveled, almost aimlessly. He had no will or desire to go to the Northwest Territory. He carried nothing but his musket, powder, shot, and salt, but he had no trouble finding food. At night he would build a small fire and sit staring at the dancing flames unable to sleep. By day he wandered through the forest, observing the beauty of the country, trying to forget Elizabeth's hard words, but they would not go away.

As he traveled, he became more and more filled with a sense of lostness. And somehow he knew that wherever he went, or whatever he did, this would not change. Day after day his mind went back to his past. He thought less now of Faith, although memories of her came at times, but he thought a great deal of Jacob. The boy's face would come before him, and the angry accusation he had made the last time he had seen him seemed to ring in his ears. Then he thought of Andrew and how close they had become—almost like a father to the boy.

One night he sat up till morning, keeping the fire going by feeding it small pieces of dried wood, listening to the sounds of the night. He heard the lonely cry of a wolf far off in the distance and felt a common kinship with him, except that the wolf traveled in a pack, he knew, and he was all alone. Wearily he extinguished the fire and traveled all morning. By late afternoon he had passed no creeks, for there had been a drought. The trees were dry, the ground itself seemed to crumble, and although Hawk had usually managed to find a spring or water of some kind, he found none as he rode along. His lips grew dry, and his tongue swelled in his mouth. He began to feel somewhat desperate, and just as he had almost given up hope for the day, he ran across a stream. It was no more than two or three feet across, and it was almost hidden by the fallen leaves of autumn, but eagerly he put his musket aside and knelt down to get a drink of water. It was cold, and nothing he remembered had ever tasted so good. But even as he drank, suddenly a sound broke through to him, and he instantly reached for his rifle, but he never touched it.

Across the creek, no more than twenty-five feet away, a deer had stepped out of the underbrush. Hawk watched with amazement as the deer seemed aware of him but did not flee. Gracefully, the deer lowered his head and drank.

As he watched the deer, Hawk was shocked to see that it had the same white mark as had been on the buck he had seen so many years ago.

That deer should be dead, he thought, almost in a daze.

The deer drank again, then without a waste of motion turned and disappeared into the heavy undergrowth.

Hawk Spencer could not believe his own eyes, but somehow he knew that deer was more than just another animal roaming the woods. He realized it was from God, and although he had never believed in visions, he had to believe that somehow this was a sign to him.

Forgetting everything else, he sat back and his mind was suddenly filled with the same memories that had been haunting him for weeks. Memories of the past, of Faith, of his parents, of his son, Jacob. He thought of Elizabeth, and of Andrew and Sarah, and Patrick. His whole life passed before him, and a great bitterness filled him. Others had attained happiness, and he realized he had thrown it away.

Hawk Spencer was a strong man, but as he sat there, he began to grow heavy and more sorrowful than he had ever felt before. To his astonishment tears of remorse gathered in his eyes. But what astonished him even more was that he had lost the hate he had had for God.

Finally, he lifted his eyes up, and cried out to God, saying, "Oh, God, I've been wrong all these years! But I'm hungry for you. Like that deer that was so thirsty for water, I'm thirsty for you. . . ."

Hawk didn't know how long he prayed, but he knew that it was a long time. Years of regret and anger poured from his broken heart as he wept and cried out for God's forgiveness. When he finally became conscious of his surroundings, it was dark. Slowly he stood up, and felt strange—clean somehow. All of the bitterness and hatred that had dwelled within him for so many years was gone. Hawk Spencer looked up and said, "Thank you, God, for coming back into my heart. I will obey you the rest of my life, Lord Jesus."

Elizabeth walked out of her cabin and headed toward the creek at the side of her home. She set down the oak bucket after filling it with cold, clear water and looked around at the familiar setting. She had been at this home of hers for over a year now, but she never tired of the magnificent view. She especially loved the scenery during this time of year. The leaves were resplendent with the vibrant colors of autumn—orange, gold, red, and yellow. The air was fragrant with the smell of fruits ready to be picked and the hint of the first cold snap.

Reminders of Hawk's presence filled all of her surroundings. Most everything at the mountain homestead had been made by his hands and brought wonderful memories of times they spent together. She could picture him working on the cabin or taking Andrew fishing or teasing Sarah. Hawk had been gone now for several weeks, and the thought of never seeing him again saddened her. She had done nothing but think of him since he left, and slowly she had come to know the truth that she did love him. However, she did not regret her decision not to marry him. After having a wonderful Christian husband like Patrick MacNeal, she was not about to settle for anything less. But she did miss Hawk's companionship.

The children were off with Abby Stevens again, and at these times she felt rather lonely. She sent a silent prayer heavenward that Hawk would find the peace of God wherever he was. No matter where he roamed, she knew he could never run from the One who was everywhere.

"I must snap out of this and get to work," she admonished herself. "The house won't clean itself!"

As Elizabeth picked up the bucket and turned to head toward the cabin, she noticed a lone figure come out of the woods and head toward her. Something about the figure looked familiar. With a small cry, Elizabeth dropped the bucket and whispered, "Hawk."

Hawk Spencer walked toward Elizabeth, leading his horse, with a determined step. He had a serious expression on his face that Elizabeth could not read. Hawk continued in that steady gait until he stood directly in front of her.

"Elizabeth . . ."

"Oh, Hawk, I thought I would never see you again." Elizabeth recovered from the shock of seeing him, but she could think of nothing to say to this man who had left her weeks before in anger for her refusal to marry him. After a long silence, she looked down and saw the bucket she had dropped. It still contained some water. Not knowing what else to say to this man she had come to care so much for, she muttered, "Would you like a drink of water?"

Hawk finally smiled, which made his dark blue eyes sparkle, and said, "After the drink I have taken from the well of Jesus Christ, I'll never thirst again."

Elizabeth suddenly understood Hawk's meaning, and the tears

welled up in her eyes and began to gently spill down her cheeks. "Tell me, Hawk."

He turned and tenderly put his arm around her as they began walking toward the creek. "Elizabeth, I have been wandering most of my life. Out there"—he pointed toward the wilderness that seemed to stretch forever—"I got to a place in my wanderings when I felt I couldn't go another step. It was at that point I knew I needed to return to the Lord. I was thirsty for something real after all these years of running. I . . . I don't understand it all, but I know the anger and hopelessness are gone now."

Elizabeth stopped and turned toward Hawk. She reached up and pulled his head down and gently kissed him. His arms went around her and he held her tightly. A moment later Elizabeth looked up at Hawk's peaceful face and knew that she was where she belonged— in the arms of the man who loved her but who now loved God more.

Notes to Our Readers

Gilbert and I want to thank you for taking this journey to America's first frontier. We have enjoyed working together to tell the story of Hawk Spencer and Elizabeth MacNeal and the characters of *Over the Misty Mountains* as they bravely stepped out—at great personal risk—to forge a new life in the untamed wilderness of the Appalachian Mountains. We hope that you will join us in the future volumes of THE SPIRIT OF APPALACHIA series as we continue their story. Andrew and Sarah, and the other settlers must work through problems with the Cherokee. And Jacob and his family are caught up in the turmoil of the American Revolution, which reaches across the misty mountains.

The history of our nation is replete with courageous men and women who undauntingly braved the obstacles that this wild frontier set before them. Together we will discover how the settlers relied on their faith to see them through all of the struggles they faced as they strived to carve out new homes on the frontier. That is why I love historical fiction. It allows us to catch a glimpse of history as it comes alive through real characters who formed the spiritual and moral fabric of our nation. It is our prayer that you will benefit from the spiritual lessons found in the pages of THE SPIRIT OF APPALACHIA series. As we learn to put God first in our lives, just as Hawk had to learn, we see that a vital dependence on Him is the only way we can find the peace and steadiness to make it through the struggles we will inevitably encounter on life's journey. He is the only *constant* on whom we can depend.

The history of the vast lands beyond the Appalachian Mountains are so rich and colorful that we thought you would enjoy knowing which characters and events in the novel are true. Little Carpenter was a leader of the Cherokee who worked for peace between the English and his people. It was his skills in diplomacy that kept the Cherokee on the side of the English for much of the French and Indian War, enabling them to concentrate on defeating the French. The Cherokee Indians did fight the English after suffering mistreatment at their hands, and they captured

Fort Loudoun in 1760. The fort was retaken in 1761 as depicted in the story. This ended the Cherokee participation in the French and Indian War, which was a major step toward ultimate victory for the English and helped to open the lands over the Appalachians for future settlements.

Daniel Boone was probably the most famous frontiersman who ever lived. The reference to his marking a tree where he "cilled a bar" in 1760 is absolutely true. The tree stood until it was blown down in a storm in 1920. A marker erected by the Tennessee DAR points out the location near present-day Johnson City.

William and Lydia Bean did establish the first permanent settlement in what is now the state of Tennessee in 1769. They settled near the Watauga River with many friends and families, and their son, Russell, was the first white child born in Tennessee. The settlement they established, Watauga, was the first self-governing territory on the North American continent.

James Robertson left North Carolina and settled on the frontier in 1770 with his wife, Charlotte. They eventually moved on to settle in Nashborough. Robertson had a large impact on the future of the area that we know today as the state of Tennessee, earning him the monikers "The Father of Tennessee" and "The Father of Middle Tennessee."

The Regulators were a group of people in North Carolina who vehemently opposed the taxing practices of the rich eastern landowners who wanted to build the governor's "palace." The political strife resulted in the Battle of Alamance, where two thousand Regulators were defeated by the smaller army of Governor Tryon. Six Regulators were hanged, and many others were taken prisoner. After being promised that they would be pardoned, six thousand Regulators surrendered to the authority of the colony. However, many of these families, fleeing the oppression, left their homes and moved to the Watauga settlements so they could find freedom.

John and Valentine Sevier and Evan Shelby are also true characters. John Sevier became the first governor of the state of Tennessee. His story as well as that of all of these people will be continued along with the stories of the Spencers and the MacNeals. Please write us in care of Bethany House Publishers and let us know what you think of THE SPIRIT OF APPALACHIA.